Also by Chrissie Manby

Flatmates
Second Prize
Deep Heat
Lizzie Jordan's Secret Life
Running Away From Richard
Getting Personal
Seven Sunny Days
Girl Meets Ape
Ready Or Not?
The Matchbreaker
Marrying for Money
Spa Wars
Crazy in Love
Getting Over Mr Right
Kate's Wedding
What I Did On My Holidays
Writing for Love (ebook only)
A Proper Family Holiday
A Proper Family Christmas
A Proper Family Adventure
A Wedding at Christmas
A Fairy Tale for Christmas

About the author

Chrissie Manby is the author of twenty-three romantic comedy novels and a guide for aspiring writers, *Writing for Love*. She was nominated for the Melissa Nathan Award for Comedy Romance in 2011 for *Getting Over Mr Right*. Raised in Gloucester, Chrissie now lives in London.

You can follow her on Twitter @chrissiemanby
or visit her website to find out more:
www.chrissiemanby.com

The Worst Case Scenario Cookery Club

CHRISSIE MANBY

HODDER

First published in Great Britain in 2017 by Hodder & Stoughton
An Hachette UK company

1

Copyright © Chrissie Manby 2017

A CIP catalogue record for this title is available from the British Library

Paperback ISBN 978 1 473 63977 5
eBook ISBN 978 1 473 63976 8

Typeset in Sabon MT by Palimpsest Book Production Ltd, Falkirk, Stirlingshire

Printed and bound in Great Britain by Clays Ltd, St Ives plc

Hodder & Stoughton policy is to use papers that are natural, renewable and
recyclable products and made from wood grown in sustainable forests. The
logging and manufacturing processes are expected to conform to the
environmental regulations of the country of origin.

Hodder & Stoughton Ltd
Carmelite House
50 Victoria Embankment
London EC4Y 0DZ

www.hodder.co.uk

To Mum and Kate

Chapter One

15th September

www.brittneysbites.com

New blog post. Status update!

Good morning, dear readers! I hope the blessings of the universe are pouring down on your head like gentle rain today. They're certainly raining down on me. Dearest readers, I am more blessed than I could ever have imagined and I'm itching to tell you why.

Those of you who have been following my little blog since I started it last September will understand what a fantastic journey I've been on. Healthy eating has always been my number-one interest and to be able to share it with you has been a privilege, but, as you all know, finding someone to share my passions away from the internet has been more of a challenge. Though I've always worked hard on my inner *and* my outer self, my essential beauty kept going unnoticed. I began to wonder what the universe had planned for me. Was I stuck in my single state because I was destined to serve the many rather than The One? Like the Dalai Lama?

Well, today all that changes. I can finally announce to you that I am changing my status (watch my Facebook page)! I am no longer single. It's no longer complicated. I am in a relationship and it's time to tell the world!

Dear readers, it's been such a whirlwind. When I met my darling BF for the first time at the beginning of the summer, I knew at once there was something between us. When I looked into his eyes, I understood I was seeing into his soul and he was looking straight back into mine. It was as though we had known each other for centuries. Do you remember that past lives reading I did in January, which revealed I was an Egyptian high priestess who gave her life for the man she loved? Well, I had no doubt that my darling BF was the reincarnation of that man. He is handsome, kind and intelligent. He's my soulmate for sure. Unfortunately, just as in my Ancient Egyptian life, the course of true love was not destined to run smooth.

Evil, small-minded people have put obstacles in our way. Society itself has tried to keep us apart with its petty rules and regulations. There have been times in the last three months when I thought I was losing my mind. I was so unhappy! But we all know that true love conquers everything and the people the universe intends to be together *will* be together, no matter what the ordinary world tries to throw at them. I always knew my Darling BF would eventually shake himself free of his doubts and the ugly chains of convention and be ready to embrace our joint destiny. *I believed*.

So, I'm going to be spending this morning doing a sage brush smudging cleanse of my apartment to ensure that every last bit of the negative energy that's been holding us back has finally been wafted off. I'm also going to be checking the Feng Shui alignment of my new double bed. You can find the most amazing allergy-friendly beds and mattresses via the link at the end of this blog post.

Did I tell you that I called love into my life with the power of Feng Shui? If you're single, get two model ducks and put them in your relationships corner. You will also need to make sure you've got space for someone to step into. Literal space in your home represents the space in your heart that you're saving for The One. I cleared out the bedside table on the left of my bed and put three empty coat hangers in my wardrobe to make clear my intention. It's definitely worked.

Yes! My Darling BF is moving in today. Thank you, Goddess. Thank you, Universe. Thank you, dear readers, for being with me every step of the way as I walk my chosen path through this wonderful world. I am blessed and I am ready! Let the rest of my life begin!

Comments:

Joolzlovesquinoa: 4 hours ago
Oh wow, Brittney. This is fantastic. Blessings really are upon you. You deserve it, sweetie! Much love.

hunnybunnydrinxgreentea: 3.5 hours ago
Grate news hun so proud of U

Yogachick45765860: 3 hours ago
Darling BF sounds like a peach. Can't wait to hear more about him! Will you be making your gluten and dairy free nut roast to welcome him into your home?

Liz Chandler: 2 hours ago
Dear Brittney, just thought your readers might like to
know that your Darling BF is still my husband. Yours
sincerely, Liz.

Chapter Two

Toast

Oh come on. Nobody needs a recipe for that . . . All right, if you insist.

Take one slice of bread. Cut away any green bits. Stick it in the Dualit. Remove before the smoke alarm goes off.

Liz Chandler did not need reminding that it had been twelve whole months since her husband Ian moved out of the family home to live with award-winning clean food and fashion blogger Brittney Blaine. She got that reminder anyway. She knew she should stop checking Brittney's blog first thing in the morning and last thing at night (and around eight to ten times in between) but it was as though she was compelled. And now she only had to type the letter 'b' into her iPhone for Safari to fill in the rest: www.brittneysbites.com. Ugh.

At least she had stopped commenting. That was surely a sign that Liz was coming to terms with the way things were. At first, Liz had bombarded Brittney's blog with messages via the comments section to remind her and her clueless readers that the life of physical and spiritual purity Brittney espoused was a sham. No amount of colonic cleansing could erase the stains on

Brittney's record as far as the sisterhood was concerned. She was a husband-stealing trollop and Liz wanted the world to know it.

Not only had Brittney stolen a husband, she had broken up a happy family. At the time the affair was uncovered, Liz and Ian's daughter Saskia was still not quite fifteen and they had a six-year-old border terrier called Ted. What were they supposed to do without their daddy?

The break-up came completely out of the blue for poor Liz. On the night it happened, when she saw Ian's car pull into the drive at four o'clock, a whole three hours earlier than usual, she'd briefly allowed herself to think he'd been planning a wonderful surprise. Their daughter Saskia was on a sleepover with her best friend Georgia. It wasn't often that Ian and Liz had the place to themselves. As Ian let himself into the house and Ted the dog rushed to greet him – even though Ian always pushed the dog away – Liz's mind was already racing with the possibilities. A bottle of wine? A take-away? Sex? No, hang on. She hadn't had her bikini line done in six months. Sex with the lights off?

Ian hadn't put his car into the garage.

Maybe they were going out!

Well. Ian certainly was.

'I'm just going to come out with it,' he said when he walked into the kitchen. 'I've met someone else. I didn't go looking for it but I found it and I've been struggling with what to do for months but now I finally know.'

'What?' Liz managed.

'Her name is Brittney and I'm leaving you to be with her.'

'Brittney?'

Ian nodded.

'Not the food blogger?'

Ian nodded again.

'Of Brittney's Bites.com? But you said . . .'

'I know what I said, Liz. But that was before I had the chance to meet her. In person she's got far more depth than you can tell from Instagram.'

'The food blogger?' Liz was having trouble finding the words.

Liz knew all about Brittney's Bites. She and Ian had laughed when they first heard about his boss's plan to do a tie-in promotion with Brittney's website. Ian worked for a company that provided dentists with tooth-whitening supplies. They were branching out into 'at home' whitening kits. Brittney's blog was the perfect place to flog them and as the nearest rep to Brittney's hometown of Exeter, Ian was charged with taking the kit to her and explaining how it worked.

'She's already got teeth like Tic Tacs,' Liz pointed out as she brought up Brittney's blog on her phone for the very first time. 'Veneers, I might add. They won't bleach anyway.'

But Brittney jumped at the chance to do the tie-in with White Up Your Life. Ian was her 'liaison'. And three months after Ian first drove over to Brittney's place with her personalised bleaching trays it seemed they were having one.

'You described her as looking like a chipmunk's head on a lolly stick,' Liz protested.

'She's much better looking in real life,' said Ian.

'What about Saskia?'

Ian at least had the grace to look slightly embarrassed

when Liz brought up their daughter, who right then was having a wonderful time with her friend, oblivious to the fact that her family was being rent asunder by her father's mid-life crisis. For what else but a mid-life crisis could explain Ian's decision to throw himself at a twenty-something who made a living from Snapchat videos of her lunch?

'We'll sort something out. I'll take her as often as I can,' he said.

Liz could already see poor Saskia standing at the school gates, scanning the horizon for her absent father, who'd been delayed at the launch of a new dairy-free nut butter.

'I'm sorry, Liz. I really am. But we only get one life and we've got to make the most of it. When you fall in love, you fall in love. You can't deny the plans of the universe. The French call it a *coup de foudre.*'

He pronounced it a 'coop de food'.

'I know it must hurt right now,' Ian continued, 'but we haven't been happy for a very long time and I think that by Christmas, you'll be glad I made this decision for us both.'

Christmas? Liz saw herself sitting alone in front of a turkey ready-meal.

Ian tried to put his arm around her in a comforting sort of way that didn't work at all. Liz shook him off.

'If you're going, go now,' she said, mustering every last bit of courage she had. 'But don't blame me if Saskia doesn't want to come anywhere near you and your gluten-free girlfriend in your new bachelor pad.'

He went.

Not knowing quite what to do with herself, Liz made

some toast. The ultimate comfort food. She didn't eat it.

The early months after that awful night were difficult, to say the least. Saskia was understandably distraught to hear her dad had moved out. She refused to go to school for a week, even though she was starting an especially important year. Meanwhile, Ted the dog watched the front door for hours on end. When Ian came to pick up a few forgotten things, both Saskia and Ted clung to his legs and cried and whined when he left again.

It was terrible. Liz had to watch their pain and try to ease it, while pushing her own distress into the background in order to be able to do so. To add to that, she had to take the blame for the whole debacle.

'What did you do to make him go?' Saskia wailed at regular intervals. Even Ted seemed sniffy with his mistress.

'I didn't do anything,' Liz protested. But inside her head the reasons came thick and fast. I got too old. I got too familiar. I knew him much too well.

Liz had seen it happen to plenty of her friends. A husband approaching middle age, dissatisfied with the way life's worked out, seeks a second roll of the dice with a much younger woman. Not that the familiarity of the tale helped Liz to absolve herself of too much blame. She was world class when it came to self-chastisement. She asked herself ten times a day what she might have done differently. Lost weight? Dressed more sexily? Stopped asking when he was planning to repaint the hallway he'd wrecked by insisting his mountain bike lived indoors?

'Don't blame yourself,' Liz's girlfriends all told her but she couldn't help it. Not when Saskia and Ted were both so very unhappy. Liz's pain at Ian's betrayal was nothing compared to the anger she felt on their behalf. If Liz couldn't protect them from sadness, who could?

One year on, Brittney reported on the anniversary of her stealing Ian away from his family on her blog.

'Darling Readers, blessings be upon you today! What a glorious day it is and it's only eight o'clock. When I woke up at seven this morning to do my chants and my asanas, my Darling BF had already left for work. But not without remembering what a special day it is for us both. Here's what I found on the kitchen table!'

There followed a photograph of a stumpy-stemmed rose in a bud vase and a card with a puppy on the front.

'I can't show you the secret message Darling BF wrote inside my card – this is a family blog (winky emoticon) – but I can tell you that it reaffirmed our goddess-made connection. I love my Darling BF every day of the year but tonight, on the anniversary of the night he moved in and we made our relationship official, I am going to make sure he *really* knows it. My gluten-free nut roast is definitely on the menu! How will you honour your connection to the people you love today?'

By having you killed? was what Liz wanted to type into the comments box. She resisted the urge and went into work.

Chapter Three

Liz had not intended to become a dental hygienist. Who does? But when it was time to leave school, the psychology course she'd hoped to join was oversubscribed. Her parents persuaded her that working as a dental hygienist was still about making people better able to face the world. And it was far better paid than most counselling. Danger money, Liz now knew.

She had grown to like her job though. Certainly, she liked the people she worked with. Her boss, Vince, was a good laugh. As a recovering alcoholic, he was slightly less a good laugh than he used to be but at least the laughter was no longer nervous. Julie on the front desk was slightly gormless but sweet and could be relied upon to ensure Liz got to read the latest copy of *Hello!* before it went into the pile in the waiting room. Meanwhile, Corinne the dental nurse was one of Liz's best friends. Like Liz, she'd ended up in dentistry accidentally. She claimed it had ruined her dating life.

'There is not one man in this town I could kiss,' she said. She'd seen inside the mouths of most of them and it was rarely a pretty sight.

Everyone in Newbay tried to get into Vince's surgery. Even when he was still drinking and you were just as likely to come out with a new hole in your teeth as get one filled. He was the only dentist in town still taking NHS patients.

Liz understood Corinne's complaint, though working at Pearly Whites Dental had been good for her love life. Once. She'd met Ian when he came in to sell Vince a year's supply of White Up Your Life bleach and activator. It didn't work very well and Vince soon switched to another supplier but unfortunately, by that time, Liz was already hooked into Ian and his way with superficial stains.

There were times when Liz found her job boring but she liked that she could do a day's work then leave the surgery and forget all about it. There was no taking work home from the dentist's office. You couldn't take the patients with you. Thank goodness. On the morning of the anniversary of Ian's sudden departure, however, Liz found herself taking *home* into work.

All the way into the office she composed snappy comments in response to Brittney's latest blog post.

'Goddess-made connection, my arse!' she said out loud while waiting at the traffic lights. The man in the car beside her looked surprised. It was still warm for September and Liz forgot she had her windows rolled down.

'Sorry!' She gave him a little wave.

Liz continued to mull over Ian's corny secret message in that ghastly puppy card while she set up and tested her equipment for the day. She was still gnashing her teeth at the thought of Ian actually bothering to put a flower in a stupid chi-chi 'bud vase' when her first appointment walked in.

'Sit down,' she said, without even saying hello.

Then she pulled the lever that made the chair flip backwards as though she was Sweeney Todd sending her client down to be made into pie. She clipped a bib around the poor chap's neck and brought up the patient's notes on her computer screen.

'Alex Barton?'

Twenty-nine years old. Lived near the train station. Worked as a chef.

'That's me,' he responded somewhat nervously.

'Any issues?' she asked.

Ian had issues. Writing silly love notes to a girl almost half his age. Letting himself be referred to as 'the Darling BF' in a blog post that could be seen by anyone. A blog post that made oblique reference to his sex life. Ugh! What if Saskia had read it?

If Alex Barton had any issues with his teeth, Liz certainly didn't hear what he had to say about them. She had him open his mouth and stuck her mirror straight in. She made some disdainful sounds that were more about Ian than the state of Alex's dentition – though poor Alex didn't know that – and got to work.

'Hold this.' Liz positioned the water jet and the suction pipe in the side of Alex's mouth and had him keep them in place.

'Goddess-made connection,' she muttered.

'Wha . . . ?' Alex tried to ask.

Liz was on auto-pilot as she scraped at stubborn tartar and prodded at Alex's gums. She might have been looking at his teeth but the picture in her mind's eye was all Brittney and Ian reaffirming what the 'Goddess' had given them. She squinted to make the horrifying image go away. At the same time, she involuntarily pressed down on the water jet pedal and nearly turned Alex's time in the dentist's chair into a water ride.

Alex spluttered upright and Liz suddenly came to.

'Oh my gosh. I'm so sorry,' she said. 'This equipment . . . I've been telling Vince it needs looking at for months.'

Both Liz and Alex knew it wasn't the equipment that needed looking at but Alex remained tactfully silent on the matter.

'It's OK,' he said. 'I must have moved.'

Alex was soaked from neck to navel. Liz handed him a wodge of blue paper towels, which had the absorbency of tracing paper. That is to say, not much.

'This is terrible,' she said. 'I can't believe what just happened.'

'It's really OK,' said Alex, squirming as Liz attempted to pat dry what she could reach. 'I'm a chef. I'm used to getting messy.'

Liz used one of the blue towels to pat her own face, which had caught some of the spray. As the realisation of what she had done finally hit her, she wanted to take a whiff of Vince's gas and lay down on the floor to die. When you had your tools in someone's mouth, you were supposed to be one hundred per cent present. This was the first time ever Liz had let her concentration slide to such disastrous effect.

It was because of him. Because of Ian. Still! Surely she should be over him by now?

She pressed the damp paper towel to her forehead and slumped in despair (as far as she was able on her ergonomic stool).

'Do you want to carry on?' Alex asked with trepidation.

'Sometimes,' said Liz, answering another question entirely, 'I'm really not so sure.'

* * *

Liz did go back to Alex Barton's scale and polish. She let him choose the music that played while she worked – he went for Coldplay, which was unfortunate, but given the circumstances . . . And then she gave him a dozen mini toothpaste tubes. Free samples from Ian's firm as it happened, though he no longer was the go-to rep for dentists in the Newbay area. Alex accepted the toothpaste gratefully – 'Can never have too much' – but then he asked Liz for a favour. He reached into his rucksack and pulled out a small pile of flyers.

'It's a bit cheeky but can I leave these?'

'Of course,' said Liz. She was just glad he wasn't thinking of suing. However, his kindness, coupled with the fact that now he was out of the chair again she could clearly see he was the hottest patient she'd had in years, was making her feel like a schoolgirl. Schoolgirl? Huh! He must think she was a daft old bag. She felt her cheeks colouring up again.

Subtly fanning herself with the flyers, Liz promised she would press them on every single one of her clients. It was the very least she could do. Only after Alex left with his clean teeth and a damp jumper did Liz look to see what he was selling.

'Beginners' cookery class. No experience required. Learn to cook fantastic food from scratch in a friendly and fun environment. Newbay Community Centre. Every Thursday 6pm.'

Hmmm. Liz had never been much of a cook herself. Seemed like a faff when you got such good ready meals from Sainsbury's. And she was a working mum. She didn't have time to cook from actual ingredients.

With Alex gone, Liz wandered into reception. She put the flyers on Julie's desk and did a few deep breathing exercises. Her next client required her full concentration.

Must. Not. Think. About. Brittney.

'Goddess-made connection!' Liz raged at the empty waiting room.

'You been on the blog?' asked Julie sympathetically. 'Seen that puppy card?' It turned out everyone in the surgery had.

Chapter Four

Alex would have gone home to change after his dental disaster but there was little point. He didn't have another decent jumper to change into. The one he'd been wearing that morning was the only one he owned that hadn't been moth-eaten into lace. Alex was dreading the winter when he would have to wear that grey jumper every day, unless something happened to alter his financial circumstances quite dramatically. He was saving for something far more important to him than new threads.

For now though, it was almost warm enough to pretend he didn't need a sweater at all. He took it off and stuffed it into his rucksack. The wet patch on the front of his shirt would dry more quickly if open to the air.

Alex had wanted to look good that day because he was planning a publicity blitz. He was going to visit every hotel, restaurant, shop and salon in Newbay, asking them to stick his cookery school flyer in their windows. He was determined to make his first cookery course work. He wondered, as he walked along the promenade, whether he had left too many flyers from his supply in the dental surgery.

But it wasn't long before he discovered how difficult it would be to persuade the local shopkeepers to display his little poster. Some of them wanted money for the favour but Alex was wary of forking out a fiver for the privilege of having his poster pinned on a shop window corkboard obscured by stickers advertising lottery tickets and electricity meter top-up cards.

The bigger hotels were a bit better. The receptionist at The Majestic said she might be up for it herself. That bucked Alex's spirits.

'Everyone is interested in cooking,' the receptionist assured him. 'Everybody has to eat, don't they?'

Alex agreed. Cookery shows were the biggest thing on television. The fuss when the BBC lost *Bake Off* showed just how much the Great British public loved to bake. Or at least loved to watch other people baking.

But with a week to go Alex had received only five email enquiries in response to having handed out hundreds of flyers. He'd duly sent out the details and instructions as to how the interested parties could ensure their places before the 'highly popular' course sold out. After that, nothing. Not one of them got back to him again. Was the course too expensive? Had he plugged it too hard? Alex could only hope that the following Thursday would not find him entirely alone in the Newbay Community Centre kitchen.

On the other side of town, John Barker was alone in his kitchen. Again. He had the refrigerator door open and he stared into it as though waiting for the friendly Hotpoint to tell him what to eat. But alas, there was no lady of the larder to reach out with a swordfish steak, and the longer John stared, the less he seemed to see.

It wasn't that there was nothing in the refrigerator.

Quite the opposite. It was actually pretty full. The ladies of the Newbay Theatre Society, aka the NEWTS, the amateur dramatic club to which John belonged, had made it their business to see he was fully stocked. After John's wife Sonia's sudden and unexpected death, Angela from wardrobe quickly arranged several of the NEWTS women into a rota to deliver fresh cooked meals to John each and every day. A sort of bespoke 'meals on wheels'. Nine months later, the food parcels were still arriving. At least, from a couple of the more determined widows.

But John couldn't keep up with their generosity – grief had stolen much of his appetite – and he quickly lost track of who'd delivered what and when and how it should be reheated. The result was that he now had dozens of unlabelled Tupperware tubs in the fridge. Half of them must be well past their use-by date but he didn't have a clue which.

Eating something from John's fridge had taken on shades of playing Russian Roulette, with salmonella taking the role of the live bullet. He pulled out two containers from the top shelf and opened them both. He sniffed at them tentatively. Sonia could always tell if something was on the turn just by taking a whiff but John had no clue. Was the gelatinous orange pasta dish in the left-hand container actually off or did it smell that way because it was cooked by Annette? Was that Thai curry meant to be green or was it mouldy? Was this the dish that had been prepared by the notoriously unsanitary Moira?

Once again, John resealed the Tupperware containers and put them back in the fridge. Then he grabbed his coat and his car keys and headed for the bar at the

NEWTS' converted church theatre. He'd have a pint of beer and a pasty there. And hope he didn't bump into any of the ladies.

Thankfully, Moira was not at the theatre that night. She had zumba on a Friday when she wasn't in a show. Instead John joined his good friend Trevor Fernlea behind the bar, intending to work a shift in return for a free Ginsters' Cheese and Onion pasty.

The bar was quiet. There was a dress rehearsal going on in the auditorium for the following week's performance of *The Pirates of Penzance*. When Trevor had to step in to read for the absent Derek, who was playing the Sergeant of Police, John was left entirely alone. He polished a few glasses and wiped the bar down. Then he set about tidying up the display case that contained leaflets about local tourist attractions and ads for upcoming NEWTS performances.

And flyers for a cookery course.

John hadn't seen those before.

He read the course description with interest.

'No experience necessary.'

Well, that was certainly him.

John knew he couldn't keep accepting the generosity of the ladies of the NEWTS forever. Not without someone getting the wrong idea. He was sure his name was already being linked with Moira's in all sorts of erroneous contexts. Trevor had asked him outright whether he was having a 'thing' with Annette. John was horrified by the idea that he might have eyes for anyone. His beloved Sonia had been gone for less than a year. Those food parcels and their accompanying rumours obviously had to be stopped.

Perhaps it was time for John to get out of the heat

and *into* the kitchen. He tucked the flyer in his pocket. Maybe he would sign up.

Unlike John, Bella Russo had grown up in a kitchen. Her father Ugo, an Italian through and through, prided himself on his cooking skills and Bella loved to watch him at his work. When she thought about her childhood she thought about her father's food. His home-made pasta. His melt-in-the-mouth melanzane parmigiana. His terrifically naughty tiramisu.

She loved to come home from school to find him in the kitchen.

'Taste this,' he would say. He'd cup his hand beneath the tasting spoon so it didn't drip on the way to her mouth. Then he cupped his hand beneath her chin as she tasted. In those moments she felt so nourished and so cherished. In the Russo household, food was an expression of love and Bella's father was the best cook in the world.

So it seemed perfectly logical that when Ugo was made redundant from the canteen at the fishing tackle factory, which was closing down and taking forty jobs with it, he should set up a restaurant of his own.

There was a small sandwich bar near the Newbay train station. The owner was ready to retire. Ugo saw an opportunity. The Russos could take over the bar and give it an Italian twist. The café already had a clientele and Ugo's mates at the factory assured him they'd be regulars too. The Russos had the money. Just about. Ugo and Bella's mother Maria had been saving for a rainy day for years. Here was that rainy day and their chance of future sunshine.

Bella, who was only twelve at the time, was right

behind her father. She listened to his plans for the scruffy old café and thought they were wonderful. It would be painted in the colours of the Italian flag. The tables would be covered with checked tablecloths. He'd install a pizza oven.

'I'll call our restaurant "Bella's",' Ugo said. 'And one day you'll be in charge of the kitchen.'

Maria had other ideas.

'We can't risk it. Those savings are all we have.'

Maria was eventually persuaded – Ugo was a very persuasive man – and the café beneath the train station did become 'Bella's' Italian takeaway. Bella cut the red, white and green ribbons her father strung across the door on the opening day. All his friends from the factory came by for a glass of free Prosecco and Ugo's world famous risotto.

The café lasted just three years before the bailiffs turned up.

'You see where your father's fancy ideas got us?' Maria said as she waved her hand around their tiny sitting room after it all went wrong. 'If I didn't have my hand on the purse strings, we'd be living on the streets. There's no money in cooking, Bella. When you leave school, make sure you get yourself a proper career. You've got the brains to do it.'

Ten years after Bella's closed down, Ugo died of a heart attack. He'd never quite recovered from the heartbreak of the café going bust. By the time he died, Bella felt she'd already lost her father long before. The jolly man she loved had become a bitter, angry stranger. Frightened by the way her father's joie de vivre had crumbled along with his ambitions, she'd worked hard at school to make sure she'd never end up disappointed and broke. Her father's failure made her see that dreams were for fools, as her mum had always known. So at thirty years old, Bella worked as a solicitor specialising in criminal law for a small Newbay firm. What career could be more proper?

There was certainly never any lack of work for a lawyer in Bella's area. Recessions might make people cut back on eating out but they had no such effect on crime figures. If anything, Bella was busier than ever during the lean times as financial stress led people to make drastic decisions and silly mistakes. As a result, Bella could be found in her office or at a police station at least six days a week. Lunch was at her desk or in the car. The sandwich bar she frequented would have her order on the counter even as she walked in the door at one o'clock. Coronation chicken on a wholemeal baguette.

For the evenings, there were ready meals.

The station café had never reopened.

On the Friday before Alex's course was due to start, Bella went to the sandwich bar at lunchtime as usual. Unusually, there was a queue. Waiting patiently in line for her coronation chicken baguette, Bella picked up Alex's leaflet from the small pile on the counter.

'Friendly and fun environment.'

Bella hadn't cooked a meal from scratch in a long time. Successful people didn't have time to cook, was the message Bella had subconsciously absorbed. Successful people followed the money. Bella was making money even if she had no time for a social life. She definitely didn't have time for a cookery course.

However, Bella folded the flyer in two and tucked it into her handbag anyway. She'd have a proper look when she got home.

Chapter Five

On Friday afternoons, when the dental surgery closed early, Liz picked Saskia up from school, unless she was going to her father's. That weekend, Saskia would be with her mum.

Liz was early so she did what everybody does while they're waiting. She got out her phone. There were no text messages except one from Vince saying that the accountant would be in the surgery the following Wednesday. Nothing on WhatsApp. Nobody doing anything interesting on Facebook (as if they ever did). Twitter was the usual round of tedious #FFs. With none of her customary online haunts providing anywhere near enough distraction as she waited for Saskia to slink out of the school gates, Liz was tempted to check Brittneysbites.com. She gave in to that temptation.

Brittney's usual routine was to post on Mondays, Wednesday and Fridays and that Friday was no exception. On Fridays, Brittney did a round-up of the things that had been 'inspiring' her that week. *Friday Inspo*, was what she called it. Brittney's Friday Inspo inevitably involved the latest designer handbag, spiralised courgettes and a picture of a sunset overlaid by a quote from the Dalai Lama.

That Friday's quote was: *Balance is key in everything we do. Dance but do your yoga. Drink wine but remember your green juice. Move but stay still.*

Liz was pretty sure the Dalai Lama hadn't said that. She was right, of course. Even Brittney knew the spiritual leader of the Buddhist faith wasn't given to pontificating about green juice, so she'd attributed that day's quote to Malala Yousafzai, the pioneering school-girl who braved the Taliban.

That day's handbag of the day was a Fendi Double Baguette, which was the closest Brittney would ever get to touching bread. Meanwhile, dish of the week was a variation on courgettini. So far, so familiar. But what really caught Liz's eye was how that courgettini was captioned.

'Cooked this for Darling BF's daughter on Saturday night.'

Which was indeed when Saskia had been at the flat in Exeter that Ian now shared with Brittney.

'She declared it delicious. Best compliment ever! #teens #healthyeating #cleaneating #courgettesforthewin!'

Liz let that sink in. Saskia – Saskia, *her* daughter – had declared courgettes delicious? Was this the same Saskia who once threatened to scoop out her own eyeball with a spoon when Liz kept her at the dining table for ten minutes after she asked to get down without first eating her veg? She had been a very dramatic eight-year-old.

Liz decided that Brittney was making it up. She attrib-uted all sorts of random BS to the Dalai Lama, Malala and Shakespeare. Why shouldn't that 'delicious' be a random attribution too? All the same, Liz was tempted to add a comment even if it would mean having to set up another new email address to do so. Or she could use Corinne's . . . Ah. She'd already used Corinne's. And Julie's. Even Vince's once or twice.

'Mum?' Saskia knocked on the driver's window. 'Mum? You've got the central locking on again.'

Liz shoved her phone into her handbag and let Saskia into the car.

'Nice day?' Liz asked.

'Nnnngh,' Saskia grunted.

Yeah. Liz was satisfied that Brittney had made that courgettini thing up. Delicious? Saskia hadn't used words with that many syllables in adult company since she turned fifteen.

Needless to say, Liz was not going to be cooking courgettini that evening. She was doing pasta the old-fashioned way. She was making Saskia's childhood favourite. Spaghetti Bolognese with gluten-*full* pasta and a non-specific meat sauce.

It would be a ready meal. But Liz would bung the container in the oven rather than the microwave. She got points for that, surely? And she'd grate the cheese herself. That almost made it artisan, didn't it?

Back at home, while Saskia chatted with her friends online, Liz laid the table for a delicious family meal. As she dished up, she imagined the Instagram picture and the hashtags. #homecookedhappiness #properfood #noneofyourcleaneatingrubbish #thisisfullofgluten #and-cheese. Brittney would have had a fit.

Liz was looking forward to the weekend. She was determined it would be a good one. An opportunity for some mother and daughter bonding time. She was sure that, like her, Saskia must be aware that it was a year since Ian left. Liz planned a conversation in which they discussed how that year had been for them both. Not just the things that had been hard but the little triumphs too. Despite all the disruption, Saskia was doing fantastically well at school. Liz wanted her daughter to know that she was proud of her for not letting the break-up of the family hold her back. She envisaged the conversation ending in a great big mother–daughter hug, like they used to have before Ian left and Saskia seemed to become a difficult teen overnight.

'It's on the table,' Liz called when the Bolognese was ready.

Three minutes later, Saskia slithered in, dragging her feet like Liz was always telling her not to, and slumped onto one of the chairs. Liz decided not to bring up Saskia's posture. Not that night. She wanted her daughter to feel relaxed and cherished. This was going to be a really lovely Friday.

Saskia stared at the plate in front of her.

'Go on,' said Liz. 'While it's hot.'

'Mum,' said Saskia. 'I really can't eat this.'

'What's wrong?' Liz asked. 'Are you feeling OK?'

Saskia nodded. 'I'm fine. But I'm sorry, Mum. This is not going into my mouth. No way.'

'Sweetheart, it's your favourite.'

'I know it used to be my favourite but do you have any idea how much sugar there is in the average portion of ready-meal spaghetti Bolognese?'

Saskia knew her mother well enough to know there had been no actual pans involved in that evening's food preparation.

'And all the other muck that goes in there. The additives and the preservatives? Do you know what they do to you?'

'Keep you looking young?' Liz attempted a shot of humour.

'Seriously, the preservatives are the worst, Mum. Did you know that if you leave a fast food burger bun on a windowsill, not even the birds will touch it and it won't start to rot for a hundred years. I bet this ready meal is exactly the same.'

Saskia offered a strand of spaghetti to Ted the dog, who sniffed at it gingerly before turning his nose up.

'See?'

'Ted has never liked anything with tomato in it. You know that,' said Liz.

'No, Mum. It's because he knows it isn't healthy. Animals don't eat things that are bad for them. That's why they don't get the diseases human beings do. It's because they don't eat processed food.'

'Ted absolutely eats processed food,' said Liz. 'What do you think Pedigree Chum is?'

'He only eats it because he has to. If you gave him a decent choice he wouldn't touch it. He wouldn't eat it in the wild.'

'He doesn't live in the wild. He lives in a semi.'

Saskia pushed her plate away. Liz tried not to react as dramatically as she wanted to. She sat down with her own plate and added a generous helping of her 'artisan' hand-grated parmesan. Maybe if she under-reacted, Saskia would stop trying to push her buttons.

'Have we got anything else?' Saskia asked.

'No,' said Liz. 'I'm afraid spag Bol is the only thing on tonight's menu at Casa Chandler.'

'Great,' Saskia huffed. 'Something even the dog won't eat.'

'Only because he doesn't like tomato,' Liz said again.

'He knows when he's being poisoned, more like! If he had the choice—'

'OK,' said Liz, suddenly losing her patience. 'Let's give him that choice.' Dinner was getting cold and soon Saskia wouldn't want to eat it because it wasn't the right temperature any more. She always insisted on her food being piping hot.

'What do you mean?' Saskia asked.

Liz got up from the table and went to the fridge. 'Exactly what I said. Watch. Ted?'

Liz called the dog over. Ted looked suspicious. He was always getting into trouble for pestering people for food and now he was being invited to look into the refrigerator? There must be a catch.

Liz perused the shelves and pulled out a Lunchables snack pack.

For six months when she was thirteen, Saskia had pretty much lived on Lunchables, refusing anything that looked vaguely organic (oh, how different Liz's world had been then). Saskia's Lunchables habit had worried Liz to the extent that she posted her concern on Mumsnet. Fortunately, the Mumsnetters agreed that when it came to teenagers you had to choose your battles and anyway the Lunchables' website claimed they were nutritionally balanced – '*Packed with on the go goodness*'.

This particular Lunchables was a ham and cheddar combo. Liz pulled off the cellophane and put the carton on the floor next to Ted's front paws. Ted looked at Liz. He looked at the Lunchables. He looked at Liz. He looked at the Lunchables. He stared at Liz as though trying to read her mind. What was going on?

'See!' Saskia was delighted. 'He doesn't want to eat it! He knows it's not good for him.'

'Ted,' said Liz. 'Eat it.'

Ted's ears popped up and he tucked into the forbidden food with glee. Cheese first.

'There you go,' said Liz. 'He loves it.'

'What? He's only eating it because you told him to! He's trained to do what you tell him.'

'Then let's see what he makes of these,' said Liz, putting a small open carton of pre-cooked cocktail sausages on the floor alongside him. 'I'm not saying anything. It's up to him to choose. And how about these?'

Liz peeled three processed ham slices from another packet and arranged them on the kitchen tiles.

'Mum,' Saskia's voice took on a warning note. 'You shouldn't do this.'

'But I need to know if you're right.'

'You're being, like, ridiculous,' said Saskia.

'I'm being, *like*, scientifically rigorous,' said Liz. 'You told me animals will not choose processed food. I'm saying, Ted, who is an animal, will eat whatever he can get his paws on.'

'But you're not even giving him the organic choice.'

'You're right. Hold on.' Liz took the lid off an organic yogurt and placed it next to the sausages.

Ted didn't know what to eat first. It was all his birthdays come at once. He was practically wagging his bottom off.

'Mum!' Saskia shrieked. 'Stop giving Ted dairy!'

'Have I proved my point?' Liz asked. She picked the yogurt up again before Ted could get to it. The ham was already gone.

'This isn't a fair experiment!'

'What other evidence do we need?'

'Do you have any idea how crazy you look?'

'Do you have any idea how crazy I feel when you turn your nose up at the food I've just cooked for you?'

'You hardly cooked it, Mum. You tipped a ready meal onto the plate.'

'A ready meal that I paid for.'

'Then you wasted your money.'

'Just like I've wasted my money on all this?'

Liz had moved onto the 'treats' cupboard. She yanked it open and pulled out a packet of Party Rings, which she tossed over her shoulder in the direction of the bin. It went nowhere near the bin but landed on the floor near the dog flap.

'You won't be wanting these either.'

A bag of Doritos followed the biscuits.

'Those were for my school lunch!'

'Too many additives,' Liz tutted. 'Same with this.'

Liz chucked a tube of barbecue Pringles onto the kitchen floor.

Ryvita next.

'Are these really good for you? Probably not.'

A tub of TexMex dipping sauce.

'Pure evil.'

'Mum!' Saskia could only squeal with horror while Liz emptied out the food stores in a frenzy. Soon the floor around the bin was covered in packets of biscuits and crisps, dry roasted peanuts, bags of flour and icing sugar and boxes of cake mix. Meanwhile, Ted chased the Lunchables carton around the kitchen table legs, determined to get every last morsel. He was having the time of his life.

'And Ted ate the Lunchables,' said Liz triumphantly. 'Animals know what's good for them? My arse.'

'Oh. My. Days,' said Saskia. 'Dad's right. You have

gone completely mad. I don't think I'm safe in your custody.'

'What?'

'You've gone mad. Just like Dad says. You don't care about Ted. And you don't care about me. You don't care about what Ted eats or what I'm eating because you want us to die early of a preventable nutrition-related disease because we remind you of your failed marriage.'

That didn't sound like something Saskia had just come up with.

'Who on earth suggested that to you?'

Saskia shook her head. Though Liz didn't really want the answer. She knew exactly where this clean-eating shtick was coming from.

'The most loving thing you can do for someone is make sure they're eating properly,' said Saskia. 'Which means you don't love Ted or me at all.'

Then Saskia got up from the table, pushing her chair back so abruptly that her share of the Bolognese toppled onto the floor. She raced upstairs and Liz chased after her to continue their argument through Saskia's bedroom door. Meanwhile, Ted, like a 5:2 dieter who's accidentally broken a fast day and thought 'sod it', decided he did like tomato sauce after all.

Chapter Six

Saskia would not come out of her bedroom all evening, even after Liz realised she was the one who was going to have to apologise. It didn't matter how much Liz pleaded and promised it would never happen again. The only thing Saskia would say to her mother was 'go away' until she finally did. Liz went straight to her own bedroom to cry without going back downstairs first. So much for her Friday night of mother–daughter bonding.

The following morning, Liz covered her eyes as she stood in the middle of the kitchen surrounded by the carnage of the night before. While Liz and Saskia argued and sulked upstairs, Ted had taken advantage of the opportunity to eat everything he could get into. If it was on the floor, it was fair game. And Liz had left an awful lot on the floor. Saskia's spaghetti Bolognese was a mere memory; Ted had just about licked the pattern off the plate. Unfortunately, he had also managed to open the Party Rings, the Doritos and the Pringles. Liz had never intended for him to eat those. He'd got into a bag of peanuts. He'd even polished off a box of cake mix, six months out of date. She wouldn't have guessed Ted would even be interested in that.

Reopening her eyes, Liz rued the cost of trying to

make a point. It was just that Saskia could be so blinking annoying sometimes and Liz couldn't help but see red when she heard Brittney's soundbites coming out of her daughter's mouth. She was sure she would have been a great deal more patient if she thought Saskia's sudden aversion to ready meals was entirely her own idea.

Liz spotted a note on the kitchen table. Saskia had already gone out.

'Going to stay at Georgia's,' she'd written in her big loopy handwriting. 'Don't try to make me come home. I haven't cleaned up because this isn't my mess!'

Fair enough, thought Liz, as she picked up the empty Pringles tube, the shining plate, the yogurt pot – Ted had jumped up to the counter for that – the Lunchables wrapper and the shredded cardboard cake-mix box. She couldn't blame Saskia for wanting to get out of the house. But Ted was nowhere to be seen either. Ordinarily, he would have stuck close by until he got his breakfast. Possibly he wasn't feeling like breakfast that day.

Ted had his own dog flap. When Saskia said she wanted a dog, Liz insisted on the dog flap as a condition of fulfilling her daughter's wish, knowing there was little to no chance Saskia would get up early every morning to let her new puppy outside to pee. The dog flap was duly installed in the back door and they all appreciated the convenience of Ted's being able to come and go by himself. Liz assumed he was outside that morning, policing the garden for squirrels and doing his early morning business.

Ugh. That was going to be another headache. What had gone in was bound to come out. Liz would need a bumper supply of doggy doo bags on their next walk. At least it was a beautiful morning.

But when Liz looked out into the garden as she started the washing up, she saw that Ted was not making the most of the mid-September sun. Instead, he was lying on his back with all four paws in the air and he did not look very happy at all.

Liz stopped what she was doing and raced out to the garden. Ted remained on his back, though he did attempt a rather feeble wag.

'Ted?' Liz asked him. 'Ted? Are you OK?'

Clearly he wasn't and he didn't need the power of speech to say so.

His stomach was the size and shape of a small tight barrel and he was making the strangest of noises. There was no sign that anything of the previous night's feast had come out yet but there was every sign that when it did, it would be hideous.

'Ted?'

He whined.

Liz rolled her dog back onto his feet. His breathing was oddly laboured. In her mind, Liz went through everything he might have eaten the night before. She knew he'd probably had too much. *Definitely* had too much by the look of the kitchen. But had any dog actually died of overeating? Didn't they sort of self-regulate? He'd left most of the peanuts. Everything he'd had was fit for humans so . . .

Hang on.

Was there any chocolate in there?

'The cake mix. Oh my god, the cake mix!' Liz said

out loud. Without even bothering to dress, she bundled Ted into the car.

At the Thomas and Thomas Veterinary Surgery, Liz insisted on being seen straight away. There was a queue of kittens and dogs and hamsters and even a goldfish in the waiting room but when Liz mentioned the C-word – chocolate that is – she was quickly hurried through.

Doctor Evan Thomas, the vet, knew there was no time for niceties. He lifted Ted straight onto the shining metal table.

'Ooof,' he said as he did so.

'Tell me what he's eaten,' Dr Thomas continued.

Growing redder with every word, Liz described Ted's diet over the past twenty-four hours, claiming she'd come home from work to discover Ted had raided the fridge. It was sort of true.

'Lunchables – cheese and ham, Pringles – barbecue flavour, a packet of Party Rings . . .'

'Are those the round biscuits with icing on?' Dr Thomas asked.

'They are.'

Dr Thomas made 'mm-hmm' sounds as he and his nurse took Ted's vital signs.

'Spaghetti Bolognese, two portions,' Liz carried on. 'Dry roasted peanuts. Eleven pre-cooked sausages. Three slices of processed cheese . . .'

'Blood pressure?' asked Dr Thomas.

'Quite low for my age,' said Liz.

'I was talking to the nurse,' Dr Thomas said.

'In the region of normal,' the vet's assistant, whose name badge declared she was Nurse Van Niekerk, replied on Ted's behalf.

'Anything else he might have eaten?' Dr Thomas turned to Liz now.

'A packet of cake mix,' she admitted. 'Chocolate, I think.'

'Of course. That's why you got ahead of Moby the goldfish.'

Liz started making her excuses. 'He's always been such a clever dog. He gets into absolutely everything. Not even those things you put on kitchen cupboards to keep toddlers away from the bleach could stop him. But I've never seen him go quite so mad. I certainly didn't know he could get into the refrigerator. I was completely flabbergasted.'

'It is quite surprising,' the vet agreed. 'OK.' He was listening to Ted's bowels with a stethoscope. 'I think what we have here is a classic case of chronic constipation. The combination of foods he ate yesterday afternoon has completely overwhelmed his digestive system and is binding up his bowels. He must be feeling very uncomfortable.'

Ted wagged his tail weakly in response.

'Is there anything you can do?' Liz asked. Constipation didn't sound *that* bad.

'There is,' Dr Thomas replied. 'He's going to need to be anaesthetised, then we'll administer a softening enema.'

'What? *Anaesthetised*?'

That *was* serious.

'Yes. There's no way to do the enema otherwise. Then once we've loosened up the blockage and he's been able to evacuate, he'll have to go on a drip for rehydration.'

'On a drip?'

'That's right. Mrs Ted . . .'

'Actually, it's Mrs Chandler.'

'Mrs Chandler, I'm going to have to ask you to hold Ted while I perform a quick manual examination. He's not going to like it.'

'Sorry, Ted,' Liz whispered, as she took hold of his furry body. 'I'm so, so, so, so, sorry. I love you, Ted. You're going to be OK, I promise.'

'Mrs Ted? I need to get to the back end.'

Liz changed her holding position.

'OK, Ted,' said Dr Thomas. 'This is not going to be nice . . .'

Nurse Van Niekerk handed Dr Thomas a fresh pair of rubber gloves. Liz could tell Ted was anxious, as well he might be. She held him a little tighter. He wriggled in her arms. His stomach made even louder noises.

'I think something's happening,' said Liz, as Ted turned round in her arms so she was once more where Dr Thomas needed to be.

'Stand back,' said Dr Thomas, who had seen this kind of thing before. Nurse Van Niekerk plastered herself against the surgery wall.

Liz was a little too slow.

What had gone into Ted's belly the previous night came out with an explosive vengeance, a fifty-decibel fart and a smell like hell.

'There,' said Dr Thomas, nodding in satisfaction. 'He'll feel much more like himself again now.'

Liz stepped back from the table and stared in horror at the front of the jumper she'd thrown over her pyjamas.

'Need these?' asked Nurse Van Niekerk, handing Liz

a bundle of the same blue paper towels they used at the dental surgery. The ones that didn't soak anything up.

'I think that's the blockage solved. Disaster averted,' said Dr Thomas.

It was easy for him to say. He'd been at Ted's head end.

'We'll make sure he's hydrated and he should be right as rain. But you need to work harder to keep Ted away from temptation. He's been lucky. I don't suppose the cake mix had real chocolate in it anyway but Ted's indiscriminate eating is obviously causing him problems beyond this attack of constipation.'

'What do you mean?' Liz asked.

'Do you know how much a dog Ted's size is supposed to weigh, Mrs Ted? Even when he isn't stuffed full of *Lunchables*?' Dr Thomas said that word with scorn. 'Ted is roughly fifty per cent heavier than he ought to be for his breed. As you've seen, Mrs Ted . . .'

'Mrs Chandler.'

'Mrs Chandler, we can't always rely on our animals to have good self-control. When it comes to eating and exercise, *you* are this little dog's self-control, his motivation *and* his conscience.'

Liz looked at the floor. Right then her own conscience was thoroughly guilty. Ted had nearly had to have an anaesthetic and an enema!

'I can't stress enough how important it is that you take responsibility. Good pet ownership is every bit as hard as good parenting. And just as social services will step in when a child is in danger, there are rules in place for the protection of domestic animals.'

Liz pressed her thumbs against her eyes to fend off impending tears.

'Mrs Ted,' said Dr Thomas in a headmasterly voice, 'I'm not sure you've been listening.'

'I have!' Liz insisted.

'I am deadly serious. Ted is your responsibility. If you don't think you can live up to that responsibility, or you fail to *show* me you can live up to that responsibility, then I will have no choice but to take Ted's welfare into my own hands.'

'What are you saying?'

'I'm saying that allowing your family pet to overeat in such a dramatic fashion is irresponsible in the extreme. Ted is overweight and under-walked. A dog of his age and breed should not be in such a state.'

'He is a little tubby,' Liz admitted.

'He is *obese*. And you have enabled him to get that way, Mrs Ted.'

'Chandler.'

'Mrs Chandler, I would be betraying my professional ethics as a veterinary surgeon if I did not insist you take action at once. I am signing Ted up for a program we run for our patients here. It's called Waggy Weight Loss.'

'Waggy What?'

'Waggy Weight Loss,' Dr Thomas explained. 'It's a free course, which takes place over six Saturday mornings. A new term starts next week. Nurse Van Niekerk will give you a diet sheet, to which you must adhere with absolute strictness. For the next six Saturdays, you are invited to come to the surgery for a lecture and a weigh-in.

'Whether you come or not is up to you,' Dr Thomas continued. 'But if you don't come and Ted ends up in my surgery again, looking as he did today, then I will not hesitate to call the RSPCA.'

Liz gasped.

Dr Thomas nodded.

Ted burped.

'We'll see you on Saturday morning.'

Chapter Seven

Liz drove back home. She sat outside the house, with Ted still in the back of the car, contemplating what she would find when she got inside. There was no avoiding it. She had to go back in. Not least because her jumper was covered in doggy diarrhoea and she knew she was stinking the car out.

Freed from the car, Ted waddled up the garden path ahead of her. He hauled himself up the front step. He was panting all the while. How had she not noticed before how fat Ted was getting? Now that the vet had drawn it to her attention in such a stark way, it was obvious. That dog was not big boned.

When Ted first came into their lives, she and Ian had been so strict with him. Saskia got into real trouble if she tried to feed Ted titbits at the dinner table. That discipline had gone by-the-by since Ian had gone to live with braless Brittney. While Ian and Saskia were busy eating Brittney's courgettini on a Saturday night, Liz, home alone, would snuggle up on the sofa with Ted, feeding him a crisp for every one she took for herself. She'd really let him down.

Feeling thoroughly ashamed of herself and lower than she had in a long while – and that was really saying something – Liz had a cheese and onion crisp sandwich for lunch. It was all that was left after Ted's big feast and she really didn't feel like going shopping.

There was no need anyway. Saskia had texted to say that she wasn't going to be coming home that night. Georgia's mum said she could stay over and they were going to eat her home-cooked vegetarian moussaka followed by a fruit salad. *Hashtag* healthy eating.

Was everyone getting their five a day apart from Liz and Ted?

To make matters worse, when Liz finally finished cleaning the kitchen and her jumper was washed and fragrant and drying on the radiator, she sat down with her iPad and a cup of tea only to read that the latest government guidelines recommended everyone eat *ten* portions of fruit and veg a day. Not five after all. Liz had always counted it as a good day if she managed three. No wonder Saskia was in thrall to Brittney and her courgettini. The thought of ten portions of fruit and veg a day was enough to make Liz turn to Wagon Wheels.

'Ugh,' she sighed out loud.

The day didn't get better. Liz had promised herself she wouldn't look at Brittney's Bites that weekend but Liz was also the kind of person who deals with feeling bad – as she did for so many reasons – by beating herself up just a little more. The moment she tapped the letter B into her browser, Brittney's Bites was there. And milliseconds later, Liz was reading Brittney's unusual *Saturday* blog post.

Which was all about feeding children and young people.

'Dear readers, you often ask me how to adapt my recipes for the younger members of your family. Sometimes children, even teenagers, can be resistant to the idea of healthy eating. They can be very set in their

ways, wanting to eat just a handful of different meals. But you owe it to yourself and to them to try to broaden their horizons. The most loving thing you can do for someone is make sure they're eating properly.'

Where had Liz heard that before?

Brittney then went on to describe a case study. 'Savannah' aged fifteen, almost sixteen. Full marks for the clever literary disguise. Not. Savannah's mother was a 'busy career woman' who 'thought' she didn't have time to cook from scratch. As a result, her daughter's diet consisted largely of ready meals and even at such an early age it was showing its effects. Irritability, fatigue and dull skin.

'Dull skin!' Liz exclaimed. As far as she was concerned, her daughter was radiant.

Brittney continued.

'When it came to food, Savannah was reluctant to step outside her comfort zone but by carefully listening to her concerns and then describing in a serious but not scary way how we really are what we eat, I was able to persuade her to swap her ready-made spaghetti Bolognese for my home-made gluten-free vegan version. Needless to say, she loved it and now, whenever she's visiting her dad (my Darling BF!) for the weekend, she asks for the healthy option. To give her anything else would be tantamount to child cruelty.'

Liz sank her face into her hands. On the back of Dr Thomas's lecture about overfeeding Ted it was especially hard to stomach.

Then she scrolled through the comments. So many people seemed to agree with Brittney. A mother's primary responsibility was to make sure her children ate properly. That 'career woman' was a bad parent to

'Savannah'. What luck her husband had got himself and his daughter (on a part-time basis at least) away from her awful influence.

'What do you think, Ted?' Liz asked the dog. 'Am I a bad mother? Was I a bad wife? Am I even a bad *dog* mother? Am I totally pathetic?'

Ted pressed his warm wet nose into Liz's hand. His brown eyes were full of sympathy despite Liz having caused him an unnecessary visit to the vet. He tried to climb onto her lap but his barrel-round tummy made it difficult and she had to hoist him up. There was no doubt he had got very heavy. How could she have let him down so badly?

'I'm going to do something about it,' Liz promised her furry friend. 'I'm going to do something about your diet and my diet and Saskia's diet too.'

The following morning, instead of her usual Sunday lie-in, Liz got up early to take Ted for a very long walk. Well, long for him. And for her, as it turned out. She wasn't at the peak of fitness. For that reason they stopped at the gorgeous retro beachfront café in Duckpool Bay on the way home and it was there that Liz spotted a flyer just like the ones her hapless patient Alex Barton had left at the dental surgery.

'Oh, he's great,' said the girl on the counter when she saw Liz pick one up. 'He worked here for a while last summer. Everything I've learned about food, I learned from Alex. He can make anything taste delicious. He cooks really healthy stuff too.'

'Hmmm,' said Liz. She took the flyer and put it in her bag before accepting her hot chocolate with squirty cream on the top.

'Do you want marshmallows?' the girl behind the counter asked.

Liz nodded. It was a Sunday and the following day she was starting a new regime.

When she got home, Liz picked up her iPad and settled down with it on the sofa. While Ted snoozed off the exertion of their walk at one end of the cushions, Liz officially signed Ted up to the Waggy Weight Loss group on the Thomas and Thomas Vets page. She was gratified to see from the before and after photos Dr Thomas had posted that her dog was not the largest pooch the WWL team had ever dealt with by a long way. There was a photograph of a spaniel as big as a Shetland pony.

After that, Liz pulled out the cookery course flyer and fired off an email to Alex Barton, saying that she'd like to join his class if there were any spaces left. She stopped short of asking for a discount in return for ten per cent off Alex's next scale and polish at Pearly Whites. He probably wouldn't want that.

Chapter Eight

There is nothing worse than setting up a cookery course only to have no one sign up for it. Actually, Alex was learning that wasn't quite true. There was something far worse than having no takers at all. Having only three, which meant Alex couldn't just bow out gracefully and pretend he'd never even tried. The course would have to go ahead. And in a teaching kitchen that could have accommodated twenty.

Ah well. Alex had to make the best of it. He couldn't make a half-hearted effort just because so few people were going to turn up. They had, all three of them, paid full price for their places and they deserved the full-price treatment. If they were happy, they might tell their friends, and the next course Alex ran might sell out. All the same, it was hard not to be disappointed. Newbay was a town of fifty thousand inhabitants. Were only three of them really interested in food? Were the rest of them already ninja cooks?

Alex laid out the equipment his three budding chefs would need on the front bench of the room's four benches, though he was sure that once they actually started cooking they would want to spread out. Beginners always needed lots of elbow room, just as he once had.

Beside each place, he laid out that day's course material. He'd decided upon a lesson structure that would allow him to teach a vital culinary skill, then demonstrate its application in a recipe which the students could take home for their supper. That day's skill was the correct and proper use of a knife. What held back so many amateur cooks was their chopping technique. Preparation was key in any kitchen and uneven chopping led to uneven cooking.

Alex checked the three knives he'd chosen for his students to ensure their blades were properly sharp. Scary as they were to look at, he knew that seriously sharp knives were actually far less dangerous than those that were slightly blunt and would slip and skid as a result. Ever tried to cut an onion with a butter knife?

The class was due to start at six. By ten minutes to, Alex had finished all the setting up. The course price included all the necessary ingredients. He checked his emails, half wanting to find that another five punters had signed up at the last minute, half wanting to find that all three of those who signed up had cancelled. Alex wasn't a novice to teaching but the teaching he'd done had been in a restaurant kitchen with students who were motivated to get it right. What would this bunch of beginners be like?

John Barker was the first to arrive. Though he was in his seventies, he had the gait of someone much younger. He was wearing a neat grey coat over a tweed jacket. He had the air of a beloved school teacher, which is exactly what he had been until he retired. History was his subject.

'I hope I'm not late,' he said, looking around the empty room in what Alex took to be confusion.

'You're exactly on time,' said Alex. 'You're the first.

Take your coat off, wash your hands and pick your seat.'

Hands duly washed, John went to choose a place on one of the back benches. A surprising move for someone used to being at the front of the class.

'It would be better if you could come forward,' Alex said. 'Make the room look full.'

John made his way to the front.

'I haven't done any cooking before,' John warned Alex.

'Then you've come to the right place.'

Next to arrive was a woman. Young. In her late twenties, perhaps. Thirty max. Around Alex's age. She had a sweet face with kind eyes beneath a rather severe hairstyle – her hair was scraped back into a bun – and she came in at a run saying 'Sorry, sorry, sorry', assuming she was holding things up. It was only a minute past six. When she saw just Alex and John in the room, she stopped dead.

'Oh,' she said. 'I'm here for beginners' cookery?'

'This is us,' Alex confirmed.

'I'm Bella. I was worried I'd be the last to arrive.'

'You very nearly are,' Alex admitted. 'You can hang your coat up over there. Then come and join us here.'

'I thought there would be more people.'

'So did I. But a smaller class makes for more personal teaching. Their loss is your gain. Have you washed your hands?'

'Sorry.' Bella pulled a face like a naughty child then headed for the sink.

'I'm going to nag you about that a lot over the next six weeks,' Alex told her.

'I need a lot of nagging,' Bella said.

The last to arrive was Liz Chandler. Alex recognised her at once from the dental surgery. She'd already apologised profusely over email for the dental chair debacle. Fortunately, that was just another funny anecdote for Alex now.

'I'm glad your jumper dried out,' she said.

'Your turn to get messy today,' Alex told her.

Liz took the last seat on the front bench. After washing her hands, of course.

'Well, this is it,' Alex finally addressed his modest crowd. 'Welcome to my Absolute Beginners' Cookery Course.' He opened his arms to take in the room.

All three students looked behind as if hoping to discover that the rest of the class had silently filled up while they were settling in.

'I'm Alex Barton,' he said. 'And I'm a chef. I've been working in food for the past eight years. I've worked in big canteens and tiny cafés. I got my training in London—'

'And you ended up in Newbay?' John asked.

The two women chuckled. Everyone who'd grown up in the faded seaside town harboured fantasies of escape.

'Yes, well. More of that later,' said Alex. 'I'm sure you'll be hearing plenty about me over the next six weeks. What I want to know is why you're here. Why have you decided to learn to cook? Why now? Why haven't you done so before? Are you really all absolute beginners? What made you decide to join this particular course? John?' Alex picked on him first.

'Well,' said John. 'I must admit I've spent my adult life being spoiled. I married a wonderful woman and she was a wonderful cook. I never lifted a finger in the kitchen because I never had to.'

'Lucky man,' said Alex.

'But nine months ago I lost my darling Sonia to a stroke.'

Liz and Bella murmured condolences. That was a pretty fresh wound.

'And while her friends and mine have done their best to take very good care of me, inviting me round to eat and bringing me stuff to heat up in their Tupperware, I think it's time I learned to stand on my own two feet again. And I don't want that to mean eating toast for the rest of my life.'

'We'll make sure of that,' said Alex. 'Though there's nothing wrong with eating toast if you stick something good on top of it.'

That was reassuring for Liz.

'Bella? How about you?' Alex asked.

Bella straightened up in her seat. She'd come right from work and she was wearing a tailored black suit that gave her an air of competence and authority. When she spoke about cooking, however, she sounded less sure of herself.

'The thing is,' said Bella, 'I feel like I should know how to cook already.'

'Why's that?' Alex asked.

'I mean, I *did* know how to cook. Cooking was my father's passion and when I was small, he was always showing me how to make this, that or the other. My twelve-year-old self could have cooked a family dinner no problem, but I seem to have lost the knack. I work long hours and when I get home, I very rarely feel like putting in another shift at the stove. But I know I eat way too many sandwiches and ready meals and that's got to be bad for my health. I suppose, what I'm looking for is to brush up on my kitchen basics so putting together something from scratch doesn't feel like such a chore.'

'We can help with that,' said Alex.

'I also know I need to expand my interests,' Bella continued. 'I don't seem to do anything but work these days. And it's always nice to make some new friends.'

She glanced shyly from John to Liz. John rewarded her with a smile.

Liz was too distracted to listen to Bella's reasons for being at the community centre that day. She was looking at Brittney's Bites.com on her phone. Corinne had alerted Liz by text that Brittney had published another new post in which she discussed her devotion to yoga and its astonishing impact on her sex life (and by extension on Ian's). Who knew that yoga tuned up muscles you couldn't even see?

'Liz,' Alex interrupted her. 'We're just talking about why we're interested in cooking. What is it that made you sign up?'

With the sight of Brittney's bottom, raised to the air in the 'down dog' position, still seared on the back of her eyeballs, Liz answered Alex.

'Knife skills. I want to learn some knife skills,' she said.

Bella and John moved imperceptibly further away.

Chapter Nine

Liz got her wish. Knife skills were the first item on Alex's agenda. After he'd established that Liz was only joking when she said that was why she'd signed up.

Bella and John relaxed once more as Liz confessed her real reasons for wanting to learn to cook.

'I've got a teenage daughter who won't eat anything I put in front of her. She thinks I'm trying to finish her off with ready meals. I do my best,' Liz said. 'But I've got a full-time job. I don't have time to cook.'

Bella nodded sympathetically but Alex assured them that everyone had time to make dinner.

'But I'm tired when I get home and I'm just not that interested in cooking,' Liz continued. 'I know I should be. I'm only doing this because of Saskia. Her father has run off with a health-food blogger and I think I'm losing out by comparison in my daughter's eyes. I'll do whatever it takes to make her believe that I love her. If that means learning to cook, I'll do it. I just want to be a better mum.'

'Thanks for being so candid,' said Alex.

Liz suspected she'd said too much.

'That's three very different reasons you've got for signing up. I wish I felt that being interested in food was the main motivator for you, Liz, but I don't mind if you're only here because you feel like you ought to be. The lessons are the same. Over the next six weeks,

I'm going to take you through the basics every chef has to learn. I'm also going to show you some excellent cheats. It's my opinion that cooking should be a pleasure and never a chore. By the end of the course I hope you'll agree. Now, shall we get going?'

Alex had the class don their aprons. John and Bella had remembered to bring their own, as per Alex's email, but Liz had forgotten hers so she had to get her spare hygienist's uniform out of the car and put that on instead. At least it was clean. Was she imagining it or did Alex blanch when he saw her dressed up for her day job?

When everyone was ready, Alex gave the traditional health and safety speech that was compulsory for every community centre session. It included where the class should assemble in the case of a fire.

'Though there's not going to be a fire,' he assured them.

'You haven't seen me cook yet,' Liz replied.

After that, Alex gave another health and safety speech, in specific regard to knives.

'These knives are as sharp as a surgeon's blade,' he said. 'But you have to treat them with confidence. Nothing will get you into trouble more quickly than acting unsure of your knife.'

Liz picked her knife up for the first time. Her collection at home comprised a blunt bread knife and three small paring knives from Ikea. They all had crooked blades. Fortunately, she very rarely tried to use them.

'We're going to be practising on an onion.'

Alex demonstrated first. Talking all the while, he picked up his own enormous flashing blade. He showed his students how they should hold it. Not by the handle, like a virgin cornered by the monster in a horror film, but with thumb on one side of the blade and forefinger curled against the other.

'To give you more control.'

Then he showed them how to keep the tip of the knife on the board as they worked and how to hold the item they wished to cut with a claw-like grip, finger-tips curled in to protect them from the edge of the blade.

With his hands in the correct position, Alex reduced his onion into slivers in a matter of seconds. After that, he demonstrated the technique necessary for dicing, cutting another onion so quickly that no one had time to cry.

'Your turn,' he announced.

Bella and John stood up eagerly, if a little nervously. Liz stared at the two onions on her board and silently christened them 'Ian' and 'Brittney'. She was astonished when Onion Ian fell into two halves at the first chop. Crikey, the knife was sharp.

'Good,' said Alex. 'Now, take it slowly. Remember everything I've told you. Each step makes the process easier and far safer. Curl your hand around the handle. Hold the blade steady with your thumb and a crooked forefinger. Not straight. You'll catch the edge. Hold the onion firmly as though you're an eagle and it's a wriggling fish. Make a claw and dig those nails in if you have to. No need to pull the face to match.'

Liz realised she was grimacing.

'Point of the knife on the board for leverage. It's an up-down motion. You're not sawing back and forth. Slowly, slowly. It takes years to reach my sort of ninja speeds.'

Liz cut the roots and the top off Ian the onion. She discarded the papery outer skin. Then she held the onion down on the board with the claws of a velociraptor. Cooking was already proving to be more fun than Liz had expected. With every pass of the knife, she was sure she felt some of her frustration being sliced away.

'Nice work,' said Alex, when Onion Ian lay in a pile of perfect pieces and Onion Brittney had met her fate by dicing. 'You've already mastered the basics of knife skills. I think I'll call you Chopper.'

'Thanks, chef,' said Liz.

But chopping an onion was just the beginning. Alex wasn't going to see that good food go to waste. The onions were to form the basis of the class's first recipe, which was to be a chicken curry.

Preparing the chicken required more knife skills and another lecture on health and safety in the kitchen. This time with regard to kitchen hygiene.

'I'm sure I don't need to remind you that you must use a different chopping board when you're preparing poultry. Veg, meat, fish and chicken should all have separate boards.'

He didn't need to remind anyone but all three students took on expressions which suggested that they each had only one chopping board at home.

'Always wash your hands before and afterwards. I know that some people like to rinse chicken in the sink before they cook with it, but that is one sure-fire way of getting salmonella all over your walls. It just splashes everywhere.'

Liz thought of her mother-in-law, Janice, who was

a chicken-washer. She liked imagining her covered in both salmonella and E. coli. Janice had not been very sympathetic to Liz when Ian moved out to be with Brittney.

Alex made sure his students prepared their chicken safely. After that, they made a curry paste.

No shop-bought paste for Alex's students though. He showed them how to make a Thai version. There was nutmeg to be grated, peppercorns to be ground.

'Nutmeg supposedly has hallucinatory qualities,' he said as an aside.

'I know,' said John. 'We tried to smoke some when I was at teacher training college.'

'How much nutmeg would you need to eat to have an hallucination?' Bella asked.

'About three of these?' Alex held one up.

'Have you tried too?' Liz asked.

Alex shook his head. 'Not my thing.'

Liz was relieved at how the class was progressing. She had worried when she signed up that her fellow students would not really be beginners at all. She thought they would be the kind of yummy mummies who had been making her feel inadequate since she met them at her NCT class before Saskia was even born. John and Bella were more Liz's kind of people. There was no faking their level of incompetence. Halfway through the class John was already sporting a blue plaster. Crying as she cut her onions at a snail's pace had quickly done for Bella's perfect make-up.

Meanwhile, Alex was rather lovely. He looked a bit like that Luke Evans from *Girl on the Train*. Though Luke Evans was gay, wasn't he? Was Alex gay? Liz pondered, as he stood behind her to help place her hands correctly during the onion chopping. He smelled delicious.

'What's that aftershave?' Liz asked.

'Oh, sorry,' said Alex. 'Did I put too much on?'

Not gay, Liz decided from the way Alex had blushed when she commented on his aftershave. But nearly fifteen years younger than she was. Not that it should matter. Corinne, whose husband had walked out when their twins were three years old, had recently signed up to Tinder.

'I'm telling you,' she'd said to Liz. 'Young guys are the way to go. They like the self-assurance of an older woman.'

Liz did her best to look self-assured as she added her chicken to the pan. Alex nodded his approval.

'Excellent work, Chopper.'

The nickname was flirtatious, Liz decided. And flattering. You didn't give a nickname to someone you didn't think could take it.

Yes, she was liking this cooking class very much.

'It's that easy,' said Alex, when they'd all assembled their dishes. 'All you have to do now is let it cook through. And that's taken us . . .' he looked at his watch. 'Half an hour from scratch. If you called your local takeaway, they wouldn't be able to deliver it so quickly.'

Alex obviously hadn't ever ordered a takeaway from Newbay's Great India Tandoori, where the curry was made in vats and the delivery driver fancied himself as the next Guy Martin. But then you only ever ordered from the GIT if you were drunk.

While Alex recapped the recipe, the sound of a

mobile phone rang out from the coat pegs at the back of the room and Bella's expression fell as she realised it was hers.

'I'm sorry,' she said to the others. 'I've really got to take this.'

'Go ahead. You're not at school,' Alex reminded her.

'I know, but . . .'

Bella sprinted to the back of the room. Liz and John tried to cover the call with conversation to give their fellow student some sort of privacy. Eventually she hung up and returned to the bench with a sigh and a shrug.

'That was work,' she said. 'I've got to go. I'm a solicitor. A client needs me at the police station.'

'Ooooh.' The other three made interested noises. They'd been wondering what necessitated the suit.

'I'm sorry,' said Bella. 'Is it all right if I leave you with the washing up?'

'I'm sure you'll get a chance to wash up at some point,' said Alex.

Bella took off her apron. 'It's been really fun so far. I feel like I've learned a great deal already.'

'You've been an excellent student,' Alex assured her.

'Thank you.' Blushing again, Bella stuffed her apron into her bag and was gone.

'Ah well,' said Alex, having watched her until she reached the door. 'I guess that's all the more for us.'

Liz was very happy not to share Alex's attention, at least.

Alex, John and Liz put the finishing touches to the chicken curry without Bella before Alex dished it up into three metal takeaway trays. He handed a tray to Liz and one to John along with strict instructions for refrigerating and reheating that definitely went over Liz's head.

'So,' Alex asked as they got ready to leave, 'will you be coming back next week?'

John and Liz both enthusiastically assured him they would.

'Tell anyone you like to come and join us,' he added as he bid them farewell.

'Well,' Alex muttered to himself as he gave the demo table a final wipe down after they'd gone, 'that wasn't a *total* disaster.'

Chapter Ten

John was quite pleased with the results of that evening's cookery class. He'd gone from never having cooked anything more complicated than beans on toast or soup from a can to putting together a real chicken curry. To think that he'd always assumed curry was complicated, which was why you had to buy it ready-made or go out to eat it. He looked forward to tucking in when he got home.

It didn't take long to get back to the house. John's mood was pretty buoyant the whole way, but as he pulled into the driveway it started to sink again.

That afternoon he'd left for the cookery course without remembering to put the hall light on for when he got back. As a result the house was completely dark, underlining the fact that there was no one inside. No one there to greet him. Not even a dog.

While Sonia was alive, even when she wasn't at home, the house had never felt empty. Her presence infused the building. The smell of her perfume lingered on her coat in the hall. She left a trail of scarves and discarded jewellery wherever she went.

John even missed the scrunched-up tissues Sonia used to drop all over the place. Over the years, they had plenty of fallings-out over Sonia's absent-minded untidiness but as much as John had hated the clutter, he hated even more knowing that when he went inside the house it would be exactly as he left it.

Without Sonia, the house was no longer a home.

John took a deep breath and turned the key. He stepped inside and almost ran to turn on the lamp on the console in the hall, like a child banishing demons with the light. He gave himself a start when a figure seemed to loom out of the darkness, until he recognised one of his own coats hanging on the stand. Still he had the urge to go back outside and sit in his car until morning came again.

'Come on, John.' He talked to himself. 'You're a big bloke. Sonia wouldn't be impressed by all this fannying around.'

He added the coat he was wearing to the other coat on the stand and couldn't help remembering how he used to get ticked off by the fact that the stand was always toppling over because Sonia used to hang *everything* on it, including her ridiculously heavy handbags. Now that it only hosted his coats, it never even wobbled but that was somehow worse.

'Oh Sonia.'

John suddenly sank down to sit on the bottom stair and spoke to the darkness around him.

'I'd give anything to have you back, my love. Anything. You could put your handbags anywhere. You could hang your coats over the bannister. You could drop as many tissues as you wanted.'

He felt a tear trying to push through. Sonia would have reached into her sleeve and pulled out a handy wodge of toilet roll with which to stop it in its tracks. John had to wipe it away with the back of his hand.

'Come on,' he said to himself again. 'Be a man, John. Just bloody get on with it.'

John went into the kitchen. With all the lights on, he was sure he was already starting to feel a little better. He put the radio on too. He listened to three minutes of a depressing debate about the NHS on Radio 4 before he turned to Classic FM. They were playing a terrible dirge. Eventually John settled on Newbay FM. The DJ was inane but at least he was cheerful, as was the music. John wasn't really listening anyway.

He put the curry in the oven according to Alex's instructions. It wasn't long before the scent of the spices infused the still, cold air. John got out a dish and waited for his creation to be ready. He cracked open a beer to go with it.

'Look, Sonia,' he said, as he placed the curry on the kitchen table. 'I cooked this myself. Maybe I'm not so useless after all.'

But he still found he had lost his appetite after only half a dozen mouthfuls. John just didn't like eating alone.

Bella was always eating alone. She couldn't believe her luck. Getting called out by the DSCC – the Defence Solicitor Call Centre – to attend a client in the middle of her first cookery class?

However, the custody sergeant was probably right to have Bella specifically called to the station for this one. Bella walked into the interview room to see a very familiar face. She couldn't begin to count how many times she had turned out on behalf of Jimmy Cricket.

'Jimmy,' she sighed.

That wasn't his real name. It was the name, nicked

from an eighties comedian, that he'd adopted for the streets, which was where he lived for the most part. Whenever the police asked for his address, Jimmy gave, 'Underneath the Pier. Newbay. Devon,' as his permanent abode.

'Evening, Miss B,' Jimmy greeted Bella like the old friend she almost was. 'I hope I didn't interrupt *Coronation Street*.'

'Not tonight, Jimmy. I was at a cookery class.'

'Cooking? What for? Are you looking for a husband?'

'As always,' Bella played along.

'I don't know why no one's snapped you up. I know I would, if I weren't already promised to Angelina Jolie.'

He grinned at her, showing all the gaps in his teeth.

Bella shook her head and smiled. Jimmy was a pain in the proverbial but it was hard not to like him. She had never seen him in a bad mood, though given the way he lived, he'd certainly be entitled to be in one.

'What is it this time?' she asked him.

'Shoplifting,' interrupted the police officer – Sergeant Mellor – who had brought Jimmy in. 'Took a pair of trainers from Sports Shooze in the precinct.'

'I was going to pay for them,' Jimmy insisted. 'I was just taking them outside to see the colour in the daylight.'

'It was already dark,' Sergeant Mellor pointed out.

'Come on then,' said Bella, knowing that it wasn't going to be simple. Jimmy was already the proud owner of an ASBO, which meant that every little misdemeanour counted more heavily against him than the last. 'Let's get this over with, shall we?'

Sergeant Mellor went to fetch three cups of tea from

the canteen. He came back with a biscuit for Bella. She looked at it longingly. She was hungry. She'd been looking forward to that curry and cooking it had certainly whetted her appetite. But Jimmy was looking at it longingly too and the policeman had not brought one for him.

'I'm not a big fan of custard creams,' she said. 'You have it, Jimmy.'

Poor Jimmy. Over the years she'd been working for Newbay Law, Bella had come to know her client's life story and she wondered if he'd ever really had a chance. He came from a chaotic home. He'd been taken into care as a seven-year-old and worked his way through eight foster placements and two children's homes. At sixteen, he decided he would rather fend for himself, which suited the local authority just fine. Except of course he couldn't fend for himself. Not in any real way. He slept rough and soon got into drugs. Who wouldn't take drugs when they had to live under Newbay pier for real? Funding his habit naturally led Jimmy into petty crime. The prison system was full of people like him. Sometimes, Bella suspected that Jimmy committed a ridiculous offence for the chance of a hot meal and a clean bed.

Bella had a clean bed ahead of her but at eleven in the evening – it took that long to sort Jimmy out and get him a place in a hostel for the night – her chances of a hot meal were greatly diminished. Checking her phone as she left the police station, she sighed. Not only had she had to leave her cookery class early, she'd missed the chance to join a couple of old schoolfriends in the pub. It was a wonder they still bothered to ask her to join them. Her mum, too, had texted, asking whether Bella 'might have time' to pay a visit that weekend. Bella felt a bubble of frustration and guilt rise in her chest. Her mum had wanted her to get a 'proper job' but she didn't seem to understand the time commitment that went with it.

Bella had started the day looking forward to feasting on a meal she had made for herself and intending to use the rest of the evening to catch up with the people she actually wanted to spend time with, rather than Jimmy. She ended the day with greatly improved knife skills, another Ginsters' pasty, and a sense that something about her life really needed to change.

Chapter Eleven

While Liz had been at her cookery class, Saskia had been at a meeting of the youth theatre group at the NEWTS. She'd only recently signed up for the acting sessions and Liz suspected her daughter was motivated less by the thought of an acting career than by the fact that the most popular boy in her class was a keen thesp.

Liz parked up across the road from the converted church theatre where the NEWTS troupe was based. Saskia was one of the last to come out. She was laughing with her best friend Georgia, who had also been struck by the acting bug. As soon as Saskia saw her mother, however, her face was like a slab once again.

'The minute you see me, you look like one of those big stone heads on Easter Island,' Liz had told her a few weeks earlier. That went down well. Saskia didn't speak to her for three days.

'Hello, darling!' Liz trilled. This time she tried to manipulate the atmosphere with a chirpy greeting. Start as you mean to go on.

'Hi, Mum,' said Saskia, as she climbed into the back. The front passenger seat hadn't quite recovered from Ted's visit to the vet and Liz hadn't had time to get it valeted.

'Good acting session?'

'It was all right,' said Saskia.

'I want to hear all about it,' said Liz, seizing upon the fact that this was already the longest conversation they'd had since Cakemixgate.

'It's not that interesting,' said Saskia.

'Everything you do is interesting to me,' Liz insisted. She looked at Saskia's face reflected in the rear-view mirror and was sure she saw a flicker of appreciation.

'I think it's going OK,' Saskia admitted. 'The group leader said she thought I had a good voice.'

'You do have a good voice,' said Liz. 'You've been a great singer since you were little.'

'Thanks, Mum.'

Then Saskia said, 'Why does this car smell? I mean other than of dog mess.'

'Oh,' said Liz. 'That will be the curry I made at cookery class.'

'You went to a cookery class?'

'Yes. I told you I was going.'

'No you didn't.'

'I'm sure I did.'

'You really didn't.'

'You must have been on your phone at the time.'

'I was *not*.'

Liz quickly recognised the conversation was already taking a turn in the wrong direction. She tried to haul it back.

'Well, I did go to a cookery class tonight and we made a curry.'

'*You* made a curry?'

'That's what I just said.'

Liz hated these exchanges in which Saskia basically repeated whatever Liz had told her in a tone of voice that made Liz sound like an idiot. It wasn't something Saskia had learned from her. In fact, Liz didn't think Saskia had ever done it before she met Brittney.

'Curry?'

'Yes. A curry. Chicken curry. Thai style. I made it from scratch. I boned the chicken. I diced the onions. I actually put together the spices. There's no shop-bought curry powder in there. It is one hundred per cent non-processed. *Hashtag healthy eating*.' Since they were at a red light, Liz took her hands off the wheel and made little quote marks in the air.

'Mum. That hashtag thing you do with your fingers really isn't funny.'

Liz could tell Saskia was having to make an effort not to smile.

'Well, I hope you don't think I'm going to eat it,' Saskia said then.

'That was the general idea.'

'I can't.'

'Why not?'

'I've become a vegetarian.'

'What? When? When did you become a vegetarian?'

This was news to Liz. Saskia had definitely eaten bacon on Monday morning when Liz cooked a pre-school fry-up in a desperate attempt to get back into her daughter's good books.

'This morning,' Saskia said blithely. 'Though I've been thinking about it for ages. We, like, watched this programme about factory farming in science? And the way they farm chickens is totally the worst. When the chicks have hatched they pick up the male ones and throw them straight into a chipper. And the female chicks that are left have a horrible life, forced to lay fifteen eggs a day until they're worn out and exhausted and they end up in your curry.'

'Mine was a free-range chicken,' said Liz. 'Never laid more than one egg a week.'

'It's still full of antibiotics.'

'It was organic free-range.'

'How can you even know that? I'm not being funny, Mum, but you really need to start thinking more about what you put into your mouth.'

'Right.'

'Seriously. I'm only trying to help you. It's important to me that you stay healthy.'

'Thanks. It's important to me that you stay healthy too, which is why I joined the cookery class.'

'You could have joined a vegetarian one.'

'Had I known you were going to give up meat by the end of the week, I might have done.'

'And perhaps if you made the effort to eat vegan and organic yourself, you might not look your age,' Saskia said in a mumble. Maybe Liz wasn't supposed to hear it. But she did and she almost swerved the Volvo into a tree as a result.

'What did you just say?'

'Nothing.'

'You said I look my age.'

'What I said was that eating organic can keep you looking young.'

'You mean like Brittney.'

'Well . . . yeah,' said Saskia, riskily.

'Saskia, Brittney looks younger than I do because she is nearly two decades younger than I am. A fact which can't have been lost on your father. She's just twenty-four years old. She could live on chips and Tizer and she'd still only look twenty-five.'

'She'd never touch Tizer,' said Saskia.

'I'm sure she wouldn't.'

Liz had recently begun to notice that Saskia had stopped joining in with her bitching about Brittney and, though grown-up, mature Liz knew it was for the best that Saskia had a cordial relationship with her father's partner, Liz wasn't sure she actually liked it. She'd preferred it when Saskia came home railing against Brittney's stupid food rules. At the next set of lights, Liz turned to her daughter and said, 'If I look old, it's because I've got you greeting my every utterance with a sigh and telling me I don't know how to feed you even when I go to the effort to grate a flippin' nutmeg. That's enough to make anyone feel ancient.'

'You still can't make me eat meat.'

'I'm not going to. You can make yourself some mung bean soup when we get home.'

'Mum!'

'I've had a long day. I don't need this. You don't want to eat my curry, you'll have to cater for yourself.'

'You're being so unfair!'

Saskia grabbed for the car door handle to make a dramatic statement by flinging herself out onto the road.

'Child lock's on,' Liz told her.

They made the rest of the journey in silence.

Once they were home, Saskia fled straight to her room, doubtless to log on and tell her schoolfriends what a witch she had for a mother. Liz found she cared less than she probably should. She had been so excited about her cookery course. So proud to come home with something more complicated than rock cakes. She had envisaged how impressed Saskia would be to hear all about the cooking process.

But she had reckoned without the Saskia who existed in real life, rather than the fantasy child she conjured up when talking about her daughter to other people. Specifically, when trying to hold her own in a conversation at work. Corinne's two kids were absolute angels. At least, that's what Corinne said. So Liz had to counter that with a version of Saskia who was thoughtful and studious and well on her way to studying Sanskrit and astrophysics at Oxford. Liz had trotted out the exaggerations so often that sometimes she forgot that particular Saskia didn't exist.

Thanks to Saskia, Liz no longer really wanted to eat the curry but she knew that if she didn't heat it up again right away, it would only languish in the fridge until it needed to be chucked out. So she tipped it out of the metal tray into a proper oven dish and set the heat according to Alex's instructions.

When the curry was ready, Liz went at it with a spoon. All the forks were in the dishwasher. Saskia was still upstairs. Ted was at her feet, watching avidly. The curry was OK but it was not as Liz had hoped it would be. Somehow it just didn't taste as good as it smelled. Liz ate about half of it then pushed it away. Ted, who recognised when Liz had had enough to eat, put a paw on her knee and cocked his head winningly.

'You're on a diet,' Liz reminded him.

He cocked his head further.

'Oh, sod it. I know you'll appreciate it at least.'

Liz put the dish containing the remaining curry on the floor. Ted tucked in eagerly, heartily wagging his tail as he did so. Feeling guilty again, Liz retrieved the now empty dish and shoved it in the dishwasher.

'You shouldn't have had that,' she told her happy dog. 'But at least if the spices give you the squits, you'll have a chance of being on target for Saturday's weigh-in.'

Chapter Twelve

When he got back home to his bedsit that Thursday evening, Alex wolfed down his share of the curry. It had turned out pretty well. He hoped his new students would think the same when they reheated their portions at home.

The class had gone quite smoothly, he thought in retrospect. The words *'Can't cook, won't cook'* and *'Please for heaven's sake,* don't *cook'* had come to Alex's mind when he first saw them practise their knife techniques and there had been moments when he thought it was all going to go horribly wrong, such as when John caught the tip of his finger, but in general all three students seemed to be enthusiastic and to enjoy themselves. Alex was happy to imagine the transformation he might make to their cooking skills over the following five weeks.

Alex was hoping for a transformation of his own in the near future. After he'd washed up his dishes, he sat down in his single armchair with a folder full of paperwork. His 'dream file' was what he called it. Inside were cuttings from magazines and newspapers, secret recipes scribbled on postcards and napkins, letters and bank statements. Application forms.

Sometimes when Alex opened up the file, he felt his heart sink. His dream seemed so far from reality. That night, however, he was buoyed up. It wasn't that the class had been a huge success – how could it be when only three people had turned up – but it had reminded him he had something to offer the world. People wanted to hear what he had to say. They wanted to taste his food.

He felt inspired enough to indulge in one of his favourite pastimes – matching a recipe to a face. When he thought about cooking for friends, he often tried to cook to their personalities. Now he tried it with his students. John Barker seemed like a traditionalist. He would be fan of a good Sunday lunch. Roast beef with all the trimmings. Maybe a beef wellington. Nothing nouveau or overly fussy. Liz Chandler, Chopper as she was now known, seemed like she would be more adventurous. She said she was a fan of Thai food. Maybe she was a stir fry. Colourful, full of energy and possibly mixed up. Definitely tasty. Bella was harder to read. Her exterior was smart and neat. Her interior was definitely more complex. He thought of a chocolate-coated ice-cream bombe but that wasn't right. No, he couldn't get a handle on Bella.

In one of the other rooms in the building, someone started to play music. Loudly. It happened most nights. All Alex could do was continue to make his plans to move on. He closed his dream file, put in his ear plugs and went to bed.

Chapter Thirteen

Saturday soon rolled around and with it, time for Ted's first session at Waggy Weight Loss.

Saskia was at her father's for the weekend and Liz had taken advantage of her child-free status to go out with Corinne on Friday night. Because her twins were still at primary school, Corinne did not get out very often, which meant that when she did, she liked to go especially wild. Liz could vaguely recall the first of at least four tequila slammers. Maybe six. Then there was the wine to 'wash the tequila down'. It was little wonder that the morning after, her mouth felt like the bottom of a birdcage. The last thing she wanted to do was get up and take Ted to his doggy weight loss club.

Unfortunately, Liz knew that she had to. It was her fault Ted had managed to get so overweight, after all. Though he seemed happy, she wanted him to be healthy too. Added to that, on Friday, she'd received an email from Nurse Van Niekerk at the veterinary surgery telling her that attendance was now mandatory if she wanted Ted to remain one of Dr Thomas's patients. The thought of finding Ted another vet filled Liz with the same kind of dread that had kept her dental patients loyal to her boss Vince during the *delirium tremens* years.

Liz hauled herself out of bed but before she got dressed she decided to give Ted a preliminary weigh-in.

If the figure was *truly* awful she would stay home and claim she had a bug. It wouldn't sound like a lie; there was one going round. She really didn't need another lecture with her hangover going on.

She took the bathroom scales downstairs. First she stood on them by herself and made a note of the number. That in itself was not so good but nothing that a week on the 5:2 diet couldn't fix. Or a week on the vomiting bug. Liz always lived in hope. Then she picked up Ted and stood on the scales with him in her arms. That number minus the first number *et voila*! Ted's weight.

Oh dear. It appeared that Ted had actually put on a couple of ounces since the cake-mix debacle. He certainly felt heavier than Liz had expected. She put him down and did the sums. Then Liz deducted half a pound for her pyjamas. That was better. Now Ted was doing well.

'Come on,' she said to him. 'Let's get this over with.'

The surgery was packed for Waggy Weight Loss. Liz couldn't get a space in the car park so she had to park on the street and walk three blocks.

'I suppose we need the exercise,' she said to Ted.

Liz would never have guessed that so many of the local dogs shared Ted's obesity battle. Not that they looked especially unhappy about it. The assembled dogs were completely oblivious to the social stigma of their condition. The assembled owners on the other hand were all too aware and expecting a lecture to boot. They looked anxious. Liz was reminded of the tension in the corridor outside the headmaster's office at her comprehensive school, where students waited on plastic chairs to be called in and admonished.

Liz couldn't find a spare plastic chair that morning so she leaned against the wall with Ted at her feet and tried to look casual.

'Is this your first time?' a middle-aged woman with a fancy chignon, who was perching on one of those walking-stick stools, asked her. She had a spherical French bulldog on her lap.

'It is. What's it like? Do we have to get weighed too?'

The woman didn't laugh. She fondled her little bulldog's velvety black ears. 'This is the third time we've been asked to sign up. It's just so humiliating. I feel like such a bad mother for getting her into this situation in the first place. Coco dreads having to get on the scales in front of everybody else.'

Liz didn't think Coco looked all that bothered. She was busy snuffling for treats in 'Mummy's' Chanel-style handbag. Meanwhile, Ted was acquainting himself with a huge golden Labrador's bum.

'Coco tries so hard,' the woman on the walking stick continued. 'She eats next to nothing and she exercises all the time. She's always so disheartened when the scales don't budge an ounce. I've tried to explain to her that it isn't her fault. She's the way she is because of genetics. But people can be so cruel, can't they?'

'They can.' Liz tried to lighten the mood. 'That's a nice name, Coco,' she said.

'For Coco Chanel,' the woman explained. Hence the handbag. 'She was also small, plucky and French.'

'Yes,' said Liz. She imagined this canine Coco with a string of faux pearls. It might have looked good against her fur.

'And yours?' the woman asked.

'Liz.'

The woman looked confused. 'But he's a boy.'

'Oh. You mean *his* name. Ted. After Theodore Roosevelt.'

Liz made that up on the spot. Ted was actually called Ted after the stuffed blue bear Saskia had loved as a toddler. They weren't great at original names in the Chandler household. The unfortunate hamster that preceded Ted had been called 'Hammy'. He died when Saskia left the door to his cage open and he met next door's cat.

'It's so important to give animals a proper name, don't you think?' The woman leaned towards Liz to indicate that Liz should probably duck down to hear what she had to say next. 'That Cockapoo over there is called Twinkle.' Coco's owner wrinkled her nose in disapproval. 'Can you imagine what he feels like when they're calling for him in the playground?'

'It must be terrible,' said Liz.

Liz thought Twinkle had bigger problems than his name. He needed a haircut for a start. His Cockapoo curls were hanging all over his eyes and he kept bumping into his owner's knees and barking indiscriminately. Probably confused by the fact that he couldn't see anything.

At least Ted wasn't much of a barker. That was a bone of contention, actually, since the unfortunate occasion when he didn't bark while someone was stealing one of Ian's beloved mountain bikes out of their garage. At the time, Liz joined Ian in wondering how they'd come to have such a useless guard dog. Now she wondered whether Ted had actually known that Ian was a philandering knobhead and decided that his bicycle was fair game. Yes. Ted was no idiot. Not like the Chihuahua on the other side of the room who was yapping and turning in circles. Liz wouldn't have imagined a Chihuahua at Waggy Weight Loss but this one was as round as a gourmet Scotch egg on four Twiglets. He was definitely not at his fighting weight.

At ten o'clock on the dot, the session officially began.

Nurse Van Niekerk was the first veterinary professional to appear. She handed out forms to each of the owners in attendance.

'Please fill in as much as you possibly can. It will help us to get a better idea of your animal's eating habits and the behaviours and situations that trigger them.'

The patients were dogs. Surely 'seeing food' was what triggered their eating? But Mrs Coco was already scribbling down 'stress, anxiety and low self-esteem' on Coco's chart. Mrs Coco had been to Waggy Weight Loss before. Was this the kind of stuff they wanted?

'Has Ted got low self-esteem?' Liz asked herself. She hoped not. Thanks to Ian, Liz had enough low self-esteem for the pair of them. She wondered if she should put that Ted's bad eating habits had become a problem after the break-up of his family. Yes. Blame Ian. That would be satisfying. But what if they had to read what they'd written out loud? There might be someone in the room who knew Ian. Or Brittney. Liz put: 'No obvious triggers. Basically, if he sees food he eats it.'

Liz finished filling in Ted's chart in about half a minute. Meanwhile, Mrs Coco and many of the other 'mums and dads' seemed to be writing short essays. That made Liz nervous. Was she already not taking it seriously enough? She wanted Dr Thomas to know that his concerns had not fallen on deaf ears.

At last, Nurse Van Niekerk began to chivvy people along. She took Liz's form, glanced at it and said, 'Thank you.' She didn't seem obviously unimpressed by Liz's brevity.

'OK, everybody. Some of you have been here before. What is this, Coco? Your fifth time here?'

'Third,' said Mrs Coco defensively.

'Third,' Nurse Van Niekerk repeated in a tone that hinted at amusement. 'Well, you at least know the ropes. And Twinkle. It's good to see you again. Time for a fringe trim, I think, Mr Twinkle,' Nurse Van Niekerk addressed Twinkle's 'dad'.

Mr Twinkle, Liz mused. That was why it was a good idea to give your dog a half-decent name.

'Let's just go around the room and introduce ourselves. I'm Nurse Van Niekerk as you know. We've already met Coco and Twinkle. Chihuahua Daddy, let's start with you.'

'This is Hercules,' Chihuahua Daddy introduced the walking Scotch egg. 'He's actually my wife's dog.' It was clearly important to him that everybody understood that.

Ted's friend the golden Labrador was called Monty. The King Charles Spaniel, whose stomach almost dragged along the ground, was called Rex. Twinkle's near twin, another Cockapoo with a slightly better trim, was called Biscuit.

Mrs Coco disapproved. 'How is he meant to avoid getting unhealthy eating habits when Biscuit is all that he hears?'

Nurse Van Niekerk came to Liz at last.

'This is Ted,' said Liz.

Ted wagged his tail at the sound of his name.

'Thank you, Mrs Ted.'

'Mrs Chandler,' Liz attempted.

Nurse Van Niekerk ignored her.

'I'm glad to see you all. Now we've done the introductions . . .' Nurse Van Niekerk glanced at her watch and then back towards the surgery, 'I think Doctor Thomas will be ready to join us now.'

A moment later, Dr Evan Thomas strode into the surgery reception area looking like a man who knew he would be played by Hugh Jackman in the story of his life. As befitted the fact that it was a Saturday, he was dressed in casual gear. Liz hadn't seen him without his sterile green overalls before. Mufti was definitely an improvement. That morning, the vet was wearing jeans and a long-sleeved checked button-down in a rather dashing lilac. The shirtsleeves were rolled up so that they tightly circled his triceps, which were not unimpressive. But then, Liz thought, being a vet was a very physical job. Lifting all those obese dogs onto the table was a workout for a start.

As she considered Dr Thomas's triceps, Liz's eyes then naturally drifted down to see whether Dr Thomas's thighs matched his arms. They did. She half nodded her approval. Which was embarrassing because when she next glanced up, Dr Thomas seemed to be looking at her in a quizzical sort of way. She rearranged her face into the expression she used for when she was attending 'continuing professional development in dental hygiene' lectures.

'Good morning, ladies and gentlemen. And owners . . .' Dr Thomas quipped.

The humans said 'Good morning' back.

'Thank you for coming along today. I'm very glad to see you've made the commitment to your animals' health. Now, you all know why you're here. I have met all of you in this surgery before and judged that your pets have a weight problem. I do not bandy the word "obese" about lightly, but trust me, on a human scale, that's exactly what your animals are.'

Liz felt herself melting back into the wall for shame. Mrs Coco held her dog tightly against her as if to protect her from the nasty man who was possibly denting Coco's self-esteem.

'Nurse Van Niekerk has already prepared a chart onto which your dogs' most recent weights have been plotted. All of you should have been on the diet for at least a week – some of you for longer – so let's see how you've been getting on.'

'It's time for the Waggy Weigh-In,' said Nurse Van Niekerk lightly, in an attempt to make it sound like fun.

'I hate this bit,' said Mrs Coco.

'In alphabetical order,' said Nurse Van Niekerk. 'Biscuit?'

The Cockapoo leapt up. So did nearly all of the other dogs, including Ted. Biscuit was clearly a trigger word for most of them.

Biscuit was four hundred grams down.

'Though I suspect at least three hundred of those grams are due to the haircut,' Dr Thomas observed.

'Bruno?'

Doctor Thomas looked around the room. There was no Bruno there. He shook his head and tutted. 'It's always the ones who need help the most. Never mind. Coco?'

Mrs Coco put up her hand. 'Of course, Mrs Coco. This is what? Your fifth time here?'

'Third,' said Mrs Coco.

Unlike Nurse Van Niekerk, Doctor Thomas wasn't having any of it. 'Come on now, Mrs Coco. Being in denial doesn't help anyone. Least of all your dog.'

Mrs Coco went bright red. Liz suddenly felt very sorry for her.

'Put Coco on the scales, Mrs Coco. We haven't got all day.'

Mrs Coco carefully, reverently, placed Coco on the weighing machine. She looked away and nibbled at her cuticles while Nurse Van Niekerk and Doctor Thomas looked at the figures.

'Five hundred grams down since the last appointment,' Nurse Van Niekerk announced after what felt like an *X Factor*-style pause of doom. Mrs Coco's face was suddenly wreathed in smiles.

'See?' said Dr Thomas. 'What tough love can do? Good work, Mrs Coco. Good work.'

Liz gave Mrs Coco the thumbs up. At least Dr Thomas was in the habit of giving praise where it was due.

'Who's next? Hercules?'

The Scotch egg was up. Mr Hercules looked suitably embarrassed as Hercules tipped the scales at a full two hundred and fifty grams over his week one target.

'Have you really been sticking to the diet?' Dr Thomas asked.

'I have,' said Mr Hercules. 'But I can't be sure about my wife. He only has to look at her and he gets whatever he wants. Pity that never worked for me.'

'Never mind,' said Dr Thomas. He patted Mr

Hercules on the shoulder. 'We're just at the beginning here. You keep on setting an example for the rest of the family. Remind them that if they really love this dog, they shouldn't indulge him.'

'I'm doing my best, Dr Thomas.'

'Keep it up. Monty?'

The Labrador bounded into the middle of the room. Well, bounded is perhaps too light a word. He moved like a bouncing bomb heading for a dam.

'Looking good,' Dr Thomas said. 'Let's see if it's just because you're wearing a particularly slimming collar.'

But no, Monty had lost a whole kilo since he was put on the diet.

'Let's give him a round of applause,' Dr Thomas said.

'Rex?' Nurse Van Niekerk called. The spaniel and owner waddled forward. Nurse Van Niekerk reminded Dr Thomas of just how heavy Rex had been when they last saw him at the surgery.

'I can already see an improvement,' Dr Thomas assured Rex's owner. Liz found it hard to imagine how Rex could have been any worse without morphing into a foot stool.

'Half a kilo,' said Nurse Van Niekerk.

Dr Thomas stooped to give Rex a scratch between the ears.

'Excellent work, my man,' he said.

Liz knew that she and Ted were next. There was only Twinkle left to be weighed.

'Ah, Mrs Ted,' said Dr Thomas.

'Mrs Chandler . . .'

Dr Thomas ignored that. 'It's very good to see you

here. No cake mix and Pringles for Little Ted this week?'

'Absolutely not,' said Liz. 'We've followed the diet to the letter.'

The chicken curry was mostly pure protein, surely? And chicken was allowed.

'I'm very glad to hear it. On the scales?'

Ted was busy sniffing at something on the floor. Liz tried to nudge him forward with her foot. He didn't move. Dr Thomas wasn't prepared to wait around. He bent down and lifted Ted up.

'Hmmm,' he said as he did so. That didn't sound good at all.

Nurse Van Niekerk looked at the number on the scales then she looked at the number on her spreadsheet. She tapped figures into the calculator on her iPhone. She didn't have to shake her head for Liz to know what was coming.

'He's up,' Nurse Van Niekerk confirmed. 'Five hundred.'

'That's half a bag of sugar,' Dr Thomas pointed out.

'He had a big drink of water before we came here,' Liz protested. 'If I could just take him out into the car park for a pee . . .'

Dr Thomas shook his head. 'You've got to take this seriously, Mrs Ted. Stick to the diet. No titbits. More walks. Advice that works just as well for us humans as for our pets.'

Liz was sure Dr Thomas's advice was pointed. She opened her mouth to protest but she'd already been dismissed.

'Twinkle!'

'How could you do this to me?' she muttered in Ted's direction.

'If Ted had autonomy, he would make better choices for himself.' Dr Thomas had heard her aside and Liz was right back to the cake-mix evening.

'Thank you,' Liz scooped Ted up, making sure to pretend it was hardly any effort, and went back to her place by the wall.

At least Twinkle failed the weigh-in too.

'OK, everybody. We'll see you next week. Keep the faith. You're all going to get to that target weight. I know it.'

Dr Thomas made a fist and gave a little gesture that was meant to represent tenacity and willpower, Liz supposed.

'Git,' she muttered.

Mrs Coco followed Liz out of the surgery. They paused on the wheelchair ramp while Mrs Coco loaded Coco into a *pushchair*.

'She gets very tired. It's all the emotion.'

'Of course. Doctor Thomas is . . . well, he's quite harsh, isn't he?'

'But it comes from a place of love,' said Mrs Coco. 'Sometimes I have to remind myself of that. Nothing matters to him more than the patients in his care. He truly is an animal lover.'

He certainly didn't seem to have much time for humans, Liz reflected.

'I'd better get Coco home,' said Mrs Coco. 'She has to have a nap before lunch.'

Coco made a strange sort of groan.

'What's that, sweetheart? Oh, I know. It's been a *very*

stressful morning.' Mrs Coco reached into her handbag and brought out a bag of doggy chocs. 'Here you are, my lovely little lady. I think you deserve one of these.'

'Mrs Coco!' came a voice that made both Mrs Coco and Liz jump out of their skins. 'I don't believe doggy chocs are on the Waggy Weight Loss diet sheet.'

Mrs Coco quickly stuffed the special choc drops back into her bag. But Dr Thomas had other ideas. He held his hand out, like a teacher confiscating a packet of chewing gum.

'Thank you. And if you have anything similar in your handbag, Mrs Ted, you can hand it over to me now.'

'It's Mrs Chandler,' Liz reminded him.

'Mrs Chandler, of course. How could I forget?' He shook his head in amusement and gave Liz a smile she might have enjoyed in any other context. 'Pringles and cake mix.'

Chapter Fourteen

After Waggy Weight Loss, Liz knew she needed to take Ted for a walk. A proper walk. The day had started off quite nicely, weather-wise, but it had turned distinctly grey while they'd been at Dr Thomas's surgery, and Liz still had a banging hangover thanks to her big night out. Corinne had texted with regard to that.

'Did I leave my knickers at your house?'

To which Liz could only respond '!!!!!!' Corinne hadn't even come back to her house. Corinne's wild approach to dating made Liz feel quite queasy. One of the night out's big topics of conversation was whether or not Liz should bite the bullet and put herself on Tinder. Liz's conclusion? No chance. She maintained that it was much nicer and safer to meet people in an organic way. Through work. Or on a dog walk.

'I'll take you out after lunch,' she promised Ted.

What was lunch going to be? For Ted, it was half a bowl of dry biscuits. For Liz. Pretty much the same. She needed to go shopping. She would have done a shop on Friday afternoon but since Saskia wasn't going to be at home that weekend, Liz thought a better investment of her time would be to get her hair done for her girls' night out instead.

Oh Saskia. The only communication Liz had had from her daughter since attempting to kiss her goodbye on Friday morning was a single word text: 'Yes' in response to Liz's: 'Are you at your dad's yet? Are you having a nice day? Please be sure to remind him that I've got a weekend training course in Plymouth at the beginning of December so we'll need to coordinate our diaries.'

'Yes.'

That was all.

Relations between mother and daughter had been frostier than ever since the chicken curry affair. Liz felt like an utter failure when she saw the contempt in her daughter's eyes. Which was often. She was so disappointed. It didn't matter how many times Liz heard or read that mother–daughter relationships often hit a bumpy patch during the teenage years, Liz had been so sure she and Saskia wouldn't end up like that.

When Saskia was little, she thought Liz was a goddess. She couldn't get enough of her. She lisped 'I love Mummy' almost as soon as she could speak. The first drawing she brought home from playgroup was a picture of Liz with long yellow hair, entitled (in the childminder's handwriting): 'To the best mum in the world.'

Little Saskia wanted to do whatever Liz did. She wanted to put on Liz's make-up and try on her shoes. She wanted to do the dusting and follow her round when she was hoovering. Ian even got hold of a model of a dentist's chair – he had connections with a company that made surgery furniture – so that Saskia could pretend to be a dental hygienist.

'Just like mummy,' she said.

Now? Not so much. Ten years later, Saskia pronounced

Liz's job 'gross'. 'What do you want to be smelling people's bad breath all day long for?'

'To pay for your iPhone?' was Liz's reply.

Saskia certainly didn't want to try on her mother's shoes or clothes any more.

'Could your wardrobe *be* any more frumpy?' Saskia muttered when Liz told her she could borrow a Fair Isle jumper for something they were doing at the NEWTS.

Liz tried to see that moment as an opportunity to learn and grow. A chance to bring Saskia a little closer. Crikey, it was hard.

'Maybe you could take me round the shops,' she said. 'And pick out some things you think might suit me better?'

Saskia didn't even answer. At least not verbally. She just raised her eyebrows and rolled her eyes.

Where once Liz had been the centre of Saskia's universe, now Ian was most definitely the parent with the upper hand. Even though he was the one who'd walked out, Liz was pretty sure Ian didn't get a fraction of the grief she had to endure. It was easy for him. Most of the time, he didn't even have to live with the bundle of hormones that was their daughter. He got her for two nights at a time. Three max. It wasn't hard to grit your teeth and get through a weekend with stony-faced Saskia if you knew you didn't have to do Monday morning as well.

And of course he was spoiling her in a desperate attempt to make up for having torn the family apart. When the three of them lived together, Ian was actually pretty good at laying down the law. Now that he was living in Exeter with the Busty Bloggette, it was all very different. Every time Ian dropped Saskia off at the former family home in Newbay, Saskia was carrying a bag from a fancy boutique that contained the sort of clothes he never would have let her wear before. The sort of clothes that Liz associated with Brittney. Stevie-Nicks-meets-a-stripper gear. Saskia's style, like her eating habits, was definitely coming under Brittney's influence.

Indeed, that Saturday, Brittney had posted a blog update entitled 'Retail therapy!'

'Can anything bring two women closer together more quickly than a shopping trip?' she asked.

'Yeah,' Liz snarled. 'You could bang their heads together.'

Liz read the blog and self-medicated with a single wrapped biscuit – pinched from a dental conference buffet – that she'd found in the bottom of her handbag. A biscuit for lunch. Brittney was probably spiralising a gherkin.

It was so difficult not to get disheartened. Liz knew that Saskia was harder on her than she was on her father because Liz was the one who was always around. Always there for her. And we all lash out at the ones we love, right? Eventually, Saskia would find her balance again and their relationship would improve. All the same, Liz wanted to be the one who was taking Saskia on shopping trips and sharing giggles over the kale power shakes. Well, maybe not the kale power shakes.

'Come on, Ted,' said Liz at about two o'clock. 'Let's go for that walk.'

It was almost the end of September. The summer crowds had all but disappeared and the beaches had been reclaimed by the locals. From May until the middle of September, the main beach at Newbay, the one which sported the newly renovated Victorian pier, was strictly off limits to animals, even if they were wearing a lead. Liz preferred the town's smaller beach, Duckpool Bay, anyway. That's where she was headed on Saturday afternoon. Dogs were always allowed on Duckpool.

By three o'clock, Liz's hangover headache was just a dull throb. With every step she took closer to the coast, she was sure she could feel even that remnant of the previous night's bad behaviour fading away. A walk really was a cure for so many things. Her back ached less the more she moved. It brought colour to her cheeks. She thought she could even feel her thighs shrinking. OK, that was wishful thinking. By the time she got to the coast road down to Duckpool Bay, Liz was feeling altogether better. She even chuckled to herself as she remembered that morning's Waggy Weigh-In. Mrs Coco's face was a picture when Dr Thomas caught her dishing out treats to her fat little pooch.

Liz was quietly determined that over the next six weeks she was going to confound Dr Thomas's expectations. This walk was just the start of it. She would make sure Ted did at least three miles a day. She would stick to the diet. She would prove to Dr Thomas that she loved her little dog. And it would be good for her too. She'd get more exercise. Meanwhile, the cookery class would help her to sort out her own eating habits. If she took the time to cook from scratch even once a week, she might be less inclined to stuff herself when the food was finally on the table.

Yes, she was going to make some changes for the

better. How long does it take to form a habit? Hadn't she recently read about it somewhere? Ah. Now she remembered. It was on Brittney's Blog. Never mind. It definitely wasn't an original thought. The Dalai Lama had almost certainly said, 'It takes six weeks to make or break a habit' in one of his addresses to the faithful. Liz was going to prove him right.

As she bent down to unclip Ted's lead so that he could run across the sand, Liz was really quite positive about what she could achieve before the end of that year. A fitter dog. A fitter self. A better mother–daughter relationship. Maybe even an Instagram-worthy cake?

Saskia would be turning sixteen at the beginning of November. Sixteen birthdays and Liz had almost never baked her a birthday cake from scratch. At least not since Saskia's first birthday when Liz and Ian hosted a special party at their home. Liz had so wanted to impress her in-laws (and her own family) with the perfect Victoria sponge. It came out like a Frisbee.

Liz heard her mother-in-law telling her sister-in-law with regard to what Ian saw in Liz, 'I understand she makes him laugh.'

'Yeah, with a cake like that he needs a good sense of humour,' said Ian's big sister Michelle.

The following year, Liz delegated cake duties to M&S and had done the same every year since.

The memory of Saskia's first birthday cake made Liz smile a little sadly. This year would be different. Since Saskia turned fifteen, Liz had been plotting how she might make her sixteenth birthday an especially big event. She'd been squirrelling away a fiver a week in a special account to make sure Saskia got a really good present. Would she want a party? Liz wasn't sure. She probably wouldn't want a party with the adults around. Liz decided instead that she would suggest they had a weekend away somewhere nice. Maybe at a spa. Saskia used to love it when Liz took her to the nail salon to get her nails done when she was little. They'd recreate one of those lovely moments in a fancy country hotel health spa place. Liz would take the birthday cake along.

She could see it now. Alex's course would help her achieve her goal. The perfect chocolate cake with thick glossy icing. #birthday #chocolate #mumforthebirthdaycakewin. She was going to ace it. Maybe she'd even do a cake with three tiers? Three tiers in different flavours? Handmade sugar flowers as decorations? Her imagination had no limits even if her cookery skills did.

Unhooked from his lead, Ted suddenly set off like a rocket.

'Ted!'

Liz looked up, expecting to see that Ted had decided to take his chances with a seagull, even though he never managed to reach them before they flew away. But, no.

Ted was not chasing a seagull. He was heading for three figures at the other end of the sand.

Chapter Fifteen

It was Ian. And Saskia. And Brittney.

What on earth were they doing in Duckpool Bay?

Brittney and Saskia were throwing some strange poses and Liz realised as she got closer that they were doing some sort of photo shoot. Ian was taking the pictures with the enormous camera he'd bought just before he left Liz. She didn't like to think of the private shoots he and Brittney must have done over the past year.

Saskia was dressed in an outfit that Liz didn't recognise. While Liz was wearing traditional dog-walking chic – her oldest jeans, her wellies and a puffa jacket that had definitely lost its puff – Saskia and Brittney were like something straight out of a Seasalt catalogue. Saskia was wearing a bright pink mac and yellow boots. She *never* wore bright colours. Never.

What were they doing there? Ian and Brittney lived in Exeter. There were beaches far closer to that city than Duckpool.

Liz wanted to turn and get out of there right away but of course Ted had already broken her cover. There was no pretending she wasn't on the beach now. Unless she pretended that Ted had escaped and gone to the beach on his own? No. That would still mean she'd have to face Ian at some point. He would bring Ted back to the house and then she would get a lecture about making sure he couldn't get out of the garden. What if he'd been run over? Etcetera, etcetera, etcetera.

Better to put on her big girl pants and get on with it. She had to be civil to the woman who'd ruined her life.

'Hello, sweetheart,' Liz said to Saskia, who grunted something in response. She did not seem best pleased to have been caught in the heinous act of enjoying herself around adults. 'Ian. Brittney.'

'What are you doing here?' Ian asked as though Liz was the one thirty miles from where she was supposed to be that afternoon.

'I'm walking the dog. What are you doing here? Aren't there any beaches closer to Exeter?'

'There are . . .' Ian began.

'But this one is the prettiest in Devon,' said Saskia.

'We're doing a photo shoot,' Brittney explained. 'For the blog?'

How Liz hated the way people like Brittney made every statement a question.

'That's why we're wearing these clothes,' said Saskia. 'Brittney gets sent all sorts of stuff by retailers who want her endorsement for their products.'

'Yes, I know,' said Liz. 'Like home tooth-whitening kits.'

Brittney at least had the grace to look embarrassed. She tucked her long brown hair behind her multi-pierced ears in a nervous sort of gesture. She seemed even younger than she was, standing there all shy and knock-kneed. Liz had always thought the knock-kneed thing was just something bloggers did for their pictures.

'So,' Liz addressed Ian. 'Saskia's photograph is going to be online, is it?'

She didn't need to remind him of the arguments they'd had over whether or not it was a good idea to put family photographs on Facebook. Since the split, Liz had wondered whether Ian was less concerned about protecting his daughter's privacy than keeping up the pretence that he was an available man. She had come to doubt that Brittney was the first woman to entice him away from the marriage bed.

'I think Saskia's old enough to choose for herself now,' Ian said.

'I suppose she is,' said Liz. Now she turned to Brittney. 'Are you getting paid for this endorsement?'

'Mum!' Saskia piped up in her 'you're so embarrassing' voice.

'I'm not,' said Brittney. 'I'm doing an honest review in return for free samples.' She trotted out the line she used at the end of some of her blog posts. 'But Saskia can keep the clothes.'

'I really like them,' Saskia pointed out.

Of course she did. Under the pink coat the electric blue skirt she wore was little more than a pelmet, as Liz's grandmother might have described it.

'Fine,' said Liz. 'It's up to you. I'll just remind you that online is for ever. You need to consider how your online footprint is going to look in ten years' time.'

Saskia exhaled so that the puff of air lifted her fringe. That subtly defiant gesture might ordinarily have been enough to earn a ticking off from Liz or Ian but the beach was no place to get into a row. Particularly since Brittney was already drawing a small crowd. A couple of young women in running gear were asking if she really was Brittney from Brittney's Bites and telling her how much they loved her recipe for split-pea hummus.

'Ted and I had better get on with our walk,' Liz concluded.

'Dad?' Saskia interrupted. 'Can we take Ted, Dad? Please? Please? He'd be great in the photos.'

'He would,' Brittney agreed. 'Good thinking, Sassy.'

Sassy?

'People love to see dogs in a picture.'

'Is that OK?' Ian asked Liz.

'I suppose.' What else could she say? She already knew that she was losing in the cool adult of the day stakes by a long way. To refuse to let Saskia have custody of her own dog would have looked mean and petty. Liz handed Ian the dog lead and the poo bags. 'Just bring him back when you drop Saskia off. And don't forget he's on a diet. He mustn't have any treats.'

She lingered until Ian said, 'We'd better get on with these photos. Before we lose the light.'

Liz took the hint. She turned to retrace her steps, walking as quickly as she could on the deep, damp sand. Tears pricked at her eyes. She was desperate to get out of sight before the dam burst. But just as she was climbing the steps to the car park and the road, she heard Ian shouting.

'Liz! Liz! Wait!'

She hesitated on the top step without turning round.

If her life had been a movie, then this would be the moment when Ian, having seen his wife acting with such dignity in the face of unexpectedly meeting his stupid girlfriend, realised that she was by far the better woman and decided he'd been a bloody fool. He wanted her back and he was prepared to make a scene of it. Pushing her hair from her face, Liz turned towards him slowly.

'Yes?' she said.

'Liz, thanks for stopping. Look, you'd better take Ted home with you after all. Brittney's place isn't really set up for animals. She's got cream carpets.'

'Of course.'

Ian handed Liz the lead with Ted on the end of it.

'Oh, and Saskia says can you make sure her PE kit is ready for Monday. Thanks.'

By the time Liz got back home, having stopped in a café for another consoling hot chocolate (Ted had one of the marshmallows), Brittney had already posted the first images from her photo session on Instagram.

'Great beach shoot today with my homies! This is my favourite image. #windscaleclothing #happydays #borderterrier #dogsofinstagram.'

Yep. The dog was in the picture, guaranteeing Brittney lots of precious 'likes'. Brittney and Saskia were jumping in the air and Ted was doing his best to keep up with them. Poor Ted, posing his heart out, only to be dismissed moments later. Discarded. Just as Liz had been. Brittney's fans didn't know about that. She wished she could go round and pee on Brittney's carpets herself.

Chapter Sixteen

After that awful weekend, Liz was only too glad to start the new working week. It went quickly. One minute it was Monday morning, the next it was Thursday afternoon and Liz, Corinne and Vince were going over the patients they had seen thus far at their regular team meeting.

'Got to leave on the dot of half five,' Liz told them. 'Cooking class starts at six.'

'Any nice blokes there?' Corinne asked.

'There are two. They're both nice. One's the teacher, Alex. But he's at least ten years younger than me, and the other bloke, John, probably fought in World War Two.'

'Oh,' said Corinne. 'Still, age is just a number.'

'In which direction? Older or younger?'

'Either. And the new cooking skills will come in useful when you do start dating again. The way to a man's heart is through his stomach.'

'Yeah. If only I'd known that Ian's stomach was crying out for sprouted mung bean salad and not steak and kidney pie.'

'What are you making tonight?' Corinne asked.

'A simple white sauce and fish pie according to Alex.'

'Oooh. One of my favourites. What time shall I be over?' Vince joked.

'I'm hoping that Saskia will eat her share of it this time.'

'I thought she'd turned vegetarian.'

'Not completely. She says she won't eat anything with a nose or a beak.'

'Don't fish have noses?' Vince asked.

'Crikey, I feel like I should know this,' said Liz. 'I'm going to have to google it.'

But there was no time before the class. When Liz arrived – with her apron this time, the one with the torso of the Venus de Milo printed on the front – her fellow students were already in their places. Exactly the same places as they had taken up the previous week. Liz had often thought it strange that people refused to move around. Still, she wasn't about to upset the status quo. She took her spot in the middle.

Alex was talking Bella through the final steps of making the curry – the stuff she'd missed when she had to dash from the class to the police station. She was nodding enthusiastically as he explained how it ought to be served.

'Hey! How did the curry go down with your family?' Alex asked Liz. 'Were they impressed?'

'Yes,' Liz said. 'I think they were.'

It wasn't entirely a lie. Ted had loved it.

'Well, I'm sure everyone is going to like today's recipe. There aren't many people who don't like a good fish pie.'

'My nearly ex-husband doesn't,' said Liz.

'Then it's a good job you're no longer cooking for him,' said Bella.

John agreed. 'Sounds like he doesn't know what's good for him.'

Liz decided she liked her classmates even more than she thought.

'A white sauce is very simple,' said Alex. 'It's the basic building block for all sorts of recipes from the everyday to the exotic. All it takes is a little patience. The recipe we're going to use today can be the foundation of a cheese sauce, a parsley sauce or a béchamel.'

'I never thought I'd make a béchamel,' said John.

'I'm not sure I ever will,' said Liz.

'You'll all get it right,' said Alex. 'First, you're going to watch me. It isn't hard at all.'

Alex did have the knack of making things look uncomplicated. It was a big part of his appeal.

'There are just three ingredients, plus a little salt and pepper. I'm going to start by melting twenty-five grams of butter.'

So far, so easy, thought Liz. Though she couldn't help remembering the last time she'd tried to melt butter, left it to itself while she checked Facebook, and ended up with a ruined pan and all the smoke alarms going off.

'When that's melted, we stir in the same amount of flour.'

Bella and John watched avidly but Liz's mind was racing again. She wondered if she would ever make a dish her daughter would actually eat. Butter and flour was vegetarian at least. Could she stick white sauce on courgettini? If she cooked courgettini, would Saskia just think she was trying to copy Brittney? Was she losing Saskia to Brittney altogether? Liz couldn't compete with the free clothes.

'I'm going to let the flour cook for a couple of minutes.'

Bella and John asked intelligent questions about the degree of heat and the type of flour. When Alex talked about grams, Liz thought about Ted. Had he lost a single gram that week or was she in for another lecture at the Waggy Weight Loss weigh-in on Saturday?

'After a couple of minutes, we take the pan off the heat . . .'

Liz gave herself a little lecture for having failed to walk Ted as often as she'd intended to. Well, bloody Brittney had put a stop to that. Liz hadn't dared walk on any of Newbay's beaches on Sunday in case she bumped into her ex, her child and his oh-so-glamorous lover on a photo shoot again. She was still fuming about that. How dare Brittney use her family – right down to the dog – to promote *her* flippin' interests? Maybe she should ask Bella about the legalities of it. Saskia was still only fifteen. Surely it was up to Liz whether her daughter's image could be used in advertising? And if it was used for advertising purposes, Saskia should be properly compensated.

'Did everybody get that?' Alex asked.

Get what? Liz assured him that she had got it whatever it was. White sauce. Three ingredients. Really how difficult could it possibly be?

Alex showed his students the smooth white sauce he had created.

'*Et voila*,' he threw in some French. 'No lumps. Time for you three to try it.'

With the demonstration over, Bella, John and Liz took up their positions again. Without hesitation, Bella and John began to melt their butter, which Alex had already helpfully weighed out. Liz followed suit. Melt butter. She at least remembered that bit, though . . .

'Heat's a little high,' Alex told her when he came to check her progress. 'Don't want it to burn before you know what's going on.'

Liz turned the heat back down.

'I think you're ready to add the flour,' Alex told Bella moments later. Liz decided she must be at the same point. They'd started at the same time. She dumped her twenty-five grams of flour in.

Meanwhile, Bella sifted her flour into the pan. As did John.

'If you sift it, you'll get a head start on the lumps,' Alex reminded them.

Rats, thought Liz. She had lumps already. But she was pretty sure she could beat them out. She used the edge of her wooden spoon to smash them just as Alex said, 'The trick with any white sauce is to be gentle.'

Liz slowed her beating right down.

'Now add the milk.'

Liz tipped in the whole pint in one go.

Alex, Bella and John all looked horrified.

'Liz! This bit is supposed to be *gradual*.'

Liz couldn't remember Alex having told them that at all. When did he say gradual?

'Sorry, sorry, sorry.' Liz stepped back from the pan.

'It's OK,' said Alex, quickly stepping in. 'We may be able to rescue it. If not, we can always start again. Just make sure you've got a couple of pints of milk handy whenever you do this at home.'

Alex took Liz's pan from the heat and tried to salvage her white sauce, while Liz pinched the top of her nose.

'It's been a long week,' she said.

'I understand,' said Alex.

'Sometimes I think I'll never get the hang of this,' Liz continued. 'This cooking thing. Isn't it like gardening, where you've either got green fingers or you haven't? My grandmother was always going on about having the right kind of hands for making pastry. I've only got the right kind of hands for making a dogs' breakfast.'

'I don't believe in that,' said Alex. 'It's an excuse not to take it seriously. Anyone can learn to cook. You just have to be prepared to be patient. All right, Chopper?'

He handed back the wooden spoon and gave her a reassuring smile. Liz shrugged shyly. Alex really was quite gorgeous. And kind. And not half so patronising as he might have been, given the circumstances. Why was he so lovely to her? She was still the only member of the class he'd given a nickname. Did that mean something?

'And there we have it,' said Alex, returning to the front of the class. 'You've all made a white sauce. Now wasn't that easy?'

'Surprisingly,' John said. 'I'm beginning to wonder why I've held you chefs in awe over the years.'

'We're held in awe?' said Alex. 'That's news to me.'

He smiled at Bella. She nodded.

'Well, I absolutely hold you in awe,' said Liz. 'Thanks, chef. I couldn't have done it without you.'

That much was definitely true.

'Don't relax yet,' said Alex next. 'You're going to make another one. And this time we're going to add parsley to use in our fish pie. Parsley and cod is a classic combination.'

'We used to get it in packets,' said Liz.

'Oh yes,' said John. 'I still would if I could find them.'

'Have you tried Iceland?' Liz asked.

'Students, please,' Alex interrupted. 'Once you have made your own parsley sauce and whipped it up into a proper fish pie, you'll never go for boil in the bag again. In any case,' he told them. 'The classical term is *sous-vide*.'

'Sounds much better when you put it like that,' Liz agreed.

'Fish pie is one of my favourite recipes. My grandmother used to make one every Friday. She was old school and it was always fish on Friday in her house.'

'We used to go down the chippy on a Friday,' John said. 'Every Friday, me and Sonia . . .' His voice tailed off.

'Food takes us back, doesn't it?' said Alex. 'The smell and the taste. One whiff of a good fish pie and I'm underneath the table in my grandmother's kitchen, reading comics and secretly eating the sweets I was meant to save for after dinner. Hoping it would be peas with the pie and not broad beans.'

'I like broad beans,' said John.

'I can show you how to make a sort of hummus using them,' said Alex.

'I'm not sure why you'd want to mess with a perfectly decent veg,' John replied. Yep. John was roast dinners through and through.

Alex quickly prepared a fillet of cod. 'You won't have to do this,' he told his nervous students as they watched him with frowning expressions. 'I've already prepared your fish for you but it's useful for you to see how it's done. Now, what's the food that takes you back? Bella, tell us a food memory from your childhood while I finish this off.'

'*Cotechino*,' she said. 'That's a pork sausage from Italy, which is where my family come from. We used to have it with lentils on New Year's Eve to bring luck for the year ahead. Dad made an excellent version, though I didn't really like lentils much when I was small. I only ate them because my Nonna said that every lentil I ate would translate into a shiny new penny in the year to come. On New Year's morning, she'd give me the big bag of change she'd been saving up all year – swearing there was a penny for every lentil I'd eaten – and I'd go with Dad down to the pier and waste it all on those shove penny machines.'

'That sounds like a lovely tradition,' said John. 'We always had duck on New Year's Eve, me and Sonia. She could make red cabbage like nobody else. She'd add slivers of apple and sultanas and raisins and some spice or herb I can't remember.'

'Coriander?' Alex suggested.

'I'd have to smell it. '

'I'll bring some in next week. Anyone got any other food memories they want to share?'

'Aubergine parmigiana,' said Bella with a sigh. 'I don't think I've ever tasted such a heavenly dish as the one my dad used to make. He would slice the aubergine so finely, it just melted in your mouth. Actually, I think aubergine parmigiana would be my choice for my last meal on death row.'

'I can't imagine you ending up on death row,' said John.

'You must have friends who could get you off,' said Alex.

Bella laughed. 'I hope so . . .' She paused and her smile faded. 'My dad's melanzane parmigiana is one of the things I miss the most.'

John quickly picked up the thread. 'If I was choosing my last meal, it would be beef wellington.'

Bingo, thought Alex.

'It's got everything, really. I love a bit of pastry and a good bit of beef. You can't beat it. Sonia used to make beef wellington if we were having a dinner party. It was a proper show-stopper. No one ever turned down an invitation to our house. A beef wellington with a good red wine. That takes me back. I'd give anything to be able to eat Sonia's beef wellington again.'

'What about you, Liz? What taste takes you back through the years?' Alex asked.

Liz shrugged. She really didn't know. She'd done all the ready-meal preparing during her marriage with Ian. As for her childhood, if incompetence could be passed down the generations, then Liz had inherited her lack of prowess in the kitchen from her parents and her grandparents before them. What she remembered about the food she'd eaten as a child was that it all tasted the same. No matter what it was. Liz's own dearly departed mother liked to boil her veg until they were all the same colour. No matter how green, yellow or orange something started out, it always ended up grey and tasting of over-salted water.

Liz struggled to answer Alex's question.

'There must be something,' he said. 'Even if it's only your favourite sweets.'

'Actually, there is one thing,' said Liz. 'On my birthday, Mum used to make these things we called traffic lights.'

'What are those?' Bella asked.

'Just sponge fingers with a layer of icing. And in the icing, three Smarties. One red, one orange and one green.'

'That sounds like fun,' said Alex.

'One of those could probably take me back. Not that I could possibly recommend them in my role as a dental hygienist.'

But for now they were making Alex's grandmother's fish pie. Alex did a wicked impression of her as he put the dish together. John, Bella and Liz all laughed but Liz found she was a feeling a little reflective too. She envied her fellow classmates and their culinary memories. It also worried her that she didn't really have any. If someone had asked Saskia right then what smells and flavours reminded her of home, what would she have responded?

Burnt toast? The smell of melting plastic from a ready-meal container that's been in the oven too long? The frightening bright green food colouring of a shop-bought Hungry Caterpillar Birthday Cake?

Well, at least Liz was making an effort to change that. She put her own version of Alex's fish pie into the oven alongside John's and Bella's. A delicious smell was soon wafting out. It was the smell of comfort and effort. Maybe this could be the thing Saskia remembered when she was finally fully grown and moved away from home?

'An excellent attempt,' said Alex as Liz brought her pie to the front table for inspection.

Liz was grateful. 'I think I'm getting the hang of this.'

'I told you you would, Chopper,' he said, adding her nickname again. 'You've got the hands for it after all.'

Was he flirting with her? Liz found herself hoping he was.

Chapter Seventeen

John was very pleased with his fish pie. It was the one thing Sonia never made. Though John was a big fan of fish of all kinds, Sonia claimed it stank out the kitchen with a smell that would linger for days, so he only ever had it when they were out at a gastro pub or at someone else's house.

Of course, Sonia wasn't around to complain any more. The thought gave John a little stab of sadness. Grief was a funny thing. Had you asked John a year before how he would have reacted to the loss of his wife, he would have guessed that it would finish him. He'd have taken to his bed and never got up again, he was sure.

In the event, it was all quite different. Yes, he'd done his share of sobbing, but nearly ten months on there were days when he didn't cry at all. He felt as though his emotions were muffled. Then suddenly the tiniest little thing would trigger him and feel like a twisting dagger to the heart.

The thought that Sonia wasn't around to complain about the fish pie turned out to be one of those tiny things. With a heaviness to his step, John let himself into the house. He put the fish pie, carefully wrapped in silver foil, into the fridge for another time.

He felt better the following morning. It was one of those beautiful autumn days, when there isn't a cloud in the sky and the air is crisp and fresh, with none of the heaviness of late summer. Good weather always made John feel more optimistic.

He decided to make the most of it and started his day with a walk along the beach. Though he was in his seventies, he was proud that he was still pretty fit and he intended to stay that way for as long as possible. In many ways, he had Sonia to thank for that. She was always very keen on staying active. For a while, she'd insisted they attended a ballroom dancing club in Newbay Town Hall but John, who was one of the few men there who actually knew what he was doing, found being in demand to dance every dance was over-whelming. He only wanted to dance with his wife anyway.

John walked to the main Newbay beach, the one with the pier. The onset of autumn was marked by the reappearance of the dogs and their owners, enjoying the freedom of the sand until they were booted off again the following spring. John had been thinking about dogs lately. He'd always wanted one. They didn't have one because Sonia was allergic. It wouldn't have been fair. That didn't matter now, of course.

The last time John was at the NEWTS, Trevor Fernlea had asked him, on the quiet, whether he wasn't slightly enjoying doing everything he wanted without having to ask permission from the missus. John took the question in the spirit in which it was intended, knowing that Trevor's wife, Cynthia, while she had been one of Sonia's friends, was best described as a termagant. Trevor could be forgiven for wondering what life might be like without her. For John, the answer was 'no'. Being able to get a dog if he felt like it, or cook fish pie at home, did not make up for what he'd lost. Not even close.

He watched a couple, perhaps in their fifties (bright young things!) embracing as they looked out to sea just as he and Sonia used to do.

'Make the most of it,' he told them silently. 'Life really is too short. You always think you've got time and then suddenly you haven't. Make sure you've said everything you want to say to each other. Never mind not letting the sun go down on a disagreement, don't let a single minute go by in angry silence. Not a second.'

The fifty-somethings began to walk back up the beach to the prom.

'Lovely day,' the woman said to John as they passed.

Not long after that, John turned for home. He was starting to feel hungry and there was a fish pie calling his name. By the time he got to the house, he was ready for it. He switched on the oven and laid the table for one. He got a beer out of the fridge to have with his lunch. He was probably over his weekly limit of alcohol units but he told himself it was medicinal. Besides, he was seventy. Any damage had been done already.

In forty-five minutes the fish pie was ready. It filled the kitchen with a smell of warmth and comfort. Sonia would have hated it but for John it brought back the cookery class and the camaraderie he was beginning to feel with Bella, Liz and Alex. He enjoyed hearing them chat and banter as they worked. He liked being around the happy energy of three younger people.

John helped himself to a large portion of the pie. He had a forkful before he got to the table. It was delicious.

Three mouthfuls later, John started at the sound of the telephone.

It was the landline in the hall that was ringing. The phone was still where it had been installed in the Eighties, back when people considered calls an intrusion so put it out of everyone's way.

John had thought about having another socket fitted in the living room but like most people, he found that the landline hardly ever rang any more. Even people of his generation had abandoned the fixed phone for the mobile. Sonia had been a big fan of texting. She and her girlfriends were always sending each other little notes. So now, whenever the phone in the hall rang out, John automatically assumed the worst. Landlines were for cold calls and bad news only. They were for salesmen you didn't want to speak to or old friends you hadn't seen in decades ringing to give you the date and time of yet another funeral.

Or . . .

Every Friday afternoon, at three o'clock precisely, the fixed line in John's house would receive a call.

John tried not to be in when it happened but that day he was caught out, sitting at the kitchen table with his lunch. The insistent ringing cut through the sound of the programme on the radio. John turned the radio off as if to confirm that he wasn't imagining it. Or as if, by being silent himself, he could hide in some audible sense from the person on the other end of the line.

He wasn't going to answer it.

They weren't really calling for him anyway, John told himself. They wanted Sonia. Of course they did.

The phone rang ten times before the answering machine kicked in. John covered his ears as the message played out in Sonia's voice. He hadn't got round to changing it. Didn't want to. It was as though erasing Sonia's message would be another step closer to erasing her from his mind.

'You're through to John and Sonia. We can't answer your call right now. Please leave a message.'

The caller did as he was told.

John kept his ears covered until he was sure that it was finished. Then he walked to the answering machine and deleted the message without listening to it first. The caller could have nothing to say that John wanted to hear.

Chapter Eighteen

After that week's class, Bella had at least managed to make it as far as home with her fish pie. She got it into the oven and onto the table and she was taking her first bite when the phone rang. She was tempted to pretend she hadn't heard it. She let the call go to voice-mail the first time. But whoever it was that wanted her was not about to give up and move on to someone else. Bella reluctantly put down her fork and picked up the next call. It was the DSCC again.

'I hope I'm not interrupting your dinner,' said the call centre worker.

'No,' said Bella. 'Of course not.'

Five minutes later she was on her way to Newbay police station again.

'Jimmy,' she greeted her favourite client with resignation. 'It's you. What a surprise.'

'We must stop meeting like this,' he agreed.

'Let me guess. Shoplifting?'

'Nope. Guess again.'

'Breaking and entering.'

'That's not my style, Miss. You know that.'

'TWOC?'

She meant car theft. Taking without consent.

'Nope,' Jimmy grinned.

'An enormous banking fraud that will bring down

HSBC and the entire global financial system?' Bella made a shot in the dark.

'You'll never guess,' said Sergeant Mellor.

'Urinating on a policeman's boots,' said Jimmy, somewhat proudly.

'Ah,' said Bella. 'That doesn't sound good.'

'I didn't know they were a policeman's boots,' Jimmy began to lay out the mitigating circumstances. 'I was on one side of a fence and he was on the other. I was having a pee when I saw these toecaps appear. I was thinking, hello, who's this then? I turned towards them. I'd totally forgotten I was still peeing at the time.'

Bella did her best not to smile. Jimmy could always make a good anecdote out of his misdemeanours but she knew that this was going to be a particularly tough one.

'What am I looking at?' Jimmy asked. 'Am I going down?'

'Depends on the policeman,' Bella admitted.

Sergeant Mellor brought Bella and Jimmy two cups of tea. Once again, she let her client have the only biscuit.

'You're trying to fatten me up,' he said.

'I don't think you need to worry,' said Bella.

Jimmy nodded in agreement. He was thin as a racing snake. 'You know what,' he said with his mouth full, 'I finally worked out where I used to know you from.'

'You used to know me?'

'Yes.'

'Well, I have attended pretty much every time you've been arrested for the past five years.'

'Before then. I mean when you were much younger. When you were still at school.'

'You knew me then?'

'Yeah. You went to the one with the blue uniform, didn't you? The one with the blue and white striped shirts.'

'The high school,' Bella confirmed.

'I know you from when you used to work in that café by the station on the weekends.'

'The station café. My dad owned it.'

'That was your dad?'

'Yes. It was.'

'Wow, Miss B. I had no idea. He's a good bloke. Seriously. He always said that so long as we didn't hang around bothering his customers all day, he would make sure we got whatever was left over when the café closed in the evening. And he was good to his word. Every night at seven o'clock on the dot, he'd drop by the bus shelter nearest the pier with a food parcel. There was always good stuff in it. Stuff we couldn't believe he was throwing away.'

'You have to,' said Bella. 'When you've got a café. You've got to stick to the rules about sell-by dates and storage.'

'They served some great food at your dad's place. I got quite a taste for pasta salad with sun-dried tomatoes.'

'No wonder the café went bust,' Bella said ruefully. While her father was making the rounds of the homeless, she would generally be at home doing schoolwork. She'd had no idea his generous gesture was such a regular thing.

'Yeah. We were all gutted when he had to close down. He was a very generous man. What's he doing now?'

'He's not with us any more,' said Bella.

'Oh, you're kidding me?'

'I wish I was. He died three years ago.'

'Awww. Miss B. I'm really sorry. Was it sudden?'

'Sort of,' said Bella. It had seemed sudden at the time but in retrospect Bella knew her father had been fading away from the day the restaurant shut down. Still, she wasn't sure she wanted to get any deeper into this conversation now. Not while she was on duty. Thinking about her father could only make her sad and it would hardly be professional to cry in front of a client.

Bella's dad was just in his early sixties when he had his heart attack. His parents – Bella's Italian grandparents – had been active well into their eighties. But something happened when the café failed. Ugo seemed to shrink into himself. He aged ten years in a day. He didn't even cook at home any more. After she moved out, whenever Bella went round she would find him in front of the television, shouting at the contestants on *Deal Or No Deal*, while Bella's mother smoked and complained in the kitchen.

'They say daughters always marry a man like their father but don't you dare hook up with someone like your dad,' Maria said. 'When I met him, I had the world at my feet. I could have married anyone. If I hadn't fallen for his charm, I could be living in the Villas by now.'

The Villas were in the smart part of town.

'But you wouldn't have me,' Bella reminded her.

'I'd have had another daughter,' said Maria. 'Who wouldn't have needed to pluck her eyebrows.'

'Mum!'

'You know I don't mean it,' Maria would say. 'You're

the best thing that ever happened to me. I just wish we'd been able to give you more. Give you a proper start in life.'

With that, Maria cast a sidelong glance at her husband in the kitchen. She still loved him, Bella was sure. She just wanted him to pull himself together. They had no idea he would never again be the man he once was.

'Yeah,' Jimmy mused. 'It's the worst, losing your dad. But you're a lucky woman, having had a father like that in the first place. Aren't too many gentlemen of that calibre around.'

'No,' Bella agreed. She certainly hadn't come across many. Not that she'd had time to look.

'But now I know he was your dad, I can see that he passed on his kindness to his daughter. What I like about you, Miss B, is that you never talk down to people like us. When you turn up at the station, you're exactly the same as I imagine you are when some posh bloke turns up at your office, wanting you to sort out his will.'

Bella didn't interrupt to tell Jimmy that wills were not her area of expertise.

'Your dad always understood that everyone has the right to their dignity and I know that you understand that too.'

Bella nodded. She did believe that dignity was a human right. She only wished Ugo had hung on to his. He might have clung on to life.

'Chip off the old block,' Jimmy murmured.

'Right then,' said Sergeant Mellor, who was back with his own caffè latte. 'Let's get this party started.'

Chapter Nineteen

On the night they made the fish pie, Saskia told Liz she didn't need a lift home from the NEWTS. Georgia's mother would be bringing them both back. Liz shrugged. She was more than happy for Georgia's mum to do the pick-up. In her fancy new Range Rover Evoque that wasn't embarrassing like Liz's ancient Volvo. Or Liz's driving style. It didn't seem to matter how Liz drove, Saskia declared it 'ridiculous'. Liz was either going too fast or too slow.

'You're going to kill me!' was Saskia's response whenever Liz went over thirty-two miles an hour.

Or, at the other end of the spectrum, 'You're driving like a granny, Mum. The police are going to pull us over to check you haven't had a stroke.'

That night, Liz was definitely driving like a granny. The fish pie she had made so carefully was the most precious cargo Liz had had in the car for a long while. She deliberated for quite some time as to how she might most safely transport it back to her house. The footwell was technically the safest place in the car. There would be nowhere for the pie to fall if she had to stop suddenly. But the footwell was also where Ted sat on his way to and from walks and Waggy Weight Loss. Liz still hadn't had the car valeted since the vet visit that landed him in that club. She certainly hadn't vacuumed the car herself.

So, she took the fish pie, wrapped in silver foil, her

apron and an old towel she'd found in the boot, and put it on one of the passenger seats in the back. All that insulation and then the seat belt. It should be fine. Especially if she drove as her old driving instructor would have wanted her to. Smoothly, slowly, looking out for obstacles at least three cars ahead. Ready to apply the brake gently and not so hard that the pie would get whiplash.

Liz drove that Volvo like she was a funeral director with a full boot. Never going over twenty miles an hour, her back straight and her eyes constantly scanning the horizon for hazards. It only took her ten minutes longer than usual to get home.

Success. The pie was in one piece. Liz gave herself a virtual pat on the back. The pie smelled delicious too. She was sure that Saskia would want some when she caught a whiff of that crispy cheesy topping. Saskia had inherited many things from her father – her sharp blue eyes, her broad swimmer's shoulders, her tendency towards pig-headedness – but thankfully she had not inherited his irrational hatred of one of the world's best comfort foods.

Liz hummed a happy little tune as she lifted the pie out of the car and unwound the towel and the apron. She had her work bag slung over her right shoulder and her dainty handbag securely across her body but she balanced the pie on her left hand like a pro as she fished out her house keys.

Liz heard Ted whining on the inside of the door as she fumbled with the lock.

'You can smell my pie,' she said to him. 'Well, you're not having any. It isn't on the Waggy Weight Loss diet sheet.'

Liz got the door open. Ted, desperate to find out what she was carrying, shot out through the gap. He barrelled straight into her legs. Liz tottered but managed, just about, to keep the pie upright and safe. 'Whooah! Teddy!' she said. 'Calm down, boy.'

Ted ran back into the house ahead of her as he always did, as if to be certain the coast was clear for his beloved mistress to enter safely. Liz nudged the door a little wider with her toe. She stepped into the hall. She tipped her shoulder so that her heavy work bag landed safely on the chair where everyone dumped everything.

'Fish pie, fish pie, for the apple of my eye,' Liz composed a little ditty as she moved further into the house.

She kicked the front door shut with an impressive backwards manoeuvre. She took off her cross-body bag without disturbing the pie dish at all. She transferred the dish from her left hand to her right hand so she could take off her coat. She was a genius. A mistress of balance. She could have been a waitress in a Michelin-starred gaff no problem.

She walked into the kitchen, cleared a space on the counter one-handed, then somehow, impossibly, at the very last minute, when she was so nearly in the clear, she tripped. There was nothing to slip on. She couldn't see what tripped her. She couldn't feel it. But something had, she lost her poise, and the fish pie hit the floor. The ceramic dish broke in two. The silver foil could not contain its contents. Ted was upon it in a minute.

Liz merely stared at the mess, her hand still in the pie-carrying position.

'No, Ted, no,' she said uselessly, as Ted began a

whirlwind clear-up mission. Liz pulled him off the pie as quickly as she could but he still got at least half of it down. And a good mouthful of the silver foil too. His poo would be glittering for weeks.

As Liz scraped the remains of the disaster into the pedal bin, Ted wagged his tail as if to say, 'What's for dessert?'

'You've just had half a fish pie that was meant to serve four. What am I going to say at Waggy Weight Loss?'

'What's for supper?' Saskia asked when she came in. 'Can I smell fish pie? I like fish pie,' she said.

'Ted had your share,' Liz told her.

'What?' Saskia went from nought to outrage in under a second. 'But I'm not late. You told me to be home by half eight. It's twenty-eight minutes past and you already gave my dinner to the dog? Honestly, Mum. That's you all over. You can't help overreacting. You're crazy. I don't even recognise the woman you've become. You've got all these weird rules and you wonder why Dad left you.'

Liz took a deep breath.

'Ted had both our shares because I accidentally dropped the pie on the floor when I was bringing it into the kitchen. Not because I had some kind of tantrum. But thank you for reminding me that it's my fault your father left me for a twenty-four-year-old. In any case, I thought you were a vegetarian.'

Saskia saw the broken serving dish on the draining board.

'Oh,' she said.

'Yes,' said Liz.

'Sorry, Mum. I didn't know. So, what *are* we having for supper?' Saskia asked.

They would have had beans on toast for supper but Saskia reminded Liz that baked beans were full of sugar. So they just had the toast.

'How was the youth group?' Liz asked.

'It was OK,' said Saskia.

'What is it you're rehearsing anyway?'

'Just a play.'

'Just a play? Has it got a name?'

'Seven Brides for Seven Brothers.'

'Oh, we did that at school.' Liz burst into a little snippet of song. Saskia winced. Embarrassing mum was at it again. 'Can I come and see you in a performance?'

'Sure. But I don't know what nights I'm going to be doing yet. Under sixteens aren't allowed to appear every night.'

'But you'll be sixteen by the time the play's run starts,' Liz reminded her.

'Mm-hmmm,' said Saskia.

'Talking of which, we've got to make some plans for your birthday. It's less than a month. I was thinking that we could perhaps go to a spa hotel for the weekend. Just you and me. We could have facials and massages and get our nails painted.'

'Nail varnish is a really fast way to get toxic chemicals straight into your bloodstream,' said Saskia.

'OK. We won't get our nails painted. Are facials still OK?'

'What weekend are you thinking, Mum? The weekend of my actual birthday?'

'Well, yes. That seems like a good idea.'

'Only . . . I was going to tell you about this later. For my *actual* birthday Dad and Brittney have said they're going to take me to London. Brittney's a finalist in a big blog awards ceremony. It's all the health, fashion and beauty blogs. Deliciously Ella is going to be there. Brittney's known her since they were both starting out. And Alexa Chung is going to present one of the awards.'

'Is she the one with the legs like toothpicks?' Liz asked.

'Mum, you think anyone who is a normal weight has legs like toothpicks. Just because everyone in Newbay is enormous doesn't mean it's right.'

'So, the one with legs like toothpicks is going to be handing out awards to the ones with brains like candy-floss.'

'What are you even on about?' Saskia asked.

'You're telling me you want to go to London on your birthday weekend. Which, incidentally, according to the diary, is one of your weekends with me.'

'Yes, but you and Dad always said that your splitting up was not going to ruin my life. You said that my needs and wishes would be first and foremost whenever you were making arrangements for where I had to be at weekends.'

Liz couldn't argue with that. It was indeed exactly what they'd said.

'And I might meet some people at the blog awards who could help me with my career, Mum. You know I want to go into fashion or health food PR.'

'I didn't know that. What happened to reading biochemistry at Warwick?'

'That was what you and Dad wanted me to do.'

'It was just a suggestion. And Dad's OK with you becoming a blogger now, is he?'

'He understands that the future is all about being online. He gets it.'

'Of course he does. He's been getting it ever since he dropped round to Brittney's with that bleaching kit.'

'Mum!'

'Look, it's your birthday,' said Liz. 'Of course you get to choose what you want to do on the day.'

'I knew you'd say that. And Mum . . .'

'What?'

'Well, the thing is, I'm going to Dad and Brittney's this weekend as well. Windscale Clothing were really pleased with our photo shoot and they want us to do another. We're going to have a make-up artist and everything this time. You didn't have anything planned this weekend, did you?'

Liz had thought she might try to mend some mother–daughter bridges by taking Saskia on a little shopping spree, but shoving thirty quid in her hand and telling her to 'go crazy' in Matalan at Newbay's out-of-town outlet shopping centre was hardly going to compete with a make-up artist and free clothes from a label whose cheapest item was a Breton-striped T-shirt costing forty-five pounds (Liz had looked).

'No. Ted and I are just going to be doing the usual. Walking, snoozing, going to Waggy Weigh-In.'

'Going to what?'

'Waggy Weigh-In. At the vet's. I told you last week.'

'You didn't.'

'The vet says Ted is a little overweight. He's on a diet.'

'So you let him eat the whole fish pie?'

'I didn't exactly *let* him. And it wasn't the whole pie.'

'Oh my God, Mum. You've let our dog get so fat he has to go to Weight Watchers.'

'It's Waggy Weight Loss.'

'Whatever. It's still totally embarrassing.'

'You could have taken him for walks more often.'

'When? I've got to do my schoolwork.'

With that, Saskia excused herself and went upstairs to check her Instagram feed.

Chapter Twenty

On Friday, Alex caught a train to Exeter for a very important meeting. He went armed with his dream file, though he didn't have an opportunity to show exactly what was inside it. The meeting went well, though, and Marianne, who had set the meeting up, told him she was pleased with how he had come across. She thought that getting the funding he needed would be a formality.

Afterwards, Marianne and Alex went for a coffee and he told her how the cookery course had been going. Marianne had known Alex for a long time and when he spoke about his pupils, she could tell at once that one of them in particular had sparked Alex's interest.

'She's great. She's so funny and yet self-deprecating. She's always joking and ready to laugh at herself, though she really doesn't need to. When she looks at me, I feel as though she's known me for years.'

'That sounds good. Any potential?'

Alex shook his head. 'I shouldn't think so. There are too many obstacles. You know what's gone on with me the past few years.'

'So?'

'Well, I don't know exactly what her relationship status is but I'm sure there must be someone in her life. She's achieved so much. She's not living in a bedsit, that's for sure. She's a proper grown-up and that makes me feel like a kid.'

'Yet you're the one who's teaching her, remember?'

'Yeah but that's different. And I don't think it will be long before I've taught her everything I know.'

'Don't do yourself down.'

'I just want to get to know her better, to know what she's thinking when she gets that smile on her face. To know what her life is like away from the classroom.'

'Only another four weeks and you could ask her to tell you all about it over a drink.'

'How could I do that? With everything that's gone on . . .'

'It shouldn't matter,' Marianne reminded him. 'That's all in the past. You're a different man now, Alex. Don't forget that.'

Alex nodded. It was easy to say.

'You're a great catch.'

'You say that to all the boys,' Alex joked.

Marianne chuckled. 'In the meantime, we need to follow up on today. The charity trustees are very keen, I can tell. What you're proposing is very exciting. I'm sure they're going to go for it. I think you should start looking for a venue.'

Alex agreed.

On the train back to Newbay, he thought about everything Marianne had said. Not just that day but over the three years he had known her. Though they'd met in an unfortunate context – from Alex's point of view at least – he had come to think of the older woman as a friend. Alex had come to realise that many of the people who chose Marianne's line of work did so to make themselves feel better, but Alex never felt as though Marianne was talking down to him. She was never patronising. She saw him as an individual who wasn't defined by his record. She was endlessly helpful and supportive. That Marianne thought Alex could be a restaurateur was a huge boost to his confidence. He wanted to make her feel proud.

'You've got a glittering future ahead of you,' she'd once said.

He wished he could feel as confident about his chances of finding someone to share that glittering time.

The train pulled into Newbay. Alex alighted with the commuter crowd and followed them out of the station. How many of them would be going home to ready meals, Alex wondered, as they headed off in their separate directions, heads down against the wind whipping in from the sea.

It was almost dark. The buildings around the station were mostly empty. No wonder people didn't hang around. But Alex's eye was drawn by one abandoned storefront in the arches beneath the tracks. He'd walked past many times but never really looked at it properly before.

'Hey! Alex!' someone shouted.

It was Jimmy. Jimmy who was always hanging out around the hostel.

'All right, Jimmy?'

'Haven't got a spare cigarette, have you, mate?'

'You know I've given up.'

'Spare tenner?'

Alex snorted.

'Fiver?'

Alex shook his head.

'Always worth asking,' said Jimmy. 'I guess I won't be getting a room in the hostel tonight then.'

'Sorry, mate.'

'Ah. You're all right. I know you're one of the good guys.'

'Are you going to be OK? It's cold tonight.'

'Yeah. I'm going to break in to one of the old shops and have a smoke.'

'I thought you didn't have any fags?'

Jimmy waggled a joint in Alex's direction.

Alex exhaled at the sight.

'Want some?'

Alex shook his head firmly.

'See you later then,' said Jimmy, heading for the abandoned café.

Alex watched him go. He watched him get the rotten door to the café open with a fairly feeble kick.

'Hang on,' said Alex. 'I'm coming in there with you.'

Chapter Twenty-One

So, Liz's plans for Saskia's birthday had been blown wide open by the revelation that she was going to the blog awards in London instead. What Saskia didn't know was that Liz had taken a risk and booked the spa weekend before telling Saskia what she was planning. And because Liz had gone for the most bargainous of bargain rates, there was no way she could change the dates of her stay or get her money back. It was Sod's flipping Law in action. Again.

Maybe Liz should have insisted that Saskia spend her birthday weekend with her mother. It really wasn't unreasonable. Ian would almost certainly have done the same had he already made a booking for anything more than dinner at Nandos. However, Liz had the feeling that insisting the birthday weekend went according to her plan would have driven a wedge the size of a bus between her and her daughter right then. Likewise, she felt she couldn't put her foot down about the photo shoot.

Saskia was so excited about it. She went straight up to her room as soon as she'd informed Liz about her plans for the weekend. She claimed she needed to get some rest but Liz was sure that Saskia would be up into the wee small hours on her phone or her laptop, telling everyone and anyone what she'd be doing at the weekend. Liz knew how embarrassing it would be for her to have to say the shoot wasn't happening after all. Liz didn't want to do that to her. She liked to see Saskia happy even if it was Brittney who was providing the inspiration.

At ten, Liz retired to her own room. She was trying not to use her laptop in bed – she'd read all about the dangers of blue light and its effects on sleep – but she was too agitated to concentrate on the book she had been reading for the past six months. A quick look at Facebook couldn't really do so much harm, could it?

If only it were just Facebook that Liz ended up looking at.

'Oh dear,' she muttered to herself as she pressed the letter B and saw the blog address on the auto-fill.

Brittney had published another post. This one was on 'relating to teenagers'.

'Dearest Readers! I hope you've had a happy day full of the universe's greatest blessings. What a week of lessons I've been having. I knew that when my Darling BF came into my life, it would mean I had to make a lot of changes. I had no idea just how many. Not least because Darling BF didn't come into my life alone. He brought with him his Darling Daughter. I'm going to call her the Darling SD from now on.'

SD? S for what? Liz wondered. Step-daughter?

'Don't get ahead of yourself,' she growled at the screen. The divorce was nowhere near done.

'My Darling BF has custody of his daughter every other weekend. When we were first together I worried that I would lose him for those weekends. I panicked that my Darling SD would be hostile towards me and making any kind of relationship would be hard. I didn't know how to relate to a teenager though it was only six years since I'd been one myself.'

Yeah, rub it in why don't you, Liz thought.

'Luckily, I found some great resources online for anyone thinking of getting into a blended family situation.'

AKA 'thinking of stealing another woman's husband'.

'I read around the subject as much as I could. I knew that what sours most daughter–step-parent relationships is trying too hard to replace the parent the step-daughter already has at home. Fortunately, I could not be more different from Darling SD's actual mother. We're almost two decades apart in age for a start. That's basically a generation's worth of difference. What that means is that I have a better understanding of the realities of millennial life, so that I know how to talk to Darling SD without sounding like I'm from another planet.'

Liz could only snort at that. Brittney seemed to be on another planet most of the time as far as Liz could tell. Planet Quinoa.

'At the end of the day, we have to remember that the wheel of life keeps turning and that just as we were once young and beautiful, our children will one day take that mantle from us. We need to teach them well so that they can make the world a better place. I feel blessed to have this young person in my life. I hope she feels blessed to know me too.'

Liz flicked the Vs at the screen.

Brittney was no longer even pretending that she wasn't trying to steal all of Liz's life. Liz had no doubt that she was even at that moment preparing a post about vegan dog food and how she was going to save

Ted from Type Two Doggy Diabetes. So long as she didn't have to do it in her cream-carpeted flat.

Unable to post her indignation because for some reason – perhaps because she had a tiny bit of shame – Brittney had disabled the comments function on her blog, Liz cried herself to sleep.

Chapter Twenty-Two

Saturday morning came around again along with Ted's second Waggy Weigh-In. Liz felt terrible when she refused the dog his usual breakfast but, like a trainer preparing her boxer for a big fight, Liz was prepared to do whatever it took to make sure that Ted fell under his target weight. Or at least had lost something. She even briefly considered trimming his magnificent whiskers. She'd heard that some athletes shaved off all their body hair ahead of an important weigh-in but there was no real chance Ted would stay still to have his hair cut. Going without breakfast was as far as Liz could push him.

'I'll give you a really big bowl of kibble when we get back home,' she promised. It didn't sound like much of a deal.

Once again, Liz was too late to get a space in the surgery car park and this time she had to park five streets away. She might as well have walked all the way from home. She was the last to arrive. Coco was already there. Liz knew that because her pushchair was positioned right outside the surgery door to ensure her delicate paws didn't have to touch the dirty ground.

This time, Mrs Coco had saved Liz a seat.

'Thank you,' said Liz as she gratefully sat down.

'How do you think you're going to do this week?'

Mrs Coco asked. 'I think Coco is going to hit her target but I can't tell you what a trial it's been to keep her on the diet. We've had some real battles. There have been tears, I can tell you. I just keep reminding her that when she gets through this she is going to be so beautiful. The chrysalis is a stage every butterfly must endure, I told her.'

That sounded like something Brittney thought the Dalai Lama would say, Liz observed.

'Most of this excess weight is just puppy fat.' Mrs Coco gave one of Coco's spare tyres an affectionate squeeze. 'It's all part of being a teen.'

'I know about teens,' said Liz.

'Isn't it the worst?'

'But it only lasts a few years. From the ages of nine until they have kids of their own, as I understand it.'

'Oh, you are funny, Mrs Ted,' Mrs Coco chuckled.

'Call me, Liz, please.'

Mrs Coco didn't offer her own name.

'How old is Coco?' Liz enquired.

'Four years this November.'

Four years? By Liz's reckoning, that made Coco twenty-eight in dog terms. Long past her puppy days. But Mrs Coco was so earnest. She cared so much.

'Teenagers can be difficult,' Liz agreed. That much she could say with authority.

Nurse Van Niekerk arrived with her clipboard.

'Good morning, ladies and gentlemen. And owners,' she said, nicking Dr Thomas's joke. 'Dr Thomas is running a little bit late this morning. We've got some very poorly patients in the recovery room today. So he has asked me to lead you all in a little light exercise before our weigh-in.'

'What?'

'Exercise!'

There was much moaning. From the owners.

'Come along,' said Nurse Van Niekerk. 'There's no need to complain. Let's get out there. It's a beautiful day.'

With that Nurse Van Niekerk led the Waggy Weight Losers out into the car park and from there to the playing field behind the surgery building. Liz knew the playing field well. When Ted was a puppy, she had brought him there for training and socialisation sessions. What a laugh that had been. Liz had paid two hundred pounds for those classes and Ted still didn't walk to heel. Which was obvious as he dragged her in the direction of the grass in pursuit of some interesting smell.

'Talk to your dog, Mrs Ted,' shouted Nurse Van Niekerk. 'That's the way to keep him at heel. Keep his attention at all times.'

'Stop embarrassing me,' Liz hissed at her pooch. Ted dragged her another fifteen metres.

Meanwhile, Mrs Coco was struggling. Coco would not step off the tarmac. She absolutely refused. It didn't matter how much Mrs Coco pulled on her dog's special harness.

'Come along, Mrs Coco,' Nurse Van Niekerk yelled over to her. 'Show Coco who's boss.'

Coco already knew who was boss and it wasn't her lovely mummy.

'I think she has a fear of grass,' Mrs Coco explained. 'Ever since she was stung on the paw as a puppy. She stepped on a bee. She won't walk on something if she can't be sure it doesn't contain biting insects.'

'Nonsense,' said Nurse Van Niekerk. 'You're indulging her, Mrs Coco. You've made her soft. Come on. We're walking the perimeter of the field three times.'

That made Mrs Coco look upset. Liz, who'd managed one circuit, dragged along like a water-skier in Ted's wake, drew level with her again.

'I'll walk with you,' she said. 'Perhaps if Coco sees Ted having fun . . .'

'It's no use. She won't go on the grass,' Mrs Coco insisted. 'Not without her pushchair. There's no point Nurse Van Niekerk shouting at me. I've tried everything I can to get Coco to change. She's just so stubborn.'

'Maybe . . . I've got an idea,' said Liz. She put her hand into her pocket and opened it to reveal three illicit doggy treats. 'Bribery. Saving the mental health of mothers since the beginning of time.'

Mrs Coco quickly snatched and secreted one of the snacks before Nurse Van Niekerk could see her. She crouched to give Coco a 'good talking to' when in reality she was just letting Coco get a whiff of the synthetic bacon-scented deliciousness that could be hers if she only played the game.

It worked. Coco took a tentative step onto the grass, following the treat hidden inside Mrs Coco's hand. Progress was still painfully slow. The other dogs were already finishing their second circuit.

While they were on their third circuit, Dr Thomas appeared. He jogged – actually, he sprinted – right across the centre of the field to meet them.

'Excellent work, everybody! This is how we keep our weight under control. Exercise in the open air. It's easy and it's free.' He did some jumping jacks. 'I'm sorry

I'm joining you all a little late this morning. We had a kitten go into a seizure. All sorted now, though. She's going to make a full recovery. I'm sure you understand where my priorities had to be.'

The assembled owners murmured their assent.

'But now you have my full attention. Until the next crisis. So let's just jog on back into the surgery, shall we, and do that Waggy Weigh-In?'

And then Dr Thomas did jog back with the ease and grace of movement that suggested he was no stranger to running and a couple of hundred metres was absolutely no big deal. Nurse Van Niekerk followed after him at a slightly less impressive pace. Though only slightly less impressive, Liz thought. And then came the Waggy Weight Losers, all of them secretly glad to be able to use their dreadfully lazy dogs as an excuse to walk more slowly.

'I would be running like Dr Thomas but . . .' Mr Hercules cast a look down at Hercules, the Scotch egg on four sticks.

The run may not have left Dr Thomas out of breath but it had left his hair out of place. He was still smoothing it back down when the Waggy Weight Losers trailed in. Liz wondered whether anyone had ever told him that he looked better when his hair wasn't strictly slicked down in the manner of a Fifties' civil servant in a BBC costume drama. Nurse Van Niekerk probably liked it like that.

'OK. Take a seat,' he said. 'Or stay standing if you feel like it. The human body is built to stand. Did you know that? It's sitting down that puts the strain upon our backs. We talk about taking the weight off our feet but we're actually putting a great deal more pressure on our spines in a sitting position. It's the same for your dogs. They were built to move. They like to move it, move it.'

Dr Thomas broke into an impression of the guy from Reel 2 Real, who'd sung the huge hit 'I like To Move It' back in the nineties. Or maybe he was channelling the singing lemur from *Madagascar*, which had been one of Saskia's favourite films. Anyway, it was obviously a line Dr Thomas had trotted out before because Nurse Van Niekerk danced along with him. As did Mrs Coco, from the safety of her seat.

It was embarrassing. But also, supposed Liz, faintly endearing to see the vet making a tit of himself. He really was prepared to do anything for the animals.

'Enough of my dad dancing,' he said. 'Let's get these puppies weighed. In reverse order today.'

'Oh no,' said Mrs Coco to Liz. 'Coco was so hoping to get it over with quickly.'

'Twinkle,' Nurse Van Niekerk called.

Twinkle stepped forward sheepishly. He was eating something he'd found on the floor. Could have been anything. Possibly rabbit droppings. He came in at two hundred and fifty grams more than he should.

'Ted,' said Nurse Van Niekerk. 'Exactly the same weight as before. Which simply isn't possible if you've been following the weight-loss plan and the exercise regime properly.'

'Have you been following it, Mrs Ted?' Dr Thomas looked Liz straight in the eye.

'Mrs Chandler,' said Liz.

Dr Thomas waved away that small consideration.

'I don't know why this is happening,' Liz said. 'I

have been following the diet to the letter. Someone must be sabotaging my efforts.'

Nurse Van Niekerk raised an eyebrow.

'Have you spoken about Ted's condition with the other members of your family?' Dr Thomas asked.

'Of course.'

'Has he escaped the garden this week? Might he be getting into somebody's bins?'

'I don't think so.'

'Then it's a matter of stepping up the exercise. I hope you like to move it, Mrs Ted.'

Liz slunk back to her place.

The rest of the dogs were weighed and measured. Biscuit was up. Monty was down. Coco was down but only by a fraction. Dr Thomas chastised, consoled and cajoled. He reminded the owners that they were their dogs' self-control. They were their animals' conscience. It was no use pretending otherwise. They had to stick to the diet and set the walking times.

'Make exercise a daily habit,' said Dr Thomas. 'Set your alarm for half an hour earlier in the morning and start every day with a stroll. You'll feel better for it too.'

The owners tried to appear interested but Liz was sure all of them found the prospect as unappealing as she did. Get up at half six for a walk in the dark before work? No thanks.

Dr Thomas brought the session to a close with a few suggestions as to websites the WWLs might like to check out.

'You're not the first ones to fight this battle,' he said. 'And you won't be the last. See you next week everybody.'

He left them with a salute. It was time to check on the kitten.

'Thank you for helping me out today,' said Mrs Coco as she and Liz walked out into the car park. 'I don't know what I would have done if you hadn't come up with that treat. Coco was really determined to stay put. I just wish I didn't have to bribe her.'

'Don't beat yourself up about it,' said Liz. 'Every parent knows you have to choose your battles.'

Mrs Coco nodded sadly as she loaded Coco into her pushchair.

'Mrs Ted, Mrs Coco,' Dr Thomas caught up with them. 'Next week I'd like to see you both making a little more progress. Perhaps Coco could even walk to the session,' he added. 'Remember, ladies. Dogs like to move it, move it.'

He boogied on by.

'A-hole,' Liz mouthed.

Mrs Coco giggled.

'He means well, though,' Mrs Coco said.

'I suppose,' Liz conceded.

'And,' Mrs Coco whispered, 'he's terribly good looking. Don't you think he looks like Hugh Jackman?'

Liz agreed with that too but she wasn't going to say so. Besides, good looking, as far as Liz was concerned, had a great deal to do with personality shining through. Dr Thomas had the personality of a sadistic PE teacher.

Still, Liz was in no particular hurry to get home from Waggy Weight Loss that day. She had nothing else planned for the rest of the weekend. Nothing but doing Saskia's laundry. Funny how that never got done at Ian and Brittney's house.

Chapter Twenty-Three

Liz loaded Ted into the car again and drove back home via the supermarket. On the way there, the manner in which Ted was nosing the passenger seat – he was sitting in the back that day – gave her an idea. He could still smell the fish pie. The fish pie she never got to taste, though Ted had obviously loved it. Oh, how she had been looking forward to tasting that dish. Maybe she should make another one? After all, no one said that she wasn't to do any cooking whatsoever between classes. It would be good practice. A great idea to consolidate what she'd learned before Alex's careful instructions got buried beneath all manner of daily thought crap.

Yes. She was going to make another fish pie.

Leaving Ted in the car with the window rolled down by a couple of inches, even though it was only twelve degrees outside, Liz headed into Sainsbury's with intent. She was going to make this fish pie extra special. She was going to add some prawns. They'd made a very simple version in the class but Alex had suggested all sorts of ways they could jazz it up.

Liz gathered the things she always needed – dog biscuits, milk (two extra pints in case of white sauce disasters), a family size bar of Dairy Milk (the one treat she had *never* given Ted no matter how hard he pleaded) – then she went to the chilled fish shelves.

Hmmm. The choice already made it harder than she'd expected. Did the base fish have to be cod? She couldn't see any.

'There's more over here,' said a voice behind her. She turned to see that she was being addressed by the man on the fresh fish counter. The man she'd been ignoring for at least the past seven years. Most people did ignore him. His fresh fish displays were very beautiful but while the whole fish, complete with eyes and tails, were compelling to look at, they were also slightly frightening if you didn't know what to do with them. The good citizens of Newbay preferred their fish to come in fingers rather than with fins.

'What are you looking for?' the fishmonger asked. 'I've got some great coley today. Or fresh anchovies? Look at these little fellas. All you have to do is make a bit of batter, drop them in the oil and seconds later . . .' He mimed picking one up by the tail and eating it whole. 'My favourite.'

'I'm after something a bit, er, bigger,' Liz said. 'For a fish pie.'

'Ah, can't beat a bit of fish pie,' said the fishmonger. 'Then you'll be wanting something like this.' He pointed at the loin of some poor sea creature. Was that a cod?

'Yes, please,' said Liz. Would he take the scales off for her? She was just about to admit that she was a culinary novice when she sensed someone step up to the counter beside her.

'Mrs Ted?'

Oh no. It was Dr Thomas. That man popped up like a blinking Hugh Jackman-shaped mushroom.

'Dr Thomas,' Liz nodded. 'How nice to see you again. And so soon.'

'Jerry,' Dr Thomas greeted the fishmonger by his first name. They were obviously well acquainted.

'Evan. Good to see you, my man. Got some special fish for you today. I was just telling, er, Mrs Ted, about the anchovies but she wants something bigger because she's making a fish pie.'

'Mmmm, my favourite,' said Dr Thomas. Evan, as he was to the fishmonger.

'She's going to start with this,' the fishmonger indicated the grey-scaled loin.

'Excellent choice.'

'I'll just wrap it up.'

He started before Liz could protest about the scales. And the bones. Were there bones in it?

'So you like to cook?' Dr Thomas asked her.

'I do,' said Liz.

'What will you be wanting to go with this?' Jerry the fishmonger asked. 'A few prawns?'

'Got to have a few prawns,' said Dr Thomas.

Liz watched helplessly as Jerry the fishmonger added six, complete with legs, heads and those whiskery bits, into a bag.

'And you'll want some of this . . .'

'Oh yes,' Dr Thomas agreed, as Jerry offered Liz the tentacle of an octopus.

'Octopus? Of course,' Liz said gamely. 'And I prepare that as usual, do I?'

'Depends what you mean by usual,' said Jerry.

Liz had the feeling he was messing with her but she did her best not to let on.

'I always add some mussels to mine,' said Dr Thomas.

'Absolutely,' said Jerry. 'And a handful of vongole too.'

'Would be rude not to,' was Dr Thomas's opinion.

The last thing Liz had intended to do was add shellfish. Wasn't that a sure fire way for an amateur cook to get into trouble?

'This fish pie of yours is going to be magnificent,' Dr Thomas told Liz. 'What time do you want us to come round?'

'Ha ha,' Liz laughed. Unconvincingly.

Suddenly Jerry the fishmonger was busy bagging up half the ocean when all Liz had wanted was a nice clean fillet of cod and directions to the frozen aisle where the ready-*peeled* prawns were kept. By the time Jerry had finished, with Dr Thomas's enthusiastic encouragement, Liz was the proud owner of a bag of seafood that would cost her twenty quid. Twenty quid! She could have bought at least five ready-made pies for that and she hadn't even started on the cheese and potato topping.

'Thanks,' she said weakly. 'Gosh, this is going to be yummy.'

'It certainly is,' said Dr Thomas. 'You've made me think I should cook a fish pie tonight as well.'

'Can't go wrong,' said Jerry.

You bloody well can, thought Liz.

'Oh, Mrs Ted, before you go . . .' Dr Thomas called her back.

Liz paused.

'It's not mentioned on the Waggy Weight Loss diet sheet but fish is just as good for dogs as it can be for us humans. Quite a few commercial dog foods are actually fish-based.'

'Are they really?' Liz half sighed.

'Yes. But even better is if you take a simple piece of

white fish or salmon and steam, bake or grill it fresh. Just remember not to add any seasoning and make sure you check thoroughly for small bones.'

'Of course.'

'Perhaps you can put a little unseasoned fish aside for Ted when you're making your own delicious supper. What a lucky family the Teds are going to be tonight.'

'Yes,' said Liz. 'Well, I must be going. Enjoy the rest of your weekend, Dr Thomas.'

'I will. I was really glad to see you this morning, by the way. I knew you'd rise to the challenge. I can tell how much you love your dog. See you next week, Mrs Ted!'

Three minutes later, Liz loaded her fortune's worth of fish into the boot of her car and slammed it shut. How on earth had she let herself be steamrollered into buying so much? What did it matter if Dr Thomas found out she was an incompetent in the kitchen? He already thought she was an incompetent when it came to looking after her dog. She couldn't sink much lower in his opinion, she was sure. And yet he'd been surprisingly friendly away from the surgery. Hadn't he almost praised her for going to Waggy Weight Loss?

She wondered briefly who he would be cooking for that evening. Nurse Van Niekerk? No, it was fairly obvious that particular crush was unrequited. Dr Thomas paid less attention to Nurse Van Niekerk's puppy dog eyes than he did to those of the real puppies who crossed the threshold of his surgery every day.

Did he have a wife? He didn't wear a wedding ring. But then, you wouldn't, would you, if there was a possibility that you might have to stick your hand up a cow's bum at some point during the working day. Did Dr Thomas do cows in any case? He'd referred to 'dad dancing'. Did that mean he had kids? Liz imagined a row of three boys arrayed in order of descending height, following Dr Thomas as he 'moved it'. Did they laugh at his antics or were they mortified as Saskia would have been? What was Dr Thomas really like?

Back home again, Liz put away her shopping. She stuck the bag of fishmongery in the fridge in one big lump, not bothering to take out the individual packages so carefully wrapped up by Jerry.

She had an awful feeling it would all go to waste. Twenty quid straight into landfill just because she hadn't wanted to look like she didn't know what she was doing in front of Dr Thomas. Again.

Liz made herself a cup of tea, sank into the sofa and contemplated ordering a takeaway.

No! She suddenly sat up straight. She'd already bought her food for that weekend. Twenty quid was twenty quid. It was enough to buy a lunch at the deli for the whole flipping week. There were whole families living on less. Liz was damned if she was going to waste it. She could make a fish pie. She'd made one before. It couldn't be that difficult to do it again. Anything Dr Thomas could do . . . Liz got out the recipe sheet from Thursday night's class and tried to extrapolate from Alex's instructions for a medium pie for two how she might go about making a fish pie as big as Moby Dick.

At least she had a big dish. When she and Ian got married, Liz had put all manner of kitchen equipment on their wedding list. They had a beautiful set of baking dishes. The big one had never been used. Not for cooking anyway. For a while, it had lived on top of the Welsh dresser, used as a catch-all for the odds and ends that didn't have another home. When Ian moved out, Liz had hidden the dish away. Every time she looked at it, she thought of the day they'd spent unwrapping their wedding presents when they got back from honeymoon.

'When on earth are we going to use that?' Ian had asked.

'When we have a dinner party,' Liz had told him.

They never did have a dinner party. That was something else that was going to change once Liz had mastered this cooking lark. Now, how did you make a white sauce again?

Liz nailed the white sauce and the pie, when it came of the oven, looked magnificent. Even better than the one she'd made in class. The potato on top was perfectly crisp and browned in all the right places. Liz wished she had someone other than Ted to show. She wished she had someone to share it with too. The finished dish was big enough for eleven rugby players and a referee. The only thing she'd left out was the octopus.

She even took a picture and put it on Instagram, making sure to 'dress the set' as Brittney had advised her readers in a blog post about what made her Instagram pictures so successful. To dress her set, Liz covered the knackered old kitchen table with a checked cloth. The dish covered the worst of the stains on the cloth. She then arrayed four napkins in a fan alongside the dish and on top of the napkins, she placed four sets of cutlery, having made sure there was nothing caught in the fork prongs first (that dishwasher was useless). Then she added a sprig of basil – not quite right but the only greenery she had to hand – and took twenty shots before she posted the best with the hashtags #homecooking #healthyeatinggoals #homeentertaining.

'See,' she muttered to herself. 'You're not the only good cook in town Brittney Blaine.' And let everyone wonder exactly whom Liz was hashtag home entertaining, eh?

A lump came to Liz's throat when she saw that the first Instagram like was from her daughter. Though she did worry that Saskia spent too much time online, on this occasion she was grateful.

Thirty seconds later Saskia had also left a comment. 'Looks like someone already ate it and threw it back up. #homeentertaining #cookingdisaster #gladIwontbeeatingit.'

Ah well.

And later that night, Liz did throw the fish pie back up.

Mussels.

She knew she shouldn't have added those bloody mussels. Bloody Dr Thomas. She'd never have even bought the mussels if he hadn't been there. It was all his fault.

'Isn't it, Ted?'

Ted, who had stolen his own portion of fish pie from the dustbin, agreed.

Chapter Twenty-Four

Liz was very glad that there was to be no fish at the third session of Alex Barton's Beginners' Cookery course. She really didn't care if she never saw a fish pie ever again. She would certainly never bother to make one. Not even if her worst enemy was coming for supper. Not that her worst enemy, Brittney #vegan-pure #vegangoddess would have touched it anyway.

Liz met John as they walked into the community centre.

'Did you enjoy your fish pie last week?' he asked her.

'Yes,' she said. She really didn't want to get into the whole saga. 'You?'

'Oh yes,' said John. 'Though it was rather a large portion for one.'

Liz nodded. So he was eating alone as well. She didn't know much about John beyond what he had told the class at their first meeting but he seemed to be a nice bloke. She hoped he didn't feel as lonely as she sometimes did.

'Whatever we make today, I'm going to take it along to the NEWTS,' he said.

'You're a NEWT?' Liz asked.

'I certainly am. Have you heard of us?'

'My daughter Saskia has just joined the youth group.'

'Oh, that's lovely. They're a very good group. One of the old members has been an extra on *EastEnders* three times. Has Saskia signed up for *Seven Brides*?' John asked.

'She has.'

'I hear they're having trouble finding the seven brothers.'

'Oh.'

'Demographics, you see. Am-dram attracts a lot of ladies of a certain age. Might have to make it *Seven Brides and Some Twins*.'

'Is that the Mormon version?'

'Exactly.' John laughed. 'Anyway, I'm sure I'll see you in the NEWTS bar when the performances start.'

'Getting pissed as . . .' Liz quipped.

John laughed as though he had never heard anyone say that before. Which was kind, Liz thought.

Bella arrived at class five minutes late that day.

'Sorry, sorry, sorry,' she was all apologies as she rushed in, wearing another smart little suit and carrying a briefcase. She always seemed faintly harassed. Liz was grateful once again that she could leave her own career firmly at the dental surgery door. Which wasn't to say that tartar wasn't a very serious business. She wished more of her patients would understand that.

Alex beamed when he saw that all three of his students had turned up again. His class may not have grown over the three weeks he'd been teaching but at least it wasn't shrinking, which meant that he must be doing fine in the eyes of Bella, John and Liz at least.

'How was your fish pie?' Alex asked then.

Liz trotted out the same flannel she'd told John.

'And you made another one on Saturday I noticed,' Alex commented.

'How did you know?'

'I follow the hashtag #homecooking on Instagram. It looked amazing. Did you add mussels?'

'Yes,' Liz groaned.

'I hope your guests enjoyed it.'

Liz didn't know where to look. Did John now think she was weird for not having mentioned the second pie? Did Alex somehow know that Liz had lied about having people over? She blushed.

'You're so brave to have people over,' said Bella. 'I always worry that I'd end up poisoning someone.'

Which was ironic, thought Liz, remembering her middle of the night dash to the bathroom.

'You won't poison anyone if you stick to the rules about hygiene,' said Alex. 'And don't do anything stupid like add a dubious mussel to the pot. If it ain't open, it ain't going in. Remember that. Never try to force a closed shell and use it anyway.'

Liz nodded along. That was exactly what she had done. She'd spent a lot of money on those mussels and at least half of them hadn't opened up in the boiling water. Was she supposed to throw them away? Yes, as it turned out.

'Right, today we're going to be working on another basic sauce. Tomato sauce. Now, to listen to many amateur and professional cooks I know, you would think that it's impossible to make a decent tomato sauce unless you were born in a Mafia household in Sicily.'

Bella smiled at that.

'That sounds like my grandmother's theory,' she said. 'But who has time to stir tomatoes picked from the foot of Mount Etna for three days just to stick it on top of some spaghetti?'

'I bet it tasted delicious though.'

'Yep,' said Bella. 'It did.'

'I'm going to get you to tell me more about it,' said Alex. 'But right now I'm going to show you the perfect tomato sauce for cheats. And it all comes down to the onions.'

Alex had already set up the three students' stations with chopping boards, an aluminium bowl and the enormous knives with which they'd learned their knife skills at the very first session. Now he handed each of them a small red onion.

'You could use any type of onion for this sauce in an emergency but if you use a small red one like this, you'll be giving yourself a head start.'

And heaven knows I need one of those, thought Liz.

'You remember how we chopped those onions three weeks ago?'

John, Bella and Liz nodded.

'Good. What we're going for today is fine slices. I'll show you one more time to refresh your memories.'

Whack. The onion was cleaved into two perfectly equal halves.

Alex's chopping had a compelling rhythm as he quickly turned those two halves into slices so fine they were all but transparent.

'Easy? Huh?'

Liz was already sweating at the thought.

'Another trick beginners often miss involves ensuring that your pans are hot before you start cooking. If you throw these onions into a cold pan, you're not going to get the caramelisation we want. At least not quickly. So, make sure your pan is hot and the oil is ready to begin its work. Then just throw those onions in, shake the pan to spread them around a little and leave them.'

'Don't you have to keep stirring them to stop them from burning?' asked John. Sonia was a big fan of stirring constantly, no matter what she was cooking. John thought that was the mark of a good cook.

'No. We want them to caramelise. If you keep stirring them around, they won't have a chance. They'll cook *too* evenly. Leave them to go a little brown around the edges first.'

The worried faces that looked back at Alex told him that it seemed counterintuitive.

'It gives us time to prepare the garlic,' he added.

Alex took a clove of garlic and covered it with the blade of the knife laid flat.

'This is how you take the skin off.'

He brought the heel of his hand down on the blade with a smart clack. When he picked up the garlic again, the skin was loose and fell away easily. He then chopped it into slices as fine as the onion.

'But I'm not going to throw it in just yet. One of the most common mistakes people make when cooking with garlic is to toss it in at the beginning with the onion. Onion and garlic may go together like mac and cheese in most people's minds but they actually need very different treatment. If you throw the garlic in with the onion and cook the onion for as long as it needs, you're going to have burnt garlic. And while there is nothing quite so delicious as garlic, there is nothing quite so awful as garlic that has burned.'

Liz could certainly attest to that.

'The smell lingers for days.'

'Yup,' said Liz. She thought she could still smell a

whiff of garlic in her kitchen though she hadn't knowingly cooked a clove of the stuff since the summer of 2014. She couldn't remember what it was she'd made but she knew it had ended in tears.

'So give the garlic a chance. Wait until your onion is almost half done.'

Alex looked into the pan where the onion had been left to its own devices.

'Perfect,' he said, shaking the pan and then showing his students something which Liz, at least, thought looked like a disaster already. She could probably manage that.

'It burned,' she said.

'No. It browned. This is what we're looking for. See how the edges of the onions are crisping up? This caramelisation is going to give us a delicious richness. Now you can turn the heat down, add the garlic and give the mixture a stir.'

Leaving the onions and garlic to mingle, Alex reached under his counter and pulled out a tin and a tube.

'Now this is the point at which the Sicilians would send for the village virgin to hand peel a half-dozen tomatoes and squeeze them into the pot with her toes. But we're going to add a tin of ready chopped. And a squirt of my secret weapon.'

He showed them the tube then squirted a snake of tomato puree onto the bowl of his wooden spoon.

'Sacrilege!' Bella announced.

'Don't tell Grandma,' Alex winked.

He tipped the tomato puree into the onions and garlic and gave the whole thing another quick stir. Finally, he added the tinned tomatoes and a sprinkling of oregano.

'And that, give or take a few minutes of simmering, is that. Of course you'll need to season. Do that gently. Too much is always harder to fix than too little. And you might want to add a few more herbs. You could add some chilli. Or some basil . . .'

Alex handed each of them a teaspoon.

'Here's your chance to taste it. You could chuck this straight over some pasta. A bit of cheese. A glass of red. There's your easy dinner. But I'm going to show you a show-stopper. We're going to do something with this.'

The three students waited to hear what was coming next.

'I've been thinking about the conversation we had last week. About the food that takes us back in time and the recipes that remind us of the people we've loved and lost. I'd like to try and recreate your special recipes with you. Bella, I hope you don't mind if the class starts with yours?'

Bella's eyes glittered. It was clear that she was moved. She shook her head. 'No,' she said. 'Of course I don't mind.'

'Then here goes. Bella, I hope this will live up to your memories.'

Alex pulled out an aubergine. It was almost as big as Hercules, the obese Chihuahua from Waggy Weight Loss. Liz had always thought there was something faintly obscene about aubergines. They certainly drew her eye at the supermarket with their wet purply shininess but she had never actually picked one up. They had an air of 'touch me and I'm yours' about them and she wasn't really sure she wanted the commitment. Now Alex handed her one of her own.

She was surprised at its texture. Spongy yet firm. Oddly familiar. Bella didn't seem quite so surprised.

'I've never touched one of these in my life,' said John.

'Then you don't know what you've been missing,' said Alex. 'Today we're going to make melanzane parmigiana. Melanzane being the Italian word for aubergine. But you all knew that.'

I didn't, thought Liz.

'So, Bella,' Alex continued. 'Tell us about your dad's version of this dish.'

'It was one of the classics on the menu at his café. It was something we ate all the time at home. Dad said he could never understand why the British didn't seem to like aubergines. For me, it was the dish I always asked for if I was given a choice. Dad would cook it to cheer me up. I remember when I was fourteen and some silly boy at school broke my heart. Dad cooked his parmigiana and we sat in the kitchen and he listened to me whine on while we ate. At the end he just said, "What does he have in his packed lunch at school?" I didn't know where Dad was going but I told him. Dairylea on white bread. Dad put down his fork and leaned back from the table. "The boy has no taste. He's unadventurous and he's going to stay that way. Never fall for a man who doesn't appreciate food, Bella. That's a man who doesn't appreciate life." I promised Dad I'd take his advice. It hasn't served me wrong.'

By the time Bella finished her story, Alex had sliced his aubergine into layers as thin as petals.

'That looks beautiful already,' said Bella.

'It looks difficult,' said John.

'Don't look so worried, John. I promise you it's really very easy. The trick is in the slicing.'

'Well, there goes mine,' said Liz.

'Come on Chopper, you're going to slice that auber-gine like a professional,' Alex said.

Liz came closer to losing a finger than she would have liked but she did manage to slice the aubergine exactly as Alex directed. The aubergine had to be fried ahead of being layered with the tomato sauce. She enjoyed painting on the oil with a pastry brush – it made her wonder if she should do an art course next – and when she cooked them she managed to get all the slices nicely transparent without any nasty burnt bits.

Assembling the parmigiana in an ovenproof dish was easy. A layer of aubergines. A layer of tomato sauce. Aubergines. Tomatoes. Aubergines. Tomatoes. Then cheese. Tearing the 'pizza' cheese (similar to but not the same as mozzarella) Alex had chosen into chunks was rather satisfying, as was grating on the parmesan. The smell that began to fill the room minutes after the dishes went into the oven was heavenly.

Surely Saskia had to like this one. It was vegetarian. It was healthy. Sort of. If you didn't think about the frying. The scent of triumph was in Liz's nose.

At the end of the class, Liz carefully loaded her parmigiana into a basket she'd found in the garden shed the previous day. That way she could carry the dish into the house without mishap. She hoped.

When everyone was ready to go, Alex handed out a fistful of flyers.

'Here's tonight's recipes sheet and,' Alex paused, 'an invitation. It's my birthday on Saturday and I'm having a little party. I'd be really pleased if the three of you might see fit to come along. It won't be very grand.

I'm having it here at the community centre. But there will be fantastic food and some great wine. I've got some friends in the business. And there'll be music and dancing if you like that kind of thing.'

'Thank you,' said John.

'Sounds great,' said Bella.

'It's very kind of you to invite us,' said Liz.

'Well, I hope to see you all on Saturday,' said Alex. 'Until then, happy cooking.'

Chapter Twenty-Five

This time, Bella was the last of Alex's students to leave the community centre. There'd been no phone call to drag her off ahead of the end of class. She helped him to tidy away the last of his equipment and waited as he locked the centre door.

'Where are you headed?' Bella asked. Alex had a big box of things to take home that night.

'West Cliff,' he said.

'I can give you a lift,' Bella suggested.

'No,' Alex shook his head. 'It must be out of your way.'

'Nothing in Newbay is really out of the way,' said Bella. 'It only takes ten minutes to get from one side of the town to the other.'

Alex insisted. 'I don't want to put you to any trouble.'

'It's no trouble,' said Bella. 'That's me over there.'

She pointed to a little blue Audi.

'Nice wheels.'

'Thanks.'

She popped the boot open.

With his kit stashed in the back, Alex climbed into the passenger seat. Bella made sure he was strapped in before she pulled away from the kerb. She was an exemplary driver and not just because she had a melanzane parmigiana in the boot.

'Wouldn't do for me to end up in the magistrate's court with a speeding conviction,' she explained.

She pulled out of the community centre car park, making sure to indicate. Alex wondered what to say next. It was strange seeing Bella in a new context. In the classroom he had his cooking to give him confidence. But in her car . . . Fortunately, Bella jumped in.

'Thank you for teaching us melanzane parmigiana tonight,' she said. 'I can't tell you how excited I am to have that to eat later on.'

'I was worried,' Alex said.

'Why?'

'I didn't know if you'd think it was weird, having to cook one of your dad's old recipes. I mean, it seemed to be something you had good memories about but I wasn't sure.'

'I have great memories of it,' said Bella. 'I would have made it myself but when Dad showed me how to make it, I never had quite enough patience to let the onions and the aubergines cook for as long as they needed before putting the whole thing together. I could never get it quite as melt-in-the-mouth as I wanted it. Until you reminded me how.'

'I hoped you'd be pleased.'

'Oh, I was delighted. That smell. It took me right back, though your cheat's tomato sauce would have caused outrage in my grandma's village.'

'Where is your grandma's village?'

'Western Sicily,' said Bella. 'Near Trapani.'

'I'd love to go there.'

'You should. *I* definitely should. I mean, I haven't been for years. We used to go every summer when I was a kid. Grandma died years ago but I've still got cousins I could visit. Never seem able to find the time now.'

'You work very hard,' Alex observed.

'It's just a desk job. It's not as though I'm slaving away over a hot stove all day. Working in a restaurant is what I call hard work.'

'Yes, but cooking's fun. And there's nothing better than watching someone enjoying something you've made for them.'

'You're right. I can't say all the people I work for are grateful,' Bella said.

'Then why do you do it?'

'It makes me happy to help someone out of a jam.'

'And you do legal aid stuff?'

'Yeah. It doesn't pay much but it's interesting and I know it's important. Everyone should be able to afford a lawyer.'

'It must be like seeing an angel turn up. I don't remember any of the duty solicitors I saw being quite so lovely.'

Bella cast a sidelong glance at him but before Alex could explain his comment, her mobile rang.

Bella had a hands-free set for her phone of course. 'I've got to take this,' she said.

It was the DSCC. Bella got more calls from them than anyone. Even her mother.

'He's asked for you specifically,' said the operator.

'I bet he did,' said Bella. 'Look, I'll be there in half an hour. I've got to do something first.'

But Alex would not hear of Bella taking him all the way back home now. Not when she had important work to do.

'But where can I leave you?' she asked. 'I've taken

you miles out of the way because of the one-way system.'

'Drop me there. That's my bus stop.'

'I feel so embarrassed. This seems to happen every Thursday night.'

'Your client needs a solicitor more than I need a lift home. Drop me here and go to the rescue, Angel Bella.'

Bella duly dropped Alex off at the bus stop, where he would stand, surrounded by his bags full of cooking equipment, for nearly forty-five minutes before a bus came. But though it was cold and damp, Alex didn't care. He was really happy. The class had gone exceptionally well that night. His little team was beginning to gel quite nicely. And Bella had offered him a lift home. She might not have been able to give him a lift home in the end but it was the thought that counted. In fact, it was probably for the best. He'd almost said too much. At least she hadn't got as far as seeing where Alex lived. Now that he thought about it, that could have left him with some explaining to do.

Bella could feel her shoulders tightening with annoyance as she drove away from the bus stop, leaving Alex and his box of kitchen equipment. Was there ever going to be an evening when her phone didn't ring with some new emergency that she simply had to attend? How had she ended up being on twenty-four hour duty for these people who seemed utterly unable to stay on the right side of the law for more than a week at a time?

Jimmy Cricket certainly seemed to think he could have Bella at his beck and call as though he was a Russian oligarch and she was the family lawyer. No matter that she might want to have a life of her own.

But then she remembered what Jimmy had said about her father and how he thought she was a chip off the old block precisely because she treated him with every bit as much respect as she would have treated someone who could afford to pay for her services. In many ways her job was really a vocation. She wasn't in it for the money. If she'd wanted money, she'd have joined a big commercial law firm in London, not a scuzzy partnership with an office above Argos in Newbay. She certainly wouldn't have put herself on the CDS rota. She was in it to help.

And yet . . . There had been days lately when she was really tired. When she wondered if there was some other way she could be of service to the people who came into her life. There was no doubt she was being taken advantage of by her boss and her colleagues, who were always coming up with excuses as to why they couldn't do the worst of the shifts. They had families. Bella didn't have time to get started on one. She didn't even have time for a date! The only men she ever met were colleagues or criminals. Until Alex.

'Evening, Miss B,' said Jimmy, when she walked into the interview room. 'I'm sorry to have to drag you here because of this misunderstanding.'

'What has Sergeant Mellor misunderstood this time?' Bella asked.

'I was only urinating into the dustbin because someone had thrown a lighted cigarette in there and I thought the whole thing would catch fire.'

'There are public toilets,' Bella reminded him.

'Shut for the winter,' Jimmy reminded her.

'Of course. Is it that time already?'

Jimmy nodded.

Bella shook her head. A local group had campaigned for the public loos on the promenade to remain open outside the main tourist season but the council claimed it was beyond their budget. It also prevented people like Jimmy sneaking into the loos with the intention of staying there overnight to keep out of the cold. It was inhuman, really.

'So, the charge is . . .' Bella looked at the sheet and sighed.

'Want a cup of tea?' Sergeant Mellor asked her.

'With two biscuits this time, my good man,' said Jimmy.

Chapter Twenty-Six

John was very pleased with his aubergine parmigiana. It wasn't a dish he had ever tried before, even in a restaurant. When he and Sonia went out for an Italian, John had usually plumped for a boring carbonara or a nice quattro formaggio pizza. Aubergine, he had always regarded with suspicion. But Alex had let everyone in the class try a bit of the parmigiana he'd made for demonstration purposes and John was surprised to discover he rather liked it. The aubergine didn't taste as he had expected and caramelising the onions had added a pleasant sweetness to the tomato sauce, just as Alex promised. The bubbling cheese on top was a real indulgence. The whole thing came together in the perfect dish for a wild, wintry night.

Or even a slightly squally autumn one, as that one was. He abandoned his plan to go to the NEWTS in favour of heading home.

John had left the light on this time, so when he let himself into the house he didn't have to make a dash for the switch. Everything was exactly as it had been at half past five. Except that the indicator on the answer-machine was flashing.

John stood over the machine. He knew that if he picked up and dialled 1471 he would be told that the number that made the last call was unavailable. Which meant that he couldn't block it but he could refuse to listen to the message so that's what he did. He cleared the message without letting it play.

However, the sight of the message indicator flashing had rattled him. He needed company. He wrapped the parmigiana back up in silver foil and took it to the NEWTS theatre bar.

Another rehearsal for the main cast of *Seven Brides for Seven Brothers* was taking place that evening. By the time John arrived, it was finished and the cast members were milling in the bar. Trevor was serving. Moira was there too. She didn't have a part in the production this time. She found it notoriously difficult to hold a note. Instead, she had been given the job of prop mistress.

Her face lit up when John walked in. John wondered if he should walk straight back out but Moira had been so kind to him. Now that he'd done a little cooking himself, he was starting to realise just how much effort it took to produce something from scratch. He was also embarrassed that he hadn't returned any of Moira's Tupperware thus far. He made a mental note to get it all washed up and ready to return the very next day.

'Trevor? Can I use the café oven?' John asked.

'Be my guest,' said Trevor. 'Though I don't know how sanitary you'll find it.'

'What have you made?' asked Moira. 'What have you got for us?'

'An aubergine parmigiana.'

'Aubergines! Don't you have to soak them for three days to get the poison out?' Moira asked.

'No,' said John. 'Turns out you don't have to soak them at all.'

While the parmigiana was heating through, John held a small audience, including Trevor and Moira, spellbound while he explained the recipe as though he had been making it for years. He did wish he'd started earlier.

The NEWTS oven was temperamental but the parmigiana came out perfectly golden.

'Oh, John. This is really tasty,' said Moira as she helped herself to a portion. 'You're a natural. When the ladies at the NEWTS hear what a good cook you are, you're going to be more in demand than ever.'

Behind Moira's back, Trevor Fernlea pulled a face that expressed every bit of the panic John was feeling.

Chapter Twenty-Seven

'Mum, what actually is this?' Saskia asked when Liz placed that evening's efforts on the kitchen counter.

'It's a melanzane parmigiana,' said Liz, savouring the roll of the words on her tongue. 'And it's completely vegetarian.'

'Ah, but it isn't,' said Saskia.

'Yes it is. There's no meat in it. No fish. No chicken. Just aubergines, onions and tomatoes.'

'But there's cheese.'

'Vegetarians eat dairy,' said Liz, trying to head off the argument.

'Er, not all dairy actually. Because not all dairy is made without killing animals.'

'You can't milk a cow if it's dead,' said Liz.

'Duh! Don't you know how cheese is produced, Mum? Sometimes they use the contents of an animal's stomach.'

'What?'

'It's true. So I'm not eating cheese any more. I'm sorry, Mum, but you really should ask me whether I can have all the ingredients before you try to make me eat something new.'

'You ate cheese on toast just last night.'

'That cheese was OK. This cheese is like . . . It's parmesan, right?'

'There's some on there, yes,' said Liz. 'Because this is a *parmigiana*.'

Saskia tapped something into her smartphone. 'Parmesan is made using rennet. It has to be made with rennet or it can't even be called parmesan. And rennet is made from the stomach of a calf.'

'Crikey.'

Even Liz didn't think the parmigiana looked so appealing any more.

'So I suppose I shall have to have toast again.'

'If you're sure it's vegetarian,' said Liz. 'I heard that the average loaf contains at least three ground-up insects.'

'You're not funny, Mum,' said Saskia.

Neither are you, Liz thought.

Liz bunged the parmigiana in the oven to warm up again while she made Saskia two slices of wholemeal toast with mashed avocado. At least she could get that right. When she came back downstairs to eat it, Saskia first took a photograph of the toast for Instagram and Liz was faintly mollified by the idea that her avocado toast had passed the picture test. It was only later that she would log on and discover that Saskia had captioned the picture. #avocadotoast #brownbits #instafail.

In the meantime, Liz managed to put calves' stomachs to the back of her mind and tucked into her class-cooked meal. She thought it was delicious. And she was proud that she had tackled her first ever aubergine. Until Alex had shown them how easy it was to prepare and cook, Liz had laboured under the impression that aubergine had to be buried in salt for at least three days to leach out some sort of poison. Where had she learned that?

Saskia slunk downstairs with her empty toast plate.

'Enjoying your calf's stomach juice?' she asked her mum.

'As a matter of fact, it's delicious,' Liz said. 'I might insist on having calf juice sprinkled over everything from now on.'

Saskia gave a world-class sigh.

By coincidence, the following day, Brittney's Bites Friday Inspo was replaced by a blog post on 'The hidden dangers of cheese', which explained Saskia's rennet revelation in full and disgusting detail. Liz read the blog while she was waiting for her first patient of the day.

'This is just another of "big food's" ways of getting us to eat their lies,' Brittney concluded. 'Like Big Pharma, they have a vested interest in getting us addicted to their products.'

She illustrated the piece with a quote from the Dalai Lama.

'You can't have a clean conscience if you don't eat clean food.'

'Funny,' Liz snarled. 'I would have thought that adultery made your conscience grubbier than the odd bacon sarnie.'

'First patient's here,' Julie called.

Chapter Twenty-Eight

That weekend Saskia was supposed to be spending time with Liz. She declined an invitation to join her mother at the Waggy Weigh-In, saying that she had to revise for a mock English Lit exam the following week. She would, however, be taking a little time off to go shopping that afternoon. She *needed* to get a new dress because on the Saturday evening she was going to her cousin's eighteenth birthday party.

Ah yes. This was Eric, a cousin on Ian's side of the family. For that reason, though it wasn't Ian's weekend to have Saskia, he would be coming to pick her up at seven on Saturday night. The party was going to be held at The Majestic, Newbay's grandest hotel. At least, it used to be grand. Rumour had it Wallis Simpson was a guest there in the Thirties. Now it was rather more 'tinsel and turkey', filled as it was by busloads of senior citizens who flooded to the coast out of season for cheap Christmas-themed mini-breaks. The Majestic started offering its Christmas menu in October.

Liz didn't know what to think about Saskia going to Eric's birthday party without her. After all, until the divorce went through, Liz was still technically Eric's aunt. She had known him since he was a red-faced baby, just two days old when she first visited him and his mother, Ian's younger sister Kerry, in the hospital. Once Saskia was born, the two cousins were an excuse for the families to get together at child-friendly venues and Liz had grown quite close to Kerry for a while. She definitely preferred her to Ian's po-faced older sister, Michelle.

Eric grew from an ugly baby into a serious sort of child. Now he was studying for his A levels. He was on track for a place at Cambridge to read physics. Liz knew all this because Ian's sister still texted her. As she did on the morning of the party itself.

'I feel really bad that you're not coming tonight. You've been there for Eric his whole life. You'd be very welcome. We'd love to see you.'

'I went ahead and made other plans,' was Liz's text response, which was almost certainly the answer Kerry really wanted to hear. Liz understood that when couples split up, families had to take sides. Kerry couldn't un-invite her brother. Though, thought Liz, she could have told him not to bring Brittney if she'd really cared.

Ah. Liz had never really liked Kerry either.

Anyway it was true that she had something else to do that evening. For once, there were two appointments in Liz's Saturday diary. Alex's birthday party was one.

'There will be plenty of food,' he'd promised.

But first, Waggy Weight Loss.

Nurse Van Niekerk was there as the warm-up act as usual.

'I've set up a new Facebook group,' she said. 'It's specifically for this cohort of WWL. I've added as many of you as I could find. I thought it would be a good way to keep the lovely community spirit we have here going through the rest of the week. We can offer each other motivational tips and fill in the group on our own progress. You could even post photographs of your dogs' dinners. It'll help to keep us all honest!'

'This is becoming a cult,' Liz muttered to Mrs Coco.

'Actually,' said Mrs Coco, 'I have been keeping a visual diary of what Coco is eating.'

'You have?'

'Yes.'

While Nurse Van Niekerk handed round a printout with the new Waggy Weight Loss Facebook page details, Mrs Coco showed Liz her Instagram feed. It was every bit as beautiful and well-curated as Brittney Blaine hoped hers to be.

'That's what your dog eats?'

There was a fillet of fish, cooked without seasoning, of course, but garnished with parsley and presented on a fine antique porcelain plate that was edged with gold leaf.

'I would have eaten that,' said Liz.

'I did eat that,' said Mrs Coco. 'I've decided that the best way to motivate Coco to eat properly is to sit down to exactly the same thing myself.'

'Yikes,' said Liz. 'Does that mean you're also eating kibble?'

'The organic kind really isn't so bad,' said Mrs Coco.

'Well, I'm not going to be joining Ted on the Waggy Weight Loss plan any time soon,' Liz assured her friend. 'I made aubergine parmigiana on Thursday night.'

'Aubergine?' Mrs Coco looked concerned. 'Don't you have to soak them for at least three days to stop them from being poisonous?'

'It turns out you don't,' said Liz. But before she had time to explain to Mrs Coco exactly how you prepared the classic Italian dish, in strode Dr Thomas, looking ready to 'move it, move it'. This time he was wearing a pink shirt with the sleeves rolled up to show off those hairy forearms, which Liz could now imagine him flexing as he made his own bread. He was definitely the type to make his own bread.

'Hello, everybody. Thank you once again for turning out on a Saturday morning. I'm delighted to see we've not lost a single participant since the beginning of the course. That tells me that you're all truly dedicated to your dogs' health and that makes me very happy indeed.'

Mr Biscuit, owner of Biscuit the Cockapoo, chanced a self-congratulatory whoop but was quickly shut down by a look from Nurse Van Niekerk. Waggy Weight Loss was not *The Jeremy Kyle Show*.

'This week I want to talk about how our pets pick up on our moods and how their habits reflect *our* habits. Stress is contagious. And in a dog that has a propensity towards it, stress can cause comfort eating, just as it does in human beings. So, I want you to ask yourselves, what has been going on in your life or in the life of your family of late that might be triggering your animal's desire to overeat?'

'To think I thought Ted was greedy just because he was a dog,' Liz whispered to Mrs Coco.

'There will be time for everyone to share their thoughts in due course,' said Dr Thomas, with a quick look in Liz's direction. 'For now, I just want you to reflect on events in the past few years and how you yourself have reacted. What do you do when you're unhappy? When you're down, do you automatically reach for the biscuit tin?'

Mrs Coco was nodding along. Biscuit, having heard his name, wagged his tail.

'Or, even worse, do you make yourself feel better by treating others? A particularly insidious trait, this one. Does giving your dog everything he begs for make you feel like a nicer, kinder person and help you to forget the bad day at work or the row you just had with your husband? Is your animal comfort eating by proxy? That is, on your behalf.'

I know what by proxy means, thought Liz. Dr Thomas really was patronising today.

'Would anyone like to share their thoughts on this particular topic now? Mr Hercules?'

Mr Hercules shrugged.

'Mrs Monty?'

'Well,' she said. 'There's no doubt I'm prone to comfort eating myself but I've never thought I could be passing it on to the dog. I thought all Labradors were greedy.'

'Mr Biscuit?'

'I haven't a clue.'

Mrs Coco tentatively put up her hand.

'Mrs Coco.' Dr Thomas looked at her encouragingly. 'Are the questions I threw out there ringing any bells for you this morning?'

'Yes,' said Mrs Coco. 'Absolutely. It made me think about the stress in my life when I was growing up. My mother was very unwell you see and I wasn't allowed to mess around and be noisy at home like the other children I knew. I had to be very, very quiet at all times. But my father rewarded me by bringing me a big bag of sweets every Friday afternoon. I've been rewarding Coco with food just as my father did me!'

Dr Thomas nodded. 'It was very brave of you to tell us that, Mrs Coco, and to admit that you might have some responsibility in how Coco's weight has got out of control. How do you feel, having made that connection?'

'I feel . . . I feel . . .'

Mrs Coco suddenly burst into tears. Nurse Van Niekerk bustled over with a box of tissues to save Mrs Coco having to wipe her nose on Coco's fur.

Liz glared at Dr Thomas. 'Is this really necessary?' she asked the room. 'Mrs Coco's upset.'

'It's OK,' said Mrs Coco, reaching blindly in Liz's direction. 'Please don't worry. I'm not upset at all.'

'You *are* upset,' Liz assured her. 'She is upset,' Liz reiterated for the benefit of Dr Thomas. 'I just don't get why we have to do this. Why can't you just tell us what we need to feed our dogs and let us get on with it without all the psychobabble?'

'Other people who have attended this course in the past have found that looking into how their own behaviour might be influencing their animals was helpful in making real and lasting changes. No one here is forced to share anything they don't want to.'

'It doesn't always feel like that,' Liz protested.

'Really, Mrs Ted, it's fine,' said Mrs Coco.

'My name is Liz Chandler,' said Liz. 'Not Mrs Ted.'

'Mrs Chandler,' said Dr Thomas. 'I'm sorry you're finding it hard to get on with our methods here at WWL.'

'Your methods are bizarre.'

'They work for me,' Mrs Coco insisted.

'If I've overstepped the mark for anybody in this

room,' said Dr Thomas, 'I'm very sorry. Mrs Coco, I apologise. Mrs Chandler, I appreciate your concerns.'

He seemed sincere so Liz backed down.

'I'm really finding it very useful,' said Mrs Coco to Liz. 'I don't mind.'

'Perhaps Mrs Ted, I mean, Chandler, is right,' said Dr Thomas. 'Let's concentrate on the immediate physical concerns facing our dogs.'

Nurse Van Niekerk had taken an executive decision and was already rolling out the scales.

'Let's do Ted first,' she said.

Liz brought him forward.

'Two hundred grams down.'

'A little less than we hoped but good work,' said Dr Thomas. 'Mrs Chandler.'

'Thank you,' said Liz.

Dr Thomas caught up with Liz and Mrs Coco as they said goodbye to each other in the car park.

'Mrs Coco,' he said, 'I wanted to make sure that you're all right.'

'Oh, I'm fine, Dr Thomas. You know me. I burst into tears at just about anything.'

'Well, if you're sure,' he said. 'And Mrs Chandler, I hope you don't really think we're out to upset anybody here at WWL.'

'I have to say that sometimes I think your manner with animals is better than your manner with humans,' Liz said.

'I appreciate the feedback,' said Dr Thomas. He looked genuinely crestfallen. 'Well, I must get back inside. I've got an operation to prep for. Hamster. Got its foot caught in its wheel. I hope we'll be able to save it.'

'Oh, Dr Thomas, so do I!' said Mrs Coco.

'Me too,' said Liz. 'Good luck.'

'Thanks.' Dr Thomas gave Liz an awkward thumbs up.

She liked him a little better for it.

Chapter Twenty-Nine

'Well, that went brilliantly,' Liz told Ted when they got back from Waggy Weight Loss. 'Your weight's not gone down enough again. Is it my fault? Are you fat because I'm unhappy?'

'Who's unhappy?' Saskia asked as she appeared in the kitchen doorway, still wearing her pyjamas.

'You're not up yet? It's almost midday.'

'Teenagers need more sleep because their brains are still developing,' said Saskia.

'Then you'd better go back to bed for another three days at least,' said Liz.

Saskia looked suitably affronted. So much so that when she asked Liz for an advance on her birthday money to buy her outfit for that evening's party, Liz immediately gave in.

'What are you doing tonight anyway?' Saskia asked, in a transparent attempt at seeming slightly interested in what Liz did when she wasn't being 'Saskia's Mum', in the hope of getting more money.

'As it happens, I'm going to a party as well.'

'Whose party?' Saskia was immediately suspicious.

'A man's.'

'Does Dad know?'

'Please, go ahead and tell him.'

* * *

Liz did not really feel like going to Alex's party any more but now that she'd told Saskia, she knew she was going to have to at least make a pretence of getting ready or Saskia would smell a rat.

So, when Saskia came out of the bathroom at quarter to seven, having been in there since five o'clock, Liz raced straight in after her.

'You're not the only one who wants to look good tonight,' she said.

'Don't forget to bleach your moustache,' said Saskia.

Liz wasted a good five minutes trying to work out if Saskia was joking. In the end, she did reach for the Jolen cream bleach and emerged from the bathroom slightly red about the top lip as a result.

'Mum, what have you done to yourself this time?' Saskia asked. 'I was joking about the bleach. Now you look completely ridiculous.'

Liz retired to her bedroom with a handkerchief full of ice cubes to hold against her lip until it went back to normal.

Soon there was just fifteen minutes until Ian arrived. He would almost certainly just park at the top of the drive and call Saskia on her mobile to let her know he was there but if there was the faintest chance that he might come to the door Liz wanted to be ready.

She stood in front of her wardrobe, still holding the ice cubes to her face, hoping for divine inspiration. Or any kind of inspiration really. *Wardro Inspo* is what Brittney would probably call it. Liz's wardrobe was more a case of *Wardro Nono*. In the end, she pulled out her old faithful – a black dress that fitted and flattered at most points on Liz's scale from thin days to fat. Accessorised with that big chunky Zara necklace Corinne had given her on her birthday, it would look passably festive. Possibly even chic.

Liz opted to style her hair in a messy bun. It was more mess than bun but she thought it had a touch of Catherine Deneuve in some Seventies' film about it. Two coats of mascara. A quick dash of blusher. A touch of red lipstick that detracted from the pinkness of her bleached upper lip.

'Are you actually wearing lipstick?' Saskia asked as they passed on the landing.

'Yes, I am,' said Liz, feeling all plucky. Then, 'Is it too much?'

Saskia nodded.

'Let me fix it.' Saskia said. She pulled Liz into her bedroom. Her secret lair. Liz was amused to see Saskia still had a poster of Justin Bieber tacked to the inside of her wardrobe door. Of course, she made sure not to mention it.

Saskia had Liz swap the red Mac Ruby Woo, which she had never actually worn outside the house, for a slick of a Lancôme Juicy Tube. Which Liz also never wore outside the house because it would never be much more than five minutes before the wind blew in the wrong direction and she ended up with her hair stuck to her mouth. Liz was the definition of low maintenance.

'That looks better,' Saskia said approvingly, having given her mother an extra coat of mascara as well. 'Almost a MILF.'

'I guess that's a compliment. How about the dress?'

'Put a belt around it? Show off your waist.'

Saskia pulled a belt from her own collection, which

was miraculously long enough. Liz immediately followed her daughter's suggestion.

'Yep, that'll do,' Saskia gave her the nod.

For once the gods were smiling and Liz was looking her very polished best when Ian knocked at the door. Yes, he actually knocked, without phoning Saskia first. Suspicious.

Liz opened the door. She could see Ian's car at the top of the driveway. Brittney was in the front passenger seat, examining her make-up in the sunshield mirror. Brittney was the kind of woman who knew about contouring. The cow.

'Is she ready?' Ian asked without preamble.

Saskia came down the stairs in the outfit she'd bought that afternoon. Liz easily spotted the twitch in Ian's right eye as he clocked what his daughter was wearing.

She knew that Ian would not be happy to see Saskia in an outfit that looked like it belonged on stage with Little Mix but he was playing 'good dad' now, wasn't he? He'd handed over all the discipline to Liz. He couldn't ruin all that hard work by kicking off about Saskia's clothes. Especially not when his girlfriend was usually dressed the same way. Probably *was* dressed the same way. They were the same generation after all. He had to lump it.

It was a small victory for Liz but it was sweet.

'You look very nice,' Ian said to Saskia.

Saskia pulled a selfie sort of face in response.

'And you,' Ian said to Liz.

'What?'

'You look very nice too. Is that dress new?'

'I bought it for our fifteenth wedding anniversary. I don't suppose you remember.'

Ian glossed over that. 'Are you going out?'

Just as she had detected the twitch of distress at the sight of Saskia's mini-skirt, Liz thought she heard something beyond the small talk Ian was making with her now. He wasn't just asking, 'Are you going out?' He was asking, '*Who* are you going out with?' And 'Are you actually going to get laid?'

'Just a party,' Liz said as casually as she could manage. 'A man I met at my cooking club.'

A man who could cook. She hoped Ian was imagining a hunk in chef's whites, whipping up some kind of chocolate cream to spread all over Liz's naked body. In Liz's imagination the chef had Alex's face. Or Hugh Jackman's. That would do.

'Right. Well, have a nice time,' Ian said. 'Come on, Saskia. We're going to be late. Your Auntie Kerry wants us there by seven thirty for the speeches.'

'Enjoy yourselves,' said Liz. 'Remember me to everybody.'

You know, she said to herself. *Remember Liz? The wife? The one you're still technically married to even though you're turning up to her godson's party with that blogging tart?*

'I will,' said Ian.

Liz blew Saskia a kiss and closed the door behind them.

It was one of the more successful encounters Liz had had with her ex since the night he moved out. She was looking good and she had managed not to say anything stupid but still Liz was surprised at how much it had taken out of her to stay so cool for what felt like so long. For a couple of minutes after Ian and Saskia left, Liz just sat on the bottom of the stairs, pressing her thumbs to the corners of her eyes to prevent any tears from leaking out. She didn't want to spoil her make-up. Not when it had gone so well.

She wondered if Ian had felt as strange as she had. Him standing there in the hallway of what had been their family home. Was he even now being assailed by memories of the times they had spent there together, as she was? It was much easier when he didn't come in, when he just called from the top of the drive. Why had he come in that night?

Even Ted seemed out of sorts. Perhaps, Liz thought, I should just stay in with the dog after all. I could make an aubergine parmigiana. Yes, Liz had bought an aubergine in Sainsbury's the previous evening, feeling a small flutter of pride as she placed it and two red onions on the checkout belt in front of a man whose basket was full of ready meals for one. She had the feeling that if she had invited him to join her for some aubergine-related entertainment, he would have leapt at the chance. That memory made her want to give herself a shake. She was never going to find anyone to share an aubergine with unless she really put herself out there. And that meant accepting invitations like Alex's at the glamorous Newbay Community Centre.

Liz was just about to get into the car when she decided she would really push the boat out. She called a taxi. She was going to get lightly inebriated. If not completely hammered. While she was waiting for the taxi to arrive she poured herself a large gin and tonic.

'For courage,' she said to Ted.

Chapter Thirty

At eight o'clock, Alex's party was already jumping. Liz was more than slightly nervous as she approached the room, which had been decorated with balloons marked with '30'. It was a long time since she'd been to a party and it was hard to walk in on her own. When she and Ian were together, they had each other to talk to. Alone, she would have no choice but to make conversation with strangers. She hoped John and Bella would turn up. This crowd looked intimidating. Liz had no idea where Alex had found so many hipsters in Newbay. He must have had them bussed in.

When she saw the rest of the guests, Liz was pleased she'd dressed up. She felt pretty good in her little black dress, accessorised as per Saskia's instructions. The lip gloss, though it was hard to keep her hair out of it, made her feel properly polished and glamorous. She was sure she caught a few appreciative glances as she made her way towards the birthday boy.

'Chopper!' Alex greeted her warmly. Liz returned his big smile with one of her own. 'I was really hoping you would make it.'

That seemed genuine, Liz thought.

Alex turned to the woman standing next to him. 'Liz is one of my star pupils on the beginners' cookery course.'

The woman nodded appreciatively. 'He's been telling

me all about it. There's nothing Alex doesn't know about cooking,' she said. And she said it in such a way that Liz wondered what she knew about Alex's other life skills and whether they were worth investigating too.

Alex was looking edgier that evening than he did when he was dressed in his white overalls for teaching. He was wearing tight black jeans and a dark blue shirt, unbuttoned to reveal an attractive amount of chest hair. Liz liked chest hair. Ian, who was very fair, didn't have an awful lot. She'd always pretended it didn't matter but there was something very primal about it. Masculine.

'Well, I need teaching a thing or two,' said Liz with a wink. Alex's friend gave her what Liz's mother would have called 'an old-fashioned look'.

'Can I get you a drink?' Alex asked.

Liz plumped for a glass of white wine. She couldn't see any spirits on the drinks table so she decided that the closest she could get to sticking to the advice about not mixing your drinks was not mixing the colours. Gin and white wine. Close enough.

'You've got a choice,' said Alex. 'My friend Joe is a wine merchant and he's brought along quite a selection. Are you a Sauvignon blanc or Chardonnay sort of girl?'

'Whatever makes me Sauvignon *blanc out* the fastest,' said Liz.

Now it was Alex's turn to give her a funny look.

'Oh! I get it.'

He poured Liz a glass of Sancerre. Though a half-glass was what it looked like to her.

'This is from a small vineyard in the Loire run by two brothers who are really into biodynamic wine. I think you'll find it's a little bit different.'

Different to what? Liz was no wine buff but she nodded along as Alex gave her the wine's potted tasting notes.

'There's a lot of fruit in there. Can you taste the gooseberries?'

'I thought it was made with grapes.'

Alex chuckled. 'There's a flinty undertone, don't you think? Great acidity.'

'I like it,' Liz confirmed. 'You can fill my glass up if you like. Save me coming back too soon.'

'But Liz,' said Alex. 'Your glass *is* full. If I put any more in, you won't be able to taste it properly, I promise you.'

'I was only kidding,' Liz said.

Alex looked relieved. 'When you've finished that, I'd really like you to try this Sancerre as well. See which one you like better.'

Somehow Liz persuaded Alex that it would make more sense if she compared the wines side by side. He poured her a glass of the second and she hovered by the bar with a glass in each hand, sipping frequently to mask her nerves.

Alex's guests were still arriving. He was a perfect host, making sure that everyone was introduced to someone they might like to talk to and that they had a glass in their hand while they were doing so. She was grateful that he hadn't forgotten her and that she was alone. He introduced her to what seemed like dozens of people.

'This is Liz.'

'Or Chopper, as he likes to call me,' Liz started saying after she finished the first two glasses of wine, accompanying the revelation with an onion-chopping mime. Alex thought that was very funny. 'At the first class, when he asked what had persuaded us all to sign up,' Liz elaborated, 'I told him that for me it was learning knife skills. I'm getting a divorce.'

'Gosh,' said a woman who had worked with Alex in London.

'Have you tried this?' Joe the wine merchant waggled a red wine bottle in her direction. She let him pour a slug into one of her glasses that was empty. So much for not mixing the colours of her liquor.

'It's a Cabernet Sauvignon from the Aconcagua,' he said.

Liz nodded knowledgeably. The Aconca-what?

'Parker's people gave it 93 points. I can understand why. It's absolutely a Parker style wine. Big. Lots of oak. A bit too high in alcohol if you ask me. I'm sure it's a winner though.'

'Hmmm,' Liz agreed. 'And I can definitely taste blackcurrants.'

Liz was finding that talking to Alex's food- and wine-fanatic friends was getting easier by the minute. Or by the glass.

'Yes,' said Joe the wine buff. 'There is a hint of blackcurrant in there, you're right. Alex, your mate Chopper really knows her stuff.'

Liz tipped her glass at Alex, who tipped his glass back at her. She went back to the wine conversation. The buff was explaining how the *terroir* in the Aconcagua made for a very different wine from those produced in the Maipo Valley. Liz nodded along but all the while she kept half an eye on Alex. Just as she was pretty sure that he was keeping half an eye on her in return.

Joe was joined by a woman he knew.

'Joe, it's good to see you,' she said.

Joe introduced the woman to Liz.

'This is Elle. She works as a sommelier in Exeter.'

Liz raised her glass.

'Oooh,' said Elle. 'What's that?'

'Cabernet Sauvignon from Chile,' said Liz.

'Lovely. Have you tried this Australian red?'

Liz knocked back the Cab Sav so that Elle could fill her glass anew.

Then Elle leaned in confidentially and told Joe and Liz, 'Can you see how nervous Alex is tonight? As I understand it, there's someone here who's rather special to our mate Al and he's desperate to make a move.'

'Who is it?' Joe asked.

'Someone from his cooking class, I think.'

Liz flicked her hair back. She glanced across at Alex. He was looking right at her. And yes, he did look nervous. Liz smiled at him then looked away in a classic flirting move.

'Would you excuse me?' she said to Joe and Elle before moving off in what she hoped was a mysterious sort of way. She gave Alex another discreet little smile as she passed him en route to the ladies'. He was into someone from his cooking class? As far as Liz knew, she was the only one from the cooking class who had made it to the party. Alex had seemed especially attentive. Was Liz about to experience the joy of passion with a younger man that Corinne swore was better than yoga for keeping trim?

Liz examined her face in the mirror in the ladies' room. Her make-up was still largely intact. Just a little bit of mascara slippage in the heat but she could soon touch that up with the wet wipes she carried in her handbag. She blotted her shiny nose with another layer of powder. She didn't need to add any more blusher. Red wine always made her colour up. After two glasses, she had a natural glow, she decided. She puffed up her hair and added another slick of lip gloss. Her hair was sticking to her lips by the time she got back into the hall where the party was taking place, but that was soon remedied.

Liz was looking good. She was having a wonderful time. She dared to give Alex a wink. He tugged at his collar. A sure sign of nerves. Yes, it was definitely her that he fancied. *She* was the mystery lady Alex's friends were all talking about.

Chapter Thirty-One

Liz met Bella and John by the buffet table.

'Hello, lovelies.' She gave them both a hug. 'Isn't this a fantastic party?'

'It certainly is,' said John.

'The food's amazing,' said Bella.

'Of course it is,' said Liz. 'With our chef in charge.'

Bella sighed. 'It's not just the way to a *man's* heart that's through his stomach. Oh look! Mini beef Wellingtons.'

'I'm having one of those,' said John.

John and Bella were filling their plates. Liz didn't pick up a plate of her own straight away. She plucked a sausage on a stick straight from its serving plate. Naturally, it was no Sainsbury's ready-cooked cocktail sausage. It was an artisan, organic cocktail sausage with a honey and mustard dip. Alex had carefully labelled everything on the table.

Liz plonked her sausage in the dip and brought it to her mouth. She made sure she caught Alex's eye before she bit into it.

'Plate, Liz?' John passed her a paper plate and napkin.

'Oh yes, thank you.' Liz delicately dabbed at her sticky lips.

'We were just saying how much we've been enjoying the cookery class. I wish I'd started earlier. I'd never

197

have let my wife do all the cooking if I'd known how much fun it was.'

'You shouldn't have let her do all the cooking anyway,' said Liz.

John looked a little taken aback. 'But she said she liked to do it.'

'I'm sure she did,' said Bella, trying to stop a fight. 'In our house, it was always Dad who was in the kitchen. He wouldn't let Mum anywhere near the stove. He said she could curdle a sauce just by looking at it. I think I inherited her ability.'

'Nonsense,' said John. 'You got the method for white sauce straight away. You have the knack.'

'Alex seems to be having a good time,' said Bella, changing the subject. 'He's got some very interesting friends. I was just talking to someone called Elle. She works as a sommelier.'

'There are lots of people who work in the wine trade here,' said Liz. 'I've been getting a crash course in wine tasting. I had no idea there was such a difference between a Sauvignon and a Chardonnay.'

'It's hard to keep them apart in your head if you have too many in a row though,' John responded.

'I think I've got a talent for it,' Liz pressed on. 'Wine tasting. I suppose I didn't know how good I was at differentiating grapes because I'd never actively compared them side by side before. What have you got there, Bella?'

'Elderflower cordial. I'm on call. I don't suppose I'll get to be here long but it was so kind of Alex to invite us.'

'John?'

John let her take a sniff at the wine in his glass. He

looked less happy when she took a big swig and noisily swilled it around her mouth.

'Cabernet Sauvignon,' she said.

'Spot on,' said John.

'I'm good,' said Liz. She took another sausage and looked for Alex so that the way she ate it wouldn't be wasted. This time she circled the tip with her tongue.

'Shall we sit down?' Bella took Liz by the elbow. 'I hate trying to eat standing up. Balancing a glass and a paper plate full of food is a sure-fire recipe for disaster.'

'I've got pretty good balancing skills,' said Liz, standing on one leg to prove it. She wobbled dramatically. 'Only kidding,' she said when she put the other foot back down. 'I'm perfectly steady. Look.'

John spotted a table and three chairs.

'Shall we set ourselves up over there?'

'Great idea,' said Bella. 'I'll see if I can get hold of a jug of water, too.'

'Now that's a very good plan,' said John.

Liz was slightly annoyed by the choice of table. It was in a corner, obscured from the rest of the room by a large pillar. John insisted she take the seat against the wall, but that meant she couldn't see around the pillar to keep an eye on what Alex was up to. How was she supposed to let him know it was all right to make his move if she couldn't see him?

'Are you having a good weekend, Liz?' John asked. 'What have you been up to today?'

'I took my dog to his weight loss club,' said Liz.

'They have those for dogs?'

'Yes, they do. It's hard. I know I've overindulged him.'

'It's difficult not to overindulge,' John agreed.

'Hey!' Liz saw Elle walking by. 'Can we have a bit more of that Cab Sav?'

Liz knew the lingo by now.

'Of course,' said Elle. She topped Liz up. John put his hand over his glass.

'I'd better not,' he said. 'You can't tolerate your alcohol so well when you're my age. I think I started to lose my tolerance when I was about forty.'

'I'll have his then,' said Liz, pushing an empty glass in Elle's direction. Who had left the empty glass on the table? Liz didn't care.

Bella returned with not one but two bottles of water.

'Here you go,' she said to John and Liz. 'Still or sparkling?'

'I'm OK, thanks,' said Liz. 'I've already got two glasses on the go.'

Bella poured out a glass of water for her regardless.

'And would you like this?' she pushed her plate of food towards Liz. 'Maybe some of the bread? I can go and get myself some more.'

'I don't want any bread, thank you,' said Liz.

'It's really nice,' Bella pushed it upon her. 'I think Alex made it himself.'

'I liked it,' John concurred. 'You should try it, Liz. And a coffee? I really fancy a coffee right now. Shall I get one for you ladies too?'

'I don't drink coffee in the evening,' said Liz.

'Tea would probably work just as well,' said Bella, with an urgent nod to John.

'Tea with milk?'

'Yep,' Bella told him.

'You can't drink tea with milk any more,' Liz told them. 'Not ordinary milk anyway. Don't you know how bad it is for you? You should read Brittney's Bites.com. She's my husband's mistress. She does yoga and would never touch a sausage. Except Ian's.'

She waved her hand around to illustrate her point and knocked one of her wine glasses off the table in Bella's direction. Fortunately, Bella was pretty quick on her feet and avoided the worst of the spill. However, in attempting to mop the mess up with an ineffectual paper party napkin, Liz only made matters worse. She knocked Bella's glass of cordial over as well.

'Oh bum,' said Liz. 'Let me get you a new one.'

Liz stood up. Bella physically pressed her back down into her seat.

'No, really,' she said. 'It's OK. I don't need any more. I don't know about you, Liz, but I find it's really easy to overdo it at a party like this where there's so much delicious alcohol going round. Especially if you don't eat before you come out and the only food on hand is party nibbles. I find I really need to line my stomach before I come out or else try to soak up what I'm drinking with some bread.'

She pushed her plate of sandwiches towards Liz once again. Liz pushed it back. Why was Bella so insistent on passing her food over? Was it like at Waggy Weight Loss? Was Bella trying to snack vicariously?

'Really, Bella,' said Liz. 'I'm trying to stay off the complex carbs.'

'There are carbs in wine,' said Bella.

'Yes, but they're not proper carbs, are they?'

'I think you'll find they are.'

'Whatever they are, I need some more of them,' said Liz.

She got up from the table. Bella looked desperately to John.

Chapter Thirty-Two

Moments after Liz sashayed off in the direction of the dance floor, slopping wine from the one glass she hadn't managed to knock over, Bella got a phone call.

'I have to take this,' she said to John.

He was used to it by now. Besides, Bella wasn't just taking a phone call in the way young people did – because she thought the caller might be more interesting than the person she was actually with – she had a good reason. Somebody somewhere needed her urgently. Bella's presence could make the difference between freedom and a night in the cells, John now knew.

Bella's face dropped as the caller spoke to her. She nodded and made affirmative noises then, eventually, she told the caller, 'I'll be there right away.'

She put the phone in her pocket and started to gather her things together. John helped her to put on her coat.

'I'm needed at the station,' she said.

'Must be nice to be wanted all the time,' said John.

Bella rolled her eyes. 'Sort of,' she said. 'I should have known I wouldn't get to be here long. I haven't even had a chance to try one of Alex's desserts.'

'I'll make sure he saves you some,' said John.

'Thank you. Will you tell him I'm sorry for dashing off? I didn't even have a chance to talk to him.'

'I'll let him know.'

'And give him this?'

Bella pulled a birthday card out of her handbag.

'And will you keep an eye on you-know-who?'

'Of course I will.'

'She's in quite a state. I get the impression there's something going on with Liz today,' said Bella. 'Something upset her earlier, perhaps.'

'Well, she's going to be upset in the morning for sure, when she wakes up with a massive hangover.'

'Try to get her to drink that tea,' said Bella. 'And some water. And eat some bread. I've got to go.'

'You stop worrying, Bella. I'll do my best.' John waved her off. Alex was soon by his side.

'Has Bella gone?' he asked.

John nodded.

'Work,' he said.

'On a Saturday?'

'I don't think the local criminals take the weekend off,' said John.

'But why is she always on call?'

'She must be very dedicated.'

'There you are!'

Alex and John were interrupted by Liz, who sashayed back towards them like she was auditioning for *Strictly*. She had a glass in each hand again. Both were full to the brim. None of those fancy wine-tasting portions for Liz. She handed one to Alex, who took it before it had a chance to spill. She toasted him.

'To the birthday boy,' she said.

'Thank you.'

'Happy birthday to you, happy birthday to you, happy birthday, Mr President!'

Liz did her best impression of Marilyn Monroe.

'Just like the real thing,' John said tactfully.

'I'm even better than the real thing,' Liz told Alex, keeping her eyes firmly on his.

Alex gulped.

'Let's dance!' said Liz.

'Sure,' said Alex. 'Why not?' Perhaps keeping Liz moving would prevent her from drinking any more wine.

Liz took Alex by both hands and boogied him backwards onto the dance floor, to the whooping amusement of his mates. While Alex jigged awkwardly on the spot, Liz was soon in full on twerking mode. She rubbed herself against Alex's thigh. She used him as a pole-dancing prop. She had the whole party watching and clapping. As far as she was concerned, she was definitely owning the dance floor. The alcohol had made Liz fearless.

Alex had to grab both her hands to stop them from wandering. Liz moved in close.

'I know,' she said in a confidential sort of way.

'Know what?' asked Alex.

'About your secret.'

'You do?' Alex didn't like the sound of that.

'Your mate Elle was talking about it and I just want you to know that I don't mind. I've always liked you. You don't have to worry about me.'

'Thanks,' said Alex.

'I don't know what the others will think,' Liz continued. 'But it's really none of their business, is it? If they disapprove, they disapprove. I don't think they will though. John and Bella both seem like open-minded people. I can't see how finding out would change their opinion of you.'

'Do you really think so?'

'Yes. They'll probably be pleased that the cat's out of the bag. I'll bet you are . . .'

The music slowed in tempo. Liz swayed closer and closer.

'You don't have to worry about me, Alex, but if you need to keep it just between us for a little while longer, that's fine too. I understand. You're working as a teacher. Your reputation is important. When you're teaching people to cook, you don't want them to be looking at you and wondering if you're fit to tell them what to do when your mind is so obviously elsewhere.'

Liz pressed herself ever closer to Alex's hairy chest.

'No,' said Liz. 'It makes perfect sense that you should keep it quiet.'

'I didn't know what else I could do,' Alex suddenly sighed. 'People have expectations of their teachers, don't they? You, Bella and John have paid a lot of money to attend my class.'

'And it was worth every penny,' said Liz. 'For me. Though I can see why Bella might be miffed.'

'You're losing me now,' said Alex.

'If it makes it easier, I could always leave the class. That way you can't possibly be accused of favouritism.'

Though the music was still playing, Alex stopped dancing. He held Liz at arm's length and asked her, 'Liz, what exactly are we talking about here?'

'Your feelings,' said Liz, quite simply. 'Your feelings for me. It's OK. You can admit to them now. Elle told me you were falling for someone in your cookery class. I would never have dreamed it might be me.'

Liz closed her eyes, waiting for a kiss. When she

reopened them, after no kiss materialised, she said, 'That's because it isn't me, is it?'

Alex put his fingers to his temples and groaned.

Leaving Alex in the middle of the dance floor, Liz blundered in the direction of the ladies' again. Of course Alex didn't fancy her. Of course not. Why would he when every time he saw her at the cooking course she was standing next to the serene beauty that was Bella? Next to Bella, Liz felt like a toad. Next to Bella she was an ancient, unattractive old lump of middle-aged woman. He wouldn't fancy her in a million years! She stared at her reflection again. This time she didn't think she'd nailed it. This time she could see all too clearly her shiny forehead, her open pores, the bright red cheeks that told her (and everybody else) that she'd had way too much to drink.

She imagined the party going on outside. Was everybody talking about her now? Were they waiting for her to come back out of the loo so they could all have a proper laugh at the forty-five-year-old mum of one (and owner of a fat dog) who thought she had a chance with a thirty-year-old chef who looked like Luke Evans off *Beauty and The Beast*?

Liz groaned again. Could her life get any worse?

Chapter Thirty-Three

It was a full fifteen minutes before Liz came out of the loos. When she did, Alex was waiting for her. He pulled her to one side with admirable discretion.

'Are you OK, Liz?' he asked. 'Do you want to sit down somewhere and talk? Have a cup of tea?'

'Oh no,' she said, trying to keep it breezy. 'I didn't realise how late it is until I checked the messages on my phone. I'm just going to call a taxi and go home.'

'Have you got a taxi number?' Alex asked.

'On my phone,' she assured him.

'Well, if you're sure. If you can't get one then I've got a card here.' He pulled a local taxi firm's card from his pocket.

'I like to use the people I know,' she said.

She couldn't face saying goodbye to John properly so she just waved to him from across the room and kept on walking when it looked as though he wanted to say something. Thank goodness Bella was already gone. She did, however, pause briefly by the buffet table. It was still heaving with food. Alex had over-catered and she was suddenly ravenous. Feeling embarrassed was definitely one of Liz's food triggers. She picked up a piece of bread, which she stuffed into her mouth, and a whole plate of charcuterie, which was still covered in cling film. If that was going to waste, then she and Ted might as well have it.

* * *

Liz felt much more sober when she stepped outside and the chilly breeze coming in across the sea hit her full in the face.

'Oh woe,' she muttered to herself. 'I made a complete and utter tit of myself. I'm never ever, ever, ever drinking again.'

She dialled the taxi number she had stored in her phone.

'It's going to be at least an hour,' the controller said.

'Ah never mind,' said Liz. It was way too cold to wait outside the community centre for an hour and Liz couldn't face going back inside. She decided that she should walk. It might help to stave off the hangover that was doubtless already on its way. It would also save her money and it wouldn't take long.

Especially if she took her stupid shoes off.

Liz's route home from the community centre took her right down to the sea front. When she got to the promenade, she turned west towards the big hotels, the biggest of which was The Majestic, where her nephew's eighteenth birthday celebration was being held.

The party was still in full swing when Liz got there. She stood outside, looking up at the windows of the ballroom, feeling like a Victorian urchin shut out of a fabulous dinner. Despite the fact that she had her own charcuterie plate if she really needed a snack.

Of course, it made her sad. When the plans for Eric's big birthday party were first mooted, some eighteen months earlier, Liz had most definitely been on the guest list. She'd helped Kerry to narrow down the possible venues. She'd discussed table plans and menus. She'd even helped Kerry listen to endless demos as she tried to find a suitable live band. And now Liz was NFI to the party she had helped to plan while Brittney – Brittney Big Boobs Blogtastic Blaine – was probably even now dancing with Liz's brother-in-law Shane. Actually, that would serve her right. Shane had hands like an octopus and breath like a cat that had eaten one.

Yeah. Maybe Liz was glad she wasn't at Eric's boring eighteenth birthday party making small talk with her boring former in-laws about their boring lives. Let Brittney try not to glaze over while Kerry bored on about her kitchen station. Let Brittney make interesting noises while Ian's sister Michelle bored on about her IBS. Let Brittney try not to spit her drink all over the table when Ian's father bored on about his plans to stand as a UKIP candidate at the next council elections. Let Brittney try to tell Saskia that she could not have another drink. Or Ian for that matter.

Liz did not envy Brittney any of that.

And yet . . .

As Liz stood outside, looking up at the windows of the hotel's winter garden, the live band that she had helped to choose struck up 'Happy Birthday'. Liz imagined the caterers carrying out the cake – a chocolate sponge whittled into the shape of the International Space Station. Liz had helped to choose that too. Liz hoped the caterers tripped up and dropped it on the floor.

'No I don't.' Liz said to herself. Of all her in-laws, Eric was actually her favourite. It wasn't his fault he'd been born into such a dull family full of so many pompous individuals. And he would always be Saskia's cousin. As an only child, it was important Saskia had that bond. When all the adults who had made Liz feel so unwelcome and miserable were long gone, Saskia and Eric would still have each other. Saskia would need someone with whom she could discuss just how weird the Chandler clan really was.

'Happy Birthday, Eric!' Liz raised the plate of charcuterie in lieu of a glass.

Inside the hotel, a cheer went up. Eric must be blowing out the candles. Eighteen candles. How time had flown. And in just a couple of weeks, Saskia would be sixteen. Liz tried and failed to contain a sob at the thought.

'Come on, old girl,' she muttered to herself like the mad lady she'd always feared she would become. 'It's time to go home. Get into bed and forget all about it. Tomorrow is another day.'

Chapter Thirty-Four

Antipasti Cinquecento

You will need: as much Italian cured meat as you can lay your hands on. A newly polished Fiat Cinquecento (2016 reg). And a grudge.

Liz decided that if she cut through The Majestic's car park, she could shave a little time off her barefoot walk home. It was already too late for her tights, but she didn't want to risk her feet any more than she had to so she hopped over the low white picket fence and started to pick her way between the Vauxhalls and the Volvos. The Chandler family loved their Volvos. The one Liz drove had originally belonged to her father-in-law. Liz had always had second-hand cars while Ian drove new. There were rows and rows of Volvos. And so many Fiat 500s! Lately they seemed to have proliferated on the streets of Newbay like a plague of Italian bugs.

Brittney had a Fiat 500, Liz remembered then. A white one, decorated with a green and a red stripe for the Italian flag. That car said everything about the difference between Liz and Brittney. Brittney was carefree and stylish. She had a touch of Italian chic. She didn't have to worry about loading daughters and their school kit into the back. She could fling an overnight bag into the boot and drive all the way down to Tuscany whenever Ian could get the time off. Meanwhile the boot of Liz's Volvo was full of Wellington boots and hockey kits and filthy towels with which to dry off the dog at the end of a beach walk.

Liz came to a white Fiat 500.

She stood in front of it, imagining the lucky owner opening the sunroof and letting her hair fly free in the breeze. What man wouldn't choose such a glamorous driver over a school mum in a filthy old estate? Even if that estate did contain his child and his dog.

'I hate you,' Liz told the car. 'I hate you and everything you stand for, Cinquecento. You think you're so fresh and funky. You don't know that one day you're going to be like me. One day you won't be driving through the hill towns of Tuscany looking for artisan parmesan made without fucking rennet. You'll be standing in the Sainsbury's car park thinking about what to make your impossible daughter for tea. You'll be old and beaten up and finished and your tits will be down by your knees.'

As she was muttering to the car, which valiantly stood by and took all the abuse she could throw at it, Liz peeled back the cling film that was covering the silver foil platter she'd taken from Alex's party. The charcuterie had hardly been touched. There were hundreds and hundreds of slices of mortadella, pepperoni, salami and delicious parma ham.

Delicately, Liz lifted one of the pepperoni slices away from the others and laid it down on the bonnet of the Fiat 500. Italian cured meats for an Italian car.

'There. That's better. I am an anarchist. I am the *anti-pasti*,' Liz made up a new verse for the Sex Pistols'

'Anarchy in the UK' as she added another three slices to make a little pork-based flower.

Then she thought it would be a good idea if she used slices to convey some kind of message. To make some words. There was just enough mortadella to write 'Slut'. She'd have to add 'Slag' in a mixture of salami and parma ham. Liz used her thumb to estimate the size of the letters and the meat she would need.

It was really quite artistic, thought Liz as she stood back to admire her handiwork, then tweaked her design to make the 'u' in slut look more rounded on the bottom. Then she folded the foil platter in half and wedged it under one of the car's windscreen wipers. Which was the point at which she realised that the dancing white light on the Fiat's meaty bonnet was coming from a hotel security guard's torch.

Chapter Thirty-Five

The Majestic's chief security guard was already telephoning for assistance.

'Crime in progress,' he said urgently into his mobile. 'Require uniformed back-up at once. Repeat. Back-up required.'

'Hmmmm?' Liz turned to find out what was going on. She thought she felt the earth turning beneath her as she did so. She was still very, very drunk.

'Stay where you are. Put your hands on the bonnet. This is a citizen's arrest!'

'What?' Liz was utterly confused again.

A police car, complete with lights and sirens, seemed to arrive simultaneously, skidding into the car park at speed.

The next few minutes were a blur for poor Liz Chandler. She tried to explain herself but the police officers – who both looked so young – weren't having any of it when Liz said that her antipasti art was merely fair comment on the owner of the car.

They discussed between themselves exactly what might be grounds for arrest. Criminal damage? Trespass? Anti-social behaviour?

Naturally, the arrival of a police car in full-on emergency response mode had not gone unnoticed by the staff and clientele of The Majestic. First, it was a just a couple of people, bored by the party inside, looking out of the ballroom window, but soon it was a whole crowd. It wasn't long before everyone in attendance at Eric's birthday party had his or her nose pressed to the glass. It was a matter of time before Ian, Brittney and Saskia were actually in the car park.

'What's going on?' Ian asked. 'Are you arresting my wife? I mean, my nearly ex-wife? Tell me what's happening.'

'If you could just stay out of the way please sir,' the younger of the young policeman said firmly.

'I will not stay out of the way. I'm her next of kin.'

'Not for much longer,' Liz snarled.

Brittney and Saskia were agog at the car with the decorated bonnet.

'What has she done?' Brittney cried.

'Your car is so painfully tasteful,' said Liz to her nearly vegan Nemesis, 'I thought the paintwork could do with livening up.'

'But that's not my car,' said Brittney.

And that was the moment at which Liz remembered that Brittney had been in the passenger seat of Ian's blue Audi when they came to pick Saskia up.

'Mum!' Saskia wailed. 'Mum, you're a lunatic. What have you done this time? Is it possible for you to be any more embarrassing?'

'Then whose car is it?' Liz asked Ian.

'I don't know,' he said. 'There are hundreds of cars just like this in Newbay.'

'But you thought it was my car,' said Brittney, pointing her non-toxically manicured finger right at Liz's red face. 'Which means you were trying to intimidate me by writing those horrible things on the bonnet. And you were doing it with processed meat! That's a hate crime. Officer?' Brittney tugged on the arm of the one who had handcuffed Liz. 'This woman has harassed me in the past and even though she got the wrong car, that was her intention again tonight. It's not just the words, which are obviously threatening. It's the fact that she's done it with salami, knowing that I am a fully committed vegetarian. The medium was calculated to cause maximum distress.'

'I don't think it was calculated at all to be honest,' said Ian. 'For crying out loud, Liz, how much have you had to drink?'

'Are you listening to me?' Brittney asked the police officer. 'Never mind finding out who owns this car, I want to report a crime here! I need you to put this woman under a restraining order. This isn't the first time she's tried to upset me. I've got a blog. Brittney's Bites dot com. You might know it. She's left hundreds of really rude comments after my post.'

'To be fair,' said Ian to his girlfriend, 'you found out that most of those rude comments were from that other blogger.'

'But she left at least twelve,' said Brittney pointing at Liz again. 'I want to report those too.'

'One thing at a time, madam,' said the officer.

'Mum?' Saskia was standing with the heels of her hands pressed into her eyes. 'Mum, for heaven's sake. What have you done? Aren't you ashamed of yourself?'

'No. I'm glad I did it,' said Liz. 'Even if it wasn't her car.'

'Come along,' the officer said to Liz. 'I think we had better take this matter down to the station before you make things any worse.'

'I'm coming too,' said Brittney. 'I'm the victim here. Ian? Tell him!'

'You'll have to come to the station under your steam,' said the officer.

'Trust me,' said Brittney. 'I will. Ian, go back inside and get our car keys at once.'

'Liz,' Ian called after her. 'Don't worry. I'll be there as soon as I can. We'll get this sorted out.'

'Are you defending her?' Brittney was furious.

'Brittney, she's the mother of my child. What am I supposed to do?'

'You're defending her. I can't believe you'd do that. Didn't you see what she did? She called me a slag! In salami!'

One of the officers made the formal arrest.

'My mum is being put in the back of a police car in front of everyone I know!' Saskia keened. 'My life can't get any worse! Please somebody tell me I'm adopted!'

Liz settled into the back seat of the patrol vehicle. It was actually surprisingly comfy. And any embarrassment that she felt being taken away in handcuffs in front of her soon to be ex-in-laws was more than made up for by the fact that when she turned to look she saw that Ian and Brittney appeared to be having a full-on row.

Chapter Thirty-Six

Liz began to get a little more concerned as the car drew closer to the police station. The joy she'd felt at seeing Ian being poked in the chest by Brittney in front of all his stuck-up UKIP-voting relatives, was quickly replaced by the dawning reality that it had only happened because Liz had been arrested.

She'd been *arrested*.

Liz Chandler, respectable dental hygienist and mother of one (and guardian of an overweight dog), had been arrested on suspicion of an actual crime. The police were going for criminal damage.

It became even more real when she found herself being escorted into the custody 'suite'. She was read her rights and her details were taken. Photographs. Fingerprints. A swab from the inside of her mouth. She had to hand over her handbag, empty out her pockets and give the duty officer all her jewellery.

This is in case I try to hang myself, Liz thought as she was asked to remove the belt Saskia had made her put on. She wasn't looking quite so chic now.

'I'll need your shoes too, I'm afraid,' said the female custody sergeant who was checking her in.

Liz handed those over quite happily. They hurt.

'And I can see a solicitor?' Liz asked.

'Of course. I'll sort that out right now,' the officer told her. 'Is there a particular one you want us to call?'

Liz thought of the solicitor who was handling her divorce. David Tucker was not on the shortlist of people she would not have minded seeing her in a prison cell. She'd only engaged Tucker's services because Corinne said he'd got her friend a really good settlement. Liz certainly didn't like him but that didn't mean she didn't want him to respect her. Best not let him see her like this.

'Does it have to be a solicitor I know?' Liz asked.

'No,' said the officer. 'We can call for a duty solicitor if you like?'

'I'd better have you do that.'

Ten minutes later, Bella Russo arrived. She was still wearing the blue dress she'd worn for Alex's party though she'd swapped her high heels for a pair of sensible flats and added a jacket that covered her cleavage.

'Liz?'

'That's me.'

'You two know each other?' the officer asked.

'We're in the same cookery class,' Bella said. 'We're friends.'

At least Bella didn't deny their connection and though Liz didn't really know Bella that well, the sight of a 'someone' that she had been coming to like very much – at least until that night's embarrassment over Alex – made the tears well up in Liz's eyes. Bella had called her a friend! It was so much more than Liz felt she deserved right then.

'Oh Bella,' she said. 'I did something awful. I'm so embarrassed. You're going to hate me.'

'Trust me,' said Bella. 'I won't. It's going to be OK,

Liz. How bad can it possibly be anyway? You haven't murdered anyone. Have you?'

'Not yet.'

'Just talk me through what happened and I'll do my best to sort it out. Tell me anything that might be relevant. Don't leave anything out through embarrassment. Remember I've seen and heard almost everything before.'

Though shortly after, Bella had to admit that she'd never heard of anyone being charged for criminal damage via the medium of cured meats.

'What can we do?'

'Well, it doesn't look like the paintwork on the car was actually damaged after all,' said Bella. 'And I don't think anyone really wants to take this any further – the CPS probably won't – but the police have got to track down the owner of the Fiat to be sure. They couldn't find him at the hotel.'

'It's a him?'

'Yes. It's possible that he was at a function there but left the car behind and got a taxi home having had a few drinks.'

'I should have done the same,' said Liz. 'Oh, why didn't I just wait for a cab?'

'You wanted to get some air,' said Bella. 'I understand.'

'Where did you learn to be so sympathetic?' Liz asked.

Bella shrugged. 'Anyway, the police will probably have to go round to the car owner's house to let him know what's happening. I'm afraid it won't be a priority. No one's been hurt and it's a Saturday night in Newbay so they'll be tied up with lots of D and Ds.'

'D and D?'

'Drunk and disorderly. But they will get onto it as soon as they can. Now, shall I get you a warm drink? George Clooney wouldn't be fighting anyone for the last espresso from the machine here but it's really not that bad. The tea, however, is appalling.'

'I don't normally drink coffee at night,' said Liz.

'Ah yes. I remember.' Bella referenced the party.

'But I suppose I'm not going to be getting much sleep anyway.'

Bella nodded. 'It can get quite noisy on a Saturday, I'm afraid.'

'Then I'll have a coffee. So this is where you come when you get called away from cookery class?' Liz commented.

'It's like a home from home.'

'It must be a very interesting job,' said Liz.

'It can be. Though I have to say, Liz, I don't think I've ever been asked to attend as interesting an arrest as yours.'

Bella brought Liz a coffee, which was far more awful than Liz had expected. Bella had obviously become inured to the muck served in the police station canteen through spending too many nights there.

'It might help me sober up a bit,' Liz suggested. 'Why didn't anyone stop me drinking so much at the party?'

'We did try,' said Bella. 'But you were quite determined.'

Now Liz remembered how Bella had kept shoving that plate of bread under her nose and the water and the cup of tea that John had gone to fetch. And that was swiftly followed by another very clear picture of Alex's face when he realised that Liz believed he fancied her. What had he thought Liz was talking about up until that point? For a while, he'd looked quite pale and anxious.

'Does Alex know I'm here?' Liz asked.

'I certainly haven't told him,' Bella replied.

Once Liz had her coffee, Bella left her alone for a while. She had paperwork to do and calls to make on behalf of several of the poor unfortunates who'd found themselves in the cells that night. Before she left though, she promised Liz she would do her very best to make sure that Liz got to wake up in her own bed.

'I don't think I'll have any trouble arguing that you're not a danger to the public.'

Bella also said that she would telephone Ian and ask him to go round to Liz's house and check on Ted.

'He'll be wondering where I've got to,' Liz said. 'Poor Ted.'

Without Bella to talk to and help keep her spirits up, Liz quickly went into a decline. The effects of the alcohol she'd had to drink at Alex's party were definitely wearing off, leaving behind the beginnings of the mother of all hangovers. So much for biodynamic wines being less likely to give you a headache. By one in the morning, Liz felt as though the world clog-dancing championship was taking place inside her skull.

And she was starting to worry. Bella had done her best to keep Liz calm, assuring her that her previously clean record, impeccable character and the fact that no one had really been hurt by the 'crime' would all work in her favour. She'd almost certainly get away with a caution. Liz was looking on the dark side though. When she shoved the tin foil tray under the windscreen wiper, she'd snapped it. That was proper criminal damage. And what if Brittney went through with her threat to have Liz charged for harassment?

Liz imagined Ian turning up at her house and scooping poor worried Ted into his arms. He'd have to take him back to Exeter – to Brittney's flat full of cream carpets – along with Saskia. Maybe he and Saskia were right now packing her a suitcase full of the things she would need for an extended stay *chez* Brittney while Liz was in the slammer? Even if Liz didn't end up in jail, would Ian use this incident against her when it came to their ongoing divorce? Would he say that Liz was an unfit mother and sue for full custody of their not so little girl? Then she really would be Brittney's Darling SD.

By half past one, Liz had convinced herself that her life was in absolute ruins. She had already lost her husband. Now, with her new criminal record, she would lose her daughter, her job, her income, her home, and her dog! Brittney Blaine would have it all while Liz ended up living under Newbay pier with the gang of homeless people who gathered there every evening, drinking Strongbow and eating out of wheelie bins. If she wasn't living in a prison cell.

As the night wore on, more and more people were brought in to the station in various states of inebriation and distress. Some of them protested noisily. They shouted and sang and banged things against the cell doors and walls. There was no way Liz would have been able to sleep even if she weren't being kept awake by feeling so frightened.

All she'd ever wanted was to have a happy family life. How had it all gone so wrong? She had failed in so many ways. Her husband had stopped loving her. Her daughter accused her of not caring enough to feed her properly. Her dog was in emergency measures because he was overweight. And now Liz was in a police cell. Turned out Liz Chandler was just no good at being a grown-up at all.

Chapter Thirty-Seven

Of all the people Alex had expected to stay at the party until the very end, he had not expected it to be his beginners' cookery course student John. How old was John? He must be in his mid-seventies at least. And yet long after everyone else had gone – they said they'd meet Alex at a club later – John was still there. He offered to help clear up.

'I've got nothing to rush home for,' he said.

'It must be hard,' said Alex. 'I mean, it must take some getting used to, not having someone to go back for when you've been together for so long.'

'More than fifty years,' John confirmed.

'Wow. It's hard to imagine even knowing anyone that long.'

'We met when we were not much more than kids.'

'How did you meet?' Alex asked as he handed John a roll of cling film with which to wrap up the spare food. Meanwhile, Alex was going to gather the empty bottles into a box for recycling.

'I was twenty,' John said. 'Living in Hertfordshire. I'd just started working at the new comprehensive – well, it was new then – that opened up on the edge of town. It was my first job out of teacher training college. I'd got my first pay packet and I decided I was going to celebrate. So me and a couple of my mates went to a dance at the town hall. Our town didn't really have any nightclubs then and the hotels were only for residents.'

Alex paused. The bottles, as he put them in the box, were making a horrible noise that made it hard to hear John talking. Alex decided it was worth hearing this story. He sat down on the edge of the table. John stopped what he was doing too.

'So you went to the dance . . .' Alex prompted him.

'Yes. Wearing my new suit. And a pair of shoes with pointy toes – winkle pickers – that were very fashionable but which were killing me by the time the dance started.'

'Were you a mod?' Alex asked.

'I was trying to be. I was never slim enough to pull it off.'

'Nah! I bet you looked great,' said Alex.

'I thought so, even though all I wanted to do was take those shoes off and stick my feet in a bucket of ice water.'

'So what happened next?'

'I was standing at the bar, waiting to be served. It had just got to my turn when this pushy girl shoved her way through and tried to catch the barman's attention ahead of me. I didn't stand a chance. I was going to point out to her that I'd been waiting for a while, when she turned to ask her friend what she was having and I turned too and there she was.'

Alex nodded to encourage John to carry on.

'It was Sonia. The woman who would become my wife. I just saw her face and I knew. I must have been gawping, because Sonia's pushy friend said to me, "Are you all right? You look like you're having a funny turn." Not exactly the pose I was going for.'

John chuckled.

'Anyway, somehow, I ended up buying drinks for Sonia, her pushy friend – who was called Esther – and their other mate Joyce. That pretty much wiped out my evening's budget. I'd have to stick to water from then on. But it was worth it. Because I'd bought them a drink, Esther and Joyce were immediately on my side. They encouraged Sonia to dance with me. She said she didn't want to. She had two left feet. I should dance with Esther instead, she said.

'But I didn't care if Sonia had *three* left feet. By the time we stepped out onto the floor to the opening strains of Ray Charles, "I Can't Stop Loving You", I was already smitten. I was sure I'd never stop loving Sonia Squires. By the time the band brought the evening to a close with Acker Bilk's "Strangers On The Shore", I had asked Sonia to marry me.'

'You what?'

'That's what she said. I'd only meant to ask if I could see her again, that was all, but my subconscious must have taken over. Luckily she said she wouldn't hold me to it but she did agree to go with me to the pictures the following week.

'I asked her to marry me for real six months after we met. Mum let me have her engagement ring for the proposal. I promised I'd get Sonia a ring of her own later on but first we had to save for a deposit on a house and the wedding.

'It took almost three years to get enough cash together. By then, Sonia was working at Sainsbury's. She joined the supermarket's trainee management team and was able to put quite a bit by. She went up to London to buy her wedding dress. It was like Princess

Margaret's from her marriage to Antony Armstrong-Jones, only the skirt and the train weren't quite so voluminous.

'We were married on a beautiful June day at the church where Sonia was christened. Esther and Joyce were the bridesmaids. It was the happiest day of my life.'

'And you just knew the moment you saw her?'

'I did.'

'That sounds like a fairy tale.'

'I know. I never would have thought it possible to fall in love so quickly.'

'Me neither, until three weeks ago.'

John gave Alex a sly grin.

'You like our Bella, don't you?'

'Is it obvious?'

'Just a bit, lad. Just a bit.'

Alex grimaced.

'I can't help it. She's just so . . . so lovely. Every time I see her I want to break into a massive grin. Though it's not just because she's beautiful.'

'That she is.'

'She's so intelligent. And funny. And she cares so much about her clients. Do you get that from talking to her?'

'Yes, I do. She's a rare sort.'

'She makes me feel all warm inside.'

'I felt that about Sonia. But I think the feeling's mutual with you and Bella, don't you?' said John.

'How do you know?'

'You're both cow-eyed when you're in the same room.'

Alex grinned.

'You've been like that from the first class. Oh, and she brought you a birthday card.'

An even bigger smile spread across Alex's face as he opened it.

'Did she put kisses after her name?'

Alex confirmed that she had.

'You should just ask her out,' said John firmly.

'I can't.'

'Why? Because of the course? Are you not allowed to fraternise with your students? We're all adults, aren't we? It's not like being at school.'

'I know but . . .'

'Well, you don't have too long before the course is finished, I suppose.'

'No, it's not that.'

'Then what is it? Faint heart never won fair lady.'

'I'm not afraid of asking her out, John. I'm afraid of what might happen if she says yes.'

'You'd go on a date and fall madly in love.'

'So we fall in love and then she finds out all about me . . . That's when the trouble starts.'

'Nonsense. With Sonia, I found that the more I knew about her the more I loved her. And she said it was the same for her too. When you love someone, you don't mind about those little quirks that would drive you mad in someone you didn't like. Sonia had this habit of shoving tissues up her sleeve. They used to fall out all over the house. Worse was when they were still in her sleeve when she shoved her jumper into the washing machine and then everything came out covered in bits of tissue.'

'I'm not talking about something like that,' said Alex.

'Then what are you talking about? Seems to me like

you're making excuses. Are you worried about not having enough money? Nobody's got enough money these days, Alex. You just get together and start working on saving up as a couple.'

'John,' Alex shook his head. 'I'm grateful for the pep talk but the skeletons I've got in the cupboard are far too big to be put before a woman like Bella.'

'Try me,' said John.

Alex took a deep breath.

'I've spent some time inside.'

John squinted just a little, as though it would help him more easily understand what Alex was saying.

'I mean I was in prison,' Alex clarified.

'How?' John asked. Then, 'Why?'

'It's the classic story of teenage rebellion. I had a great family but I fell in with the wrong crowd. I wasn't academic and I struggled at school so I got through by hanging out with the cool kids and pretending I didn't care if I didn't get any qualifications. I got my validation from them. I did stupid stuff to make them laugh. Pranks. Vandalism.'

John winced.

'Shoplifting. Underage drinking. Smoking. Smoking weed. The more risks I took, the more they respected me. So I took bigger risks. You know how it goes.'

'I've seen it happen,' said John.

'Of course. You were a teacher,' Alex said. 'But then I got a reputation outside school too and I suppose you could say I was groomed by some really hard nuts. Adults. They had me do them a few favours. They paid me far more than my mates were getting for their Saturday jobs. I was flattered and I was an idiot. It seemed like a game. I was having a ball. I never thought I'd get caught. But I was and I ended up doing time.'

'What for?'

'For handling stolen goods. TVs, laptops . . .'

'And you went to prison for that?'

'I did. I was eighteen. I got six months.'

Alex's shoulders slumped at the memory. He exhaled loudly.

'What was it like?' John asked.

'Not quite the holiday camp the *Daily Mail* would have you believe.'

'I don't imagine it was.'

'But it was exactly what I needed. I worked in the canteen and that turned out to be the thing that saved me. Finding my passion.'

'Your melanzane parmigiana doesn't taste like prison food,' said John.

'I should hope not.'

'It must have been hard,' said John. 'Being so young.'

'I only had myself to blame. Anyway, I learned my lesson pretty fast and I was determined I was never going back. But even though I only got six months, the repercussions were endless. It changed so much. When I came out, my family were great but I couldn't stay in London. There were too many people I had to avoid. And I couldn't get a job. At least not where I'd grown up and people thought they knew my story.'

John nodded.

'I had to get away so I moved to Exeter and got taken on by a voluntary scheme that helps ex-offenders. My liaison – Marianne – got me an in at one of the hotels, working as a washer-upper to begin with. I ended up cooking there for a couple of years. After that, it was easier to get the next job and the next. Marianne's remained a friend. She put me in touch with the woman who runs this place, just as the guy who was supposed to be running the beginners' cookery course dropped out. That felt like serendipity.'

'You've got luck on your side,' John agreed.

'I hope so. As I look back on it, I can see that even when my life looked like it was going really wrong – like when I got arrested – it always turned out to be a blessing in disguise. I've certainly been lucky when it comes to meeting people willing to give me a second chance here in Devon. But you can see why I can't ask Bella to go out with me. I've got a criminal record. And she's a flippin' solicitor. She spends her life getting people like me out of trouble. She doesn't want to date an ex-offender.'

'Why don't you give her a chance to decide?' John asked. 'It's a long time since you were inside, Alex.'

'Twelve years,' Alex said.

'You were a kid. You made a mistake and you paid for it. There's plenty of kids who go off the rails. You had the misfortune to get caught.'

'God knows what I would have done next if I hadn't been.'

'It doesn't bear thinking about. But the fact is, you didn't end up going down that road. You did your time and you've kept your nose clean since.'

'I have.'

'And like you said, you've always been lucky when it comes to getting second chances. Why should that luck run out now?'

'Because not everyone is as understanding and open-minded as you are, John.'

* * *

John helped Alex to clean and tidy the room at the community centre and listened to more of Alex's story, but he declined the invitation to go on to the club and catch up with Alex's other friends.

'I've already stayed out way longer than I usually do.'

'I'm really grateful to you for staying to help me get this place sorted out,' Alex told him. 'And for listening to me, as well. I don't think I've changed my mind about asking Bella out yet but I do feel better for having talked to you. Every time someone like you – someone I respect – hears my story and doesn't freak out, it helps me to believe that maybe one day I'll be able to put it all behind me and just be known as Alex the chef, rather than Alex the chef who used to be a drug dealer.'

'You're getting there,' John assured him.

'So, I guess I'll see you on Thursday night,' said Alex.

'Wouldn't miss it for the world. What are we cooking?'

'Ah. Next week's recipe is just up your street.'

Alex put his hand on the older man's shoulder.

'Thank you for not judging me,' he said.

John got into his car for the drive home. As he adjusted the rear-view mirror, he gave himself a start. It was as though someone was in the back seat, looking straight at him. Judging him somehow. Of course it was only his own reflection and the troubled expression was all his too.

The conversation John had had with Alex was not one he had expected or could have imagined having before it actually happened. It was a brave move on the part of Alex, being so honest and candid about his past. He'd risked a great deal in telling John the truth about his time in prison. It wasn't the sort of thing you mentioned lightly. Most people would have found it a shock and perhaps even felt slightly betrayed they hadn't known sooner. However, John had found it easy to tell him the past didn't matter. He'd done his time. He'd wiped the slate clean and he deserved the chance to build himself a bright new future. Alex didn't have to drag his history with him. John meant it when he said that.

'You've done your time. You're officially rehabilitated. Isn't that the word?'

And yet John remembered a time when he'd argued just as hard that the stain of criminality was permanent. Giving people like that a second chance, a third chance, a tenth, eleventh, twelfth chance was just foolish. It was madness to keep doing the same thing, expecting a different result.

'For Christ's sake, John, have a heart!'

That's what Sonia had shouted at him before she went up to bed and he slept on the sofa for the first time in their marriage. He could hear her shouting it now.

Chapter Thirty-Eight

It was nearly three in the morning when Bella came back. She looked almost as tired as Liz felt.

'Good news,' she said. 'The police caught up with the man who owns the Fiat 500 and he says he doesn't want to press charges. I can't say I blame him. I expect he just wanted to go back to bed.'

'What does that mean?' Liz asked.

'It means you're getting a caution and then you're free to go, once we've filled in a few forms.'

'But what about Brittney and the harassment claim?'

'I don't think you need to worry about that. Ultimately, it wasn't her car you decorated. And I think your husband might have had a word.'

'You spoke to him then?'

'Yes. He's staying at your place tonight, with your daughter and the dog.'

'And her?'

'You mean the blogger? I don't think so. He didn't say that she was.'

'OK,' said Liz.

'Shall we get you out of here then?'

'Yes, please. I can't say when I woke up this morning that I had any idea the day would end with a jail break.'

The caution was delivered and signed. Fifteen minutes later, the officer on the front desk returned Liz's property and she was officially signed out.

'How are you getting home?' Bella asked.

'I suppose I'll get a taxi.'

'Tell you what, I've finished my shift on call. I'll drop you off if you like.'

Liz was pathetically grateful. She hadn't relished the idea of calling her local mini-cab firm and asking them to pick her up at the police station. That said, neither did she particularly relish the idea of going back home. Not if Ian was there, even if Brittney wasn't. She was grateful that he'd stepped in to rescue Ted from a night alone but she didn't want to have to discuss the events of that evening. Not now. Not while her head was still pounding and she was pretty sure she looked like a mess and smelled even worse.

'If you like,' said Bella, reading Liz's mind, 'you could stop in my spare room until the morning.'

'Won't that be a nuisance?'

'Not at all. It'll give you a chance to put yourself back together a bit before you face the next round of questioning.'

'That would be so helpful,' said Liz. 'I don't suppose Ian is going to be half as kind to me as those policemen were. Or you.'

'You'll have to excuse the mess,' said Bella as she let Liz into the passenger side of her car. 'I'm afraid I use my car as a travelling office.'

Indeed, Liz had to move a pile of files off the seat before she could sit down.

'And kitchen and dining room,' Bella added, as Liz gingerly picked up a pasty by one corner and put it into the footwell. 'I'm sorry. I always seem to be working. I keep promising myself I'm going to take the car to that valet car wash down by Tesco's but I never seem to have the time.'

'My car's not much better,' Liz admitted. 'Life's too short to worry about whether or not your car's clean enough to eat your dinner off.'

Bella chuckled.

'It wasn't that funny,' Liz said.

'I was just thinking about what you did with all that Italian sausage, Liz. It really was the most creative piece of revenge.'

'If only I'd chosen the right car.'

'Probably a good job you didn't.'

Bella lived in the west of the town. As they drove back past The Majestic, Liz sank low in her seat even though the lights were out and the guests at her nephew Eric's birthday party had long since gone home.

'You made that party for most of them,' Bella commented when Liz reiterated how ashamed she was to have humiliated herself in front of her in-laws.

'Yeah. It will go down in history as the night I finally cracked. Most of them already hated me anyway.'

'So who cares what they think? There's no point worrying about the opinions of anyone who doesn't actually like you, is there? Or you them?'

'Good point.'

'Here we are,' said Bella, pulling up outside a modern block of flats.

'This is nice,' said Liz.

'I bought it almost five years ago. As you'll see, it's still a work in progress. I just never seem able to find the time to get round to doing any decorating. Or even putting up proper curtains,' she added, as she ushered

Liz into the sitting room. A bedsheet was tacked over the window.

'The neighbours must think I'm a total skank.'

'Who cares what the neighbours think?'

'You're right.'

'Are you sure it's OK for me to stay here?'

'If you don't mind sleeping on a futon. I just thought you should be properly sober and rested before you face your family. I know how tricky families can be.'

'You're very wise,' said Liz.

As Bella and Liz drank herbal tea to help them sleep, they got to know each other a little better. Bella had taken off her make-up. Without it, she looked very young and incredibly pretty, thought Liz with a slight pang. And she was so kind. It was no wonder that Alex had fallen in love with her. Liz wondered if Bella even knew what effect she had on him.

'When did you know you wanted to become a solicitor?' Liz asked.

'I don't know if I've got there yet!' Bella replied. 'I mean, I don't think there was ever a moment when I said to myself, this is it. This is the job I was made for. I just seemed to get on the path. My mum was quite keen on it. A law degree. Law school. Police Station and Magistrates Court Qualifications. And now here I am. The successful career woman. Who doesn't even have time to put up proper curtains.'

'Curtains aren't all they're cracked up to be,' said Liz.

'It'd still be nice to have some with actual curtain rails. I'm forever having to stick those sheets back up with drawing pins. I could probably have handwoven some curtains and whittled the curtain rails in the time I've spent on my temporary fix.'

'But you must be earning enough to get someone to come and sort it out for you?' Liz suggested.

'I suppose I am. But I'd still have to track them down and arrange for a day when I could be here to let them in.'

'Yeah,' Liz sighed. 'It sucks not having a man about the house for that sort of stuff.'

'I don't know. At least I get free rein on the colour scheme.'

'And you like your job,' Liz went back to that.

'Yes. I want to help people. That part of my job is the best. There's real satisfaction to be had in knowing that you've made someone's life a little better.'

'Like you did mine tonight.'

'It was my pleasure. You're far easier than a lot of my clients. But . . .'

'I wondered if there was a but,' said Liz.

Bella frowned. 'I'm sure there must be other ways I could be contributing that aren't quite so time-consuming and occasionally soul-sapping. Being a solicitor pays the bills but I feel like there's more to me I need to express.'

'How do you mean?'

'It's like there's a creative streak inside me that's determined to come out. It's why I signed up for the cookery course. I used to love cooking when I was small.'

'Where did your dad cook?'

'We had a café near the train station.'

'You mean Bella's?'

'That's the one. It was named after me.'

'I used to go there all the time. The food was amazing. Best in Newbay,' said Liz.

Bella smiled sadly.

'But it didn't work out.'

Bella told Liz the full story of Bella's, the train station café.

'After the café failed, Dad just seemed to lose interest in life. I could see that the light had gone out of him. But I didn't really understand why. I listened to the way Mum talked about the whole thing and ended up agreeing with her. Dad had been silly to think he could go it alone. If he'd done what she asked and worked for someone else all along, he wouldn't have ended up so unhappy. I didn't realise that it wasn't that he'd failed that bothered him, it was the way the rest of us looked at him when he did.

'Mum's view on life was always that you had to do whatever it took to stay safe. To make sure you had a roof over your head and the bailiffs were never knocking on the door. Being secure to Mum was everything. But the older I get, the more I wonder if that really is everything. If you never take any risks, where does that leave you? What's it like to look back over a whole life of taking the easy, safe option? To look back over a life where every day was pretty much the same. Every week. Every year.'

'I think I know what you mean. It's playing on your mind.'

'It is. I can't help feeling I let Dad down.'

'You didn't, Bella. You were a kid.'

'But all those things he taught me. The way he saw the world. I turned my back on the things he tried to show me. And food for him really was about love. No wonder he felt so abandoned.

'I need to make some serious decisions about the

way my life is going to be. I've got to find a balance and right now I'm just about as far off balance as I could possibly be. I need to find my passion. I want to feel about my job the way Alex so obviously feels about his.'

'He's doing what he loves,' Liz agreed.

'My dad would have loved Alex,' Bella said. 'The way he talks about food. They could have had such great conversations. In fact, he reminds me of the way Dad was, before the café failed.'

'He's a good man,' said Liz. 'A kind heart and generous.'

'He's one of those people who lives life in full colour,' Bella said, her face softening as she thought of him. Her frown fading into a smile.

'You could do that too,' Liz assured her. 'Live in full colour.'

'I'm not sure I've got the guts.'

'You spend your life fraternising with Newbay's most notorious criminals.'

'Like you?'

'Exactly. I'm sure you've got the guts for anything.'

'Alex makes me feel as though it might be possible.'

Liz wondered whether now was the moment to tell Bella about Alex's feelings.

'But what about you, Liz?' Bella changed the focus. 'What are you going to do next? I can give you the names of some great counsellors if you want to talk to a professional about how your divorce is making you feel.'

'Just having you look after me tonight has been as valuable as years of counselling,' Liz said.

'You don't have to do it all alone.'

'Thanks. Neither do you.'

Liz glanced at the clock. It was almost four in the morning.

'We'd better get some sleep.'

'Good idea.'

The two women embraced.

'The best thing about our cookery course is the people on it,' said Liz.

'Yes,' said Bella. But Liz knew Bella was thinking about one person in particular.

Chapter Thirty-Nine

At ten o'clock on Sunday morning, Liz showered and dressed in a pair of jeans and a sweatshirt borrowed from Bella and took a taxi back to her own home. Ian's car was still in the driveway when she got there.

'Where exactly have you been all night?' he asked.

'With a friend,' Liz said.

'Which friend?'

'I don't have to tell you.'

'A man?'

'Maybe.'

'Are they going to charge you?'

'The police? No. Just a caution.'

'Good.'

'Look,' said Liz. 'Do you mind if I come in? To my own house? I don't particularly want to have this conversation on the doorstep.'

Saskia was at the top of the stairs listening. When she saw her mother, she exclaimed her distress and flounced straight back into her bedroom. It seemed that only Ted was really pleased to see Liz. He threw himself at her legs and sniffed at the unfamiliar jeans she was wearing with great curiosity.

'You made a complete fool of yourself last night,' said Ian.

'I know,' said Liz.

'You embarrassed me in front of my whole family.'

'Mm-hmm.'

'You were more drunk than I have ever seen you.'

'I was.'

'Where did you go to get that drunk? Who were you with? Why didn't he make sure you got home safely after letting you get that hammered? Were you roofied, Liz? Is that what happened? Did someone slip you some Rohypnol? Did the police give you a blood test?'

'I wasn't roofied,' said Liz. 'Don't be ridiculous.'

'How do you know? Where did you pick up your date? On Tinder?'

'I wasn't on a date,' Liz admitted at last.

'Oh.' Liz was sure she saw relief in Ian's eyes at that. 'Then where were you?'

'At a party. For the guy who runs my cooking class. I had a bit too much to drink and I was walking home past The Majestic and couldn't help feeling a bit sad at the thought that my nephew and godson was turning eighteen without me.'

'It wasn't much of a party,' said Ian. 'Eric and all his mates just sat around in corners with their iPhones.'

'I expect Saskia loved it then,' said Liz.

Ian agreed.

'The band you picked was good,' he added. 'Though Brittney said they didn't play anything she could dance to. Not even Take That was good enough for her. She thinks nineties' music is for old people. Like us.'

Liz couldn't help smiling at that.

'Put the kettle on, Ian,' she said. 'You know where it is.'

Ian moved to the counter where the kettle lived. Ted followed him, hoping for a titbit.

'Get lost, you fat mutt.' Ian brushed him away before

checking his trousers were unsullied by Ted's paws. Ted returned to sit by Liz. She fondled his velvety ears as she watched her soon-to-be-ex looking for a teapot. Liz hadn't really moved anything around since Ian left. It was just that he'd never really spent much time on food or drink preparation while they were together. Not enough to make tea with his eyes shut, as Liz might have done.

'How do you have your tea?' Ian asked.

'Same way I always had it,' said Liz.

He returned to the kitchen table with two mugs and put the milk alongside, still in the bottle. He was hedging.

'I was worried about you in the cells,' said Ian. 'I didn't like the thought of you being there on your own.'

'It was OK,' said Liz.

'It was horrible not knowing what was going on. I couldn't sleep until I heard you'd been let go. I'd have come to pick you up but I didn't want to leave Saskia on her own.'

Liz nodded. 'That was the right thing to do.'

'Look, Liz,' Ian sighed, 'I had no idea you still felt so strongly about Brittney. About me leaving. I thought you were over trying to upset her. I suppose I thought you were over *us*.'

'I am,' Liz assured him.

Something flickered in Ian's eyes again. Doubt? Disappointment?

'Ian, I really don't know what came over me. It just seemed like a laugh. I had the antipasti . . . there was the car . . . I'm allowed to have my opinion on your girlfriend, aren't I? Even if she did me a big favour by taking you off my hands.' Liz winked.

'I suppose.'

'Talking of which, it's probably time we gave our solicitors a prod. To get the divorce moving.'

Ian, who had been taking a sip of his tea, spat it out again.

'Went down the wrong way,' he said. 'What did you say?'

'We need to get the divorce squared away. It's been a year since you moved in with Brittney now and we both need to clear a path for the future. I'm sure Brittney would agree.'

Liz could feel the shake in her voice. She hoped Ian couldn't hear it. 'I don't think there's any point waiting any longer. If you're willing to divorce on the basis of your adultery, we could have everything done in a few months.'

Before Ian could respond, his mobile, which was face down on the table, vibrated with a text message. He read it.

'It's from Brittney. I've got to go,' he said. 'She's still really upset by what happened last night. The sooner I can get back to Exeter the better. We'll talk about the other thing soon, yeah?'

'Of course. Thanks, Ian. For staying here with Saskia and Ted.'

Your daughter and your dog, Liz thought.

'It was the least I could do.'

Ian went upstairs to say goodbye to Saskia. He gave Liz an awkward sort of kiss on his way out to the car.

It was three in the afternoon before Liz saw her daughter again. Saskia spent most of the day upstairs, furiously messaging her friends. When she came downstairs she had a face like thunder and informed her mother: 'Mum, I can't even think about talking to you so don't try to make conversation. I have never been so embarrassed in my life. You do know that the story is already online, don't you?'

'Is it?'

'Someone at the party took a picture and put it on Instagram. Someone else took a video. It's gone viral, Mum. Everyone in Newbay knows you're a nutter now. Make that everyone in the entire world. I can't believe you'd do this to me.'

'I wasn't trying to do anything to you, sweetheart.'

'I am going to get so much shit for this on Monday morning. I'm already getting shit for it left, right and centre. I've had to deactivate my Facebook account. I'm not even looking at Instagram. I've had to take myself off WhatsApp. Do you know what everyone is calling you?'

'I'm sure you're going to tell me.'

'They're calling you a *sausage-bothering bunny boiler*.'

Liz blanched.

'Oh, Mum. Are you ever going to grow up? Are you ever going to accept the fact that Dad's with Brittney now?'

Liz gave a little shrug.

'I'm sorry, love. I had too much to drink. But I think I learned my lesson.'

'You never ever think about me, do you?'

'I think about you all the time,' said Liz, but Saskia had already flounced from the room again.

When Liz finally dared check her own email, she found that Saskia was not the only one who was getting stick for what had happened the previous night. Liz's inbox was full of messages.

'Liz? Was that really you with the car?'

'Elizabeth Chandler! What have you been doing?'

'Liz! Call me straight away you nut job!'

Many of the messages were congratulatory. Liz knew plenty of women who had also been usurped by younger models who said they were positively inspired by what Liz had done to the Fiat 500. 'So much more creative than writing "slapper" on the bonnet with your lipstick,' said Corinne, referencing something she might have done in the past.

Liz wrote back. 'Thank you. I'm not sure everybody sees it that way though. What do you think Vince is going to say tomorrow morning? He's going to have to let me go, isn't he? Who's going to want to have their teeth cleaned by a bunny boiler?'

As it happened, Liz didn't have to wait until the following morning to find out what Vince had to say on the matter. He called her on Sunday afternoon and was kind and solicitous when he asked how she was after her night in the cells.

'It wasn't the whole night but it's not an experience I ever want to have to repeat. Look, Vince, they let me go with a caution but I perfectly understand if there's been too much bad publicity to make my place at the surgery tenable.'

Vince made a sympathetic sound. 'Liz, I would never let you go over something like this. You didn't kill anyone. You had a small moment of madness while you were in your cups. Heaven knows, I had enough of those myself before I found AA. I'm only where I am today because I was lucky enough to have some truly good people in my life. People who know you can't judge anyone else unless you've walked a mile in their shoes. I've been in your shoes, Liz, and I'm not going to judge you. If people want to take their dental business elsewhere, that's up to them. But you and I both know that we're the only decent NHS practice left in Newbay. Our customers aren't going anywhere. And I hope the same goes for you.'

'Thanks, Vince.'

Her boss's kindness made Liz feel like crying again.

By lunchtime on Monday, Liz's Saturday night misdemeanour was almost old news. Though she did get a call from a journalist from the Femail section of the *Daily Mail* asking if she would be willing to be photographed in a universally flattering sheath dress for an article about the top ten best acts of revenge. Liz politely turned the offer down. She just wanted to fade back into anonymity. Maybe in time she would be able to laugh at herself. Right then, she didn't really feel like it.

Then, just as she was finishing up at the end of the work day, she got an email from Dr Thomas at the veterinary surgery. Liz clicked it open, expecting to get a lecture about the dangers of feeding your pets on processed meat. She got one of those. She also got this:

'Dear Mrs Ted/Chandler, In view of recent events, I have decided to discharge Ted from Waggy Weight Loss and ask that you do not attend my veterinary surgery again in the future. I'm sure you understand. I wish both you and Ted well. Yours sincerely, Dr Evan Thomas.

P.S. It is not advisable to feed your dog on any

commercially produced cured meats that may have undergone treatment with sulphur.'

Liz could hardly believe what she was reading. The pompous idiot. How dare he?

Liz wrote back in the white heat of anger. 'I shall be very happy to avoid your stupid veterinary surgery from now on. How very mean and self-righteous of you to respond to my private business in such a small-minded way. Personally, I can't believe that you would put Ted's health at risk over a matter that simply does not concern you. Yours sincerely, Mrs Chandler/Ted.'

She got an email by return.

'Actually, it does concern me,' wrote Dr Thomas. 'That Fiat 500 was my car.'

Chapter Forty

Oh no. Liz clapped her hand to her forehead. She remembered now how Bella had told her the owner of the car had been very sweet and understanding. That's why Liz hadn't thought for a moment it could possibly be Evan Thomas, the uber-vet.

'I'm so sorry,' Liz wrote back at once. 'I had no idea.' She took a deep breath before she continued. 'I understand that I may have caused some damage to one of the windscreen wipers. I would of course like to recompense you for that.'

Dr Evan responded: 'Yes, you did break one of my windscreen wipers but I wasn't going to pursue the matter any further because it's clear to me that you've got enough problems without my adding to them by demanding compensation.'

Enough problems! Liz bridled at that. 'I don't need your charity,' she replied. 'Send me an invoice.'

'I really don't want your money,' wrote Dr Thomas.

'I insist,' wrote Liz.

Liz flicked the Vs and blew a raspberry at the screen. The pompous git.

The truth was however, Liz felt sick. Though she and Dr Thomas had been exchanging words only virtually, they had been doing so in real time and the idea of him being angry with her right in that moment was rather upsetting.

Oh, why did she have to reply to his first email at all? She could have just taken Ted to another surgery with a nice kind vet who liked people as much as he liked animals. She'd never even have had to know that the Fiat was Dr Thomas's car. Now she had to find another vet and pay for the windscreen wiper. Why oh why had she let him wind her up?

She thought about phoning him. That's what she should do. Because maybe right then he was consulting his lawyer to see whether he could still press charges about the car. Yes. She decided she would phone. Get the whole thing sorted out asap. Face to face. Sort of.

Nurse Van Niekerk answered the call. 'Thomas and Thomas Veterinary Care.'

'Can I speak to Dr Thomas?' Liz asked.

Though there were two Thomases in the name, there was only one at the practice.

'Who's calling?'

Suspecting that she might be in a blocked list, Liz thought quickly. 'Mrs Coco,' she said.

Fortunately, Nurse Van Niekerk didn't need any more than that. She didn't want Mrs Coco's real name. Liz was put straight through.

'Ah, Mrs Coco,' said Dr Thomas, when he picked up. 'I was just about to call you. I've had another look at the scan results and I'm afraid it's exactly as we thought. No wonder poor Coco has been so resistant to exercise. She must have been in terrible pain. The only solution I can think of is the operation we discussed when you came to the surgery yesterday. Now, before you say anything, Mrs Coco, I know you were worried about the financial implications. It is a very expensive procedure but I'm certain that it would improve Coco's quality of life quite dramatically and for that reason . . .'

Liz tried to interrupt.

'Please, let me finish. Mrs Coco. I want to tell you something. Mrs Coco, I was inspired to become a vet by my father, who as you know was a vet himself. He always told me that you can judge a man by the way he treats animals and on that basis, I know you are a woman who feels and cares very deeply indeed. When my father died last year, he left me a sum of money, which I have put into a trust for the treatment of animals whose owners can't afford my usual fees. I'd like Coco to be the first beneficiary. With your permission, I'm going to do her operation *pro bono*.'

'Wha—' Liz began. But then she heard the urgent ringing of what sounded like a fire alarm in the background at the surgery.

'Animal ambulance coming in, I'm afraid, Mrs Coco. We'll talk about getting Coco's operation in the diary tomorrow.'

And then he was gone, flying into action (with his sleeves rolled up, no doubt).

'Oh no,' thought Liz. But it wasn't her fault he hadn't drawn breath for that entire phone call, was it? Liz wondered what she should do. Poor Mrs Coco was probably sitting at home right now, worried sick about her dog. She needed to know what Dr Thomas had said, which meant that Dr Thomas needed to know he had been saying it to the wrong person.

Liz called the surgery back.

Nurse Van Niekerk picked up the phone.

'Nurse Van Niekerk, this is Liz Chandler. Mrs Ted—'

Nurse Van Niekerk put the telephone straight down on her.

'Witch!' Liz hissed at the ring tone.

She had to write an email.

'Dear Dr Thomas, I just called your office and did a very silly thing. I told Nurse Van Niekerk that I was Mrs Coco. It wouldn't have mattered but you obviously believed that to be the case and didn't give me a chance to explain otherwise. You just told me the details of your plans for Coco and her operation. I know it's none of my business, but I have to say, I'm very impressed by your plan to provide free veterinary care to those who can't afford it. It's an extremely kind thing to do.'

It was. Liz felt humbled by what she had heard Dr Thomas say that afternoon. He could have used the inheritance he got from his father to do all sorts of things. He might have travelled the world, splurged it on luxuries, got himself a bigger car. He was a very tall guy to be pootling around in a Fiat 500. Instead, he had chosen to set up a trust for those less fortunate than he was. And Liz had only found out about it by mistake. That was the true test of altruism as far as she was concerned. He wasn't just showing off about it willy nilly.

And poor Coco. Liz had sneered at Mrs Coco for pushing that dog around in a baby's chair but she had obviously been doing her best. Coco wasn't just greedy and overindulged, after all. She had something wrong with her. Liz wondered what it was but thought it probably wasn't polite to ask.

Liz finished her message.

'I'll await your email regarding the cost of the windscreen wiper. With very best wishes, Liz Chandler.'

Her heart sank when a few hours later Dr Thomas replied in just one line. 'Thank you for letting me know.'

The brevity spoke volumes of his disdain.

Chapter Forty-One

By Thursday, Liz's fifteen minutes of fame were pretty much up, she thought. Hoped. Prayed. Everyone she had expected to see the video footage of the car on Facebook had seen it. Meanwhile, Ian had informed Liz, by text, that he had asked Brittney not to mention the incident on her blog. 'Just keep your head down,' he said.

In some ways, the other internet attention hadn't been all bad. She'd heard from people she hadn't heard from in years. Her moment of embarrassment had given them an excuse to reach out to her. She'd caught up with lots of gossip from her university friends. Among those who reached out was an old boyfriend, which was flattering. Sort of. Liz wasn't sure quite how she was supposed to respond to his question about whether she 'enjoyed' being tied up in those handcuffs. She decided she would pretend she'd never seen the email and leave it at that.

She allowed herself to think that everything was getting back to normal but there were three people she had to make her apologies to first. What she didn't know was that they were just as anxious to make things right again.

Alex looked mightily relieved to see that Liz had come back to the class.

'I was thinking you might decide against it. I should never have let you leave the centre in such a state,' he said. 'I thought you were getting a taxi. I should have made sure.'

'I should have stepped in too,' said John.

'It's OK,' said Liz. 'You both tried. I think it was inevitable that I'd end up doing something like I did on Saturday night at some point. It's been brewing for a very long time. I needed to get it out of my system. Thank goodness I had Bella to get me out of any serious trouble.'

Bella gave her the thumbs up.

There was small pause before Alex said, 'The CCTV video of you decorating that car was one of the funniest things I have seen in my life. You were like a modern artist creating a masterpiece. So much care went into the placing of that meat.'

John agreed. 'Someone at the NEWTS showed me on his phone. Full marks for creativity, Liz.'

'It was the best call out I've attended in my entire career,' said Bella.

Liz gave her fellow cooks a little bow.

'Ok, guys,' said Alex, once Liz had recapped the story of her terrible half-night in the cells. 'Let's get to work. Over the past three weeks you've picked up three very important basic cookery skills and you've applied them with great aplomb.'

'Good word,' said Liz, trying it out for herself.

'You've learned about knife skills, how to make a basic roux and how to make a tomato sauce that you can use as the basis for all sorts of recipes, like Bella's dad's parmigiana. Today we're going to learn how to cook something for John. A beef Wellington.'

'Oh,' said John. 'That's lovely. But Sonia always made it look so complicated. We're just beginners.'

'She was just trying to keep you in the dark, John. It doesn't have to be difficult. And no, Liz, you don't need special hands to be able to make the pastry. I'm going to show you a version of this recipes that's easy to make and still impressive. You'll be the host or the hostess with the mostess if you serve this at your next dinner party.'

'I don't think anyone I invited round to mine would show up after this weekend,' said Liz.

'Perhaps if you promised to write an apology in beef,' Bella suggested. 'I bet more than a few people of your acquaintance secretly think you're a hero, Liz,' she added. 'You only did what we'd all like to do given half the chance.'

'However, it would be a waste to do anything other than eat this particular piece of beef,' said Alex, bringing them back to the lesson.

'There isn't enough there to write anything really rude,' Liz remarked when she saw the piece that Alex had placed at her work station.

'Aren't all the best swear words four letters?' Alex asked.

Bella laughed with a gusto that was entirely out of proportion to Alex's joke but now that Liz and John both knew how Alex felt about her, they were very glad to see the way she lit up in his presence. The way she hung on his every word and giggled at the lamest of jokes. Liz couldn't bear a grudge against Bella for having stolen Alex's heart. Not when she was such a kind and generous person. Not when he was clearly exactly what she needed too. From now on, Liz would be rooting for Bella to get the guy.

'OK,' said Alex. 'Here goes.'

Just as for the other weeks, Alex had done the shopping for his pupils. He explained to them that the beef they were going to cook with was from the butcher favoured by all the good local chefs he knew. It was grass-fed, organic.

'No wonder this course cost so much,' said John.

'I promise it will be worth it. Now, the first thing we need to do is sear the beef. You're going to work at the same time as me today because there's chilling involved between each stage and we'll never get it done otherwise.'

The class, already wearing their aprons, each stepped up to their hobs. They watched as Alex showed them the searing method. He seasoned the beef before adding it to a pan glazed with a little olive oil.

'Just thirty seconds a side. We're colouring the beef, not cooking it.'

Alex laid his beef on a plate to cool a little while he made sure his students weren't going too far with their searing.

'Perfect, Bella,' he said. She beamed.

When all three students had seared their beef correctly, Alex had them brush the meat with a delicate layer of mustard.

'Not too much, Chopper! Unless you want to make your guests' eyes water.'

Liz scraped half of her mustard off.

While the beef was set aside to cool, Alex showed them the next stage. He chopped a couple of shallots into tiny pieces. He put a generous helping of mushrooms into a food processor and pulsed it until it was a sort of pesto. Together with the shallots, this was then cooked to reduce the moisture.

'Why do we need to cook everything before we put it together?' Liz asked. 'It's all going into the oven at the end.'

'And if you haven't cooked the mushrooms, you'll end up with a soggy mess,' Alex said. 'Which is why we're also going to add a layer of Parma ham.'

'What could you write with that, Liz?' John teased. She poked her tongue out at him.

While the mushrooms and shallots were cooling, Alex had the students cover their chopping boards with cling film, onto which they laid out the ham in a single thin layer. The second layer was to be the mushroom paste.

'Put your beef in the middle and carefully roll the ham and mushroom layers around. Remembering you're not going to be cooking the cling film,' Alex added, just as Liz finished making a cling film Swiss roll.

'Chopper,' he helped her start again. 'What am I going to do with you?'

Once the beef, ham and mushroom rolls were complete, Alex took all four and put them in the deep freeze for a speedy chill. While that was happening, they prepared the pastry. It was puff pastry, ready-made.

'Because life's too short,' said Alex.

'Sonia made her own pastry,' said John.

'Tell us more,' Alex said. 'Tell us what this dish means to you.'

261

'I'll tell you about the first time Sonia cooked this for me,' John began. 'I was going after a promotion. I wanted to impress the headmaster at the school where I worked so I invited him and his wife to dinner. Sonia spent a week going through her cookery books looking for something suitably posh to serve them. It was the Seventies. The prawn cocktail years.'

'I'm glad you didn't say prawn cocktail was your favourite food, John,' said Bella.

'That's what she made for starters that night, I think. Anyway, this headmaster was a bit of an old bastard – 'scuse my French – so I was very anxious that everything went right. When the Saturday of the dinner party came, Sonia spent the whole day cooking. I didn't help, of course. I didn't know where to start. I could only lay the table and polish the glasses. But that didn't stop me from fussing about and offering Sonia my useless opinion all day long. By the time my boss arrived, she was thoroughly fed up of me.

'But Sonia knew how important the evening was to me so when we were within earshot of the boss and his missus, she was sweetness and light. In the privacy of the kitchen, it was very different. We were squabbling like a couple of children. I thought she was drinking too much. She thought I was being pompous. She told me I was being a terrible suck-up and if that's the way I was at work, she wasn't sure she liked it. She said my boss was an old misogynist and it was rubbing off on me. She actually snorted when I told our guests that the main dish of the evening had been chosen in honour of the headmaster's favourite general.

"You didn't choose anything I've cooked tonight,"

she said when we were in the kitchen again. "You're acting like I'm some irrelevant little skivvy."

'This was as she was getting the beef Wellington out of the oven. It looked magnificent. She was going to serve it on a bed of watercress. She laid it out and as she turned round to put her oven gloves back on their peg, I picked the dish up and made for the dining room. I knew she'd be angry but I wanted my boss to associate me with all that evening's triumphs. I pushed open the dining room door with my foot and went to walk in. I pushed too hard and the door swung back too fast. It bounced off the hinges and came back to whack me as I was stepping over the threshold. I dropped the bloody Wellington on the floor.

"I think you just met your Waterloo," said Sonia when she saw and my boss laughed for the first time that night.'

'Brava, Sonia!' Bella, Liz and Alex applauded.

'Did you get the job?' Liz asked.

'I did. After that cock-up the evening went very well. But I never tried to take credit for Sonia's hard work again.'

'You're doing it for yourself tonight,' said Alex.

The pastry was ready and the meat was chilled. The four cooks lay the meat in the centre of the rolled-out pastry, which was brushed with egg yolk to make it stick when it was wrapped around the beef and parma ham.

'Now ordinarily,' said Alex, 'I'd let this parcel chill for another quarter of an hour but the caretaker will be after us before long.'

So Alex had the students wrap their parcels in cling film again and put them back into the chiller ahead of going home.

'You can cook them there.'

Meanwhile, Alex's beef Wellington, glazed all over, went into the oven prematurely.

'Delia would have a fit,' he said. 'We're almost guaranteed a soggy bottom.' But Bella, Liz and John thought the finished product looked and smelled delicious.

'Yours will be even better,' he assured them, as they all took a small slice to try.

'I can't believe I've made a beef Wellington,' said John.

'It was easy, wasn't it?'

John pulled a clean handkerchief from his trouser pocket and dabbed at his eyes.

'I can't thank you enough, Alex. Watching you putting it together and then trying it myself, it was like we were, I don't know, somehow getting in touch with Sonia. I don't believe in all that afterlife stuff but it was almost as though she was standing at my shoulder when I was putting the Wellington together. I could feel her love all around me. It felt like a proper tribute to her. Thank you.'

'I felt the same when we made my dad's parmigiana,' said Bella. 'Thank you, Alex.'

'Your turn next week,' Alex said to Liz.

'Well, I apologise in advance if we're going to be boiling vegetables to within an inch of their lives, because if my childhood had a flavour it was definitely overcooked.'

'Ah, Chopper,' said Alex. 'Don't you worry. I've already been thinking about an update on those traffic lights of yours.'

Chapter Forty-Two

John had thought about taking his beef Wellington to the NEWTS – he could have finished it off in the oven where they warmed up the pasties – but he decided against it. He was down on the rota to man the theatre bar on Saturday night so he'd see everybody then anyway. What he needed was some time in front of the TV. Keeping himself busy was making him tired. Also, the beef Wellington he'd made was not so big and he wanted to make sure he savoured it himself. And perhaps Alex's gift of this particular food, and the memories that came with it, were best served in a place where John wouldn't be embarrassed if he couldn't stop the tears. He really had felt as though Sonia was alongside him that evening. He wanted to keep that feeling for as long as he could.

He let himself into the house, humming one of the songs from *Seven Brides for Seven Brothers* as he did so. He found that humming to himself until he got the radio or television on helped to make the transition from outside world to empty house a little easier. He paused in the hall to take off his coat. He couldn't help but glance at the answering machine on the hall console table.

It was flashing. The indicator light suggested there were two messages.

'Listen.' He heard Sonia's voice.

Putting down the tray of beef Wellington next to the phone, John took a deep breath and pressed 'play' instead of delete.

'Have you been involved in an accident?' said the first message. John quickly stopped that one in its tracks. It was the next message he wanted to hear.

He held his breath while it played out.

'Dad? Dad? Are you there, Dad? It's David. Please pick up. You won't be able to call me back on this phone. It's outgoing only but the main switchboard number is in the book. If you call that and tell them who you are, they'll probably come and find me. I need to talk to you, Dad, and I think you probably need to talk to me too.'

John nodded. He did need to talk. It was time.

Chapter Forty-Three

Bella didn't quite make it home after the cookery class before her phone rang. It was the DSCC. Jimmy Cricket was in again and he was kicking up a terrible fuss. He said he wouldn't talk to anybody except Bella. Sighing and trying not to think about how hungry she was after all that hard work in the kitchen, Bella said she'd be at the station as soon as she could.

This time, Jimmy had been brought in after being found in an act of vandalism. He'd got hold of a can of red spray-paint – pinched from the local DIY store – and was in the middle of using it to decorate the side of the toilet block that was closed from the end of September when a couple of police officers strolled by. Jimmy had thrown the can away and legged it but the officers were faster than he was and they caught him red-handed, as it were. Jimmy's hands were still covered in paint when Bella arrived to sit in on his interview.

'Can we get something for Jimmy to clean up with?' she asked the custody sergeant.

Bella's first thought, given where Jimmy had been caught, was that perhaps the graffiti he'd been spraying was related to the council's mean yearly closure of the prom's only public convenience when the pier itself was shut. But no. Jimmy's gesture was not one of protest but of passion.

'I was spraying a heart,' he said. 'And our initials.'

'Whose initials?'

'I've got a new woman in my life,' said Jimmy. 'I did wait for you, Miss B, but you're always too busy at work.'

She smiled at that. 'Whose fault is that?' she asked.

'I've met this woman called Morgan Le Fay,' he said.

'Like in the Arthurian legend?'

'That's the one. She's a tarot reader.'

Bella nodded. There was a tarot reader who set up a stall on the prom most afternoons. She was quite popular with some locals. They thought she had the eye. Unfortunately, Jimmy explained, she had not foreseen the authorities stopping her benefits after she stopped a job centre worker to try to sell him some heather, and now she spent most nights beneath the pier.

'But we're going to get our own place,' said Jimmy. 'Her and me. She's given me something to live for. I want to be a better man for her. I'm going straight, Miss B.'

'You can start by laying off the vandalism,' said Sergeant Mellor.

'I'm very glad to hear it, Jimmy,' said Bella. 'Because you're not going to be able to call on me for much longer.'

Both Jimmy and Sergeant Mellor looked at Bella quizzically.

'I'm planning a change of career. I've decided I'm handing in my resignation tomorrow.'

Up until she said it out loud, she wasn't actually sure she had made up her mind. Now she had.

'I'll have to work out my notice over the next few weeks,' she continued. 'But that's it. You won't be seeing me round here any more if I can help it.'

'Aww, Miss B, I don't know what I'm going to do without you. What are you going to be instead of Newbay's best solicitor?'

'I think I might train as a cook.'

That too had just come into Bella's head. Why did it sound so right?

'Like your dad!' Jimmy at least was delighted. 'See, I told you you was a chip off the old block. You're going to do him proud.'

'I hope so.'

Bella could already imagine her mother's tense, tired face, pinched into despair at the thought that her daughter was saying goodbye to a decent, steady job. However, she hoped that underneath her mum's concern, a little bit of her would be pleased. Maybe even proud. And she had the right to choose how her life turned out, didn't she?

'You can be anything you want,' was what her dad had once told her. 'We only live once. We've got to make sure we enjoy the ride.'

'Well, good for you, Miss Russo,' said Sergeant Mellor. 'I'm retiring myself in the spring. Thought I might look into landscape gardening.'

'That sounds good.'

'I've loved being a policeman but it's time for me to unleash my creativity.'

'I'm going to do that as well,' said Jimmy. 'I've always wanted to be a painter.'

'That's lucky,' said Sergeant Mellor. 'Because someone needs to repaint the wall of the toilet block on the prom.'

'Come on,' said Bella to her favourite client. 'Let's get this graffiti thing sorted.'

Chapter Forty-Four

Alex also took a phone call on his way home from class that evening. It was

Marianne, the volunteer worker he now counted as his friend.

'Good news,' she said. 'That unit you told me about? It's still available and the leaseholders are open to the possibility of letting you have it at a special rate for two years while the details on the rest of the station development are finalised.'

'Are you serious?' Alex asked.

'It's a win–win situation for them. The place is empty and it's only getting into a worse state with each winter that passes. You'll be doing them a favour.'

Marianne told Alex what the costs would be.

'It's only temporary but it's a start. We need to get another meeting with the trust in the diary as soon as possible. If everyone is in agreement, then you could be in there as early as Christmas.'

'This is amazing.'

'Are you ready for it?' Marianne asked.

'I am so ready.'

'Good.'

'And thank you, Marianne, for giving me a second chance.'

'Are you kidding? How could I not? You're a great guy, Alex, and I want to see you succeed. Everybody does. And who doesn't deserve a second chance?' She paused. 'Did you ask that woman in your class out yet?'

'Maybe next week,' Alex promised. 'Now that you've called with the news, I've got something special in mind.'

Chapter Forty-Five

Soon it was Friday again. Liz was thoughtful as she finished the working week. Nurse Van Niekerk may have officially asked Liz to leave the Waggy Weight Loss Facebook group but what Nurse Van Niekerk didn't know was that the group's privacy settings were woeful and thus Liz was able to lurk anonymously, avidly scanning the page for news of Coco.

Of course, Mrs Coco had posted about Coco's hip operation. It was a congenital hip deformity that had been making Coco find walking so difficult and contributed to her weight problems. The operation would take place on Friday morning. Dr Thomas would be performing the work. Liz wondered how long it would take. She could hardly concentrate on her own work. She started obsessively refreshing the page from about midday onwards, hoping to see that Coco was out of theatre and into recovery.

It was four o'clock before Mrs Coco posted that Coco had come round from the anaesthetic and was doing well. Dr Thomas chipped in with a comment to say that he was very pleased with how the operation had gone and he hoped to see Coco up and about again within just a couple of days.

'With her new bionic hip, Coco will be known as Coco the Superdog from now on.'

Liz felt a surprising amount of relief when she read

that. She had no idea until then how much affection she had grown to feel for that little dog and her eccentric mama. She wanted to leave a message to say that she was pleased for them both but of course she couldn't do that on the group's page. Instead, she sent Mrs Coco a private message, saying that she'd heard 'on the grapevine' that Coco was having a procedure.

Mrs Coco wrote straight back. 'Thank you, Mrs Ted. We were all very scared this morning but Dr Thomas – Evan – worked his magic and Coco will be back on her paws before you know it. He is such a good man.' Mrs Coco underlined 'such'. 'He cares so much for his patients. I'm not supposed to tell anyone this, but he did Coco's operation for free. He said he wouldn't hear of me paying, which was a huge relief because I couldn't have afforded such marvellous care otherwise.'

'That is very sweet of him,' Liz replied.

Dr Thomas had yet to send Liz an invoice for the damage to his car. In all likelihood he had been too busy to get to a garage. Liz found herself hoping that the charcuterie had had no lasting effect on the paintwork on his bonnet. Ian had always been so adamant that if a bird pooped on your car you had to try to get the muck off before it dried. Did cured meats contain the same nasties?

Liz wondered if she should send Dr Thomas another email to prompt him but she decided against it. He would be in touch with her. Until then, as Vince always said, perhaps it was a case of 'least said, soonest mended'. The fastest way for everyone to forget what had happened on the night of Alex's party was to stop talking about it.

* * *

'Got any plans for this weekend?' asked Vince, as they closed up the surgery.

'Nope,' said Liz. 'Not even Waggy Weight Loss this weekend.'

Vince knew why that was.

'It doesn't mean you and Ted can't keep following the diet,' he pointed out. 'One of the most important things I've learned over the past year is that the worst way to respond to a fresh crisis in your life is to let it derail your good intentions altogether. If you have a drink, it doesn't mean you're never going to get on top of it. It's the same for diets. Exercise regimes. Anything. You can't let screwing up once stop you from following through. You have to keep your eye on the bigger picture. Start again. Day by day.'

'Thanks, Vince.' She gave him a kiss on the cheek.

'Day by day,' Vince reminded her.

Now that the year was on the downhill stretch, it was already dark by five o'clock. The glow of lights from the other houses on her street made Liz feel like that Victorian urchin again. Two years ago, she was on the inside. She would have been in the kitchen, making supper for her husband and child, indulging the family dog with treats he wasn't supposed to have. She would have been part of a picture of domestic bliss.

Except that it wasn't ever really like that. Liz would have been reheating a ready meal for a teenager who could hardly bear to speak to her. Feeding treats to a dog that was already unhealthily obese. All while her husband met his lover in a health food café in Exeter. How many times had Ian worked late during his last year in the family home? How many times had she believed him? Even when he was at home, Ian preferred to be upstairs in his study 'answering important emails' than snuggled up on the sofa with his wife.

Would it have been better to try to sustain all those lies just to keep the status quo? Life might not be perfect, but at least Liz wasn't kidding herself any more. Now that everything she'd cherished had been stripped back to what it really was, Liz could see what really needed to be done. There was no more bad news waiting to ambush her like dry rot waiting beneath the polished floorboards of a beautiful home.

Liz let herself into the house. Ted greeted her as though she was back from a round the world trip.

'At least you'll always love me. It's been a long day, hasn't it?' Liz agreed with him. She was going to talk with Vince about the possibility of taking a longer lunch hour so that she could come home in the middle of the day and take Ted for a walk. He deserved much more of her attention.

Saskia wasn't at home. It was one of Ian's weekends. He would be picking Saskia up from her rehearsal at the NEWTS' theatre that night before taking her to Brittney's pristine cream flat. Saskia was still barely talking to Liz after the humiliation of the previous weekend. She claimed that she could not walk down the school corridor without someone making a reference to salami. Liz had 'ruined her life'. Again.

Ordinarily, Liz's weekends without Saskia were quiet affairs if Corinne hadn't managed to persuade her former husband to spend some time with their twins. That weekend was set to be especially quiet. It didn't mean it had to be miserable though. So long as she stayed away from Brittney's Bites.com.

Liz did not stay away from Brittney's Bites.com.

It was Friday. It was time for Friday Inspo. Didn't everybody need some?

Liz scrolled down through Brittney's post. She was still waiting for some sort of comeback regarding the Fiat fiasco but Brittney's Friday Inspo was fairly innocuous. There was a handbag – a 'bargain' mini cross-over body affair by Philip Lim that could really only be considered a bargain if you were prepared to shoplift it. There was a recipe. Vegan hot dogs in a quinoa bun. Just right for Bonfire Night. Perhaps you could use them as kindling.

However, there was no quote from the Dalai Lama. That Friday, Brittney had written an essay. Liz settled in to read it.

'Greetings, dear readers! How has the universe been blessing you today? Have you remembered to thank the goddess for all that she has given you and your beloveds?

'Autumn can be a very melancholy time of year. It feels as though things are coming to an end but the important thing to remember is that every year must have its seasons. If we didn't have an autumn and a winter, we wouldn't have spring and summer. However, the past few weeks have felt like autumn in my heart as well as in the world at large.

'Dear reader, I've been struggling, I can tell you. Though I know that we can always close the door on negativity – especially that of other people – by surrounding ourselves with light, I was really finding it hard. When you find out that someone has got such a high level of hatred for you – hatred is the only word

I can use to describe it – as I discovered someone had for me, quite unjustifiably . . .'

Liz scoffed at that.

'. . . it can feel as though they are actually aiming real arrows at your heart.

'Some of you know that I have come under severe psychic attack these past few weeks and I worried for a while that my darling BF did not have my back. That has changed. There are still a few real world legal details to iron out, but after that we will be moving forwards again. You'll hear about every step of our journey and you'll see the pictures too. My Darling BF and I have agreed that it's time to make a stronger commitment . . .'

Liz almost snorted a mouthful of tea across the computer screen.

Brittney's post could mean only one thing. Ian must have asked her to marry him. Those 'few real world legal details' must be referring to Liz and Ian's divorce. Was an engagement ring the price Brittney had demanded for keeping the salami debacle out of the courts?

'No,' Liz muttered. 'No, no, no.'

But when Liz read Brittney's post again she could only come to the same conclusion. Ian was going to marry Brittney the blogger, the twenty-four-year-old he had once described as looking like a lolly stick with a chipmunk's head. How far they'd come from the night when he came home from first having met her and they both laughed at one of her vegan vlogs? The laugh was only on Liz now.

Or it would be if she didn't pull herself together.

Brittney hadn't actually said she was getting married.

Deepening commitment could mean anything. Ian would have to ask Saskia before he pulled out any engagement ring and Liz was pretty sure that no matter how much Saskia liked being in Brittney's fashion shoots, actually having her as a step-mother would be another thing entirely. Yes. Liz was sure Saskia wouldn't approve.

She read the post one more time. It shouldn't matter to her. Hadn't Liz told Ian that it was time they moved on properly? They'd been apart for a year. It was over. And wasn't that for the best? Was Liz's self-esteem really so low that she still wanted Ian, who had treated her with such disrespect, to change his mind?

She sent the link to Brittney's latest post to Corinne to get her opinion of it. Did she think Brittney was talking about a wedding?

'Wishful thinking,' was Corinne's response. That made Liz feel a little better.

'Step away from the computer,' Corinne continued. 'You'll drive yourself mad. Or should that be "madder"? ☺'

Corinne was right. Liz turned off her computer and went downstairs to the kitchen. At least she didn't have to cook anything. She'd saved the previous night's beef Wellington, knowing that Saskia would not want any. They'd eaten pasta with tomato sauce (made to Alex's recipe). Saskia had complained that it 'didn't taste like normal' but she ate it all the same.

Liz turned on the oven and watched the clock impatiently as the uncooked pastry grew crisp and golden. Ted joined her and did his best to remind her that beef was his favourite thing.

'You can't have pastry,' Liz told him. 'You may no longer be a member of WWL, but you're definitely still on the diet.'

She poured some kibble into his bowl. Ted made it clear from the way that he looked at Liz that he was thoroughly unimpressed. He went back to watching the oven.

'You can have some broccoli if you like?' Liz told him as she put some on the stove for herself.

Ted's glance was utterly disdainful.

Liz was just sitting down to eat her dinner when the doorbell rang.

It was eight o'clock. Not terribly late but still a little late to pay a visit unannounced. Liz frowned. She would not be happy if it was a Jehovah's Witness or a salesman. But Ted had not barked. In fact, he was wagging his tail. Ted would ordinarily be trying to tear a hole in the door to get at a salesman's jugular. It must be someone that Ted, and by extension Liz, already knew.

Liz turned on the porch light to illuminate her caller. She recognised the slightly stooped posture at once.

It was Ian.

Chapter Forty-Six

'What are you doing here?' she asked as she opened the door just a crack.

'Nice to see you too,' said Ian.

'Why didn't you call to let me know you were coming over?'

'I thought I'd surprise you.'

More likely, Liz thought, he was worried that Brittney would check the call records on his phone.

'I might not have been in,' Liz said.

'Saskia said you would be.'

Of course. Ian was going to pick Saskia up at the NEWTS after her rehearsal. He hadn't come miles out of his way. He had an hour to kill and he probably didn't want to put his hand in his pocket to buy a pint in the NEWTS' bar.

'Well, can I come in?' he asked.

'Sure. It's still half your house. Technically.'

Ian's nose started twitching as he took off his coat in the hall.

'Something smells good. What have you been cooking?'

'A beef Wellington,' said Liz.

Ian's expression told her he was impressed.

'Isn't that quite advanced?'

'Not at all.'

Ian followed her into the kitchen. Ted brought up the rear after sniffing Ian's jacket to check for treats.

'I haven't eaten beef in months,' said Ian. 'I know this vegan diet is good for me but . . . your dinner smells really good, you know.'

'Do you want some?' Liz asked.

'Can I?'

'There's enough for two, I think.'

'Then I'd love some, thanks. I'm ravenous.'

'So long as nobody tells Brittney, eh?'

Ian grimaced.

Liz got out two plates.

This was the first time Liz had eaten with her husband since the night before he left to live with the Blogger. She tried to remember what they'd had on that unremarkable night before Ian detonated the grenade that would blow their marriage to pieces. It was a Thursday, so they'd probably had lasagne. A Charlie Bigham's lasagne. With their rustic packaging, Charlie Bigham's ready meals were easily as good as home cooking. At least that was what Liz used to tell herself. Ian certainly hadn't complained back in the day. Before he was introduced to the delights of quinoa.

Arranging slices of beef in pastry on Ian's plate, Liz thought back to that last supper and wondered if she should have known what was coming. But no, she was pretty sure Ian hadn't been off his food.

While Liz put the finishing touches to their supper, Ian had seated himself in what had always been his chair. He didn't know that since he'd been gone Liz had adopted it as her own. It was the best seat in the kitchen, facing the window onto the garden but with its back to the radiator. Liz let Ian have it. It would be hers again soon enough. At least until those few 'real world legal details' were sorted out. Liz had been hoping for a property price crash that would allow her to buy Ian out of his half of the house when their settlement was through. Newbay prices had been spiralling ever upwards as people moved out of the unsustainably expensive big cities and gentrified the smaller ones instead.

It was odd to see Ian at his end of the table again. How many times had they sat opposite one another like this during their fifteen-year marriage?

'I think this is the first time you've cooked for me,' said Ian.

'No it isn't,' Liz said.

'I mean from scratch. Using proper ingredients. Not by getting things out of tins and packets.'

'Then I suppose you're right.'

'Apart from the baked avocado you did when we were first going out?' Ian chuckled. 'Who bakes an avocado?'

'I saw it on television.'

'Was it on a sitcom?' Ian asked. Liz gave him a look to remind him that he didn't get to tease her any more.

Ian switched his attention to the beef. 'This tastes great. I'm amazed you stuck it out with that course. I thought you hated being in the kitchen.'

'I guess you don't know everything about me any more,' Liz said.

'I guess I don't,' said Ian. He looked a little sad at that, she thought.

'Thank you for calling off the attack dog,' said Liz.

'What do you mean?'

'I mean thank you for persuading Brittney not to press charges.'

'I didn't. She spoke to a lawyer at the station. Someone called Isabella, I think, who told her she didn't really have a case. She said that in order to prove someone has libelled you, you have to convince the jury that the defendant has actually said something untrue.'

Liz's mouth twitched into a smile though she was a little alarmed at the risk Bella seemed to have taken for her.

'Oh, well, it's good news for me,' she said.

'Yes. The last thing I wanted was for you to be dragged through the court. They'd have gone over everything, wouldn't they? The affair and all that.'

'I suppose they would.'

There was a lull in the conversation as Ian tucked into the beef Wellington again.

'This is really good. Eating red meat again after all those months on bean sprouts, I mean. I feel like it's already making a difference. God, I hate bean sprouts.'

'I didn't think you were supposed to like them. I thought they were supposed to make you feel virtuous.'

'I don't feel very virtuous,' said Ian. 'Not at all.'

He paused with a piece of beef halfway to his mouth. He put it down.

'Liz.'

Ian made an awkward grab for her hands across the table. Liz was still holding her knife and fork. He waited while she put them down then took her hands properly at last. 'Liz . . .'

'What is it?' she asked.

Were there tears in his eyes?

'Liz, I've made a terrible mistake.'

She remained silent, to give him a chance to apologise just as she had always dreamed he would.

'I didn't want to leave you.'

'But you had an affair.'

'It wasn't meant to be a big thing.'

'Just a *coop de food*?'

'I don't know why I said that,' Ian told her. 'I suppose
. . . well, I suppose I didn't feel like I was getting much
attention at home.'

'What with me going out to work all week to earn
half the money to pay for the house and supporting
our daughter . . .'

'I get that now. I'm sorry. But please let me finish. I
was a fool. I allowed myself to be flattered by Brittney's
attentions. I didn't think it would get serious. She was
so young and . . . well, vacuous. I fancied her of course
and I was amazed she fancied me. I thought she would
end up getting tired of me before any real damage
could be done.'

'Then why didn't you call it off when it was obvious
she was getting serious?'

'Liz, she told me she was pregnant.'

Liz took a deep breath. Her head swam as though
she was drunk again. 'Pregnant?'

'She told me she was going to tell you. I knew that
would be the end of everything so I let her persuade
me that I had to tell you myself and then I had to do
the right thing by her.'

'But she wasn't pregnant? Unless there's a secret baby
you're going to tell me about now.'

'No. She missed three periods because she wasn't
getting enough iron and the bloating was just due to
all the beans.'

'You're telling me our marriage was effectively ended
by legumes?'

'I really believed she was pregnant, Liz.'

'But you've stayed with her since you found out she wasn't.'

'How could I leave after that? Finding out she wasn't having a baby very nearly unhinged her. She went into a depression. She's been fragile ever since. You can't tell from her blog but she's been really down. I couldn't walk out on her with everything she was going through.'

'I suppose not.'

'But I want to leave her now, Liz. The events of the past few weeks have made me realise that I can't spend the rest of my life with her.'

'And?'

'I think I want to spend it with you.'

It was everything Liz had wanted to hear for so long. But though the words were right, there was something a little off about the whole situation. She chewed her lip.

'You want to come back home?' she asked for clarification.

'I do,' Ian nodded enthusiastically.

'To this house?'

'It is still *our* house,' Ian reminded her. 'But I don't have to move straight back into the master bedroom, Liz. I understand if you don't want that. I'm willing to do my probation as it were. I can move into the spare room.'

'That's got my home gym in it,' said Liz. Though she never actually used it.

'You can put that in the dining room. I'll move into the spare bedroom. I won't be here every night anyway.'

'You won't?'

'I meant to tell you. I've been allocated a bigger sales area in the latest shake-up. I'm covering the whole of the south-west from Bristol right down to Lands End now. There will be times when it's silly for me to try to get home every night. And when I am here, that doesn't mean that you have to stay home and cater for me.'

'OK,' said Liz.

'I understand that we've both changed over the past year. You've probably got used to having your freedom.'

'I think I have,' said Liz.

'Then I won't encroach on that. All I ask is for a chance to be back in the heart of my family. Just think of those Sunday mornings we used to have. Bacon butties for you, me, Saskia and Ted. Those were my favourite times.'

Liz remembered them rather less fondly. Sunday mornings were the one time of the week when Ian 'cooked' (unless they were having a barbecue). In order to make his 'world famous' bacon butties, Ian would use at least three pans and get spatters of bacon fat over everything. Naturally, having 'cooked' Ian considered himself excused from washing up. He also seemed to have forgotten that Saskia was now a vegetarian. Even a vegan when someone important was watching.

'Will you think about it, Liz?'

She nodded. 'Yes.'

'But we won't tell Saskia just yet, right?'

'So that means you're going back to Brittney's tonight?' Liz asked.

'Yeah,' said Ian. 'I need to give you some time to think. But regardless of what you decide about us, I'm going to tell her it's over this week. I swear I am.'

'If you bring Saskia back here after her rehearsal, so you and Brittney can have a bit of privacy, you could tell her what's going on this weekend.'

'Yeah. I would but . . . but it's not a good time for Brittney.'

Too right, thought Liz. She's just all but announced her engagement on the *interwebz*.

'She's got some important blog convention coming up.'

The convention that was taking place over their daughter's sixteenth birthday.

'I don't want to drop my bombshell at such a big moment for her career. That seems unfair.'

'Yes,' Liz agreed. 'But there's never a right time, is there?'

Ian glanced at his phone, ostensibly to see the actual time. Liz noticed that he had a couple of text message notifications. Ian didn't check them but when he put his phone back on the table, he placed it face down so that Liz couldn't see the screen.

'I've got another fifteen minutes before I need to pick Saskia up. Any chance I could have some more beef?'

'Won't Brittney smell it on your breath when she kisses you?'

'She doesn't kiss me any more,' said Ian.

Chapter Forty-Seven

Later, as she washed up two plates instead of one, Liz wondered what on earth had just happened. Was Ian serious about wanting to come back? He seemed to have given some deep thought to how it might work. All that stuff about staying in the spare room though. What was that really about? On the one hand, Liz knew she should be impressed that he'd realised she might not want him to move straight back into the master bedroom. On the other hand, she couldn't help wondering why he hadn't pushed it. If he wanted her back, didn't he want her *body* and soul?

Did she have the right to refuse him the spare room anyway? The house was still in both their names. If she didn't let him come back, a judge certainly might.

Oh, it was all she'd ever wanted. Her ideal life. Her husband, her daughter, her dog, all safely cocooned inside their lovely family home, which they would no longer have to sell to complete the settlement. And yet . . .

Ian had scrunched up his paper napkin and left it on the table as he always did. Even though he had blown his nose on it. Liz was surprised at how irritated she felt by her nearly ex-husband's appalling table manners. She'd forgotten how bad they were.

Was Liz ready to face that every day again?

When Ian first left, Liz thought she would never get

used to a life without him. He had been a part of her day-to-day existence for seventeen years. It felt as though her adult life really began when she met him. It was with Ian that Liz had shared so many firsts. She went on her first foreign holiday with Ian. They bought their first house together. They had their first child together. Ian's revelation that the timing of his leaving was down to the fact that Brittney thought she was pregnant had been a wake-up call. At forty-five, Liz didn't expect to have any more children. She had found Saskia's baby years such hard work that she didn't fret over the thought that she might not go through that again. But that didn't have to be the case for Ian. There were plenty of younger women who could keep on producing his progeny if that's what he wanted.

However, in the past twelve months, Liz had experienced a whole new raft of firsts. The first time she had to put the bins out (Ian was always very traditional about that). The first time she had to take a meter reading (he never trusted her to get it right). The first time she had to take her car for an MOT (he was sure the garage would rip her off if he didn't take it in for her, though he knew just as little about cars as she did). The first time she holidayed alone with their daughter (that was a disaster, but never mind). The first time she cooked a fish pie (another disaster). The first time she had been arrested (though technically, Ian had been there for that).

It was an entirely different list of firsts and experiences Liz might not have chosen for herself but she had survived them all and they had made her a stronger person. Never again would she worry about the car making a funny noise or the towel rail in the bathroom not heating up evenly. Liz knew what to do in both those circumstances and many more besides. And if she didn't, she could always find someone to ask. She'd cultivated quite a few 'handy people' over the past twelve months.

For a while Ian's departure had left Liz feeling like she was losing a limb – she felt helpless and abandoned – but without even really noticing it, she had changed and grown and become a woman who was perfectly capable of looking after herself, her daughter and their dog. She didn't need a man to do life's 'heavy lifting' any more, so if Liz was going to have a man in her life, she wanted him to be there to be her best mate and her lover. She wanted him to be there so that she had someone to laugh with. Someone to hold. Someone to kiss.

Liz thought about Ian's assertion that Brittney would never find out he'd been eating beef because she didn't kiss him any more. At least the last six years of Liz and Ian's marriage had been a kiss-free zone, no matter what Ian had eaten. It wasn't Liz who'd stopped wanting the affection. If Ian came back, would the affection miraculously come back too?

With the washing up finished, Liz sat down at the kitchen table with a cup of tea. She sat in Ian's seat, which was now her seat. If Ian returned, she'd have to give up the comfort of the radiator at her back and the garden view. How had he ended up bagging the best seat anyway? Liz thought of her boss Vince and his wife Bernie. At the surgery's Christmas dinner, Vince always insisted that Bernie have the better seat, looking into the room. Bernie was his princess.

'I want to be someone's princess,' Liz said out loud.

Ted put a paw on Liz's knee, in a gesture that said, 'You're mine.'

'Oh Ted,' she scratched the little terrier behind the ears in the way that always sent him into a happy trance. 'What are we going to do? Do you want Ian to come back? Do you miss him? Would he take you for better walks than I do? He never used to take you for walks, did he? I'm sure he'd make you stick to the diet though.'

Ted was not much help.

The bottom line was Liz wasn't entirely sure she wanted Ian back and she wasn't convinced he really wanted to come back either. Not for the right reasons. Not because he woke up one morning and realised that he was missing the love of his life. Liz began to suspect that if there hadn't been a spare bedroom in the Chandler family home, Ian might have been looking elsewhere.

Chapter Forty-Eight

'Good weekend?' Corinne asked when Liz walked into the surgery on Monday morning.

'I suppose so,' said Liz.

'Did you get laid?' Corinne asked, as she always did.

'Fat chance.'

'You should go on Tinder.'

'You should get lost. Anyway, Ian asked if he could move back home.'

'What?'

'He says he wants to leave the blogger.'

'What! Oh my days, Liz.' Corinne grabbed Liz by the arm and steered her into a quiet corner so they could gossip without Julie hearing. 'What happened? And what did you tell him?'

Liz recounted Friday evening's events, finishing with, 'I told him I'd think about it.'

'That's right, girl. You make him sweat before you let him come home. And make sure you lay down the law before he gets his feet under the table. This is your chance to get it right, Liz. Catch him now, while he's at his weakest. He'll agree to anything. I'd demand a renewal of your vows for a start. And a nice new eternity ring to go with them.'

'I hadn't even considered the possibility of getting jewellery out of the situation,' said Liz.

'Oh, but you must. How will the bastard ever learn

his lesson if it doesn't cost him lots of money? You need diamonds, my girl.'

'I really don't,' said Liz.

'Whatever. When's he going to tell her?'

'He says he's got to wait for the right moment. She's got some big blogging convention coming up and he doesn't want to upset her before then. He doesn't want to ruin her career as well as break her heart.'

'If only he'd given you the same consideration,' Corinne pointed out. 'Didn't he leave you the week before we went to the Dental World Fair in Nottingham?'

'He did.'

'I remember. You were in pieces.'

'I didn't have to get up on stage or anything.'

'So? You ought to tell him that if he's leaving her, he's leaving her. If he's coming back it's you he needs to be thinking of now.'

Liz nodded vaguely. It was an odd sensation. Liz wondered if she was feeling as Brittney must have felt when Ian told her he was going to end his marriage. On the one hand, Liz's dream was coming true. The days until Ian came back should be like the days on the advent calendar. But Liz couldn't help thinking about the row that would have to happen first.

Oh, that was Brittney's lookout. She had knowingly got involved with a married man. She had stolen him away from his wife and his daughter. And his dog. Now she was getting a taste of her own medicine.

Corinne gave Liz a high-five. 'I knew he'd come back to you,' she said. 'You rock.'

Before she started work, Liz logged on to Brittney's Bites. There was nothing to suggest that Ian had dropped his bombshell yet. Brittney had merely posted a picture of that morning's healthy breakfast, complete with instructions on how to make her super-food muesli, which worked out to cost about the same per ounce as gold, once you'd bought all the raw ingredients at your local Holland and Barrett.

Disappointed by Brittney's blog, Liz logged on to Facebook to do a little light stalking of the Waggy Weight Losers. There was good news from the latest weigh-in. Hercules had hit his target weight. Twinkle the Cockapoo was the week's biggest loser, which was a surprise. And there was a photograph of Coco, wearing a great big canine choirboy collar designed to stop her from picking at her stitches. She was photographed sitting on the grass outside the surgery with Dr Thomas crouching beside her. He looked so pleased with his patient's progress. Liz couldn't help smiling.

Once again, there was no mention of the fact that Dr Thomas had done the operation for free. He was keeping his generosity safely under his hat.

Liz found herself enlarging the photograph so that she could get a better look at Dr Thomas's eyes. The nice eyes that twinkled when he laughed at the antics of the Waggy Weight Loss dogs.

'Who's that?' Corinne asked, walking in and looking over Liz's shoulder. 'He's gorgeous. Did you meet him on Tinder? No wonder you don't know whether you want Ian to come home.'

Liz abruptly clicked the screen closed.

'Give over,' said Liz. 'I was just trying to get a closer look at the dog.'

Corinne just gave her 'the nod'.

'Can we have one more girls' night out before Ian

leaves her and moves back home?' Corinne asked. 'A farewell to your singledom? It'll be like a second hen night.'

Corinne had been at Liz's actual hen night. Liz had only hazy memories of that party and they were all highly embarrassing. Vow renewals and the prospect of a second hen night seemed strangely unappealing. It was all a bit Katie Price.

'We'll go back to that Mexican place,' said Corinne. 'Tequila!'

Before Liz could make her excuses, her first patient of the morning arrived.

Derek was an ageing punk, who took a very un-punk interest in his oral hygiene. He was a regular in Liz's chair and absolutely unimpeachable when it came to brushing and flossing. There was rarely very much for Liz to do.

Derek asked if Liz would play 'Firestarter' by The Prodigy while she was giving him his scale and polish.

'Louder,' he said, when she started with the Sonic Pic.

Liz hadn't listened to The Prodigy in a long while. It reminded her of when she and Ian first started seeing each other. When he was still living with his old girlfriend in Totnes and they had to meet up on the sly. The Prodigy was one of the CDs Ian played when he drove Liz to deserted beaches for illicit snogging sessions.

Liz wondered what had happened to the girlfriend from Totnes. Kat, Liz thought her name was. Ian had taken at least four months to find the right time to say he was leaving her. He told Liz that Kat took their break-up badly. He said she refused to let him have a lot of his stuff, which necessitated him having to go round there on a regular basis for a while in an attempt to persuade her to relinquish his shirts and CDs. Now Liz wondered whether Ian had actually moved out when he said he did. He had done a lot of 'business trips' in the weeks after he first left a toothbrush and holdall full of worn-out underpants at Liz's.

Already that day, Ian had sent Liz three texts. It was the most communicative they'd been since the beginning of their separation, when Liz texted Ian around fifty times a day to remind him that he was an arsehole and he'd left her for a bitch. The tone of their communication was somewhat different now.

'Hope you're having a nice day!' Ian wrote almost before the day had started.

'Just thinking about you and how you're getting on.'

'Had any more thoughts about what we talked about on Friday night?'

Liz started to type a response to the third text but it struck her halfway through that she still didn't really know what she was thinking. And then her next patient arrived downstairs. A new patient, according to the schedule on Liz's screen. Thomas Evans.

As she pulled up his details, Liz realised she was busting for a wee. She asked Julie on the front desk to show Thomas Evans in and settle him into the chair while she nipped to the bathroom. When Liz came back, Thomas Evans was obscured by the back of the reclining seat. Talking all the time, Liz tipped back the chair – still a bit Sweeney Todd – and simultaneously flicked on the stereo, which was still playing 'Firestarter' at full volume.

When Liz leaned over her new patient, he stared up at her with frightened eyes.

'Mrs Ted!' the vet exclaimed.

Chapter Forty-Nine

'You're not Thomas Evans.'

It was Dr Evan Thomas. Trust Julie. She was forever getting things the wrong way round, especially if people had surnames that could be Christian names. She always had one eye on an article in *Hello!* when she was tapping things into the electronic diary.

The vet sat up, looking worried and clutched at his collar in a protective sort of gesture.

Liz turned off the music.

'Sorry, sorry, sorry,' said Liz. 'I had no idea the music was going to come on so loud. I had no idea the Firestarter CD was still in there.'

'And I had no idea the hygienist was going to be you,' said Dr Thomas.

He didn't look happy about it. Fair enough. He did know Liz as a careless dog owner and a salami-wielding psychopath after all.

'Well,' said Liz. 'I'm sorry to have surprised you. You do have the right to walk if you want to. I'll understand if you do. We won't charge.'

'No. No. No,' said Dr Thomas, settling back in the seat again. 'I need to have my teeth cleaned and I don't want to wait for another appointment. I have a busy schedule. I have animals to treat.'

'In that case . . .'

Liz put Dr Thomas into the prone position again.

'But I would prefer not to have to listen to "Firestarter".'

'What do you want instead?' Liz asked. 'You can have anything except Coldplay.'

'Why no Coldplay?'

'Do you really have to ask? My office, my rules.'

'OK.'

'And don't say Ed Sheeran either.'

'Got any Chopin?' Dr Thomas suggested.

Liz pulled up some Chopin Nocturnes. She talked Dr Thomas through the breathing exercises she gave her patients in times of stress (even if she was more stressed than he was by this point). He took to them like a yoga master.

'I do something similar for my cat owners,' he said. 'They tend to be nervous of needles.'

'OK,' Liz said. 'I think you're ready. Open up.'

With only a little residue reluctance, Dr Thomas opened his mouth.

Liz winced at the sight of his molars. Deliberately. At first sight they actually looked pretty good but she didn't want him to know that.

'Is there a problem?' Dr Thomas asked.

The temptation was to tell him there was a big one. She had Dr Thomas in her chair. She was in charge now. She could put her instruments in his mouth and tell him exactly how he'd made her feel over the past few months of Waggy Weigh-Ins and his high-and-mighty attitude to her having covered his car in cold meats. This was karma in progress.

However, Liz reminded herself that Dr Thomas's reaction to her having covered his car in cold meats was actually to attempt to pretend the deeply embarrassing incident had never happened. He'd not asked her for any compensation until she forced him to reveal his interest and told him he was a pompous ass. Then, while she was pretending to be Mrs Coco, she had seen a whole other side to him. A man who put the welfare of animals well above his own financial gain.

'Actually, your teeth look very good,' said Liz. 'You obviously look after them well.'

Dr Thomas's face visibly relaxed.

'I'll just give you a little tidy-up.'

So Liz didn't use Dr Thomas's vulnerability to get her own back for having been made to feel so small in so many ways over the past couple of months. She did, however, take the opportunity to try to explain herself. She guessed that she might never have another chance and there was something about Dr Thomas that made her want him to understand what had driven her to the salami incident. She wanted him to know that she wasn't a bad person. Temporarily mad, maybe, but not truly awful.

'The thing is,' she said, while she suctioned the water from his mouth, 'the last year has been a really tough one for me, Dr Thomas. My husband left me for a much younger woman and trying to keep our daughter from suffering too much in the fallout was so much harder than I ever would have thought. There was no outlet for my own distress. When you spoke about how we project our own psychological issues onto our animals, that really touched a nerve. I didn't want to admit it, but I realised poor Ted *had* become the focus of my unhappiness. I was overfeeding him because I wanted him to love me more than Ian. I wanted to be sure that I wouldn't lose him too. It was bribery.'

Dr Thomas nodded. He couldn't do much else.

'I took against you unfairly from the start. When you told me that he had to go on a diet, I suppose that was a threat to my ability to keep Ted on my side. If I had to discipline him, then he would stop loving me. That's what I thought.

'I was spiralling out of control. That night, when I decorated your Cinquecento with salami, I was really suffering. I'd waved my teenage daughter off to a family party I wasn't invited to even though I helped to plan it. When my husband picked her up, he had his new girlfriend in the passenger seat of the car, in my place, going to spend the evening with *my* in-laws. I tried to make myself feel better by going to my cookery teacher's birthday party but it was full of really young, attractive people and that made me feel even worse.'

Dr Thomas tried to say something.

'You're very kind,' said Liz, assuming he was just trying to tell her that she was young and attractive too. 'But I really didn't feel that way. So, when I was walking home I was sad and angry and still really rather drunk, and I wanted to lash out in my pain.'

'Nnnngh,' said Dr Thomas.

'I know, I should have known better,' said Liz. 'I can only beg for your forgiveness.'

Dr Thomas desperately tried to signal his forgiveness with his eyes.

'The irony is, now my husband tells me he wants to come back.'

Dr Thomas's eyes suddenly narrowed.

'Yeah. I'm not sure what I think about that.'

Liz paused and looked off into the distance with the suction pipe still in Dr Thomas's mouth. He struggled to be free of it.

'Oh sorry,' she said, turning the pump off. 'You can rinse now if you like.'

Dr Thomas sat up. He looked at Liz seriously.

'I said too much,' she said.

'No. No. I feel honoured that you opened up,' he said. 'Mrs Ted. I mean, Mrs Chandler . . .'

'Call me Liz.'

'Liz, I—'

Dr Thomas tried to say something but Liz headed him off.

'I know you didn't want to hear about my love life. But I needed you to know I'm not always such a nut job. It's been a tough time, that's all.'

Dr Thomas nodded.

'I'm so embarrassed,' said Liz.

'There's no need to be.'

'And now I've got this big decision to make. After everything we've been through this past year, can Ian and I really make a go of it again?'

'Mrs Ted . . .'

'Liz!'

'Liz! Yes, of course. Liz, I've not always been so good at human relationships – I'm aware you've noticed that – but I can offer you one piece of advice that has never let me down.'

'What's that?'

'Trust in your dog, Liz. Trust Ted. Dogs are very rarely wrong about people. I can tell from the way Ted interacts with you, that you're a soft-hearted woman underneath.'

'Really?' Liz flushed.

'But how does Ted interact with your husband? And how does your husband interact with him? Is there affection there? Love? Respect? The way people treat animals speaks volumes about their personality. That's what my father taught me.'

'I know,' said Liz, remembering the time she'd impersonated Mrs Coco and got Dr Thomas's life story by deception.

'So, what does Ted think?'

Liz cast her mind back to the last time Ian had been at the house. Ted was not as enthusiastic about Ian as he had once been. And hadn't Ian pushed Ted away, fearing for his fancy trousers? He didn't want them covered in paw prints and hairs.

Liz thought it was Brittney's influence. With her cream-coloured flat, she'd drilled it into Ian that cleanliness was next to godliness. The Dalai Lama had probably said that. But then Liz had a sudden stabbing memory of Saskia's babyhood. Of Ian coming home from work and refusing to take his baby for even a minute so that Liz could dash to the bathroom because Saskia had chocolate around her mouth. He would not take her until she'd been wiped clean. Liz remembered Saskia's face as she tried and failed to charm Ian into a cuddle. Liz still found it impossible to resist her daughter's soft round cheeks. But Ian . . .

'I've upset you,' said Dr Thomas, misreading Liz's expression of sadness.

'No,' she said. 'Not at all. What you said makes perfect sense.'

But could she act on it?

'I hope you make the right decision for *you*,' said

Dr Thomas. 'Now, how is Ted?' he asked. 'Are you sticking to the diet?'

'Of course,' Liz assured him. Then she joked, 'Only half a box of cake mix the at weekends.'

Dr Thomas grinned at the memory. 'Your face when that situation exploded . . .'

'Don't remind me.'

'Funniest thing I'd seen in years. Tell me, Liz, now that we're friends again. How did Ted really come to eat a whole box of cake mix and those Lunchables?'

'That's definitely a three-Martini story. As in that's how drunk I'd need to be to tell the truth. I don't think we're at that stage of our friendship yet,' replied Liz.

'If Ted really can open a fridge, I'd love to see it. It'd make an interesting paper for The Institute of Canine Biology.'

'Ted can't really open a fridge,' said Liz.

'I didn't think so. I can see I'm going to have to buy you three Martinis.'

'I still need to buy you a windscreen wiper. You didn't ever send me the invoice.'

'How petty would that have been? Let's say we're quits on that.'

'Thank you.'

'In the meantime, come back to Waggy Weight Loss,' said Dr Thomas. 'I know Mrs Coco would love to see you there. Me too.'

'We'll be there,' Liz assured him. 'But only if you promise to floss.'

Chapter Fifty

For the last but one session of the beginners' cookery course, Alex had prepared a very special recipe. He'd already cooked Bella's melanzane parmigiana. A great main course or starter. For John, he'd prepared the beef Wellington. A fabulous centrepiece for any special meal. For Liz, it had to be dessert.

Liz had been wondering all week how on earth Alex was going to turn her food memories into something he could actually teach. The traffic light biscuits she'd told him about were the kind of thing you 'cooked' with small children on a wet afternoon. Well, it wasn't cooking was it? Just food assembly.

Liz picked up the tube of Smarties Alex had placed on her chopping board. She helped herself to a couple while the others got ready to begin. There were sponge fingers too. And icing sugar. Were they really going to make her mother's birthday speciality? Was that it?

Alex asked the class how they'd fared with finishing their beef Wellingtons at home. John said he'd enjoyed his. Bella admitted that she'd been swept up with work and hadn't had time to eat it. Liz said she was pleased with how hers had turned out. She didn't tell the class that it might have won her husband back.

'So today,' said Alex, 'we're going to prepare the final part of our three course meal of recipes. Liz's traffic lights.'

'It'll only take three minutes,' said Liz.

After all, how hard could it be to put some icing on a sponge finger?

'We're not doing that,' said Alex. 'At least, that's not the whole recipe. We're going to make traffic light tiramisu.'

Tiramisu, or 'Pick Me Up', one of the world's favourite puddings. It was so ubiquitous that it was hard to believe it had only been invented in the nineteen-sixties.

'Which means that I have no compunction whatsoever in giving it a thoroughly English twist.' Alex shook the Smarties. 'However, we'll start in the traditional way.'

Alex poured a cup of coffee for each of his students but the coffee was cold and not for drinking. It was for dipping the sponge fingers. In another bowl, he had the students mix mascarpone and Cointreau. 'Because we're going to pick up the taste of the orange Smarties.'

'The orange Smarties don't actually taste of orange,' said Bella. 'All Smarties taste the same. It's just a trick of the mind. You see the colour orange and orange is what you think you taste.'

'I'm not having that,' said Liz, insisting on an instant taste trial, which even she had to agree was inconclusive.

'It doesn't matter,' said Alex. 'The Cointreau will make up for it.'

He splashed a slug into each students' mixing bowl.

'This is an easy version of tiramisu,' he told them. 'The ones you get in Italy are made with whipped eggs.'

'That's how Dad used to do it,' Bella agreed.

'I hope he'd approve of this version.'

'I'm sure he would,' said Bella.

Bella and Alex shared a soft sort of look that made the other two students smile soppily.

'OK, mix the mascarpone and Cointreau together until it starts to soften. Add a bit more orange juice if it's not getting smooth enough. If it looks like it's curdling, just keep mixing. It'll soon bind together again. What do you think of the scent of that?'

Already the smell had Liz wanting to lick her fingers.

Alex showed them how to layer the sponge fingers soaked in the coffee with the creamy mascarpone in a glass.

'Save at least one of the sponge fingers for the decoration.'

Liz cursed as the first of her sponge fingers soaked up too much coffee and fell apart.

'Don't worry about making it too perfect,' Alex said when he saw that John was fretting over not having even layers. Liz's bench was covered in blobs of cream. Bella had a splodge on her cheek.

'May I?' Alex asked her permission to wipe her face clean. She stood still as he tenderly ran his thumb across her cheekbone. John and Liz sighed.

'I don't need to tell you how we're going to be decorating this,' said Alex, getting back to the pudding.

A sprinkle of icing sugar and three Smarties.

'Red comes at the top,' John had to remind Liz.

'No wonder I've got six points on my license.'

Alex had them put their desserts in the freezer while they tidied up their benches.

If only Liz had known that cooking could be a pleasure. She thought of her mother, always in the kitchen but always harassed and unhappy about it, cooking meat, veg, fish and puddings until they were all exactly the same shade of grey. As a result, Liz had never had any expectation that she might be able to produce something that actually tasted nice or that she might enjoy herself while she was at it.

And yet, as she ate the traffic light tiramisu, Liz had a lump in her throat that wasn't due to bad cooking. She could picture quite clearly her mother's smile as she placed the traffic light biscuits in front of Liz on her birthday. They may have been simple but they had been made with love, that was for sure. A mother's love. Endlessly forgiving and unconditional.

She wanted Saskia to have memories like that.

'What do you think?' Alex asked. 'Does it take you back, Liz?'

'It's the Cointreau that does it. Mum used to put that in my bottle.'

The others took a moment to realise she was joking.

'Yes,' Liz said. 'It does take me back and it makes me sad. It makes me think of all the things I should have said while I had the chance. I wish I'd told her I loved her every day. I wish I'd made her this pudding. I can't believe I've never learned to cook up until now. My daughter is almost sixteen and she's never had a birthday cake baked by me. If you don't count the one for her first birthday that came out like a cow pat. Doing this course has made me realise that I can cook after all. And I like doing it. And it's shown me how important food is to all of us. I don't want my daughter's, and maybe my grandchildren's, abiding taste memory of me to be something created in a lab for the Sainsbury's ready meal range.'

'Then you can make them traffic light tiramisu,' said Alex. 'Though maybe go easy on the Cointreau.'

The four happy chefs finished off their pudding together. It was almost nine o'clock by the time they finished eating. The community centre caretaker was hovering, keen to be certain that the place was locked up on time. He was momentarily placated by a taste of the tiramisu but he was soon back again, reminding Alex that the cookery course was, strictly speaking, only meant to take place between half six and half eight.

Alex duly brought the session to a close.

'Ladies and gent, as you know, our cookery course must come to end next week. I've enjoyed working with you all so much and I'd like to make next week's session really special. How do you feel about a graduation dinner?'

'Will we get certificates?' Liz asked.

'Perhaps. But I was thinking what would be really nice would be for each of you to bring a guest to the class next Thursday. They can sit at the table and have a nice glass of wine while we prepare a special dinner to eat together here instead of taking the food home.'

'Sounds good,' said John.

'I'm up for it,' said Liz.

'Me three,' Bella confirmed.

'Then all we've got to do is decide who's cooking what. And who we're going to invite to eat it. We'll all bring a bottle of wine and some nibbles. There are plates and glasses and silverware here, of course. It would be nice to have a tablecloth. Does anybody have one?'

'I can bring one,' said John. 'My wife was always buying tablecloths.'

'I can bring a pair of candlesticks,' said Liz. Like her big fish pie dish, Liz's candlesticks were an unused wedding present.

'I'll bring flowers,' said Bella.

'This is coming together,' said Alex. 'Any idea as to who you might bring along as your guests?'

All three students were silent, looking hopefully to the others to leap in with their suggestions.

'Boyfriends? Girlfriends?' Alex asked.

Liz and John knew at once that Alex really only wanted to know who Bella was going to bring along.

'I don't have either of those,' she said at last. The relief on Alex's face was comically palpable to Liz and John.

'Then bring a friend,' he said.

Chapter Fifty-One

Though she still had another four weeks to work out her notice, that Friday was to be Bella's last night on the CDS rota, and for once it was turning out to be a quiet one. She felt quite restless as she sat in her living room, waiting for the phone to ring. She was trying to read, but couldn't find the concentration it required. She turned on the television. There was nothing she wanted to watch. Five minutes flicking through the channels convinced her that she had missed nothing all those nights she spent down the police station. Real life was so much more surprising.

Bella made herself a cup of tea. Putting the kettle on was usually a sure-fire way to make the phone ring. If that didn't work, then sticking something in the microwave definitely would. Bella pulled a frozen spaghetti Bolognese out of the freezer. This was the last time she would eat such rubbish. From now on she would have the time to shop and cook properly. For that reason, she was looking forward to this last indulgence. She'd have no more excuses for eating so much processed stuff after that night.

The spaghetti needed to be cooked on max power for five minutes. Bella watched as the black plastic tray turned in the orange light. One minute, two minutes, three minutes, four minutes, four minutes and thirty seconds, four minutes and forty seconds, fifty seconds . . .

Ring!

As if by magic, Bella's mobile started buzzing as the microwave pinged to tell her dinner was ready. She snatched her phone up, while simultaneously popping the microwave door to stop it from beeping. A smile spread across her lips as she saw that the call was from the Defence Solicitor Call Centre. She would have hated to spend her last night on duty sitting at home.

Leaving the spaghetti in the microwave, as she had left so many ready meals cooked and uneaten before, Bella pulled on her coat and headed out into the misty November night.

She was expecting to see Jimmy Cricket when she got to the station. She was not expecting to see him on the wrong side of the desk. Or should that be the right side? The side where people who hadn't been arrested waited to be seen.

'Jimmy? I thought . . . Shouldn't you be in one of the cells? I got a call from the CDS about you. Haven't you been arrested?'

'Not tonight, Miss B.'

'Then what am I doing here?' she asked.

'We're taking you out,' said Jimmy. Sergeant Mellor appeared. He was wearing not his uniform but a grey woolly jumper over a pair of jeans and a checked blue shirt. It struck Bella that she had never seen him out of uniform before. Just as he had never seen her out of the smart formal suit that she wore in her professional life.

'What's going on?' she asked him.

'We've had reports of unusual activity near the town

centre,' Sergeant Mellor said. 'I think we ought to go and investigate.'

'And I'm to come with you?'

'You can resist if you like,' said Sergeant Mellor. 'But it would make all our lives easier if you didn't.'

Bella smiled at the phrase she had heard him use so often in other more usual contexts.

'Then I suppose I'm coming with you,' she said.

The unlikely trio walked out of the station together. Jimmy seemed especially excited.

'I've got to go on ahead,' he said. He sprinted off into the night.

'We'll catch him up,' said Sergeant Mellor.

'I have to admit I'm a little bit concerned,' said Bella. 'Where exactly are you taking me?'

'No need to worry, Miss B. I'm a policeman.'

Bella chuckled. 'You know, I find that no comfort whatsoever.'

'We just wanted to make sure your last night on call was a memorable one,' said Sergeant Mellor. 'Jez from your office is covering for you.'

'And you're taking me out on the beat? I don't think I'll be much use to you if anything kicks off,' she said.

They turned up East Hill Road, the one that led to the railway station. Bella knew the road well, of course, though she rarely went up there any more. If she was ever going out of Newbay, she drove. It usually worked out cheaper apart from anything else. But there were other reasons why she rarely took the train unless she had to. Station Parade was a street full of ghosts for her. She turned to Sergeant Mellor but he was texting someone.

'Just letting them know we're on our way.'

'Them?' Bella echoed.

'I'm not saying any more,' Sergeant Mellor said. 'But you need to put this on now.'

He reached into the back pocket of his jeans and pulled out a cat-shaped eye mask.

'It's my wife's,' he said by way of explanation.

'I don't know if I want to put this on.'

'I'll make sure you don't fall over,' said Sergeant Mellor. 'There isn't far to go.'

Slowly, Bella placed the mask over her hair and wore it like a visor for a second. She tipped her head on one side.

'Bella,' said Sergeant Mellor, 'how long have you known me?'

'OK,' said Bella, pulling the mask over her eyes. 'I trust you.'

Sergeant Mellor lent Bella his arm and they continued on their journey. Though Bella did trust her friend and former colleague, she walked slowly. This was all so surreal. Where was he taking her? Why had Jimmy gone on ahead? Were they really heading for the train station?

Sergeant Mellor turned Bella around a couple of times and it made her less certain of their direction. There was nothing near the train station. Not really. A few of the less illustrious hotels. No restaurants. No pubs where people might be waiting to send her off with a well-deserved drink.

'We're nearly there,' said Sergeant Mellor.

Bella felt the ground beneath her feet change from smooth tarmac to a rougher surface. Gravel. Like the surface of the overspill car park at the railway station perhaps. Yes. They were definitely there.

Bella stood her ground and refused to move any further. 'Until you tell me where you're taking me.'

'Just a few more metres,' Sergeant Mellor cajoled.

'I'm not moving.'

'You'll spoil the surprise. I've got to get you in exactly the right place. Please,' he added.

'OK,' said Bella.

She let him lead her for about ten more steps, then they stopped and at last he said, 'Now you can uncover your eyes. When you do, just look straight ahead. And try not to scream.'

Chapter Fifty-Two

There was no danger that Bella would scream. The sight that greeted her when she took off the lavender-scented cat mask rendered her speechless.

It was the café. Her dad's café. Bella's. The café where she had spent so many of her happiest times growing up. But it was no longer boarded up as it had been for the past fifteen years. The boards had been taken down and the broken glass they hid had been replaced. Someone had touched up the woodwork in the exact same dark green her father had chosen. Ivy trailed from new window boxes. Candles lit the interior so that it glowed like a fairy cave.

The name above the door was still hers. The mystery decorators had repainted that too.

'Oh my goodness,' Bella finally breathed.

'This is where I leave you. They're waiting for you inside,' Sergeant Mellor told her. 'Go on in.'

Jimmy Cricket was by the café door. While Sergeant Mellor had delayed Bella by leading her round the houses on the way from the police station to the railway station, Jimmy had changed from his usual greasy parka into a smart white overall. It had 'Bella's' embroidered on the breast pocket. Jimmy opened the café door and gave Bella a low bow.

'Miss B. I've saved you your favourite table.'

Indeed it was her favourite table – the one right in

the window. Bella was about to ask Jimmy how he knew but then remembered he must have seen her there many times. It was where she sat to do her homework when the café was empty as it so often, sadly, was.

Jimmy pulled out a seat so that Bella could sit down. She took in the rest of the transformation of the café that had been empty for so long. The interior was not quite so polished as the outside. It was still a work in progress. The tiles on the floor were cracked and broken. The paint was peeling. But whoever Jimmy and Sergeant Mellor had been working with had done a pretty good job of clearing up and in the flicker of the candlelight, the place looked shabbily chic rather than just plain shabby. Music was playing from an old cassette player on the counter. Someone had thrown a checked tablecloth over the table in the window and brought blankets too, that Bella could wrap up in as she sat.

'No heating yet, I'm afraid,' said Jimmy.

'What have you been doing here?' Bella asked. 'How did you get inside? Who paid for the glass in the window?'

'Too many questions. You'll find out all in good time,' said Jimmy.

He took the cloth napkin from the table in front of Bella and, with a flourish that looked well practised, he placed it on her lap. Then he handed her a menu. Handwritten.

'Tonight's special . . .' Jimmy began. 'Well, it's all special but there isn't actually a choice.'

'Am I having dinner here?'

'I hope so,' said Jimmy. 'The chef's been working very hard.'

'So there *is* a chef?'

'Of course.'

Bella tried to get up to look into the kitchen but the door was shut and Jimmy insisted that she remained seated in any case.

'May I get you an aperitif?'

'What have you got?' Bella asked.

'Whatever you want,' said Jimmy. 'So long as it's Prosecco.'

'Then Prosecco it is. It's my favourite anyway.'

Jimmy returned with a bottle and a glass. He seemed to struggle with the cork. Bella asked if she could help.

'Nah,' said Jimmy. 'If anyone can get the cork out of a bottle, it's me. I've had enough practise.'

He picked up a knife from the table.

'Jimmy!' Bella protested. 'You'll hurt yourself.'

'The French call this the sabre method,' he told her as he ran the knife along the bottle's seam before whacking it against the cork which flew out in a fountain of spuma. Jimmy managed to catch a little of the fizz.

'Here's to your retirement, Miss B,' he said, as he chinked the half-empty bottle against her full glass and took a swig.

'Thanks, Jimmy,' said Bella. 'Though I'm not retiring yet. Just changing direction.'

Bella heard a loud expletive come from the kitchen. She tried to place the chef's voice but couldn't, beyond the fact that it was definitely a man.

'Sounds like the chef needs me,' said Jimmy, disappearing into the back where Bella's dad had once been in charge. While he was gone Bella had time to read the menu.

She didn't recognise the handwriting but she recognised all the recipes. There was cotechino and lentils as a starter. An aubergine parmigiana. A tiramisu. Bella soon decided she knew exactly who was behind the kitchen door. She stood up.

Jimmy returned with a bowl of olives and a plate of antipasti. He put his hand on Bella's shoulder and gently pushed her back into her chair.

'I've got a speech to make. From the foothills of the Italian foothills of some-such and some-such,' said Jimmy, in a pastiche of a waiter in an altogether smarter establishment.

'Thank you.'

Bella nibbled at a hunk of parmesan that was as good as any she had tasted. She tried to get more out of Jimmy. How was he involved?

'I've got this mate,' Jimmy said. 'I want to tell you his story. He was a good bloke but he fell in with a bad crowd.'

'You mean you?' Bella teased.

'Nah. This was before he met me. It was years ago. When he was a kid. Anyway, he got into trouble for handling stolen goods and he did a spell inside. Six months. Turned out to be the best thing for him. He got clean, he got straight and he got a qualification in cooking skills.'

'And then?'

'When he got released he moved to Exeter and started looking for work. He stayed at the hostel where I was for a while. He made us some fantastic grub. About six months ago, I bumped into him again here in Newbay. Small world, I said. Only he's doing much better for himself than I am now. Then last month, I told him about this place. I told him how your dad used to run it and how he would bring any spare food down to the bus shelter at night. I told him it was probably your dad's generosity that sunk the place as well.'

Bella smiled a little sadly.

'He said he was looking to open a restaurant so he got in touch with the freeholders and they let him have a two-year lease. Now he's going to reopen it and give me a job.'

'Who is this foolish person?' Bella asked.

'I think he's going to join you after dinner. Now if you'll excuse me, I have work to do.'

Jimmy disappeared into the kitchen again.

Bella chewed her lip as she considered what Jimmy had just told her. If the chef was who she thought it was, had he really been inside? It didn't seem possible. Yet, Bella knew that all sorts of people fell foul of the law. They weren't all bad to the bone. Far from it. Take Jimmy for a start. And so many of those people, given a second chance, gave their very best in return. What was the story here?

Jimmy returned with the cotechino. Bella struggled to keep the tears from her eyes as she ate one of her father's signature dishes in the restaurant that had been his life's dream. She could see herself as a young teen again, leaning against the fridge in the kitchen while he cooked. The contentment in his face as he turned towards her and asked her to taste the lentils. He cupped his hand under her chin as she ate.

'Not too salty?'

'Always perfect,' she assured him.

'Like you, my favourite girl.'

'Your only girl!'

She thought of her grandmother, promising her that every lentil eaten would mean a coin on New Year's Day. She thought of her mother, worrying they would end up penniless.

Next Jimmy brought out the aubergine parmigiana. Perfect food for a damp November night. The dish she always asked for when she was off school because she was unwell. The cheese on the top was her favourite part. Her father would let her have the cheese from his portion as well.

The cheese on top of this parmigiana was perfectly cooked. The aubergine was sliced so finely as to be transparent. Bella could see the effort that had gone into every stage of this recipe. The tomato sauce was as good as her grandmother's.

'Tell the chef that the food is really excellent,' Bella said to Jimmy.

'He'll be glad to hear that.'

'Tell him I'd like to tell him in person!'

'All in good time,' Jimmy promised.

'I don't think I can wait,' Bella called, wanting the man in the kitchen to hear her.

To accompany the food, the chef had chosen a wonderful wine. It wasn't Italian but it complemented the food very well. And it had her name on it. It was from the Bella vineyard in the Napa Valley.

'Leave as much as you like,' said Jimmy, when Bella seemed to be slowing down. 'None of it will go to waste.'

Bella noticed Jimmy taking a forkful of the parmigiana for himself as he carried her half-finished dish back to the kitchen. Whoever it was that was planning to take Jimmy on as a waiter was going to have his work cut out explaining the finer points of working in a restaurant, but she thought he would be popular with the guests so long as he could stay out of trouble.

'Would madam like a moment or two to reflect and digest before dessert?' Jimmy asked.

Madam thought she probably should but she was too keen to find out whether the chef was who she thought it was. It had to be him. It had to be Alex. She would have put money on it. If he was waiting until the end of the meal to come out of the kitchen, Bella saw no point in delaying.

'I'll have it now,' she said. 'I'm sure you want to knock off.'

'I'm washing up once you're done,' Jimmy explained.

He brought out the tiramisu, carefully layered perfection in a stubby glass, like the ones in which they used to serve water in the school canteen. There were no Smarties decorating this one but in the hint of Cointreau Bella saw the unmistakeable mark of her teacher.

'Tell Alex this is my favourite,' she said.

'How do you know it's him?' Jimmy asked. His face told her she'd hit the mark.

'He gave himself away in every mouthful,' she said. 'Tell him that it's all been wonderful and I can't wait to thank him in person.'

She had a sense that he was listening at the door.

'In fact, I'd like to share this tiramisu with him.'

Chapter Fifty-Three

Behind the kitchen door, Alex was indeed listening to the conversation going on in the dining room and he was every bit as nervous as a chef in a starred restaurant knowing there's a critic from *The New York Times* at the best table. More nervous. For Alex the stakes were much higher. He'd asked Jimmy how Bella had reacted when he told the story about how he came to be in the café that night. How had she looked when he mentioned that his new boss had spent time inside?

'She looked how she always looks,' said Jimmy. 'Like nothing you say would ever shock her. Like she's always going to do her best by you, no matter what you've done.'

'You mean, she looked how she does when she turns up after you've been arrested?'

Jimmy assured Alex that was a good thing but Alex couldn't help thinking that the expression Jimmy read as calm and unshockable was actually simply professional and resigned.

Had he done the wrong thing? When Jimmy told him the history of the boarded-up café by the train station, it had seemed like fate. Fate had brought Bella to his class and it had brought him to the café. It was a sound business proposition too. That was what he had told his backers at the rehabilitation trust. The old warehouses behind the station were being redeveloped as luxury apartments. The people who worked on the building project would need somewhere to eat. The people who moved into the finished flats would appreciate a casual yet stylish local. Everybody liked Italian food.

But perhaps Alex had overstepped the mark. This place held promise to him but for Bella it must contain melancholy memories as well as happy ones. After all, the original Bella's had failed.

'Are you sure she doesn't look sad?' he quizzed Jimmy.

'Miss B never looks sad,' Jimmy told him. 'She puts a brave face on everything.'

'Jimmy,' said Alex. 'That doesn't really help.'

She'd responded to Jimmy's suggestion that she wait a little for dessert by telling him that she wanted to eat it straight away. Alex wondered if she was just trying to get out of there as quickly as possible.

'Why don't you go and ask her?' Jimmy said at last.

Alex stepped out of the kitchen and Bella did her best to look surprised, though she was nothing of the sort. Of course it was him. She'd been sure almost as soon as she saw the café all lit up with those candles. She'd known for certain when she ate the parmigiana. Alex looked nervous. Bella realised that she was feeling nervous too. She gestured towards the other chair at her table.

'Sit down, chef,' she said.

Alex took his seat. Like Jimmy, he was wearing a white jacket with 'Bella's' on the pocket. What Bella didn't know was quite how significant that single word was to him. When Alex first put the jacket on, he told himself, 'You really are. Bella's that is. She's got your heart in her hands. Let's hope she wants it.'

'This has all been amazing,' Bella said. 'But how did you do it? Is the kitchen reconnected?'

'I've got a camping stove out the back. And a freeze box. And a blow torch for doing the cheese on top of the parmigiana.'

'I thought it was especially crispy.'

'It's amazing what you can do with a blow torch.'

'How did you get in here?' Bella asked. 'Jimmy told me some story. Did you really break in?'

Alex laughed at the idea.

'I didn't have to. I'm taking over the lease,' he said. 'For the next two years. I'm being backed by a charity who are helping with the rent and the set-up costs. I'm going to open a café staffed by ex-offenders. Like Jamie Oliver did.'

'Ex-offenders like you?'

Alex nodded. 'I should have told you before.'

'Why would you? It wasn't any of my business.'

'I thought it would change how you looked at me.'

'I understand that,' Bella said.

'*Has* it changed how you look at me?'

'No,' she assured him. 'But this has.' She gestured around the candlelit room.

Alex held his breath. He still wasn't sure whether she was happy about it.

'I can't believe you chose this place. My dad's old café. And what you're going to do with it . . . it's . . .'

'Does it upset you?' Alex asked.

'No. No. Your project is exactly the sort of thing Dad would have done if he'd had the chance. It's a beautiful idea.'

'When Jimmy told me that he used to see you here every day after school, I knew I'd found the right spot. It could be really great. I bet it was great.'

'It was.'

Alex poured himself a glass of the red wine he'd chosen with Bella in mind. 'We should have a toast to your dad.'

'To Dad,' Bella chinked Alex's glass. 'He would have loved this. Here's to your new café.'

Bella toasted Alex.

'Is it OK if I call it Bella's again?' he asked.

Bella looked into her glass. She wiped at her eyes with the back of her hand.

'I've upset you,' said Alex. 'You're crying.'

'I'm not upset,' said Bella. 'At least, not in the way you think. I know that you'll do something wonderful here. You've already worked miracles with a tablecloth and some candles. It's just that this place was so much part of my life. And my dad's life.'

'It could be part of your life again.'

'How?' Bella asked.

'You said you wanted to use the skills you've picked up over your years in law to help people. You could do that here. I've got plenty of people who can wash up, lay tables and make a decent tomato sauce. You could be the business brains. You could give people legal advice when they drop in. And when you've done all that, you could cook.'

'I promised my mother I would never go into the restaurant business,' Bella laughed.

'I promised my mother pretty much the same thing. But we only get one life. Best to make it your own.'

'You're right about that. That's exactly what my dad would have said.'

Bella sat up straight.

'I can't believe I'm sitting here. When I was a kid, I used to imagine that one day I would have a really grand restaurant in London, like the one Dad worked in when he first came out of the army. I would be there every night, greeting my celebrity guests, working out which of the great and the good should get the best table.'

'The best table is always the one *you're* sitting at,' said Alex.

With his heart in his mouth, Alex reached for her hand across the checked tablecloth and lifted it to his lips.

Bella looked as though she was about to say something but the words didn't come. They looked at each other, searching each other's eyes for a deeper message. This was the moment. If Alex let go of Bella's hand now, it might be gone forever.

Suddenly Bella pulled Alex to her across the table and kissed him passionately.

'Oi!' came a shout from Jimmy in the kitchen doorway. 'This isn't that kind of establishment!'

Chapter Fifty-Four

Liz was unloading the supermarket shopping when she became aware, with the sixth sense we all have that something is going on behind us, that a car had pulled up across the top of the drive. When she turned to see the white Fiat 500, Liz's heart gave a small flutter that betrayed an awful lot about what she had been thinking. And about whom. But this Fiat 500 did not belong to Dr Evan Thomas. It belonged to Brittney The Blog Tart Blaine.

Brittney was glaring at Liz from her place behind the wheel. Liz could almost feel the hatred shooting from Brittney's eyes like lasers. This must be the moment, she thought. Ian must have told Brittney that he wanted out. And he must have told her where he was going.

After what felt like a whole minute of hard staring, Brittney climbed out of the car and slammed the driver door shut, making sure to lock it as though she had arrived at Liz's house for a friendly sort of visit and expected to be a while. Or as though she thought Liz lived in an especially bad area.

'I want to talk to you,' she said as she stepped onto the drive.

'OK,' said Liz. 'Talk away.'

There was no point telling Brittney to F off. That would immediately shift the conversation into nuclear gear and that's not what Liz wanted on the doorstep. Her bat sense told her that curtains were already twitching in the houses to the left and the right of her. There couldn't have been anyone on the street who didn't already know about the antipasti incident. Now here was an identical car. Was this the Salami Slut? would be the question on her nosey neighbours' lips.

Brittney stalked down the drive, twisting her ankle as she did so. She was wearing a pair of deeply impractical high-heeled trainers, which the fashion bloggers periodically declared '*le dernier cri*' before, as Brittney was wont to do, they ended up with a twisted ankle and went back to flats.

'Ow,' said Brittney.

That afternoon she was a far cry from the beautiful, composed eco-goddess of her website. Her eyes were red. She looked as though she had been crying for a week.

'You bitch,' was her next gambit.

'Er,' said Liz, indicating with her eyes that they were probably being overheard.

'You stole my fiancé.'

'Your *fiancé*?'

'Yes.'

'You mean, *my* husband?' Liz pointed out. The divorce was still not final. 'You can't be engaged to someone who's still married to someone else.'

'Whatever. You've stolen him from me.'

'I think in legal terms, I've merely taken repossession of my own property,' Liz responded.

'He's nobody's property.'

'In which case, he gets to do exactly what he wants, right? Look, Brittney, I don't think this has to be a long conversation. I don't know what's gone on between you and Ian, but if he's chosen to call off your relationship, I can promise you I had nothing to do with it. I gave up trying to change Ian's mind a long time ago. If he wants to come back here – to his house – it's entirely of his own free will. I haven't dragged him back here against his wishes by the use of crystals and feng shui.'

Brittney's eyes narrowed as Liz mocked her.

'You shouldn't want him back anyway,' Brittney responded. 'Not after all the things he said about you. If you knew—'

'I'm sure you're going to fill me in,' said Liz. She had that sinking feeling.

'He said you'd let yourself go,' Brittney began. 'He said you had a stomach the texture of porridge.'

'As a result of giving birth to his child.'

'He said that making love to you was like making love to a beanbag.'

'What?'

'Lumpy and unresponsive.'

'That's enough,' Liz said.

'And you're letting him move back in after that?'

'It's still half his house,' said Liz, attempting to keep her cool. 'Look, is there anything I can actually do for you, Brittney? Only I need to get all this food into the freezer before it starts to thaw out.'

'Ah yes. The kitchen goddess,' Brittney sneered. 'Not.'

Liz raised an eyebrow.

'Why he would want to come back to this,' Brittney indicated the carrier bags on the floor by the car, 'is beyond me. When he left you he was on the verge of becoming a diabetic.'

'Then I'm grateful to you for having got him back on track.'

'I cared for him far better than you ever did. I nurtured him body and soul.'

'With your goddess-made connection.'

'Don't mock me,' Brittney told her. 'Your small-minded conventionality is what drove you and Ian apart. It won't last, him coming back to you. It won't last. Three weeks of food like this.'

'It's just frozen veg, which retain more of their nutrients than veg shipped unfrozen . . .' Liz tried.

'And sex with an unresponsive bean bag means he'll soon be back to me.'

'For wild goddess sex and mung beans?'

Thank goodness Saskia was at the NEWTS and didn't have to see or hear any of this, Liz thought.

'Ian likes mung beans!' Brittney roared.

'Oh come on, Brittney. No one likes mung beans. Not even the Dalai Lama.'

'Don't bring him into it!' Brittney screeched.

And with that, she delved into the nearest carrier bag – which happened to be one full of fresh vegetables – and pulled out an avocado. She hurled it in Liz's direction. Liz ducked. The avocado bounced off the Volvo, leaving a visible dent. It really wasn't ripe.

'Brittney,' Liz said in the voice that used to work on Saskia, when she was two and having a tantrum over the Petit Filous. 'Let's not let this get out of hand.'

But Brittney was already reaching for her next weapon. A packet of vine tomatoes. Without taking them out of her packaging, she hurled them at Liz's head.

'Stop it!' Liz cried as she dodged the missile.

'I will not stop it!' said Brittney, as she picked up a baking potato.

'Not that,' said Liz. 'That could really hurt me.'

'Like you've hurt me!' Brittney caught Liz a glancing blow to her shoulder with the spud. Then she picked up the aubergine and Liz knew she had to take action.

Quickly, Liz ducked down and found some ammunition of her own. As it happened, Liz had a bag full of tins. She picked up a tin of ready-chopped tomatoes. No. She couldn't throw that. A tin was a serious missile. She didn't want to kill Brittney. She just wanted her to stop. While Brittney rained more potatoes, the aubergine and a bag full of organic lemons on Liz's head, Liz rifled through the nearest carriers in search of anything that wouldn't take an eye out. She came up with a yogurt.

'Not organic!' she said, as she ripped off the foil and let the yogurt fly.

She caught Brittney in the middle of the chest. Yogurt splattered all over her dry-clean only sweatshirt from Windscale's latest collection. All one hundred and fifty quid's worth of it, Liz knew.

'You!'

Brittney sent another potato to the side of Liz's head. It caught her right above the ear, making her stumble against the car. Liz recovered enough to find a tub full of mini-mozzarellas. They'd do no lasting damage except to the fabric of Brittney's silk athleisure track pants.

'I hate you!' Brittney bawled at her. 'I hate you, I hate you, I hate you!'

'I hate you back,' Liz assured her, fending Brittney off with a French stick as she came in for the kill with a melon. Liz sank down onto the floor next to the car. She could hear Ted going berserk on the other side of the front door. If only he really was as good at opening doors as she had lied in the veterinary surgery when trying to explain his cake-mix binge. Liz looked up at the melon, which seemed to grow to the size of the moon as Brittney raised it high above her. How ripe was that melon? Which would split first? The fruit or Liz's skull?

'Brittney! No!' came a shout behind them. 'Put the melon down!'

Saskia had come home.

Chapter Fifty-Five

Brittney dropped the melon onto the drive. Liz was giddy with relief as she saw the melon bounce and roll away. Like the avocado, it wasn't ripe. It might even have been capable of killing her. Clinging on to the side of the car, Liz got to her feet. Saskia was standing next to Georgia. Both girls' faces were the picture of shock.

'I was going to ask if Georgia could stay here tonight if that's OK with you . . .' Saskia said to Liz but as the gravity of the situation sank in – this was no ordinary food fight – Saskia turned to Georgia and said, 'Another night?'

Georgia made a hasty retreat, though her mother, who had dropped the girls off, took a while to pull away from the kerb.

'What's going on?' Saskia asked. 'Why is half the shopping splatted on the wall? Has Dad left you?' she addressed Brittney.

'For this bitch,' Brittney jerked her thumb in Liz's direction.

'You mean my *mum*?' said Saskia.

Liz felt a huge flood of love towards her daughter for that.

'Can we take this inside, please?' Saskia said then. 'I really don't think you want the neighbours to see you two fighting. As if my life were not full enough of embarrassment already. I don't know what I did in a past life but it must have been really bad to deserve ending up between you two.'

'Sassy!' Brittney protested.

'Brittney, please. That's not my name.'

Liz and Brittney followed Saskia inside like a pair of school children. Liz was not sure how she felt about having Brittney in the house, especially since she was dripping yogurt. As far as she knew, Ian's lover had never stepped over the threshold. Though of course it was entirely possible that they'd trysted there before Ian had the decency to leave. Ted didn't seem that surprised to see her. He tried to lick Brittney's knees.

'So this is what he's coming back to?' Brittney sobbed, as she pushed Ted away.

Liz kicked a basketful of dirty laundry under the kitchen table so that it wasn't in view.

'It's his home,' said Liz. She found a small mirror in her handbag and used it to examine the damage caused by Brittney's direct hit with a potato. She was going to have a big bruise for certain. Did she really want this woman in the house? Was there any need for the conversation to carry on?

'My flat is his home,' Brittney insisted.

'Not any more, it seems,' said Liz.

'Look, shut up, both of you, about where Dad belongs,' said Saskia suddenly. 'Just shut up and sit down. I've got something to tell you both.'

'What?' Liz and Brittney both snapped.

'Dad has been playing you. You, Brittney. And *you*, Mum. Brittney, I'm afraid he really does want to leave you. He's worried that you want too much commitment.

335

But Mum, I don't think he wants to come back here for the right reasons. He wants to come here to save some money while he finds himself somewhere else to live. He's got another girlfriend.'

'What?' Liz and Brittney said at once.

'I guessed that something was going on when he got all weird about his phone again. The way he was when he was getting ready to leave Mum for you,' Saskia told Brittney. 'And then he started having to work away from home all the time.'

'He's been given the south-west area manager's job,' said Brittney.

Liz agreed.

'No he hasn't,' said Saskia. 'Honestly, the pair of you can be so gullible. Dad's got a girlfriend. In Totnes.'

'Totnes!'

Liz at once pictured Kat, the ex-girlfriend, in her Birkenstocks and her cheesecloth dress.

'How do you know that?' Brittney asked.

'Dad didn't know how to get to the NEWTS theatre from Exeter so he asked me to put the address in the sat nav. And the last place he'd visited was an address in Totnes, which was not a dental surgery. I checked it on my phone. It's a little terraced house and it's registered to one Katherine Newton.'

'The cheesecloth girl. Have you thought about becoming a private detective?' Liz asked.

'It doesn't mean anything,' said Brittney. 'There are all sorts of reasons why he could be going to see someone in Totnes. There's a bespoke jeweller there,' she said significantly. 'Perhaps she's called Katherine.'

Liz tutted. 'I don't think so.'

'I overheard him on the phone,' said Saskia, 'and he

definitely wasn't taking an order for dental whitening products.' In one line she delivered the coup de grace to Brittney's dreams and confirmed Liz's worst suspicions.

'Bastard,' muttered Liz.

'So there's no point the two of you arguing over him. He doesn't care that much about either of you.'

'I knew it,' said Liz. 'When he said that he wanted to come home but thought it would be fairer on me if he didn't move back into the master bedroom. And he pre-empted the whole having to sneak out all the time thing by saying he had that new job. Ah well. Good job he hasn't moved his stuff back yet. Totnes. I knew there was unfinished business there.'

Brittney was taking it altogether more badly. She sank to the floor dramatically and appeared to faint. When he saw what was happening, Ted rushed over to revive her by licking her face. And more of the yogurt off her sweatshirt. That soon brought Brittney round. But because she had chosen to faint under the kitchen table, when she sat up to avoid Ted's ministrations, she cracked her head, which made her howl, which made Ted even more determined to comfort her. Utterly defeated, Brittney lay back down on the floor and let Ted take off all her make-up with his exfoliating tongue.

Liz and Saskia looked down at their visitor. Saskia shook her head and murmured, 'Sad.'

'I know how you feel,' Liz told Brittney. 'I really do.' She offered Brittney her hand. Brittney refused it.

'Oh, get up, Brittney,' said Saskia. 'It really isn't that bad.'

'I've got a blog post about summer weddings all

ready to go,' Brittney wailed. 'It's being sponsored by the Bridal Fayre at The Majestic.'

'I can see how that might be embarrassing,' said Liz.

'Ooooh.' Brittney sat up. She covered her face with her hands. Ted was still desperately trying to comfort her. Finally Brittney buried her face in his fur and snorted. 'I've made such a fool of myself.'

'Use this as a learning experience,' said Saskia, treading dangerously close to being annoying.

'Let me get you a cup of tea,' said Liz. 'Though I'm afraid I haven't got any macadamia nut milk or whatever it is you bloggers drink.'

'Semi-skimmed is fine,' said Brittney in a very small voice.

It was not how Liz had expected to be spending her evening. She thought she would be getting the spare room ready for Ian's arrival the following day. Now that she knew he was probably in Totnes and not in Bristol, as he had claimed, she didn't feel inclined to change the linen. She felt inclined to open a bottle of Chardonnay. With Brittney.

Liz would never have guessed that she would ever have Brittney sitting at her kitchen table. She would have been downright flabbergasted if anyone had told her that she would be holding the woman's hand across the checked cloth, watching her cry big snotty tears about the man they'd both loved and lost.

'It gets better,' Liz assured her. 'I promise you, right now you may think you can't live without him but you totally can.'

'Totally,' Saskia agreed.

'You lived without him before you met him, didn't you? You don't actually need him at all. You're a young, independent, and, much as I hate to say it, beautiful woman. Saskia tells me your blog is really taking off. You've got bigger fish to fry than Ian Chandler.'

'He told me that he loved me.'

'I'm sure he meant it at the time.' Liz was kind.

'He told me that he had never met anyone like me before.'

'I'm sure he meant that too.'

'What has that woman in Totnes got that I haven't? What is she giving him?'

'It's probably what she isn't giving him,' said Liz. 'Right now, in the first flush of romance, she's not making any demands. She thinks she's having a nice little fling. As soon as she needs Ian to be there for her in any real way, he'll be off.'

Liz turned to Saskia. 'I'm not sure you need to hear all this, sweetheart.'

'Mum,' said Saskia, 'I'm under no illusions about Dad any more. Not after I heard him on the phone. I mean, I love him and I always will, but while he's all right at being a dad, he's awful at being a partner. I get that now.'

'What will I do?' Brittney asked.

Brittney was like the dormouse at the Mad Hatter's Tea Party, drifting in and out of the conversation and spending a lot of the time with her head on the table.

'Do what you always tell people to do when they ask for advice on your blog,' said Liz. 'Set your intentions. Clear your mind of negative thoughts. Ask for help from the universe to find your true purpose and achieve your dreams. And don't tell me that your dream is to be married to a short, tubby, balding, unfaithful dental equipment sales rep from Newbay.'

Brittney managed a sort of laugh. 'When you put it like that . . .'

Half an hour later, Brittney announced that she was leaving.

'Are you sure that you're OK to drive?' Liz asked.

Brittney admitted that she wasn't sure at all.

'Then you're not going anywhere. Not tonight. There's a spare room with your name on it right here.'

So Liz did end up changing the linen in the spare bedroom after all.

'And there's a glass of Chardonnay too.'

'Is it organic?'

'It's alcoholic. Who cares?'

Brittney didn't argue with that.

Chapter Fifty-Six

The following morning, Brittney composed a blog post from the spare room at Liz's house, while she sipped a cup of tea, with normal semi-skimmed milk, delivered to her by Saskia first thing. Liz was sitting at the kitchen table when she got the Google alert to say there was news on Brittneysbites.com.

'We spend so much of our time asking the universe to give us what we want,' Brittney wrote. 'What's been revealed to me over the past twenty-four hours is that sometimes we don't really *know* what we want. Often what we want is not necessarily what's good for us – like eating a whole packet of Oreos. When that happens, the universe will do what it can to set us on the right path and sometimes that manifests itself as the thwarting of our dreams.

'Just twenty-four short hours ago, I thought that my dreams were slipping out of my grasp and I was desperate to hold on to them any way I could. They'd been so dear to me for so long. I was prepared to do anything to make sure they happened. But, dear readers, I was pushing on the wrong door. I wanted a life that was never supposed to be mine and the more I wailed that it wasn't fair, the more the universe resisted me.

'What I thought were my dreams brought me to a very bad place. I was prepared to ride roughshod over the lives of other people to get what I wanted. Until the universe sent me an angel – three angels, in fact. Two in human form and one furry – to show me exactly where I was going wrong.

'When we need them, we will find friends in the strangest places. All we have to do is be quiet for long enough to allow them to give us the message they have been sent to bring. If we can be humble and hear harsh truths, they will only make us stronger.

'Last night, I heard some very harsh truths. I discovered that my Darling BF is not everything I thought him to be. I blamed the other people in his world for the way he was behaving, when, in reality, there is only one person making him act the way he does and that's him. At the same time, there's only one person making me react the way I have been and that's me.

'From now on, I'm taking ownership of the way I live my life. I'm still going to set my intentions and ask the universe for help to reach my goals but I will no longer ignore the road signs that tell me when I'm heading in the wrong direction.

'As I've said to you on this blog before, every day is a chance to start afresh. What are you going to let go of today, in order to move towards your bliss? I'm starting with my Darling ex-BF.'

Comments:

Joolzlovesquinoa : 3s ago
Oh wow, Brittney. This is powerful stuff. Live your truth, babes!

hunnybunnydrinxgreentea : 30s ago
Luv it hun really pleased 4 you

Yogachick45765860: 2 mins ago
Sounds like you've been touched by the goddess.

LizChandler: 4 mins ago

Good for you, Brittney. There are better days ahead for
all of us, I'm sure. With love from your angels. Saskia,
Ted and Liz.

Chapter Fifty-Seven

So Brittney was going to move on with her life. After breakfast – a meal Liz had never expected to share with her husband's lover – Brittney told Liz that she was going straight back to Exeter to clear what remained of Ian's stuff out of her flat. She asked Liz if she might borrow some of the empty cardboard boxes that were stacked in Liz's spare room.

'Of course,' said Liz.

She helped Brittney load the boxes into the car.

However, the events of the previous evening left an uncomfortable question in the air. Now that Brittney was determined to clear Ian and his collection of *Top Gear* magazines out of her life for good, where would said magazines and errant husband end up? As far as Liz knew, Ian was still expecting to move back into the spare room. Was Saskia expecting the same? Liz was tremendously relieved when she received a text from Ian saying, 'Supply chain issues in Bristol. Going to have to stay here until they're sorted out. Might not be back until Sunday night.'

Supply chain issues. That was a new one. Liz still didn't let Ian know he'd been rumbled. She was grateful for the extra time to think. She responded, 'That's fine. Don't work too hard!'

Had Liz only herself to think about, the decision would have been simple. One of the many things she had been turning over in her mind since Dr Thomas's visit to the dental surgery, was what he'd said about animals showing you who people really are. She'd pushed it to the back of her mind at the time, but when Ian had come over to eat the beef Wellington, Ted had not been himself. He'd not cozied up to Ian as he might once have done. Had Ted sensed that something about Ian's proposal was off? Liz realised that like Ian, she'd been pretending that his coming back was a good idea. Doing it for Saskia's sake really. She'd known all along that it wasn't what she wanted. Her own animal instincts about Ian's lack of sincerity had been shouting it loud.

On Friday evening, Saskia had a NEWTS rehearsal. Georgia's mother was going to bring her back, which meant that Liz had all evening to prepare herself for the conversation they were going to have to have. It also gave her time to make one of Saskia's favourite meals. From scratch.

Saskia decided that spaghetti Bolognese was her favourite dish long before she could even say it. When she was really little – about four – she would demand 'spag Bog', if she was ever given a choice. Specifically, what Saskia was asking for was a little tub of spag Bol from Marks and Spencer's ready meals for children. Start them young.

Well, there was no need for that any more. Liz knew how to make a tomato sauce now. She knew how to make sure that pasta didn't overcook. And she knew what to substitute for meat if your daughter was still a vegan. Liz wasn't sure whether seeing Brittney drinking tea with semi-skimmed had put an end to that. Whatever, Liz could rustle up a veggie version of the dish Saskia had always asked for.

She laid out the ingredients on the kitchen counter and began, while Ted watched with interest from his basket. He was slowly but surely getting used to the idea that he could no longer expect a biscuit if he climbed up next to Liz on the sofa of an evening. A piece of carrot peel would have to suffice.

Liz chopped her onion as though she had been chopping onions her entire life. She let it brown in the pan, no longer panicking that it would burn before it browned. She read the instructions on the vegan mince substitute and added that to the mix. She took a spoon and tasted the results. It really wasn't bad. Oh, she hoped Saskia would like it.

The smell of the food she'd made with such love filled the kitchen and Liz's heart.

At half past eight, she heard the sound of Saskia arriving home. She heard a car door slam and Saskia's cheery goodbye to her friends. Ted was already at the bottom of the hall, wagging his tail off as he waited to greet his joint first favourite member of the family.

Saskia came in, bringing the cold autumn air and the smell of the sea with her. She threw her bag down onto the chair where everyone tossed everything. She sounded in a good mood as she asked, 'What's cooking, Mum?'

'Spag *Bog*,' said Liz.

'I can't believe I used to say it like that,' said Saskia.

'It was cute.'

'Is it . . .'

'I've made a vegan version using a meat substitute that Brittney recommended on her blog as it happens.'

'Wow. Thanks, Mum.'

Liz waited for the but. There was no but.

'I even got vegetarian parmesan,' Liz added.

'Yummy. It smells really good,' said Saskia. 'I'm just going to change into my PJs, if that's OK.'

'Nothing like dressing for dinner,' Liz replied. 'Of course it's OK, sweetheart. Wear what you like.'

When Saskia came back down five minutes later, dinner was on the table.

Liz let her eat half before she opened the conversation.

'Saskia, we need to talk about your father.'

'I know.'

'I'm sorry you had to hear me and Brittney both bad-mouthing him last night.'

'I told you, I understand. And I was the one who let you both know what he's really up to.'

'The problem is, he still thinks he's coming to live here.'

Saskia nodded.

'And I'm not sure I want that to happen. We all know now that he's not coming back here to be with me. He just wants somewhere to stash his stuff while he carries on with Miss Totnes.'

Saskia nodded again

'All I ever wanted was for the three of us to be a happy family,' said Liz. 'I want him always to be there for you but I don't want him to pretend he wants to be there for me too if he really doesn't.'

'What are you saying, Mum?'

'I'm saying that I want to tell your dad that it's best if he doesn't move back in.'

Liz watched Saskia's face closely for signs that she was upset.

'I want to go ahead with the divorce. I understand that means we'll probably have to sell the house so your dad's got money to buy a place of his own but I promise you we'll find somewhere just as nice.'

'Mum,' Saskia laid her cool hand on top of her mother's. 'It's OK. I'm sixteen in a week. In two years' time I'll be off to university and after that who knows where I'll want to be. I mean, I'll always come back and see you but the chances are I won't want to live in Newbay any more. I understand that you need to plan for a life without me and without Dad. You have my blessing to do whatever you want.'

'Do you mean that?'

'Of course I do. Mum, I could tell from the moment you told me that you weren't really sure about having Dad back. I suspected you were only considering it because of me. That's why I turned Sherlock on him, to find out if he was really leaving Brittney because he wanted us to be a proper family again.'

'I'm sorry you felt you had to do that.'

'I'm glad I did. I don't want him to use you, Mum. Especially not now. Not after the year you've had without him. He shouldn't get to swan back in after putting you – and me – through that. You've always devoted yourself to us, me, Dad and Ted. It's your turn to say what you want.'

'When did you get so wise?' Liz asked.

'I've always been wise,' said Saskia.

'You just don't always show it.'

'Ditto,' said Saskia. 'Like when you gave Ted the Lunchables.'

'Least said about that . . .' Liz reminded her.

'Right, I'm going to call your dad and tell him he'll have to stay somewhere else,' said Liz.

Saskia nodded.

'Thank you,' said Liz. 'I know you and I don't always see eye-to-eye but I'm very proud that you're my daughter.'

'And I'm proud that you're my mum. I know I haven't been a great daughter the past twelve months. I've been angry and I blamed you for Dad leaving. Now I know what really happened I'm sorry for taking his side so much of the time. It must have been hard for you too and you hardly ever showed it.'

'I just wanted you to be happy. You and Ted. Because I love you.'

'And I love you. You're the funniest, loveliest, most open-hearted Mum I could ever wish for. And now you know how to cook too. You're practically perfect.'

Liz squeezed her daughter's hand.

'What do you think of it?' Liz dared to ask. 'The vegan spag Bol?'

'It's great,' said Saskia. Then she added, 'But it would be even nicer without the cardboard-flavour meat substitute.'

Chapter Fifty-Eight

On the morning of the day he would see his son David for the first time in eighteen years, John cleaned his car. He knew that Sonia would have insisted on it. This was a special occasion after all. He needed to make a proper effort.

John was there early. He'd been worried that he wouldn't be able to find the place and he didn't think he would want to ask anyone for directions. In the end, he had to. The sat nav, which was always Sonia's domain, kept sending him round and round in circles. He had to clear his throat three times before he could even say the address he was looking for but the woman behind the counter of the garage where he asked didn't even flinch.

'You need to keep going up this road for about another mile,' she said. 'The parking's difficult though so you might want to start looking a few streets out. Saturdays are the day when everybody visits.'

'Oh, I'm not visiting,' John said. But the woman wasn't really interested.

David had been such an easy child. At least when he was small. He never got into any trouble at junior school. The reports he brought home were full of glowing praise for the effort he made with his school-work and his polite and sunny nature. John and Sonia were tremendously proud of him. He even won a prize one year.

It started to go wrong when he was in secondary school.

John blamed himself. He thought that David felt he had to muck around at school to make up for having a teacher as a parent. But it got worse. Outside school he started hanging around with a really bad gang. Drug users and pushers.

How could John's perfect son have turned into a drug addict? And how could they turn his life around again? John tried to ban the crowd of reprobates David ran with from the house. Even his girlfriend, who was another addict herself. Sonia was endlessly kind, endlessly understanding, but after David was convicted of being part of a plot to bring drugs into the country from the Netherlands – a huge haul worth tens of thousands, which made all the papers – John didn't know what else they could do.

Sonia advocated more patience but John disagreed. 'Tough love,' he told her. 'That's what he needs. We need to make him understand how much he's hurt everyone involved. It's only when he sees that he's got nothing left that he'll make the effort to stand on his own two feet.'

David's girlfriend had already washed her hands of him. Her parents paid for her to attend rehab in another city.

Sonia tried to keep everything together. She wrote to her son every day.

'We're all he's got, John. I want to be there for him.'

John refused to drive her to visit him. David was put in a prison near Bristol. Four hours from where they lived. John agreed with Sonia that they should move to be closer to him – that was how they'd ended up in Newbay – but he still would not go near. John and Sonia rowed every time she came back from visiting him.

Eventually, Sonia said she'd stopped going.

John shrivelled inside when he thought of the times she'd said she was visiting an old schoolfriend when really she was travelling across the country to see their son, navigating buses and trains and lonely taxi rides to get to him, when John could have driven her door to door. It was the only lie she ever told him and she told it because he made her feel she had to.

John was glad that David had told him he didn't need to go into the prison itself that day. Instead, he was to wait outside. David would be released at around noon.

John was parked up by half eleven. The remaining thirty minutes passed so slowly and they were full of memories. Of David as a child. Of Sonia. Of the unhappiness of the past few years.

Then suddenly there he was. Older than when John had last seen him of course, by some eighteen years. The clueless twenty-two-year-old who had gone away was now almost forty-one. He was thinner, too. He had hardly any hair. He took after John in that regard. But he was still recognisably David. Still that bounce in his walk that caused Sonia to nickname him Tigger when he was small.

John had worried over how this reunion would play out. His own father was a strict Edwardian. Though John had never really doubted his father's love for him, there hadn't been much in the way of public displays of affection. They were more likely to shake hands than hug. John had tried to be less uptight, but it wasn't easy. He was still more likely to tell David to pull himself together than scoop him into a cuddle if he fell and hurt his knee.

The past few months had changed John. Something about losing Sonia had finally chipped away at any hard covering he had. Meeting Liz and Bella and Alex had shown him that he wasn't unlovable. All he'd ever needed to do was reach out. That was all he needed to do now.

David came out of the prison gates and stood blinking, as though finding the daylight too bright and the real world too big for him after all that time he'd spent away. He looked up and down the street. Possibly, he was finding it hard to connect John the pensioner with the man his father had once been, just as John was surprised to find that he was now the father of a distinctly middle-aged man.

'David,' he called at last. 'David, I'm over here.'

And that familiar smile spread over David's face. 'Dad.'

John stuck his hand out and they shook on it. David used the leverage to pull his father into the hug they both really needed.

John drove them both back to the house in Newbay. David hadn't ever been to the house where his parents had lived for so long.

'Been waiting for you to come and help me with the painting,' John said.

'I can do that, Dad.' David jumped at the chance to let John know he was capable of working.

They had lunch in the kitchen. John had made sandwiches. David's favourite, as he remembered it. Cheese and pickle. David seemed to savour every mouthful.

'I can't tell you how good it is to eat something other than prison food.'

'I thought prison food was getting better.'

John told him about Alex.

'You've been learning to cook?'

'A man can't live on sandwiches.'

'I don't know, these are pretty good.'

The conversation was a little awkward. John wanted to know everything about David's time inside and yet a big part of him also wanted to pretend it hadn't happened. So they talked about what John had been doing the past few years. Up until the point at which Sonia died.

'They would have let me come out for the funeral,' said David. 'But I didn't think you'd want me there.'

'I should have insisted you come to say goodbye,' said John.

'I prefer to remember her as I last saw her anyway,' said David. 'She came to see me on my birthday.'

Just three days before she died. John had thought at the time that she seemed tired.

'I just wish I could have told her my good news,' David continued. 'But I didn't know until a month later.'

'What good news?' John asked.

'I've been in touch with Vicki,' said David. Vicki was David's old girlfriend. The one who'd gone off to rehab when he went inside. 'She wrote to me out of the blue.'

'How's she doing?' John asked.

'She's a mum. She was pregnant when I got arrested.

354

I had no idea. She didn't tell me. Nobody did. Dad, she had a little girl. She's nearly eighteen. She's your granddaughter. Her name is Madison.'

John felt the room spin around him. He leaned forward onto the table, burying his face in his hands.

'Dad?'

David placed his hand upon his father's shoulder.

'Dad, are you OK? I know this is a shock.'

'You're telling me,' said John. He straightened up. David looked instantly relieved. 'Why didn't she let you know she was having a baby?'

'You know what I was like, Dad. Would you have chosen me for the father of your grandchild? Vicki's parents persuaded her that the best thing to do was cut all contact. I'm not even on the birth certificate because we weren't together when the baby was born. There was nothing I could have brought to a baby's life back then. And then Vicki got married to someone else and they had two more kids. They were a family. She didn't need me. Madison had a dad.'

'So what changed?'

'Madison got older and she wanted to know the truth. Vicki decided it was time to let her know it. She's nearly an adult after all.'

'And have you met her?'

David nodded. 'She came to see me inside. It's not the best way to meet your daughter but it was wonderful.'

John nodded.

'She's really clever. She's doing her A levels. She wants to study psychology. She's doing really well. Though no thanks to me, of course. Oh Dad, I'm so grateful that she even wanted to meet me.'

'Are you going to see her again?' John asked.

'I am. Do you want to come with me? I know she'd like to meet you too. I've got a photo.'

David dug into his rucksack and pulled out an envelope. 'Lots, actually. Vicki printed out loads of pictures from all the years I've missed. Look at this one, Dad. Doesn't she look like—'

'Your mum. Sonia. Yes, she does.'

John couldn't help smiling at the familiar face, passed down to another generation. The eyes, nose and lips he knew so well, living on in their grandchild. It was like magic.

'She must get her brains from Mum too. God knows me and Vicki never had any.'

'You were young,' said John. 'And it sounds like Vicki's grown into a great woman. Your mum always liked her.'

'I just wish Mum had known.'

John nodded. He felt as though his heart was breaking again as he thought of all that Sonia had missed out on. She'd always wanted a grandchild. Life was so unfair.

'She would have loved Madison, wouldn't she?' said David.

'Yes,' said John. 'She would.'

And she would have told John to do his best to welcome the girl into the family. He could almost hear her saying it. Sonia would not have wanted him to miss this chance to make up for lost time. He would tell Madison what a wonder her grandmother had been. He'd love their granddaughter enough for the both of them.

'Madison is going to love you too. Granddad,' David assured him.

Chapter Fifty-Nine

It was Saturday morning and time for the final session of the autumn term of Waggy Weight Loss Club. Liz decided it would be a good idea to put Ted through a home weigh-in to give her some idea of what she would be facing when he took to the scales in front of Dr Thomas and Nurse Van Niekerk.

This time, when Liz stood with Ted in her arms on the bathroom scales, she did not subtract anything for her clothes.

'I think it's going to be OK,' she told her wriggling dog when she saw the numbers. 'I think the diet is finally working.'

She put Ted back down on the floor.

'Good luck at Waggy Weight Loss,' said Saskia as they headed out. 'Ted's looking really good, Mum. I'm sure he's lost weight this time.'

Liz agreed. Safe in the knowledge that she had already weighed him and the scales concurred. 'Fingers crossed,' she said.

That morning, Liz decided that she and Ted would walk all the way to the veterinary surgery. It was a beautiful late autumn day and she was determined that she would not miss an opportunity to help Ted shed even a milligram. Every little counted.

The car park at the surgery was not as full as it

had been for the first few sessions of the club. Liz guessed that her fellow Waggy Weight Losers were of the same mind. They all wanted to graduate. With honours.

Liz knew from having read Nurse Van Niekerk's update on the Facebook page, that there would also be prizes for the dogs who had lost the most weight over the course of the term. She wasn't especially hopeful for Ted's chances in that category but who knew. Twinkle in particular, had yo-yoed in weight throughout the WWL experience. He might well have blown the previous week's progress with a dustbin raid.

Or maybe not . . . There was Twinkle and Mr Twinkle, putting in one last lap around the playing field before the weigh-in began. Twinkle looked especially wild-eyed. Liz would have put money on Mr Twinkle having refused his dog breakfast.

'Hercules! And Mr Hercules,' Liz greeted the Chihuahua and his owner at the surgery door. 'Are you ready for this?'

'Yes,' said Mr Hercules. 'Though I don't think Herc's got any chance in the biggest loser category. Overweight as he was, because of his size he just didn't have the most weight to lose.'

'I'm assuming Dr Thomas will be working out the biggest loser by percentage lost,' said Liz. 'Otherwise none of us can compete with Twinkle.'

'What do you think?' asked Mr Hercules, casting a side-eye towards the big-boned Cockapoo and his owner. 'I think he's put some back on.'

'Maybe,' said Liz. She hadn't realised Mr Hercules was so competitive.

'Going in?' Mr Twinkle was suddenly beside them. They all trooped into reception and bagged the three remaining chairs.

There was no sign of Mrs Coco. Liz assumed that Coco had been signed off WWL after her operation. All the others were there. Ted did the rounds, sniffing bottoms in a particularly friendly way. The owners merely nodded at one another. They understood what was at stake. There was no fraternising with the competition on the human side.

At ten o'clock precisely, Nurse Van Niekerk bustled in with her clipboard.

'Ladies and gentlemen,' she addressed the dogs. 'Owners.' They were all used to the joke by now. 'Thank you all for coming in for this last session of Waggy Weight Loss. I'm really pleased to see you all here today and I know Dr Thomas will be too. He's just attending to a very special patient and then he'll be right with us.'

Less than half a minute later, the door from the surgery opened and Dr Thomas walked in. Followed by Mrs Coco and Coco herself.

Their appearance prompted a spontaneous round of applause. Not least because Coco was walking, and far more enthusiastically than the other WW Losers had ever seen her walking before. Her stumpy tail let everyone know how happy she was. Ted gave a squeak of delight to see his friend.

'Coco is going home today,' said Dr Thomas. 'But not before she's seen you all get your Waggy Weight Loss certificates.'

Mrs Coco gave Liz the thumbs up behind Dr Thomas's back.

'Let's get on with it shall we? In alphabetical order . . . Biscuit!'

All the dogs jumped up.

The weigh-in was tense. Everyone was so keen to see their dogs succeed. Thankfully, no one had gone backwards but there was disappointment in store for some. Biscuit was still too heavy. So was Monty, the golden Lab. Ted, much to Liz's relief, was just about on target. Hercules was doing especially well. But not well enough.

'The winner for being this term's biggest loser is . . . Twinkle!' Dr Thomas announced at the end of the weigh-in after, as Liz had predicted, weights had been adjusted for size. 'Let's have a big round of applause for Twinkle.'

Everyone except Mr Hercules obliged.

Twinkle's prize was a very fancy dog toy.

'For you to play with on the common,' said Dr Thomas to the dog. 'Remember that exercise is key to keeping that weight off.'

Nurse Van Niekerk played a blast of 'Move it, move it'.

'But Twinkle is not the only winner today. I know that making sure your dog sticks to a diet can be every bit as difficult as sticking to a diet yourself. And, just like humans, our dogs are all individuals who gain or lose weight at their own pace. It can be disheartening when you're not losing as much as the dog next door. That's why I have decided to award a prize for effort. Mr Hercules, would you please step up?'

The dog toy Dr Thomas presented to Hercules was almost as big as the dog itself.

'We can trade this in for something smaller,' Dr Thomas suggested.

'No,' said Mr Hercules. 'This will be just fine. Hercules is stronger than he looks. He's a big dog in a small dog's body.'

Hercules snatched the toy and dragged it into a corner, like a sabre-tooth tiger defending a mammoth bone.

'OK, everybody, there are certificates for the rest of you too. In no particular order . . . Biscuit!'

All the dogs jumped up again.

Ted was called to receive his certificate last of all.

'It's good to see you back here,' Dr Thomas said to Liz.

'We made our target weight,' said Liz.

'You certainly did. I knew you would. I could tell the first time we met that you're a determined woman and you care about your dog. He cares about you too,' Dr Thomas added.

'He's been a tower of strength,' Liz admitted. 'And I will try to make sure he sticks to a healthy eating regime from now on, so that you never have to see us again, Dr T.'

'That would be a pity.'

Liz noticed that Dr Thomas, Evan, was still holding her hand. He hadn't dropped it since they posed shaking hands for the WWL Facebook page.

'Well, you could come and have your teeth cleaned more often,' Liz suggested.

'I was hoping we might see each other in a rather more relaxing context than that. I still want to hear that three-Martini tale . . .'

Nurse Van Niekerk cleared her throat.

Dr Thomas let go of Liz's hand.

'Right, everybody, that concludes this session of Waggy Weight Loss! All that remains is for me to remind you that the praise of someone we love tastes far sweeter than any dog snack and if you really can't stay off the snacks, don't forget to move it, move it!'

Nurse Van Niekerk did the dance one more time. Unenthusiastically.

'Have a great weekend, everybody,' Dr Thomas said.

Liz followed the rest of the owners and their dogs out into the car park, where they chatted about their dogs' achievements and made plans for a reunion at some point in the future. They'd certainly keep up the Facebook page.

'Got to keep each other honest,' Mr Hercules told Mr Twinkle.

'I'm so glad Coco is better,' Liz told Mrs Coco.

'It's all thanks to Dr Thomas,' said Mrs Coco. 'That man is so devoted. He really is just wonderful.'

'Yes, he is,' Liz finally agreed.

Liz helped Mrs Coco load Coco into the car then she started her walk back home. About halfway there, she stopped to send an email from her phone.

'What are you doing next Thursday night?'

'What are you suggesting?' came Dr Thomas's response.

Chapter Sixty

Thursday. The last session of the beginners' cookery course and the graduation dinner.

Bella's mum was already waiting when Bella pulled up outside the house at six. She'd dressed up. She was wearing her favourite outfit. A cream-coloured silk shirt she'd had for years – since Bella's father had bankrupted them, Maria knew how to make things last – with a neat grey pleated skirt. When she saw that Bella was wearing her jeans, she tutted.

'I thought you were taking me somewhere special,' she said.

'I am, Mum. 'It's just that I'm going to get a little hot and sticky.'

'What? Why?' Maria was confused. 'Why will you be getting hot and sticky? Where are we going? What are we doing? I thought we were going out to dinner.'

'We are,' said Bella, as she opened the passenger door for her mother to get in. 'It's just that I'm making the dinner.'

'You're what?'

'I'm making the dinner. Don't look so surprised. I've been having cooking lessons.'

Maria's head snapped round.

'I started last month. I'm not exactly cordon bleu standard yet but I'm getting there. I'm really enjoying it. I'd forgotten how much I like to cook.'

Maria was tight-lipped.

'Like your father,' she said eventually.

'Yes,' said Bella. 'Just like Dad.'

They drove to the community centre in silence. Bella half expected her mother to demand they turn around but she didn't. How could she? Bella had invited her to dinner, that was all. They'd managed to ignore the tension in the house over the café's failure for years. Why should they have a huge bust-up about it now? Yet Bella knew she had to say something.

She found a space in the car park but before they got out she told Maria that she had to tell her what she'd been thinking. After all, she'd realised over the past six weeks that the café and what happened to it had shaped the rest of her life. She'd listened to her mother's anguish and followed her advice to get a 'proper' job because of it. Bella had spent a decade in that proper job and it had brought her security – if you could call her unfinished flat security – but it hadn't brought her the happiness she'd assumed security also promised.

'Mum,' said Bella, 'the restaurant didn't fail because dad was some kind of loser. It failed because of the prevailing economic climate. It failed because the bank he was borrowing from wouldn't give him any leeway to suspend or reduce his payments when the recession hit. It failed because he was a good person who wouldn't have dreamt of stiffing his suppliers to keep himself out of a hole. It failed because he was trying to bring high-end Italian food to Newbay at a time when most people still though spag Bol was exotic. If he opened his restaurant today, it would be different.

It wasn't his fault. If you want to trace it right back, the café failed because of the bankers and the lawyers. The people with the "proper jobs" who never took a risk except with other people's lives.'

Maria looked straight ahead.

'Dad deserved our love and support and sympathy. He was broken by what happened. We could have put him back together. Instead, we went with the bankers' line that the café failed because he was a failure too. We let him down when he needed us most.'

Maria was silent for a while. Then she said, 'Not we, Bella. Me. Me. His wife! You were always so proud of him. It was me that should have been different. I should have stuck by him through thick and thin. But, sweetheart, I was so scared. Your father was busy feeding the homeless of Newbay while I knew how close we were to losing our own home. If one of us hadn't taken a hard line, we'd have been out on the street. The café was dragging us down. I know it broke his heart to have to close it. It broke mine too.'

Bella had never heard her mother say that.

'I grew up poor, Bella. I didn't want that for you. I didn't want you ever to have to worry about money. That's why I was so pleased when you got your place to read law. The world will always need lawyers.'

Bella couldn't help laughing at that.

'Absolutely,' she said. 'So long as they keep writing laws that are too difficult for anyone without a law degree to follow. But I'll tell you what's certain, Mum. The world will always need food. And it will always need great chefs.'

'As your father was.'

'As I hope to be, Mum.'

Bella took a deep breath.

'This possibly isn't the right time to say it but it might come up in conversation tonight and I want you to know before someone else tells you. I quit my job a couple of weeks ago.'

'You what?'

'I quit my job. I know it was steady and paid reasonably well and all those other things, but it was sucking the life out of me. The weeks and months and years were blurring into one long stream of police interviews and ready meals. I know you've always wanted me to find a nice man and settle down. Well, I didn't even have time to date. I certainly didn't have time to think about my creative side. Never mind my clients. I was the one facing a life sentence. Was I supposed to keep doing the same thing, week in week out, until retirement?'

'This is all very sudden.'

'Not for me. I've been thinking about it for years. The last six weeks have just shown me what might be possible and given me the courage to go for it.'

'But what are you going to do instead?' Maria asked. 'How will you pay the bills?'

'I'm going to learn to cook properly. Alex, whom you'll meet tonight, is going to reopen Bella's.'

'What?'

'I've decided to throw my lot in with him. He's taking me on as an apprentice.'

Bella would tell her the rest of the story later on.

Chapter Sixty-One

It was to Maria's credit that she agreed to walk into the community centre after that. Later she would say it was because in Bella's admission Maria saw a flash of her poor husband Ugo's passion and realised that while she'd been a bad wife through the lean times, she still had a chance to be a supportive mother. And Bella seemed so happy and Alex seemed so . . . well, lovely and handsome and nice. He welcomed Maria so warmly, that she knew she had to put her reservations aside.

While the students' guests sat at the table, sipping the champagne that Bella had brought along, Alex, Bella, John and Liz set to work, chopping, dicing, stirring, frying, roasting, baking and generally making a mess. That didn't matter. They all knew by now that if you can't make an omelette without breaking eggs, you certainly can't make focaccia without getting flour and semolina all over the place. Neither could you make a fish pie without getting a prawn on the floor.

'It's a shame Ted isn't here,' Liz commented.

'Ted's not to be encouraged to beg in the kitchen,' Evan, Liz's guest for the evening, reminded her. 'Not even for what I'm sure will be a fabulous fish pie.'

'Yes, vet,' Liz gave him a cheeky wink.

Meanwhile, John had brought two guests. He would never have believed how quickly a situation can change.

A week earlier he'd been estranged from his only son, having pushed him away when he ended up in prison for a drugs' bust so enormous John thought he would never get over the shame. Now John's son was sitting at the table in the community centre and next to him, John's granddaughter, the girl he didn't even know existed.

Madison had jumped at the chance to meet her grandfather. She'd spent almost her whole life wondering what he and Sonia were like. Until her mother's change of heart, Madison had assumed her grandparents weren't interested in her. She was desperately sad to have missed the chance to meet Sonia and so she was especially glad to have the opportunity to get to know John. John for his part was immediately enchanted by the young woman. She not only looked like Sonia, she had her grandmother's ready smile and easy temperament. She was quick to laugh and soon had John eating out of the palm of her hand.

As he took his eyes off the stove for a moment and looked at the table to see Madison chatting earnestly with Liz's friend the vet and Bella's mother, John knew he could not be more proud. To think that he might have missed it all through stubbornness was unbearable.

Alex appeared behind John and put his hand on the older man's shoulder.

'Looking good,' he said of John's efforts.

John reached up and squeezed Alex's hand in response. Alex didn't yet know how much he had helped John. If it hadn't been for that conversation after Alex's birthday party, John might never have picked up the phone to David. Though he had felt like a hypocrite at the time, John now knew that the things he had said to Alex that night were true. Everyone deserves a second chance and it wasn't just David who was getting one. John was getting his second chance too. He hoped that if Sonia was looking down on him, she was proud.

A little later than expected – there had been a lot of banter between the guests and the trainee chefs – the first course of that evening's meal was on the table and Alex took his place at the head of it. Before he invited the people gathered there to tuck in, he asked if he might say a few words. Everyone agreed that he should.

'I'm not a religious person,' said Alex. 'I haven't said grace since I was at school, but sitting here with all of you today makes me feel incredibly grateful. When I took on the beginners' cookery course, I thought it would just be an easy way to make some money while I waited for the opportunity to do something more interesting. I looked forward to passing on some of my knowledge but I had no idea of the things that *I* would learn along the way. I had no idea that as well as some cash and CV points, I'd make some wonderful new mates. Mates I hope will stay in my life for a very long time.' He looked at Liz, John and Bella in turn. 'For that reason, I'd like to raise a toast to Bella, John and Liz. May tonight be the first of many fantastic dinner parties for the three of you. Not just my students but *my* teachers and my friends.'

Chapter Sixty-Two

Birthday Cake

*Four eggs, eight ounces caster sugar, eight
ounces self-raising flour, eight ounces margarine,
2 tsp. baking powder.*

*Break eggs into mixing bowl and add sugar,
flour, baking powder and marg. Mix until well
combined. Divide mixture between two tins and
bake for twenty-five minutes at Gas Mark 4.
Remove from oven. Inspect. Despair. Discard.*

Evan pronounced himself extremely impressed with
Liz's cooking skills and he volunteered himself to be
guinea pig when Liz next attempted a fish pie. It had
come out during the graduation dinner that Liz's fish
pie had ended in disaster for both her and Ted.
However, much as she was pleased that Evan wanted
to taste her cooking again, Liz had a much more important critic in mind for her next foray into the kitchen.

A week after the graduation dinner, it was Saskia's
sixteenth birthday.

Since Ian had been forced to come clean about his
true feelings (or not) for Brittney (and by extension for
Liz), the London weekend that Saskia had been looking
forward to so much was no longer on the cards. Liz

told Saskia that she could go to the blog awards if she still wanted to, but Saskia said it no longer felt like the right thing to do. Brittney wanted to put Ian behind her and having Saskia there at the blog awards with her probably wouldn't help.

'In any case, Mum,' said Saskia, 'I'd prefer to spend the weekend with you.'

Result! Liz was not going to have to waste that expensive spa weekend after all. Saskia was very much on for two days of lolling about in a bathrobe, eating salad and getting her nails done now.

The spa would be all about detoxing, of course, but Liz planned to sneak in one particular piece of contraband – that birthday cake she'd promised herself she'd create for Saskia's big day. The one that would make up for fifteen years of shop-bought cakes from Marks and Spencer.

Alex provided Liz with what he described as a 'foolproof' recipe.

'You really can't go wrong,' he said.

He still didn't know Liz that well.

Liz's first attempt at the cake came out exactly as her last attempt fifteen years earlier. It was as flat as a cow pat. It didn't seem to have risen at all.

The second attempt was just as woeful. Liz must have put the tray into the oven slightly wonky because that cake came out two inches deep on one side and just half an inch deep on the other.

The third attempt was burned. Liz got distracted by a phone call.

The fourth attempt was just like the first.

Liz phoned Alex. 'Are you sure baking skills aren't

passed down in the genes? My mother definitely didn't have them.'

Alex encouraged Liz to keep trying. Add another egg. More baking powder. Whisk the mixture for longer. Nothing seemed to work. And within an hour Saskia would be home. They were supposed to head straight for the spa as soon as she changed out of her school clothes.

Liz faced the prospect of having no cake to take on their special weekend. She'd run out of ingredients and patience.

Liz stood in front of the cupboard where she kept sugar and flour and looked for emergency supplies and inspiration. She hoped to find a forgotten box of pre-prepared cake mix. What met her gaze was a box of icing sugar, a packet of sponge fingers and a tube of Smarties.

Liz and Saskia were very good on their first day at the health spa. They ate a clean breakfast and did two back-to-back exercise classes (which was more than Liz had done since Saskia was born). In the afternoon, they both had manuka honey facials, full body exfoliations and got their nails done. Liz went for a delicate nude shade. Saskia went for black. It was quite pretty though.

At the evening meal, Liz and Saskia chose from a menu of extremely virtuous calorie-counted options, which were all delicious.

'I feel like I'm missing something,' said Saskia as they walked back to the room they were sharing.

'It is your birthday,' said Liz. 'Are you missing a cake?'

'You haven't got me another one of those caterpillar

things from Marks and Spencer have you?' Saskia asked in a way that suggested she'd been over those a great many years ago.

'Something much better,' Liz promised.

'Traffic lights!' Saskia exclaimed when Liz opened the Tupperware box. 'Oh, Mum.' She bit one in half right away.

'Hang on,' said Liz. 'I was going to put a candle on one of them and sing "Happy Birthday".'

'Please don't sing, Mum,' Saskia said.

Liz was crestfallen.

'Only joking,' Saskia said. 'But Mum, this is the best kind of birthday cake ever. They remind me of Grandma,' she added, wiping a burgeoning tear from her eye. 'Grandma couldn't cook but she was the best at giving hugs. Like you are. Traffic lights were her signature and now they're yours. When I have kids, I'm going to make these instead of a birthday cake.'

And just like that, a culinary tradition was born.

Epilogue

A year later Liz was still cooking and growing more adventurous with every meal. Particularly since Saskia had decided that she wanted to learn to cook too. She'd given up on her acting and instead enrolled in the same course that Liz had taken at the community centre. Alex wasn't teaching the course any more but a young chef called Daniel was. Saskia and Georgia had terrible crushes on the poor bloke who spent the lessons pretending he was oblivious to their teenage fervour.

Ted, too, was keeping up the good work. He was still hovering at his target weight, having finally come to understand that Liz would no longer be expressing her love for him through the medium of Marks and Spencer's ready-cooked cocktail sausages. Instead, he had to settle for her praise and a tummy rub, which turned out to be just as nice. Exactly as Evan had always said.

Liz and Evan were taking things slowly but Liz had come to appreciate Evan's quirky ways. She understood that his love for animals did not preclude him from loving another person at all. He'd just needed to find the right kind of person. Someone who wasn't scared to occasionally bark orders in his general direction. And Liz finally told Evan the true story of the cake-mix debacle over three Aperol Spritzes at Bella's.

Alex and Bella were making a fantastic job of

running the little café that was soon the place to be for Newbay's trendy crowd, who dropped in for aperitivi on their way home from work.

John was also a regular customer. He brought his son David, who had moved in to live with him. Sometimes they were accompanied by Madison, who aced her A levels and won a place at Exeter University, which brought her much closer to her father and granddad.

Meanwhile, Ian moved back in with his old girlfriend Kat, the one from Totnes. Twenty years apart had changed their relationship for the better and Ian even suggested to Saskia that Miss Totnes might be the one to help him get over his fear of commitment at last. Liz found to her surprise that she wished her now ex-husband well, despite all the trouble he'd caused her. And Brittney.

Well, Brittney's Bites did win an award at the grand blogging conference in London. With 'best health and sustainable fashion blog' all over her headers, Brittney was going from strength to strength with her combination of home-made health food, fashion bargains and made-up Dalai Lama quotes. Those misattributed quotes still drove Liz nuts, but she did appreciate the sentiment of one of them, which said:

'Great love is like great home-made food. They're both much better shared.'

Did the Dalai Lama say that? Probably not. But that didn't mean it wasn't a quote worth living by.

Acknowledgements

For their professional support, their friendship and their love during the writing of this novel I'd like to thank: super-agent Laetitia Rutherford and Megan Carroll of Watson, Little Ltd. Uber-editor Emily Kitchin, and Thorne Ryan, Alice Morley and Jo Myler of Hodder and Stoughton. Copyeditor Gabby and illustrator Emma Block. Fellow writers and fabulous friends Victoria Routledge, Alex Potter, Bernie Strachan, Amanda Brookfield, Michele Gorman, Lauren Henderson, Serena Mackesy and Mike Gayle. My old school pals, Jane Wright, Helena Cutler and Jo Medcroft. My beloved family, Mum, Kate, Lee, Harrison and Lukas. And last but not least, Mark, my dearest dear. Thank you all from the bottom of my heart.

Do you wish this wasn't the end?

Join us at www.hodder.co.uk, or follow us on
Twitter @hodderbooks to be a part of our community
of people who love the very best in books and reading.

Whether you want to discover more about a book
or an author, watch trailers and interviews, have the
chance to win early limited editions, or simply browse
our expert readers' selection of the very best books,
we think you'll find what you're looking for.

And if you don't,
that's the place to tell us what's missing.

We love what we do, and we'd love you to be part of it.

www.hodder.co.uk

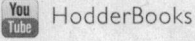 @hodderbooks

HodderBooks

HodderBooks